New York Times
bestselling author

DEBBIE MACOMBER

"Will captivate and charm
her legions of readers."
Jayne Ann Krentz

"[Is] charming and touching by turns."
Elizabeth Lowell

"Will touch the lives of every reader."
Lori Copeland

"[Is] warm, funny, and uplifting."
Romantic Times

"Debbie Macomber is one of our
premier storytellers."
Anne Stuart

By Debbie Macomber

Someday Soon

DEBBIE MACOMBER

Sooner Or Later

AVON BOOKS

An Imprint of HarperCollins*Publishers*

FIRST EDITION

ISBN-13: 978-0-06-112158-6
ISBN-10: 0-06-112158-4

06 07 08 09 RRD 10 9 8 7 6 5 4 3 2 1

Someday Soon

To Jane McMahon
A friend for all seasons
Knowing you has blessed my life

Acknowledgments

I loved writing this story. Most of you realize that no book is a single person's effort. Each endeavor has a multitude of contributors. From the beginning of this project I have felt incredibly blessed. I'd like to thank those who helped along the way.

I deeply appreciate Karen Solem and Carolyn Marino for allowing me the freedom to write something completely different. Mercenary and angels. It's a wonder they aren't pulling their hair out over me.

My agent, Irene Goodman, is the best cheerleader any writer could ever have. Thanks, Irene, for sticking in there with me.

My family deserves special thanks, too. Especially my husband, Wayne, who after nearly twenty-seven years still loves me, even though I make him pack his own lunch. My children, Jody, Jenny, Ted, and Dale—I'm so proud of you, I could just burst. Now all you need do is supply me with grandchildren.

Prologue

The screaming had stopped. The shouts, the shots, the terror, were over. Now all Deliverance Company had to do was escape, and every detail of their route had been carefully planned.

Cain McClellan had never been comfortable with this mission, although it was similar to ten others he and his men had handled over the years. It wasn't anything he could put his finger on, other than a feeling. One that caused the hair on the back of his neck to stand straight on end. They'd been lucky, damn lucky. In twelve years he'd never lost a man.

Deliverance Company was good. His men were some of the best trained commandos in the world. That was why they were paid so handsomely.

Only something wasn't right, and Cain knew it. He was a man who lived and died by his instincts, but Tim Mallory and his other men had proved him wrong. Thus far.

The rescue, their specialty, had gone off like clock-work. Deliverance Company was in and out of the jungle compound in seconds, leaving the Nicaraguan govern-ment troops stunned and confused. That was exactly the way they'd planned it. By the time the Sandinistas fig-ured out what had happened, Cain and his men would be long gone.

The man they'd saved, a CEO for a big-time manufac-turing company, had been in the wrong place at the wrong time and fallen into hostile hands. Very hostile hands. The United States government's options were limited, trapped as they were in political red tape. Cain had been contacted early on by the conglomerate. Such missions were his specialty.

The helicopter was due any minute. According to their plan, the men of Deliverance Company had split and were scheduled to rendezvous in a designated area at fifteen hundred hours.

The eerie feeling returned, the sensation that said something was about to go terribly wrong. Cain's instincts had saved his life more than once, and he didn't take this feeling lightly. He stopped abruptly and looked around.

"Come on," Mallory urged, rushing past him. "We don't have time to waste."

The sudden impact of the explosion knocked Cain to the ground. He landed hard, on his face, and his mouth filled with the slick taste of blood. Shock and pain welled inside him as he staggered to his feet. His breath rasped painfully in his lungs.

Only when he was upright did Cain understand what had happened. Mallory had stepped on a land mine, the force of which had ripped through his right leg and hip. Jagged flesh and bone were exposed where once a healthy, whole man had stood. The acrid stench of explosives hung in the air, mingled with that of blood and sweat. The smell of death hung over them like a winter fog before the smoke cleared.

The ominous sounds of gunfire crackled in the background.

"Leave me," Mallory ground out from between gritted teeth. He gripped his leg with both hands and looked over his shoulder. Cain didn't need him to say anything to know the Sandinistas were quickly gaining on them.

"I'm not going anywhere without you." Cain moved toward the fallen man, surprised by how hard it was to remain upright. His steps wove one way and then the other.

"You haven't got time to waste." It went without saying that either they reached the rendezvous point on time or the chopper left without them.

"It's too late for me," Mallory mumbled, fighting to stay conscious.

Cain reached him, and one glance told him the injuries were massive. He didn't take time to investigate further. He reached for Mallory, preparing to lift him onto his shoulders.

"I've lost too much blood. I'll never make it." Mallory's voice faded as he drifted toward unconsciousness. "Don't risk . . . "

A bullet whizzed past Cain's head as he heaved Mallory's two-hundred-plus pounds onto his shoulders. Blood drenched his shirt and ran down both his arms like a waterfall. Staggering under the weight, Cain strained and raced with his burden toward the meeting point.

"Let me die," Mallory pleaded, sucking in deep breaths in an effort to remain conscious. "The leg's gone, man, and so am I."

"Not yet you aren't," Cain shouted. "You're going to make it."

"I'd rather die."

"Not while I'm around, you won't."

A bullet caught Cain in the arm, a flesh wound, the pain as searing as if someone had branded him with a white-hot poker.

The copter was in sight, its massive blades whirling, stirring up dust and excitement. The sound was deafening, but Cain swore he'd never heard anything more beautiful in his life.

1

Her first mistake was agreeing to attend this Christmas party. Her second was downing a glass of champagne and then, for courage, another.

Her third error in judgment was remembering Michael.

The only reason Linette Collins had agreed to come was that it was easier to give in to Nancy and Rob than argue.

It was well past time for her to socialize again, they claimed. Long past time for her to grieve. Only no one had told her how she was supposed to grow another heart. No one had told her all the time she'd been granted to mourn her husband was two short years.

Her heart had been rubbed raw in the time it had taken leukemia to claim her young husband's life. Since Michael's death the days had blended together, one twenty-four-hour period dragging into the next until the weeks and months had blurred together in a thick fog of disenchantment.

Linette had gotten on with her life, the way everyone said she should. She went to work every day. She ate. Slept. She managed to do all that was required of her and nothing more, simply because she hadn't the energy. Or the inclination.

Then, out of the blue, when she was least expecting it, she'd found peace. A shaky sort of acceptance that teetered, then, gradually, with time, righted itself.

This serenity happened as if by magic. She woke one morning and realized the pain she'd constantly carried with her didn't seem quite as heavy. The doubts, the fears, the never-ending litany of questions, faded. Unsure of how it had happened, Linette had graciously accepted this small slice of peace, this unexpected reprieve, and clung to it tenaciously.

Each day the feeling had grown stronger, and for the first time in months she felt whole. Almost whole, she amended.

But when she'd stepped into this Christmas party she hadn't been prepared for the festivities to hit her quite this way. The fun, the singing, the laughter, reminded her forcefully that it had been almost two years to the day since Michael's death.

"I'm so pleased you came," Nancy said as she squeezed past Linette. Her sister-in-law smelled of cinnamon and bayberry and looked incredibly lovely in her sleeveless winter green velvet gown. Linette's own white wool dress didn't fit as well as it should. She'd done what she could to disguise how loose it was with a narrow gold belt.

"I'm pleased I came, too," Linette lied, but it was only a small white one and unfortunately necessary. She sipped champagne and forced herself to smile.

"Did you sample the hors d'oeuvres?" Nancy asked. "You must! I spent hours and hours assembling those little devils. Try the teriyaki chicken bits first. They're wonderful." She pressed her fingertips to her lips and kissed them noisily.

"I'll give them a taste," Linette promised.

Without warning, Nancy's arms shot out and hugged Linette long and hard. When she drew back, Linette noticed tears shimmering in her sister-in-law's eyes. Nancy's lower lip quivered as she struggled to hold in the emotion. "I miss him so much," she said, choking out the words. "I still think about him. It doesn't seem like it's been two years."

"I know." Instead it felt as if several lifetimes had passed.

Linette squeezed Nancy's hand. It often happened like this, her comforting others. How ironic.

"Oh, damn. I didn't mean for that to happen," Nancy murmured, pressing her index fingers beneath each eye while she blinked furiously in an effort to keep the tears from spilling down her cheeks.

"It's only natural you should miss Michael," Linette offered, briefly wrapping her arm around Nancy's waist.

"It just hit me all at once that he was gone. I'm sorry, Linette, the last thing you need is for me to remind you of Michael, especially tonight. This is a party, we're supposed to be having fun." Nancy reached for the champagne bottle and Linette's glass. She sipped from her own glass, then laughed lightly. "He'd want us to celebrate."

That was true. Michael had always been generous and loving.

"Oh, my," Nancy said a tad breathlessly, turning around abruptly. Her startled eyes flew to Linette's. "Tell me, how do I look?" she asked, nervously brushing her hands down her skirt.

Linette blinked, surprised by Nancy's lack of confidence. "Great."

"You're sure?"

"I'm positive. Why?"

"Rob's boss and his wife just arrived."

"You don't have a thing to worry about," Linette assured her.

"My makeup's okay?" She dabbed at her cheeks.

"A beauty queen would envy you that face."

Nancy laughed. "Rob's up for promotion, you know."

Linette didn't, but the news wasn't a surprise. She'd often admired her brother-in-law for his intelligence and ambition.

With a toothpaste-ad smile on her lips, Nancy left, and Linette glanced at her watch once more. Ten more minutes, she decided, and then she'd make an excuse and leave. Silently she'd slip back to life without Michael.

The minute Cain arrived at the Christmas party, he'd noticed her. Like him, she was alone. Uncomfortable. Eager to escape. She was a lovely thing. Petite and fragile. He found himself studying her almost against his will. It wasn't that she was strikingly beautiful. "Winsome" came to mind, although it was an old-fashioned word and not often used these days. But then, she seemed to be a quaint kind of woman.

It was almost as if she'd stepped out of another time and place. Perhaps it was the sense of being lost that he felt. A sense of being alone and slightly afraid, uncomfortably aware of being out of place.

Not afraid, he decided. The more he studied her, the more he realized this woman had walked through a deep, dark valley. He wasn't sure how he knew this, but he'd come to trust his intuition. She sipped from the champagne glass and briefly gnawed on the corner of her lip. Watching her made Cain wonder if she'd made her way completely across that valley. Maybe he should find out. No. He decided to leave well enough alone.

Carrying his drink with him, he slowly made his way through the crowd to find a secluded corner. Andy Williams crooned a Christmas ditty from a nearby speaker.

Cain hadn't been keen on attending this get-together. This was what he got for giving in to curiosity and looking up Rob Lewis. They'd been good friends in high school, and he was interested to see what had become of his buddy since they'd both left the thriving metropolis of Valentine, Nebraska.

Years before, Cain and Rob had been the local football heroes. Cain was the quarterback and Rob his favorite wide receiver. Frankly, he'd enjoyed his brief stint as a celebrity.

Following graduation Cain had gone into the military and Rob to college. They'd talked a couple of times in the years since, a card at Christmas with a few lines, but that was the extent of it.

Since Cain was in San Francisco getting Mallory set up on a rehabilitation program for his hip and knee, it only made sense to catch up with his longtime buddy. In a moment of goodwill and—all right—weakness, Cain had agreed to drop in on this Christmas party.

He was uncomfortable in crowds. He'd never been one to exhibit many of the more refined social graces. He felt out of place here. Sipping his Jack Daniel's, he returned his gaze to the woman who'd garnered his attention earlier.

Why not, he decided as he stepped around the sofa. It was Christmas, and it'd been a good long while since he'd felt this strongly attracted to a woman. He wove his way between two couples who were attempting to sing a favorite Christmas carol in German and failing miserably. They seemed to be enjoying themselves, and Cain found them amusing.

"A half hour," Cain said, slipping next to her. She stood close to the fireplace, holding the fluted champagne glass in both hands.

"A half hour?" she repeated, gazing at him with wide brown eyes. Doe eyes, big, trusting, sincere.

"That's how long you'd decided to wait before you quietly left."

Her gaze widened. "How'd you know?"

The whiskey burned the back of his throat. "Because that was how long I'd decided to wait before I left."

She smiled then, and he was amazed at the transformation the simple action brought to her delicate features. It was if the sun had peeked from behind a thick, dark cloud, spilling sunshine. Her eyes brightened and her lips quivered softly.

"I'm Cain McClellan," he said, holding out his hand to her.

"Linette Collins."

"Hello, Linette." The name sounded vaguely familiar, and he frowned in an effort to remember where he'd heard it. Possibly from Rob, who'd attempted to match him up for the evening.

"You don't work with Rob, do you?" Her attention drifted to his hair, and he realized the high and tight military cut told her he probably wasn't a stockbroker.

"Rob and I are longtime friends," he answered without elaborating. "What about you?"

"Nancy and Rob are my brother- and sister-in-law."

"You're married?" His gaze shot to her left hand. Her ring finger was bare, but the indentation of a wedding band was clearly visible. It was then that Cain remembered where he'd heard her name. Rob had mentioned Nancy's brother had passed away a couple of years earlier and suggested Cain meet the widow. He'd declined.

"My husband died," she explained unnecessarily.

Cain felt a sudden need for another drink. He clinked his ice against the side of the glass and stared at the melting cubes. "Can I get you anything?" he asked, gesturing toward the bar.

Linette set aside her empty champagne glass. "Nothing, thanks."

Cain left her and headed across the room. He wanted to kick himself for being so inept. It was apparent she was ill at ease; perhaps she wanted to talk about her late husband and had been looking for a willing ear.

It didn't matter, because the moment she'd announced she was a widow, he'd grown so uncomfortable that he'd made an excuse to leave her. The thing was he hadn't known what to say. That he was sorry? That sounded phony. Hell, he'd never met the man.

Circumstances such as these made him regret not leaving for Montana at the first opportunity. Instead he'd lollygagged around San Francisco, looking up old friends and making a fool of himself.

When Cain had a fresh drink, he turned and discovered Linette hadn't left the party. He was pleased she'd stayed. He hadn't wanted their conversation to end abruptly, but he wasn't sure what more he had to say, either.

He studied the bright red stockings hanging from the fireplace mantel and casually walked back to her side. Her gentle smile reached out to greet him.

"Something amuses you?"

"Nancy," she responded, which was no answer whatsoever.

He looked around for Rob's wife, not finding her.

"She mentioned you," Linette elaborated. "I just realized you were the one she'd wanted me to meet."

"Rob tried to line me up with you as well."

"Nancy did this whole song and dance about it being two years since Michael . . . and that there was this old school buddy of Rob's who was in town."

Cain grinned, thinking it had been a good long while since he'd had reason to smile about anything. "I guess we showed them."

"I guess we did." Linette laughed softly and waved her hand in front of her face. "Is it hot in here, or is it just me?"

Standing in front of the softly flickering fire might

have had something to do with why she was uncomfortably warm, but Cain didn't mention that. Instead he took her by the elbow and guided her outside to a small balcony that overlooked San Francisco Bay. The lights on the Golden Gate Bridge outlined the well-known landmark, illuminating the skyline in a postcard-perfect silhouette.

A cool breeze drifted off the water, and the sky was crowded with stars that seemed determined to dazzle them with their brilliance.

Linette gripped hold of the balcony railing with both hands, closed her eyes, and tilted her head upward. When she exhaled, her shoulders sagged appreciatively.

"Nancy said something about you being out of the country a lot of the time. That must be hard."

"It's my job," he said.

"You don't miss home?"

In the last year, he hadn't thought about the ranch enough to miss it. Nor had he hurried to Montana when the opportunity arose. He was a man without ties, without roots. That was the way it had to be.

"I'm too busy to think about it," he answered after a moment, and looked to her, wanting to divert the subject away from himself. "Do you work?"

She nodded. "I own a knitting shop called Wild and Wooly, on Pier Thirty-nine."

A knitting shop. It fit. He could easily picture Linette snuggled up on a rocking chair next to a fireplace, her long needles clicking softly as she expertly wove yarn. He found the image inviting, as if she'd asked him to cozy up next to her.

Cain wished he could pinpoint what it was about

Linette that conjured up fantasies of domestic bliss. Homespun women didn't generally appeal to him.

It was the season, he decided, when goodwill toward men flourished and a man's thoughts turned to hearth and home. Christmastime seemed to bring out the best in people, himself included, he reasoned, willing to accept the explanation.

"Would you care to dance?" Linette asked him.

"Dance? Me?" Her invitation flustered him. He flattened his hand against his chest as the excuses worked their way up his throat. "I'm not much good at that sort of thing," he managed after an awkward moment.

"Me either. But we don't need to worry about making fools of ourselves, out here." She held up her arms, and before a second protest could form, she was in his embrace.

He tensed, but she didn't seem to notice. Tucking her head under his chin, she hummed along with the music, and gradually he relaxed.

Their feet made short, awkward shuffling movements until Cain realized that there was actually some kind of rhythm to their motions.

The tension slowly eased from his limbs, and he pressed his chin against her temple. She smelled of wildflowers and sunshine. He'd never held anyone more incredibly soft. So soft, she frightened him. He absorbed her gentleness the way a thirsty sponge did water. With her in his arms, he could close his eyes and not see the mangled bodies of men who'd died at his hand. With her he heard the soft strains of joyous music instead of the screams of dying, bitter men as they cursed him on their way to hell.

His grip tightened, and she trembled. Pulling her flush against him, he felt her breath moisten the column of his neck. The tips of her breasts caressed his chest, and Cain closed his eyes and savored the feel of a woman in his arms. Linette clung to him, too. He realized, gratefully, that her hold on him was as tight as his on her.

He knew what was happening. He could spend a few hours with this woman who was lovely and pure and forget who and what he was. He could relish her softness and ignore the bitterness of the truth and the hard life he'd chosen.

All this wasn't one-sided. Linette could hold him and forget the man she'd loved and lost. He was her haven just as she had become his.

As much as he'd like to deny it, Cain needed this woman's touch. He was desperate for her gentleness. His heart, perhaps even his soul, needed this time with her.

The music ceased, but he kept moving. It felt too damn good to have her in his arms. Linette broke away from him, and for an instant he resisted, tightening his grip until he realized what he was doing.

Irritated with himself, he dropped his arms and stepped back. Linette Collins made him weak, and that was something he couldn't allow.

"Thank you," she said softly. She didn't need to say it had been a long time since anyone had held her. He knew. This wasn't the kind of woman who bed-hopped. She'd deeply grieved the loss of her husband. Cain also knew she'd grieved alone, without seeking the solace of a lover.

In one way, Cain envied her husband. There would be

no one to mourn his passing. No one to stand over his cemetery plot and weep. That was the life he had chosen. The way it had to be. There was no room for gentleness in his life. Not now, not ever. Not if he planned to survive. And he did.

For what?

The question came at him like the pinpoint beam of a laser slicing through his mind. All at once he hadn't a clue why he found it so damned important to stay alive. He had no immediate family. No heirs.

As far as money went, he could retire now and it would take two lifetimes to spend what he'd accumulated in the last several years with Deliverance Company.

By tacit agreement, he and Linette wandered back to the party, which seemed to be in full swing. Without a word, they went their separate ways. Which was for the best, Cain reasoned. Linette was a sweet thing and deserved happiness. It wasn't likely she'd find that with him. By nipping this attraction in the bud, he was doing her a kindness.

Cain caught sight of Nancy and Rob dancing on the other side of the room. Small clusters of groups were involved in chitchat, something at which he felt completely inept. With little more than a backward glance, he retrieved his coat and left. Later, he'd send Rob and Nancy a Christmas card and thank them for the party. He was half tempted to mention meeting Linette, then decided against it.

In the hallway outside, waiting for the elevator, he sensed someone's approach. It shouldn't have surprised him to find Linette rounding the corner, but it did. She seemed startled as well, and her round eyes widened.

"So we meet again," he said.

When the elevator arrived, they stepped aboard together. He pushed the button for the lobby. Stepping back, he studied the woman who stood before him. Within a matter of seconds, they would each go back to their separate lives.

Cain experienced a sense of desperation that was foreign to him. Even worse, he felt like a world-class fool. If Mallory knew what he was thinking, or Murphy, Bailey, or Jack, either, they'd lock him up until this bout of insanity had passed. Men like Cain simply did not become involved with women like Linette Collins.

On the ground floor, Cain watched Linette hurry across the street and climb inside her car. He stood rooted, unwilling and unable to move as her Toyota turned the corner and disappeared from sight.

After a moment he drew in a deep breath, then headed toward the rental car he'd picked up at the airport three days earlier.

His name was Cain, and right then he felt aptly christened. His namesake had been the son of Adam and Eve. The first child born outside the gates of paradise.

2

Linette was busy at her shop early Saturday morning when the phone rang. Although she wasn't due to open for another half hour, she reached for the receiver and tucked it between her ear and her shoulder as she unloaded skeins of brightly colored cashmere wool.

"Wild and Wooly," she said automatically.

"I wish you hadn't left the party so early," Nancy mumbled on the tail end of a yawn. It was apparent she had recently rolled out of bed.

"I had to be to the shop this morning," Linette explained. She hadn't slept well, but only because she couldn't stop thinking about Cain McClellan and the short time they'd been together. She toyed hesitantly with the idea of asking her sister-in-law what she could tell her about Cain. So much as a hint of curiosity about the other man might prove to be potentially embarrassing.

Nancy was sure to make something out of Linette's inquisitiveness.

If Linette were a little more sophisticated, a little more at ease with the opposite sex, she might have found a subtle way of quizzing Cain himself. She hadn't because he hadn't seemed keen on talking about himself. What questions she had asked had received answers that were evasive and vague. She'd noticed how he'd quickly turned the conversation to subjects away from anything personal.

She knew he was in the military. Nancy had told her that much when she'd first mentioned him. Linette speculated that his work was involved with intelligence. Probably top-secret stuff that prevented him from discussing details. Funny she could spend so short a time with him and feel as if she understood him.

Like her, he was alone. Like her, he needed someone to hold.

In the entire two-year period without Michael, Linette had never felt more alone than she did now. At first she'd assumed it was because the anniversary of his death was approaching, but gradually she realized it was the Christmas season itself.

"Did you enjoy the party?" Nancy asked, cutting into her thoughts.

"Very much." Thanks to Cain. Forcing her attention back to Nancy, she asked, "How did everything go with Rob's boss and his wife?"

"Great. They're nice people," Nancy said, and then, turning to the apparent reason for her call, she added, "Didn't I see you talking with Rob's friend?"

"Yes, we found each other despite your and Rob's best

efforts to keep us apart," Linette said with a small smile.

"I saw the two of you one minute and the next thing I knew you'd both disappeared." Linette pictured Nancy jiggling her eyebrows suggestively.

"We left. Cain's not much of a party person either."

"So you snuck off together," Nancy said, her voice dipping with implication. "That's great."

Before Linette could correct her sister-in-law's impression, Nancy spoke again. "How about the two of us getting together for lunch this afternoon? That way you can tell me all about you and Cain, and I'll let you in on my own little secret."

"There's nothing to tell," Linette protested. "Besides, I don't know if I can get away. The shop's been terribly busy, and I don't feel like I can leave Bonnie alone, especially on a Saturday." It sounded as if she were hedging, but what she said was true. Since this was the last weekend before Christmas, it could possibly be the busiest day of the year for her shop. Lunch would consist of a bite or two of a sandwich between customers.

"I'll pick up something and bring it to you, then," Nancy argued. "I'm dying to hear what happened between you and Cain McClellan."

"But, Nancy—"

"Don't argue. I must say, he's a hunk."

"But—" Before Linette could explain it might be a wasted trip, Nancy had hung up.

Replacing the telephone receiver, Linette sank onto the chair by the cash register. She loved Nancy and deeply appreciated the support and love Michael's sister had given her, but she didn't want to discuss Cain McClellan.

He'd come into her life briefly, and it was unlikely they'd meet again. Ships passing in the night and that sort of thing. He was a man without an anchor, and she was a dock. A concrete dock. Stable, permanent, lasting. Even if they had struck up a relationship, it would be a long-distance one. He'd told her himself he was only in town for a few days.

Linette's prediction about this being the busiest sales day of the year proved to be accurate. From the moment she unlocked the door, she was inundated with customers. Many of the handcrafted items she'd knitted over the autumn months had already sold, but the limited number of wool scarves and baby blankets left were gone by ten that morning.

"Has it been like this every Christmas?" Bonnie asked, sinking onto the chair and removing her left shoe. She rubbed her toes and mumbled something about getting what she deserved for wearing new shoes.

"I don't remember," Linette said.

"Linette," Bonnie said, and exhaled sharply. "I'm sorry. I forgot. It was Christmastime when your husband died, wasn't it?"

"Don't worry about it," Linette said quickly, not wanting to discuss Michael. She liked Bonnie, who was in her mid-fifties and grandmotherly with short gray hair and a thick waist. Her face was round and warmly hospitable. It helped that Linette's lone employee had been knitting for years herself and was knowledgeable about the craft. Linette felt lucky to have her.

The bell above the door jingled, and Bonnie automatically replaced her shoe. "I'll get it," Linette said, pressing her hand against her employee's forearm. "Pour yourself a cup of coffee," she said. "You deserve it." They'd been so busy, neither of them had taken time for a coffee break.

"You're sure?" Bonnie asked, glancing longingly toward the back room.

"I'll be fine."

Linette realized she'd spoken too soon. This latest customer was Nancy. "You're not the least bit busy," her sister-in-law admonished.

"You should have been here ten minutes ago," Linette countered. She straightened a row of white wool, replacing it inside a brightly painted wood bin stacked beneath a large picture window overlooking Fisherman's Wharf. Linette loved the view the window afforded her. With its colorful fishing fleet, the wharf reminded her of a quaint Mediterranean seaport. There'd been plenty of times when she'd gazed out this very window, transported to a world outside her grief.

"I brought goodies," Nancy said, holding up a grease-stained brown paper sack. "The deli packed us sandwiches and enormous dill pickles."

"I didn't think you liked dill pickles."

"I don't," Nancy said casually, "unless I'm pregnant."

It took Linette far longer than it should have to make the connection. "You and Rob are having a baby?"

Nancy's eyes brightened with tears, and she nodded enthusiastically. "I didn't want to say anything until after Christmas, but I can't keep it a secret any longer. We'd almost given up trying. Christopher's eight, and we were beginning to think we couldn't have more children when, whammo." She tossed her arm into the air, grinning broadly. "Another rabbit bit the dust."

The two women hugged, and to her surprise Linette felt tears filling her own eyes. She knew Nancy and Rob wanted another child, but neither one had mentioned a baby in so long that she wasn't sure what they'd decided.

A baby.

She and Michael had yearned for children, but early in their marriage they'd decided to wait a couple of years. Every aspect of their lives together had been carefully planned. All too soon, however, Michael had been diagnosed with leukemia. Afterward everything had changed. The days came and went, the seasons ebbed and flowed and every sunrise had become a sunset as Michael's life became consumed with dying.

"Be happy for me," Nancy said, hugging her close.

"Of course I'm happy," Linette said, wondering at Nancy's apprehensions.

"It's just that . . . well, I know how badly you and Michael wanted a child, and I guess I was afraid you might feel like you'd been cheated."

"How could I possibly feel cheated, having loved Michael? I'm sorry we didn't have children, but I'd never begrudge you and Rob your happiness. I'm thrilled for you both."

"Thank you," Nancy said, rubbing the moisture from her face. Her shoulders shook, and it took a moment for Linette to realize Nancy was laughing, not weeping.

"I cry so easily lately. Rob doesn't know what to make of me."

Knowing how Rob idolized his wife, Linette strongly suspected he'd think he'd married the most perfect woman in the world no matter what she said or did. Especially now.

Bonnie wandered out from the back room, bringing a freshly brewed cup of coffee with her.

"Bonnie, do you think I can steal Linette away for a few minutes?" Nancy asked, and looped her arm through Linette's.

"Might as well," Bonnie said with an agreeable smile. "We seem to be experiencing something of a lull, but I don't expect it to last long."

Linette led the way into the back room, which was stacked with empty boxes, most of the skeins of yarn having been sold even before the boxes had had a chance to be emptied.

A badly scarred wooden table stood against the concrete block wall with two equally dilapidated chairs. Linette couldn't remember where they'd found the set, but it had been a welcome addition to their small space.

Nancy claimed the ladder-back chair while Linette scrounged up paper plates and two clean coffee mugs.

Nancy drew out thick sandwiches from the brown paper sack. They were subways covered in wax paper and held together with large toothpicks, with gaily decorated tops.

"Did I mention my appetite's improved?" Nancy said, smiling gleefully at Linette. "Pickles aren't the only thing I find appealing. I swear if this continues, I'll resemble the Goodyear blimp by July."

Linette inspected her half of the sandwich and discovered three different kinds of meat and an equal number of cheeses, plus the usual lettuce, thick slices of tomato, and a variety of other goodies, including sliced green olives.

"All right, tell me about you and Cain," Nancy instructed now that she was settled.

"I already explained there isn't much to tell," Linette said. Juice ran down her forearm when she took her first bite of the dill pickle.

"I saw the two of you together, remember?" Nancy insisted. "And then you were gone. Where did you take off to?"

"Nowhere. We rode down in the elevator together and went our separate ways."

"That's all?" Nancy sounded terribly disappointed.

"What do you know about him?" Linette asked, her curiosity overriding her hesitation. She would have preferred to keep any inquisitiveness low key and any questions indirect. Linette feared Nancy would leap on Linette's interest in Cain and make something out of it that it wasn't.

"Rob and Cain attended high school together."

That much Linette knew.

"Cain went into the military after graduation. From what Rob said, he's only talked to Cain twice in the last twenty years. The first time was about a year or so after Rob was out of college. Cain phoned him and they chatted. Apparently he was a member of the Special Forces and had spent a good deal of time in Asia."

"Asia?" Linette repeated slowly.

"That's what Rob said. When I quizzed him, he couldn't recall much more of their conversation, which is understandable seeing that it was several years back. Apparently some of their friends have asked about Cain over the years, but no one's heard from him. When it came time for their class reunion, no one had an address for him. Apparently Rob's the only one he's kept in contact with from his high school days.

"When Cain phoned last week, Rob was thrilled. The two met for lunch, but Rob said Cain skillfully managed to steer the conversation away from himself."

"He did that with me, too."

"From what little Rob was able to glean, Cain's involved in some kind of undercover activity that consists of rescuing political hostages."

A chill raced up Linette's back.

"You'd think he'd be ready to retire soon. He's got in twenty years or more by now."

He wasn't ready. Linette hadn't a clue how she knew that, but she did. Cain was a man who enjoyed living on the edge, who felt a rush of excitement when he could look danger in the face and not blink.

"He didn't ask to see you again?" Nancy spoke as if she suspected Linette were holding back vital information.

"No." Cain McClellan had come into her life like the softest of whispers and disappeared before she'd had the opportunity to decipher his message.

Cain knew Francine Holden was the perfect physical therapist for Tim Mallory the moment he laid eyes on her. He also knew Mallory wouldn't agree with him. The highly recommended therapist was a no-nonsense professional who wouldn't put up with any of his friend's usual guff. If Francine Holden was only half as good as Dr. Benton claimed, his colleague had a chance of regaining the use of his right leg. Something that had seemed impossible eighteen months earlier.

It wouldn't be easy, but then nothing in his business ever was. Thank God Mallory was a fighter. If not, he would have died in a Nicaraguan jungle. Francine wasn't a shy, retiring soul whom Mallory would easily intimidate with his temper tantrums and wildly swinging moods.

"Dr. Benton recommended you highly for the job," he said to the woman who sat across from him. Sitting didn't disguise her height. Cain guessed she was close to six feet, with a build that resembled that of a weight lifter. She'd need strength if she was going to be lifting Mallory around. Francine wore her long blond hair in a French braid that stretched halfway down the middle of her back. Her eyes were blue and wide, by far her most striking feature, set deep in a face that was remarkably plain.

"May I see your friend's latest X rays?" she asked, ignoring his compliment. When Cain handed them to her, she held the first set up to the light. "How'd this happen?" she asked.

Cain weighed how much he should tell her and decided he'd be doing them both a disservice with anything less than the truth. "The damage to the knee and hip are the result of a booby trap."

"Booby trap? You mean as in a land mine?"

"Something like that." Cain shifted back on his chair and crossed his legs. "We were in Central America at the time, on a mission."

Slowly her intensely blue eyes left the X rays to connect with his. "What agency were you with?"

"None. We're mercenaries."

"Doing what?"

He shrugged, unwilling to give her any more information than necessary. "What we were paid to do."

"I see."

Cain watched her reaction, surprised that she revealed none, at least none he could read.

"How many reconstructive surgeries has your friend been through?" It was back to business, and Cain was impressed with the casual way in which she responded to the information.

"Ten surgeries in the last eighteen months."

She motioned to the X ray. "When were these taken?"

"Two weeks ago."

"What's your friend's mental state?" she asked before handing him back the film.

"About what you'd expect," he said evasively. Mallory had already gone through a handful of therapists. The latest hadn't lasted more than two days.

"In other words he's depressed, angry, and has done his best to shut out the world."

Cain felt his lips quiver involuntarily with a smile. "Something like that."

"I'm not a miracle worker, Mr. McClellan."

"All I'm asking is that you give it a shot. I'm willing to pay you top dollar." More if need be. Mallory was a good friend, damn good. Perhaps the best Cain had ever had. He hadn't left him in the jungle to die, and he wouldn't desert him now, either.

"It isn't a question of money," Francine returned smoothly. "It has to do with grit and spirit. I've been a therapist several years, and I've seen a number of cases similar to your friend's here. At this point he doesn't care if he lives or dies. What happened to his body can't compare with the damage done to his soul."

Cain was amazed by how accurately she'd analyzed Mallory's emotional state. "Can you help him?"

"Maybe. Maybe not. It's up to him," she said thought-fully. "I can make a more accurate assessment once I meet him."

"Great." Cain eagerly sprang to his feet. "Let's take care of that right now."

A brief smile brightened her plain features. "Have you told him I'm coming?"

Cain hesitated. "No."

"Good."

"It's probably better he doesn't know you're a thera-pist," Cain suggested, preferring to delay another of Mallory tantrums. The minute his cohort learned that he'd hired another therapist, there was sure to be trouble.

"We won't be able to keep it from him long," Francine said evenly. "He'll figure it out soon enough."

She was right. One look at this titan of a woman and Mallory would know exactly why he'd brought her to meet him.

From the glint in her deep blue eyes, Cain guessed this was a woman who thrived on challenge. All the bet-ter, because Mallory was going to demand every ounce of fortitude she possessed.

He led her through the house he'd rented on Russian Hill. Taken with the panoramic view of the Bay, Cain had also liked the countrylike lanes and terraced houses. Perhaps he was thinking the atmosphere would help Mallory, but if that was the case, the high rent area had been an expensive mistake. Mallory had made a prison out of the back bedroom.

Greg, Mallory's attendant, was leaving the room as they approached. He looked from Cain to Francine and then back at Cain.

"He's having a bad day," Greg announced. His expression suggested they'd be better off returning at a later date.

"As long as he's in the shape he's in now," Francine said without waiting for Cain to respond, "every day's a bad day."

Greg smiled and nodded. "Good luck," he said as he stepped away from the door.

Cain knocked once and walked inside without waiting for a response. The room was dark, and it took a moment for his eyes to adjust to the lack of light. Mallory was sitting in the corner farthest from the door, with a blanket over his legs. The once robust man had lost seventy pounds in the last year and a half. His eyes had shrunk back into his head, and his hair was long enough to brush his shoulders. At a glance, he looked like hell. Cain wanted to shout at him, tell him to snap out of this, but he wasn't the one with a shattered hipbone and a knee that had been blown all to shit.

Cain could walk out of this house. Mallory couldn't stand up, let alone walk. It was easy to make judgments from this side of a wheelchair. Feeling helpless, Cain did what he could, but it seemed like damn little.

"I'm not in the mood for company," Mallory muttered.

"I brought someone for you to meet," Cain said. It would take more than a sour mood to get rid of him.

"Another time, perhaps." Mallory's voice was strained, the frustration and anger leaking through the words.

Francine moved away from Cain and reached for the light switch, flipping it on. The room was instantly bathed in a warm glow.

Automatically Mallory's hands went to shade his eyes,

and he cursed under his breath. Cain watched as his friend's angry glare connected with the therapist's gaze.

"Hello, Mr. Mallory," Francine said brightly, "I'm Francine Holden."

Mallory glared disdainfully at Cain as if he'd stabbed him in the back. "Get rid of her."

"Now, Mallory—"

"I said get rid of her."

"I could get offended, but I won't," Francine said, chuckling. Cain swore he heard a tinge of glee in her laugh and loved it. This was going to work out far better than he'd hoped.

"We're going to become friends, Mallory," Francine said. "Real good friends. For the next two months, I'm going to stick to you like glue, and when I'm through with you," she said, firmly planting her hand on her hip, "I guarantee you won't be sitting in a dark room with a blanket over your head to close out the world."

Mallory ignored her. "All I want is peace and quiet. Is that so much to ask?" he demanded. Cain could almost feel the anger emanate off Mallory in waves. "It's the season, you know."

"Your muscles can't wait while you sit around feeling sorry for yourself." Francine lowered her gaze to his mangled left leg, peeking out from beneath the blanket. Mallory covered it quickly. "Every day without therapy, you risk never regaining the use of that leg. You want to walk again, don't you?"

For the first time Mallory focused the full force of his attention on her. "I don't need you."

"That's where you're wrong. You've never needed anyone more in your life."

Mallory responded with a low snicker.

"We'll get started first thing this afternoon," Francine announced, speaking to Cain. She pushed up the sleeves of her thin sweater as if she could hardly wait to get going.

"Cain?" Mallory pleaded silently for assistance, but Cain purposely looked away. A minute passed before a string of abusive threats colored the air.

"I'm pleased to see you have such an extensive vocabulary," Francine said. "I imagine you'll be using it over the next couple of months. Judging by those X rays, this isn't going to be easy. I promise you one thing, you'll never work harder in your life. But by the time I'm finished with you, you'll be walking. Now," she said, her words bright and cheerful, "are you man enough to accept this challenge, or do you want someone who'll tuck you in at night and read you bedtime stories for the rest of your life?"

"Cain, I'm warning you," Mallory said between clenched teeth. His eyes were as dark and menacing as Cain had ever seen. "Get rid of this Amazon."

"I won't do that," Cain said mildly. "She may be your last chance."

"I don't want this," Mallory muttered, and rubbed a hand over his face. "And I don't want her." He gestured toward Francine. "If you think I need a woman, fine, send me a woman, not Attila the Hun."

Cain glanced at Francine, wondering if Mallory had offended her. Apparently not. Her face remained expressionless.

"Don't worry," she said, "we just need to get to know each other better. Before long we're going to be real good friends."

"Don't count on it," Tim Mallory muttered.

"Oh, but I am," she countered, grinning broadly as she walked out the door.

Cain followed, waited until there wasn't any chance Mallory could hear him and asked, "What are his chances?"

"Good," Francine said without hesitating. "Very good. He's got plenty of spunk. Trust me, he'll need every ounce of that tenacity. We'll start right away."

Cain paused. "I apologize for the things Mallory said."

"Don't worry about it," was her automatic response, but a look flashed in her eyes that told Cain his friend's words had hit their mark. "I know I'm no raving beauty, but that's not why you're hiring me."

Perhaps not, but if she could bring Mallory out of this depression and help him walk again, Cain would believe she was the most beautiful woman in the world.

3

Cain needed to do some Christmas shopping. That was why he'd come to Fisherman's Wharf. At least that was the excuse he'd used when he found himself wandering aimlessly along the waterfront.

The harder he worked to convince himself his being there had nothing to do with Linette Collins, the more obvious the truth became. Hell, he could have arranged for damn near anything he wanted over the phone with little more than a credit card and a catalog number.

The only reason he was on the wharf was the ridiculous hope he'd catch a glimpse of Linette. Just one. Without her knowing. Why he found it so necessary to spy on her, he didn't know. Didn't want to know.

As it happened, he located her yarn shop tucked in a corner along Pier 39, the window display as charming and inviting as the woman herself. He stood outside several moments, his hands buried in his lambskin-lined jacket.

Uncomfortable emotions came at him like poisoned darts, infecting him with all the might-have-beens in his life. He'd chosen this lifestyle, thrived on the challenge. No drug could produce the physical or emotional high of a successfully completed mission. No drug and no woman.

Then why was he standing in the cold like a lovelorn teenager, hoping for a glimpse of a widow he'd met briefly one night at a Christmas party? Clearly there were a few screws loose. The military had a word for this: battle fatigue. What he needed was a few uninterrupted days by himself to put his life back in the proper perspective.

Montana. Christmas was the perfect excuse to escape for a few days. It was long past time that he visited his ranch. He heard from the foreman he'd hired every now and again, but it had been well over a year since Cain had last visited the five-thousand-acre spread.

His strides filled with purpose, he walked along the pier until he saw a sign for World Wide Travel. After stepping inside the agency, he moved to the counter and waited his turn. A smartly dressed professional greeted him with a smile and arranged for his airline ticket to Helena, Montana. The only seats available were in first class, but Cain could well afford the extravagance. It was a small price to pay to escape San Francisco and the beautiful widow who'd captured his mind.

Experiencing a small sense of satisfaction, Cain tucked the airline ticket into the inside pocket of his jacket and continued on his way, moving down the waterfront and farther away from Linette. Farther away from temptation.

He was just beginning to think he had this minor curiosity licked when out of the blue, he saw her. For a moment it felt as if someone had inadvertently hit him against the back of the head. He went stock-still.

From the way her shoulders hunched forward he could see that she was tired. She stood in line at a fish and chips place, working to open the clasp of her shoulder bag. The wind whipped her hair about her face, and she lifted a finger to wrap a thick strand of dark hair around her ear.

The smart thing to do was to turn around, without delay, and walk away as fast as his feet would carry him. He'd gotten what he wanted. One last look at her, without her knowing. His curiosity should be satisfied.

Even as his mind formulated the thought, Cain knew just seeing Linette again wasn't nearly enough. He wanted to talk to her and get to know her. He wanted to sit down across a table from her and discover what it was about her that made a man who'd built his life around pride and discipline risk making a world-class fool of himself.

Linette was exhausted. She couldn't remember a day when she'd done a more brisk business. Instead of celebrating over the highest gross income achieved in a single workday, she felt like falling into bed and sleeping for a week. She wanted to ignore Christmas, the hustle and bustle, the joy and goodwill.

It was Nancy's news, too, Linette realized. It wasn't that she begrudged Rob and Nancy every happiness. She was thrilled for them. Yet it was all so painful. She ached for the child she'd never have with Michael and all the dreams they'd once shared.

Christmas, coupled with the anniversary of Michael's death and the news of the baby, weighed down her heart as surely as if it had been tied with concrete blocks and carelessly flung into the Bay.

As she advanced toward the take-out window, Linette realized she wasn't hungry. What appetite she'd had vanished. Stepping out of line, she secured the clasp of her purse and turned to head up the wharf.

It was then that she saw Cain. Linette's heart gave a short, rapid-fire reaction. As much as she didn't want to admit it, he'd been in her thoughts most of the day.

His eyes locked with hers as if the distance, the shoppers, the crowded sidewalk and endless traffic, in no way separated them. As if all she had to do were reach out and, like magic, he'd be standing there, directly in front of her.

At precisely the same moment they started walking toward each other, their gazes continuing to hold them as effectively as an embrace.

"Hello." Cain spoke first.

"Hi." She smiled, or at least attempted one. "Fancy meeting you here."

"I had to come down to pick up my airline tickets."

"You're leaving?" It shouldn't have come as any surprise. Cain had never hid the fact that he was in town for only a few days. San Francisco wasn't his home.

"I'll be back shortly after the first of the year."

The news sufficiently lifted her spirits, although there wasn't a single reason to believe she'd be seeing him then. Or ever again, for that matter.

"You changed your mind?" he asked, inclining his head toward the fish and chip stand.

"Yeah. I was looking for something quick and easy. But by the time I arrive home, the fish will be cold and soggy." That wasn't the whole story, but it was close enough to the truth to satisfy him.

By tacit agreement they started walking. The aroma of fresh fish and thick-cut French fries floated toward them as they strolled along the pier.

"The fish and chips wouldn't be soggy if you ate them right away," Cain said. His hands were buried in his coat pockets, and he condensed his steps in order to keep pace with her much shorter stride. "I was headed that way myself. Would you care to join me?"

Linette hadn't been expecting a dinner invitation, and his offer took her by surprise. "Thank you, I'd enjoy that." She'd enjoy anything that helped her through the loneliness, helped her through this night. Rushing back to her apartment, which stood empty and dark, held no appeal.

His hand cupped her elbow as he led her, not to the fish and chip stand as she expected, but to the restaurant, a well-known and expensive seafood place that catered to a heavy tourist trade.

Because of the hour, they were put on a waiting list and told it might be as long as forty-five minutes before they could be seated. Cain didn't seem to object and Linette didn't, either.

He suggested they wait in the bar, and she agreed, although she wasn't much of a drinker. The lounge was as crowded as the restaurant, but they managed to find a table. An attractive waitress took their order. Cain asked

for a Jack Daniel's, and Linette opted for a glass of white
wine.

"Busy day?" Cain asked once they were settled.

"Frantic was more like it. There was a lull every now
and again where Bonnie—she works with me—and I
could take a breather, but those were few and far
between. How about you?"

He hesitated as if he weren't sure how to answer her.
"I attended to business matters."

She noticed how he turned the conversation away
from himself and quizzed her once more about the yarn
shop. She answered his questions, but she was deeply
disappointed. It was more than obvious that he had no
intention of lowering the steel facade he wore like plate
armor, to share any part of himself. He was a good lis-
tener, but after thirty minutes she ran out of things to
say.

As time passed it became more and more difficult to
carry on a conversation. Linette finished her wine and
set the glass on the small round table.

"Would you care for another?" Cain asked.

"No thanks." She made a show of looking at her
watch. "Actually, I think it might be a good idea if I
headed home. It's later than I realized, and . . . ," She let
the rest fade. Making excuses, even plausible ones,
wasn't her forte. "Perhaps we could have dinner another
time."

Cain's gaze narrowed with confusion as she stood.
"Sure," he said. He took out his wallet and left a generous tip for the waitress. He hurriedly spoke to the recep-
tionist on his way out the door.

Linette hadn't intended for him to follow her outside.

"It was good to see you again, Cain," she said, eager to be on her way. She turned, her steps as fast paced as she could make them. His eyes seemed to bore into her back, and it was all she could do not to whirl around and confront him.

Weaving her way in and out of the pockets of pedestrians, Linette made good time. She'd gone four or five blocks and was just outside the BART station when she heard Cain call her name.

Briefly closing her eyes, dreading a confrontation, she hesitated and then turned around. He trotted across the street. "One question," he said as he braced his hands against his knees and struggled to regain his breath. "Was that a brush-off?"

"It's me," she said, more than willing to accept the blame. "I've had a rough day. Nancy stopped in to tell me she's pregnant and it's almost Christmas." She was speaking so fast, the words nearly collided with one another on the way out of her mouth. "Forgive me if I offended you, but I didn't have the energy to sit through dinner and listen to myself all evening." By the frown he wore, she realized her explanation served only to baffle him further.

"Listen to yourself?" he asked.

"It's apparent you're not interested in sharing any part of yourself with me. Don't misunderstand me, if you don't want to talk, fine, that's your prerogative. It's just that I'm tired and hungry and depressed and not fit company. Not tonight." She clung to her purse strap as if it were a lifeline, eager to be on her way.

A car, not unlike any other, raced past them. Linette saw a youth toss something out the window. His action was followed by several loud bursts of noise. Before who or what had fully registered in her mind, Cain lunged for her, gripping her hard about the waist. Twisting so that he would receive the brunt of the impact, he pushed her toward the sidewalk, which came racing up to meet them. She landed with a thud atop him, bouncing slightly with the force of the fall.

Her breath jammed in her lungs as shock and panic shot through her.

"Are you all right?" Cain asked, brushing the hair from her face as if that would tell him what he needed to know. His touch was gentle and light, although she noticed his hand trembled.

She couldn't answer him, couldn't force the words past the sheer terror that had gripped her throat. Instead she wrapped her arms around him and clung. With her heart thundering in her ear, she sank into the safety of his arms, the warm haven of security.

"I'm sorry," he whispered repeatedly, his hands stroking the back of her head. "I thought it was something else. Apparently it was only firecrackers."

She nodded, her pulse hammering against his chest. Her breath came in rapid bursts as she struggled to regain her composure.

"I didn't mean to frighten you."

Gradually she gained control and eased herself away from him. "I'm fine." She wasn't, but she would be in short order.

He stood and helped her to her feet. A crowd had gathered around them, firing questions. Cain ignored them as if they were alone, ignored the questions and offers of assistance. Linette heard whispers about crazy kids, tossing fireworks into the street like that.

Cain wrapped his arm around Linette's waist and gently led her away.

"I'll drive you home," he said. In no way were the words in the form of a question. She saw the strain on his face.

"I'm fine," she reiterated. Perhaps she was now, but she wasn't so sure of Cain. The self-directed anger radiated from him like the heat from a sunburn.

He helped her inside his car, and when he climbed in the driver's seat, she rattled off her address. She noticed the hard set of his jaw and the way his hands tightened around the steering wheel.

He didn't say a word on the ten-minute drive to her apartment building.

"I think we can both do with a cup of strong coffee," she said.

His eyes hardened as if he weren't sure he should accept her invitation. "I've done enough damage for one night, don't you think?"

She raised her hand to her face, to brush away a strand of hair, and realized she didn't want to walk into the cold, dark apartment, surrounded by silence, surrounded by memories. Not tonight. Not alone. Like the night of the Christmas party, they needed each other.

"Come up with me." The words were barely audible, and she wondered if he heard her. His hands tightened until his knuckles went white before he reached for the key and without another word turned off the ignition.

Linette led the way into the elevator and down the long, silent hall to her third-floor apartment. She unlocked the door and turned on the light. Inside, she removed her coat and hung it in the hall closet with her purse.

Cain removed his jacket and draped it over the end of the leather sofa, as if to say he wouldn't be staying long. He scanned the room and zeroed in on the framed photograph of Michael she'd placed on the fireplace mantel.

Linette moved into the compact kitchen, but Cain gently but firmly sat her down at the octagon-shaped glass table in the dining room. "I'll make the coffee," he announced. He assembled the pot within minutes and started rummaging through her refrigerator. "When was the last time you bought groceries?" he asked, taking a carton of eggs from the top shelf.

She assumed the question was rhetorical, but she answered him anyway. "Last week . . . sometime."

Before she could ask what he was doing, Cain had scrambled eggs and buttered toast. He set the plate in front of her, poured them each a cup of coffee, adding sugar to hers. Then he pulled out a chair, twisted it around, and straddled it. "I'm sorry about what happened earlier. I don't have any excuse, other than to say I acted out of instinct."

Linette had already discerned as much.

"I've been in this line of business for too many years not to react to the sound of gunfire, or in this case a string of ladyfingers."

Linette cradled the coffee mug between her hands and let its warmth revive her. "I know. Nancy told me you were part of Special Forces."

He studied her for a few moments. "What did you mean when you said Nancy's pregnant and it's Christmas?"

Linette's shoulders sagged with defeat. "You're doing it again," she said with an exaggerated sigh.

"Doing what?"

"Turning the conversation away from yourself."

"I am?" He seemed surprised. "All right, fair is fair. Answer my questions and I'll answer yours."

Linette told him about Nancy's visit earlier that afternoon. "My husband and I badly wanted children. I don't expect you to understand. I'm not entirely sure I do myself, but it's like this big hole inside me started bleeding again. I thought it had healed."

Cain sipped his coffee. "Your husband's the man in the photo on the mantel?"

"That's Michael. He died of leukemia two years ago on December twenty-third."

"Ah, so that's what you meant about it being Christmas."

"Yes. It's my fault he lingered as long as he did."

"Your fault?"

She nodded. "He'd been in a coma for a month before he died, and there was no hope. You see, I refused to let him die. I'm convinced the sheer force of my will is what kept him alive. I sat by his bedside for weeks, refusing to leave for more than a few minutes. I feared that without me there, he'd slip away. I couldn't allow that, I couldn't let him die on me, not when I so desperately wanted him to live. And so I clung to him, clung to the hope of a miracle."

She lowered her gaze, reliving those terrible weeks in her mind. "With faith the size of an avocado pit, I expected God to heal Michael. He did, of course, but not the way I anticipated. Michael's free of illness now. It took me a long time to understand that.

"It wasn't until it was almost Christmas that I realized what I was doing to my husband. Michael was ready to go, had been ready nearly the entire month he'd been in the coma. He was waiting for me to release him. When I did, death came quickly. It may sound odd, but it came as a friend and not the bitter enemy I'd imagined."

Cain stood and, taking his coffee with him, started to pace her kitchen.

"Since the anniversary of his death falls so close to Christmas, it's all the more difficult. You see, everyone seems to want to make the holidays better for me. I feel like I'm being suffocated with attention. Everyone tries so hard to pretend Michael isn't really gone. It's like they're playacting that he's away on a business trip or something like that. His parents have had a hard time accepting his death.

"For the past two years, they've insisted I join them for Christmas. I love Jake and Janet, but they're still grieving themselves, and as much as we care for each other, it's all so uncomfortable."

"What about your family?"

"They're on the East Coast, and my parents are as bad as Michael's. At least with Jake and Janet, I'm only trapped a day."

Cain sat down once more. "All right, ask me anything you'd like."

"Anything?"

He nodded.

Now that she had free reign, Linette wasn't sure where to start. "How old are you?"

He laughed. "Thirty-six, and you?"

"Twenty-nine."

"What brings you to San Francisco?"

He heaved a heavy sigh. "One of my men was badly

injured eighteen months ago. He's required several extensive surgeries since, and the best hospital and surgeons were here."

"How's he doing now?"

A frown of deep concern creased Cain's brow. "Physically, about as well as can be expected, but mentally he's having a hell of a time. I hired a new physical therapist for him this afternoon, and hopefully she'll last longer than the others. I have a feeling Francine's just what Mallory needs."

A smile courted the corners of his mouth when he mentioned the other woman's name, causing Linette to wonder about the physical therapist. Francine was a feminine name and conjured up the imagine of a sleek, attractive woman who'd managed to capture Cain's attention. If Linette hadn't known better, she would have thought she was jealous of a woman she'd never met, over a man she barely knew.

"Where are you stationed?" she asked abruptly, wanting to change subjects, sorry now she'd asked.

This too gave him pause, and frankly she wondered why. It wasn't as if a military base should be any secret. "I'm out of Miami."

It certainly wasn't any place close, she noted. "You're a long way from home, aren't you?"

"A very long way," he agreed, his voice low and strained.

Linette had the feeling he wasn't speaking about the distance between San Francisco and Miami, either. He was out of his element with her, too. He wasn't accustomed to consoling grieving widows or answering questions about himself. He was a man who issued orders and expected complete and immediate obedience.

"Anything else?" he asked when she wasn't immediately forthcoming with another question.

She shook her head.

He downed the last of his coffee and set the mug in her sink. "I'll leave you, then. You're sure you're all right?"

"I'm fine." She was now.

Cain reached for his jacket and started toward the door. Linette followed him. "Thank you for bringing me home."

"No problem."

"And thanks for listening." She normally didn't spill out her heart like that or burden another with her grief. She'd needed him, and in some strange way she realized he needed her just as badly.

The desire to touch him was suddenly so strong that she gave in to it. She lifted her hand and pressed it against his cheek. His hand joined hers, and he moved his head slightly so that he could kiss the inside of her palm.

"You're going to be fine."

"I know." And she did. But every now and again, mostly when she wasn't prepared, something unexpected would find its mark, reminding her of all that she'd lost. This very day was a good example.

Cain's eyes studied hers carefully. "I'd like to kiss you."

"I wish you would," she confessed.

He smiled and so did she.

Before another second passed, she was in his arms and his mouth covered hers. As if this were where she belonged, had always belonged, Linette melted against him, savoring the feel of his strength. His mouth was hungry and hard, his kisses heady and deep. Before long she was clinging to him. The pleasure was so keen, it frightened her.

Expertly he moved his mouth over hers, molding her lips with his own. When she sighed, he deepened the kiss and touched his tongue to hers. She welcomed this small invasion with shy touches of her own. Her body was heating up, embarrassing her with a need she'd long denied. She felt empty and aching. She hadn't thought these sensations were possible with another man. She hadn't expected this, hadn't anticipated this.

By the time they broke apart, Linette was convinced desire and need were written all over her face.

Cain stared down on her as if he too had been taken by surprise, as if he were as shocked as she by their bodies' responses to each other.

"Good night, Linette," he said finally.

"Good night, Cain," she whispered, praying the dazed, hungry look had vanished from her eyes.

Slowly, as if it demanded all of his strength to leave her, he opened the door. He stepped into the hallway. "How about dinner tomorrow?" he asked abruptly as if the invitation came as a surprise to him.

"All right."

"I'll come by here at six."

"Perfect."

He left, and she closed the door and leaned against the hard wood. Her knees were shaking, but it wasn't any lingering effect of her adventure that evening. It was the aftermath of Cain's kiss that left her trembling.

At the fireplace, Linette picked up the photo of

Michael and stared at the lovingly familiar face for several moments.

"I like him a whole lot," she told her dead husband, and then, because she believed it was important, she added, "I believe you would have, too."

Sagging onto the sofa, Linette pressed the photo against her chest and closed her eyes. For the last three years she'd felt as if she were living out her life in the eye of a storm. The winds had died down in the last few months, the hailstorm of fears pummeling against her had tapered. And the thunderstorm she'd suffered at Michael's death had eased to a light drizzle.

She smiled to herself, amazed at how fanciful her thinking had become of late. After replacing the photograph, Linette returned to the kitchen. She hadn't eaten the eggs Cain had scrambled for her. Now she reheated them in the microwave, sat down at the table and enjoyed the meal. It was the first time a man had cooked for her in a very long while.

4

Cain tossed his car keys in the air and caught them in his left hand. From the way he was acting, one would assume he was a love-starved teen. Hell, that was the way he felt. He paused then, struck by the realization of what he was letting happen. Wanted to happen.

Linette Collins was dangerous.

Not only to his sanity, but to his very life. Cain had seen it happen often enough to other men to know the danger signs. Yet here he was making the same choice, the same mistake.

He was damn close to losing his own fool head. And all over a woman. Only Linette wasn't an ordinary woman. She possessed special powers. She must in order to tie him up in knots a sailor couldn't undo.

Cain was good at what he did. Damn good. From the time he was in Special Forces, he'd heard that he was a natural. What that meant, he'd decided years later, was that he didn't give a damn whether he lived or died. It all boiled down to one thing: He had nothing to lose.

It was this that had given him an edge, the steadiest hand, the clearest head. Now that he'd met Linette, he understood what this advantage had cost him. Over the years, the price had been exacting and demanding.

Roughly, he didn't give a tinker's damn about anyone or anything other than Deliverance Company and the all-encompassing, all-important mission.

He'd held Linette and kissed her, thinking . . . hell, he didn't know what he'd been thinking. Clearly he hadn't been, otherwise he would have known better, would have taken one look at her and run as fast as his legs would carry him in the opposite direction.

A woman like Linette would muddle his mind, would mire his reflexes. A woman like this would be the death of him. Then he'd leave this world as lonely and as miserable as when he'd entered it. It wasn't much of a legacy.

What frightened Cain most was how desperately he needed her. Linette Collins, the gentle widow, had the power to cure his heart. She had the power to cure him of a lifetime of not giving a damn.

Cain sat in his car and thumped his fist against the steering column. He had an idea. A crazy one in light of what he'd been thinking, but one that had presented itself and wouldn't let go.

Before he could change his mind, he climbed out of the car and hurried back into Linette's apartment building. Instead of waiting for the elevator, which he considered too slow, he raced up the three flights of stairs, taking the steps two and three at a time.

He was panting by the time he arrived outside her apartment. Drawing in several deep breaths, he waited until his heart had calmed before he rang her doorbell.

Although he didn't see it happen, he was certain Linette checked the peephole before unlatching the deadbolt lock.

"Cain?"

"Listen," he said, struggling to sound nonchalant and relaxed, "I just had an idea. Why don't you spend Christmas with me in Montana?"

"Spend Christmas with you in Montana?" Linette repeated slowly.

Cain was beginning to think this might not be such a brilliant idea after all. "You were telling me how difficult the holiday is for you. I'm offering you a solution."

"But . . . "

Apparently she didn't know what to think of his suggestion, because she blinked several times and stared at him with a dumbstruck expression.

"I've got a ranch house there with plenty of bedrooms, so you don't need to worry about sleeping arrangements. I'm not expecting anything more than your company for a few days." He couldn't believe he was doing this. Couldn't believe he was tossing his heart out on a slab for her to either accept or reject.

Perhaps he was trying to make up for all the Christmases he'd missed as a kid, with a father who guzzled every dime he'd ever earned. Somewhere in a hidden corner of Cain's heart, a little boy was waiting for the Christmas tree and the home-cooked turkey with all the trimmings. He'd believed that child had long since matured to manhood, but apparently all it took was the warmth and gentleness of a beautiful widow to reawaken the long forgotten childhood fantasy.

"Listen," he said, feeling more foolish by the minute, "think about it, and when we meet tomorrow evening, you can let me know. It's just an idea, and if you'd rather not come, then it isn't a big deal."

Without waiting for a reply, Cain turned away, wishing now he'd taken more time to consider what he was doing before traipsing upstairs and taking the bull by the horns.

"Cain."

He whirled back around.

Linette had stepped into the hallway. She looked vulnerable and uncertain. "I'll be happy to go."

He shouldn't be this pleased, but he was. Ecstatic. Already he'd determined that Linette was dangerous. Yet here he was inviting her to his home, opening his heart and his life to her softness. He might as well pull the pin out of a hand grenade and drop it at his own feet. All he had to do now was wait for the explosion.

"How soon can you leave?" he asked, burying his hands in his pockets in an effort to resist the urge to kiss her again.

She gestured weakly as if she weren't sure how to answer him. "Tomorrow, but I'll need to make the arrangements with Bonnie, and I need be back before the twenty-eighth."

"No problem."

She grinned then, and Cain swore he'd never seen anyone with a more beautiful smile.

"You'll call me in the morning?"

He nodded, and took two giant steps backward.

"Good night, Cain."

"Night." It wasn't until he was in his car that he realized he was whistling. He stopped abruptly, wondering what madness had overtaken him. It didn't matter if this craziness had a name, Cain decided. He couldn't remember a time when he'd been this happy.

Francine dressed carefully for her second encounter with Tim Mallory. Not that she had a vast wardrobe to choose from. Her closet contained mostly white uniforms of tops and slacks that afforded her freedom of movement. For the occasional interview and business meeting, she kept a couple of tailored suits on hand, but nothing spectacular.

She wore her hair the way she always did, pulled tightly away from her face in a long French braid that stretched halfway down the middle of her back. She didn't bother with makeup. Never had, even as a teenager. Nature hadn't given her an attractive face, and with nothing to enhance, she figured why go to all the bother.

She parked her car in the driveway and hopped out, taking her gym bag with her. She was eager to get started on this case. She'd always thrived on challenge, and something told her she was going to enjoy working with this particular patient.

Generally she would have preferred starting Monday morning, but the longer they waited before beginning the exercises, the greater the chance Tim Mallory's muscles would atrophy. She'd know soon enough how much his leg muscles had already degenerated.

Tim Mallory might think he was some he-man soldier, but she'd demand every ounce of grit the mercenary ever believed he possessed.

When she arrived at the house, Greg, his personal assistant, opened the door for her. "It's Sunday," he said, looking surprised to see her.

"I know. How's the patient?"

The beefy young man shrugged. "About the same. Cantankerous, angry, and in a generally bad mood."

"Be prepared, then," she said, casting the assistant a sympathetic glance. "Because it's about to get worse. Much worse."

"You're kidding, I hope."

"I wish I was. Come and get me in an hour, and bring ice bags and two aspirin."

"For Mr. Mallory?"

"No," she said with a chuckle. "For me. Mallory and I've only met once, but I can tell this guy's going to give me a migraine."

Greg laughed.

Francine didn't wait for him to show her the way, she already knew the mercenary was holed up in the back bedroom. Probably with the lights off, buried under blankets because the lack of circulation in the lower half of his body left him chilled inside and out.

She found him just where she'd suspected she would.

"Hello again," she said brightly, flipping on the light switch and moving into the bedroom with the determination of a Mac truck.

"What the hell are you doing here?" Tim demanded. He sat up in the bed and grabbed the clock off the bedstand. "It's barely nine."

"I prefer to start early. Beginning Monday morning, I'll be here at six. We'll have your first workout before breakfast."

"Wanna bet, sweetheart?" His dark gaze hardened, daring her to defy him. She noted his eyes were dull with pain and rimmed with fatigue. Her best guess was that he wasn't sleeping much and had the appetite of a bird. That too was about to change.

Francine flattened her hand against her hip. She didn't like being referred to as "sweetheart," especially in that tone of voice, but mentioning it was certain to guarantee he would continue.

"Do I wanna bet? Sure, I'd be willing to place a wager on that."

Mallory eyes flared, as though he'd welcome the opportunity to send her packing. "Any time, any place."

"Great," she said gleefully. "We'll make it easy. You get out of that bed and walk me to the door, and I'm out of here. Until that happens, big boy, I'm going to be your shadow. I promise you, you'll never work harder than in the next several months."

His blunt features flushed with anger. "I can't walk," he said between gritted teeth. "And you damn well know it."

"Not now you can't, but you will in time."

"Can you guarantee that?"

"No," she returned evenly, unwilling to pull any punches. "But you're going to have to give it your best shot, and I'm here to help you." Rolling up her sleeves, she smiled at him. "Let's get started."

"I don't feel like it." The anger in his eyes intensified as he glared at her.

"I don't suppose you do. No one does, and I'm not going to lie to you, Mr. Mallory. There's going to be pain, plenty of it. For a time, you'll hate me." She rolled the empty wheelchair away from his bedside.

"I already do."

She grinned and promised, "But not nearly as much as you will."

By the end of the first hour of gently working the stiff muscles of Mallory's legs, rubbing them down to encourage the circulation, Francine was invigorated. As she worked, she explained what she was doing and why. She wanted to reassure him there was a payoff for the pain she inflicted on him. From Mallory's tense silence it was unlikely her patient had received the message.

Francine had enough experience to know this procedure wasn't painless, but after the first few protests, Tim lay on his back, his eyes closed, his expression cast in stone.

"How much longer?" he asked after the first hour. His face glistened with sweat, and his chest heaved as he struggled against revealing his discomfort.

"I'm almost finished," she said, working the calf of his injured leg. She elevated it slightly, and as he rolled his head to one side, she saw that he'd gritted his teeth. There was no joy in witnessing pain. It was never easy to see another suffer, no matter how cantankerous the patient. More often than not, her lecture on the benefits of the exercise were for her own ears. She needed to be reminded of the eventual outcome for all this agony.

By the end of the session, what little energy Tim Mallory possessed had vanished. Greg arrived, and

Francine asked that he help Mallory out of his clothes and into his swimming suit.

Her patient lifted his head off the sweat-drenched pillow. "I thought you said we were through."

"We are. But now that I've got the circulation going in that leg, I want to put it to use."

"I'm tired."

"I know." She'd wager he was a lot more than tired, but she couldn't allow her sympathy to show.

"Not today."

"Greg," she said, "have him to the swimming pool in fifteen minutes."

The young man grinned and nodded. "I'll see that he's there."

"Good." With that she reached for her gym bag and left the room. She heard Tim protest the minute she was out of the room, but he didn't stand a chance of winning this argument, and he knew it. The mercenary might not willingly own up to it, but he had few options. Eventually acceptance would come, but from what she knew of Mallory's personality, he'd hold out as long as he could.

One thing was certain, he didn't have much energy left to put up much of a fight. At least for now.

Linette's first impression of the ranch house was that it looked like something out of a television western. *Bonanza* revisited. The two-story log structure, nestled against the backdrop of the Rocky Mountains, looked as inviting as a port in a storm. An apt description in light of the fat snowflakes lazily drifting down from a thunder blue sky.

"It's beautiful," she told Cain.

"I called ahead and had the kitchen stocked, so there'll be plenty of chow. John Stamp's my foreman, and his wife, Patty, promised to check everything over and have the house ready when we arrived." Cain glanced her way. "Are you tired?"

"Not in the least." They'd spent the majority of the day hopping from one airport to another, and when they'd finally landed, they'd had to drive nearly three hours.

Cain had phoned Linette bright and early that morning and asked if she could make a ten o'clock flight. After a moment of panic, she'd assured him in a calm voice that it wouldn't be a problem, and thanks to Bonnie, it hadn't been.

"I'm more hungry than anything," Cain said.

Gourmet cooking was one of Linette's favorite things. She hadn't been doing much of that lately, not when she was cooking for one. Now she looked forward to impressing Cain with the smooth way she handled herself around a kitchen.

Cain pulled the Bronco into the detached garage and helped her out of the passenger's side before hauling their luggage out of the back end.

The lights from inside the house glowed brightly like beacons of welcome. Linette reached for her cosmetic bag and followed Cain through a thin layer of freshly fallen snow to the house. Several inches had already been shoveled off the pathway.

The door was unlocked, and Linette sighed inwardly at the rush of warm air that greeted her. When Cain had mentioned the ranch house, she hadn't a clue it would be this beautiful or this inviting. From the entryway, she saw a fire flickering gently in the massive stone fireplace. A stairway rounded up one side to a hallway, leading, she suspected, to a series of bedrooms.

Cain removed his coat and hung it in the closet before helping her out of hers.

"If you take care of the luggage, I'll see what I can do about rustling us up some dinner." Eager to explore his beautiful house, she didn't wait for his response.

While Cain carried their suitcases up the stairs, Linette wandered into the kitchen. She stood, awestruck, just inside the door. This wasn't an ordinary kitchen, but a chef's dream. Sparkling copper kettles hung from above a large gourmet island. The appliances looked new, and a quick investigation revealed a walk-in cooler and a six-burner gas stove.

It didn't take Linette long to realize nothing was required of her. Dinner was already prepared and waiting for their arrival. Apparently Patty Stamp had seen to that along with everything else.

Cain soon joined her. "Dinner's ready," she announced.

"That was quick," he teased.

They ate at the dining room table, which was set with pink linen napkins and a centerpiece made of freshly clipped holly and cinnamon candles. Neither felt obligated to carry the conversation. Linette suspected it was because they didn't feel the necessity to fill the silence with idle chatter. Perhaps, like her, Cain didn't know what to say.

Cain helped her with the dishes, and afterward they drank coffee in front of the fireplace in matching wing-back leather chairs. As he sipped from the ceramic mug,

Cain read over some business papers John Stamp had left for him to review.

The fire mesmerized Linette; the flames licked noisily at the logs, and every now and again they'd spit and sizzle as if undergoing some great debate.

Intermittently her gaze drifted to Cain, and she thought about what her parents had said, the warnings they'd issued when they'd learned she was spending the holiday with a man she barely knew. Yet she felt none of their concern.

Cain must have felt her scrutiny because he raised his eyes to her. His gaze softened as it met hers. His look was gentle, almost loving. Neither spoke. For her part, Linette wasn't sure she could. All she knew was there was no place else she would rather be than right here with Cain McClellan sitting at her side.

"I'm not being good company, am I?"

"On the contrary," she hurried to say. "I'm perfectly content."

Her in-laws hadn't known what to say when she'd announced she wouldn't be joining them for Christmas after all. Linette knew she'd stunned them by telling them she was traveling with Cain to Montana. Michael's mother had swiftly phoned Linette's, and within fifteen minutes Linette had received a call from her concerned parents. Once she'd explained how she'd met Cain and what she intended to do over Christmas, her mother had been left speechless. Unfortunately Betty Lawson's silence hadn't lasted long, and Linette had been forced to listen to a tense lecture about the wisdom of her actions.

Apparently both Michael's parents and her own felt

she was making a foolish mistake. She couldn't trust her own judgment, they feared. She wasn't herself. Grief had clouded her thinking.

Perhaps they were right.

Linette had certainly never done anything like this before, but then she'd never met a man like Cain McClellan.

She yawned and decided to rest her eyes a moment. She must have been more tired than she realized and drifted off to sleep, because the next thing she knew Cain was whispering close to her ear. Her eyes fluttered open, and she found him standing next to her chair.

"I'm sorry to wake you, but you'll be far more comfortable upstairs."

She smiled sleepily and yawned. "I suppose you're right."

"I'll go up with you," he said, offering her his hand. He guided her up the stairs and escorted her to the bedroom he'd had readied for her arrival. He pointed out his own room, which was at the far end of the hallway. Linette didn't know whether to be relieved or disheartened that his bedroom was so far removed from her own.

"Can I get you anything?" he asked, poised in her doorway.

"No, I'm fine."

He nodded, and it seemed to her that he wanted to say something more. The look in his eyes intensified, and he hesitated before adding, "Good night, then."

"I'll see you in the morning."

"Speaking of the morning," he said, leaping on the excuse to linger.

"Yes?"

"I thought we'd cut down a Christmas tree and decorate it."

Linette's heart gladdened at the prospect. "That sounds like fun."

The strong sexual attraction between them spit and sizzled much like the logs had earlier. Nor could Linette deny what was happening to her body. A tingling awareness spread through her, leaving in its wake a desire she'd shared only with one other man.

Linette realized that Cain was a full partner in these feelings, but like her, he was bewildered and unsure.

"Good night," she said with a sigh.

He swallowed tightly, nodded, and turned away.

Cain wandered back down the stairs. Settling back onto the chair he'd recently vacated, he rubbed a hand down his face.

Linette deserved more than he could offer. Already she'd made it clear that she wouldn't be satisfied with the bare bones details of his life. She wanted to know it all.

He couldn't tell her about Deliverance Company.

It was necessary to shield her from the reality of who and what he was. Not knowing would protect her from the worry. Protect her from the harshness of what he did for a living.

After watching Michael die, Linette was a woman who cherished life, and he was a man who often foolishly risked his own. He could think of no way to explain what he did. There wasn't a chance in hell of making her understand, so he hadn't tried. And wouldn't, because every moment with her was too painfully precious to destroy.

The snow fell relentlessly through the night. Cain woke to look out at a thick blanket of the powdery substance. He was in the kitchen drinking his first cup of coffee when Linette joined him the following morning.

She was dressed in jeans and a thick cable-knit sweater. He'd never known a woman could look this naturally beautiful without makeup. Afraid she'd notice how he couldn't keep his eyes off her, he poured her a cup of coffee. She smiled her appreciation when he handed it to her.

"Did you sleep well?" he asked, hoping she had. For his own part, he'd tossed and turned most of the night, tormented by the knowledge that she was only four doors away.

"Like a log."

"Good." Toast popped up from the toaster, and he reached for it, then buttered the twin slices. "John will be by first thing this morning to go over some business matters with me."

"I'd like to meet Patty," she said.

"From what John said, she's just as anxious to meet you."

No sooner had he spoken than there was a polite knock against the back door. John let himself inside, followed by his wife of ten years. Cain watched as Patty's curious gaze moved past him to dwell on Linette. He might have been wrong, but it seemed Patty took one look at Linette and her eyes gleamed with approval.

Cain introduced the couple, and Linette shook hands with them both.

"Did you get a chance to read over those papers?" John asked. He was tall and rangy and wore his cowboy hat low on his head. Patty was short and slightly stocky, with shoulder-length blond hair and blue eyes. The two expertly managed his spread. When Cain had first purchased the place, he'd urged the Stamps to move into the main house. They'd declined, choosing instead to live in the smaller house reserved for the foreman. Cain maintained a small herd, but John had been urging him to build it up, claiming beef prices were better than they had been in a number of years. Cain was taking the advice under consideration.

As he became involved in a lengthy conversation with John, he noted Linette and Patty talking as if they were longtime friends. Every now and again he caught a word or two of their conversation. From what he gathered, Linette was asking Patty about Christmas dinner. Apparently she planned on cooking it herself.

Hard as he tried, Cain couldn't keep his eyes away from Linette. Soon John, who was eager to prove his point, realized it was useless.

"This is the first time you've ever brought a woman to visit," he commented dryly. "Are you and Linette serious?"

Startled, Cain snapped his attention away from his guest. "No," he said abruptly, perhaps too abruptly, because the women stopped talking and looked at him expectantly.

"We're going out to cut down a Christmas tree this morning," Cain said, breaking the strained silence.

"Then we won't hold you up. Come on, John," Patty urged. "These people have more important things to do than talk about purchasing a few more head of cattle."

Cain walked the couple to the door and thanked Patty

for having thoughtfully seen to their dinner the night before. He casually mentioned how good the roast had tasted.

"Linette already thanked me," she said, blushing with pleasure at his compliment. "I shouldn't have traipsed down here first thing this morning," Patty went on to say apologetically, "but I couldn't help being curious about your lady friend." Her gaze narrowed as she studied him. "She's a good woman, Cain. I hope you're considering settling down. It's time for you to start thinking about a family." With that she turned and walked away.

It was time all right. Time to have his head examined, Cain decided. That he was foolish enough to live out a schoolboy's dream was one matter, but having his foreman's wife advise him to marry and start a family was enough to turn his blood cold.

"You ready to go find a tree?" he asked gruffly after the couple had left.

"Any time," she assured him.

By the time Cain located a hand saw and found a sled and rope, the sky had turned an angry shade of gray. "It looks like it's going to start snowing again," he said, wondering at the wisdom of their gallivanting through the woods.

He did this sort of thing routinely, but he didn't know how well Linette would hold up to the physical demands of hiking in the snow. He was about to suggest that perhaps this wasn't such a great idea after all when he saw the disappointment flicker in her eyes.

"It'll be fine," she insisted. "We'll cut down a tree and be back before you know it."

"All right," Cain relented, mainly because he didn't

have the heart to disappoint her. Whatever common sense he possessed had taken a flying leap toward insanity the minute he'd met this woman. Why stop now?

Fortunately a copse of trees grew close by. Any one of those would serve nicely. They could walk there and back without much difficulty, he decided.

"This one will do," he said, coming upon the first tree the appropriate size. He reached for the hand saw when Linette stopped him.

"It's too short," she insisted. "And one side isn't as full as it should be."

"Too short? Not full enough?"

"Yes! Besides that, you'll be able to see that you cut down a tree from the house. It'll spoil your view."

It would be a cold day in hell before one blasted fir tree would ruin his view. He wasn't likely to notice the loss of a single six-footer when he owned a forest full.

"All right," he said with limitless patience, "you choose."

Apparently this was what she'd been waiting for him to suggest, because she dragged him halfway up a mountain and down another before she discovered the ideal Christmas tree. Frankly, Cain didn't know there could be so much wrong with so many trees. He would have been perfectly happy with any one of a thousand she'd singularly dismissed for one ridiculous flaw or another.

To think he'd been worried about her physical endurance. By the time she'd made her choice, he was both hungry and tired.

"You're sure about this one?" he asked. One thing was clear. If he ever spent another Christmas with Linette Collins, he was buying a tree in town. And he was purchasing it without taking her with him.

"Positive," she said, and her cheeks glowed pink and healthy.

He hunkered down and sawed away at the trunk, grumbling under his breath. This was his reward. All his life he'd dreamed about cutting down his own Christmas tree. He'd never realized it would be this damned difficult.

He stood when he'd finished and discovered Linette had vanished. "Linette," he called, his heart pounding hard and fast. It would be just like the damn fool woman to wander off and get lost.

"Linette," he called a second time. Concerned, he scanned the area as the sense of dread filled him. He left the fallen tree and glanced toward the sky, sure they were about to encounter a blizzard.

When he didn't get an answer, he shouted louder, this time cupping his mouth in order for his voice to carry farther.

"Cain."

Relieved, he whirled around. The snowball's impact caught him square in the chest. For one moment he stood frozen in surprise. It didn't take him long to recover. Before another second had passed, he'd scooped a ball of his own.

"That wasn't wise," he said. She didn't appear to believe him because he was bombarded with three other snowballs in quick succession. He was amazed by the accuracy of her throws.

"Anyone who stands around and waits to be hit deserves what they get," she called out. "Some soldier you turned out to be."

Cain was quick enough to duck behind a tree this time. The snowball slammed against the bark, spraying his face with snow. Cain laughed outright. This was what he got for trusting that little she-devil.

It didn't take him more than a few minutes to work his way through the woods and sneak up behind her. He watched her for several moments, peeking out from the tree, attempting to locate him. It never occurred to her that he could be less than ten feet behind her.

"Linette." He spoke her name softly and let the breeze carry it as though it had been whispered by the angels themselves.

Linette stiffened, her attention keen.

He said her name a second time.

She swung around and blinked incredibly large eyes at him. "Cain? How'd you get there?" She made it sound as if they'd somehow become separated during a Sunday school picnic.

He bounced a snowball from one gloved hand to the other. "You certainly had me fooled," he said, smiling gleefully. "And all along I thought you a sweet and gentle soul."

"But I am." Once more she fluttered her long lashes at him.

"Who would have guessed a woman so beautiful would possess such a wide streak of malice?"

"You shouldn't have complained."

"Complained?" He lightly pitched the compacted snowball in the air, catching it with one hand.

"About the Christmas tree," she said. He noticed the way she was edging away from the tree and guessed she was planning to make a run for it.

"I never said a word," he countered.

"Maybe not out loud, but you were mumbling a

number of times, and what you didn't mumble you were thinking."

He laughed, because she'd read him so accurately.

She pitched one last snowball at him, then turned and ran like a jackrabbit, ricocheting from one tree to the next and yelling at the top of her lungs.

The snowball missed him completely. He dropped the one he was holding and took out in a dead run after her. Her agility and speed amazed him, but she was no match for him. He reached her within seconds and grabbed her about the waist.

Laughing, they both went down in the snow. She lay sprawled atop him, but he quickly reversed their positions, pinning her beneath him. Her eyes had never been more clear. They sparkled with laughter and life. Her chest heaved as she smiled up at him.

"You deserve to have your face washed with snow," he told her, holding her hands above her head. "And I'm just the man to do it."

"I'm so sorry," she said in a totally unconvincing lie. "I don't know what came over me. You were cutting down the tree and muttering when all at once this voice inside me said you needed to be brought down a peg or two."

With his free hand, Cain lifted a paw full of snow and held it above her face. "If you're planning to talk me out of washing your face, you'd better come up with something more convincing than that."

Laughing, she squirmed beneath him in a useless effort to escape. "It'll never happen again," she promised, then made the mistake of snickering.

"Until next time, you mean," he told her sarcastically. She squirmed again, buckling under him. He sincerely doubted that she knew the effect her movements had on him. Even through several layers of clothes, he could feel her body rubbing against his. His reaction to her was strong and immediate.

"Cain," she pleaded.

"You owe me," he said, his eyes holding hers.

Linette went still, her chest heaving, her eyes laughing. All at once the amusement drained out of her, and she gazed up at him and asked, "Wouldn't a kiss do just as well?"

5

Louis St. Cyr wasn't going home for Christmas. A visit on New Year's didn't appeal to him, either. Why should he rush to the loving arms of his family? In Bayamon, the small Caribbean island his father ruled, he was known as "Sonny" or "Junior." He was tired of fitting into the background of his father's ambitions. Tired of living his life to suit his family.

In France he was his own man, and he didn't need his mother's pampering or his father's tedious advice. He didn't need the hassles that went along with being the son of a wealthy landowner turned politician.

His mother had pleaded with him to reconsider, and his father, the great and mighty leader, had threatened to cut off his hefty allowance. But Daddy wouldn't, and Louis knew it.

After all, it was his father who'd insisted he attend the University of Paris at the Sorbonne, his own alma mater.

And to think that in the beginning, Louis had balked. He'd wanted to attend Harvard University in the United States, but that was a battle in a long list of battles he'd lost. But no more.

Moving away from his family was the best thing that had ever happened to Louis. He wasn't giving his mother an excuse to drive him home just because she wanted him available for a silly Christmas party.

One small taste of freedom and Louis discovered the elixir to be habit forming. Daddy could push all the buttons he wanted, but Louie boy wasn't responding.

Besides, he was in love. What red-blooded nineteen-year-old would turn down an invitation to spend two glorious weeks with a gorgeous blonde named Brigette? Not Louis.

The nymph had planted herself in his life and in his bed, and he had no intention of allowing her out of either. He might even marry Brigette, he decided. That would make his father sit up and take notice, especially since they'd long since chosen his bride for him.

Angelica was beautiful and the daughter of a longtime family friend, but Louis and Angelica had grown up together. Louis's tastes were far more adventuresome these days. He couldn't imagine Angelica doing the things in bed that Brigette had.

Louis lay on his back and studied the ceiling tiles. A slow, satisfied smile came to his lips. Brigette was asleep at his side, her blond hair spilled over the thick feather pillow. One shapely leg was sprawled atop a thin sheet, and she breathed softly, her breath gently teasing his ear.

All his life Louis had done what his family requested.

All his life he'd accepted that they knew what was best for him. Never again. He was his own man. How much of a man was something Brigette had taken great delight in proving to him.

Until he'd met his French mistress, his sexual experience had been limited. Brigette had taught him well, and he was a fast learner. In all the years he'd dated Angelica, the only thing she'd allowed him to do beyond a few chaste kisses was to taste her breasts. Then she'd acted as if she had done him a favor for which he should be eternally grateful.

Content, Louis reached for Brigette's lush breast, filling his palm with its fullness. His thumb grazed the nipple, which pearled to a hard peak. She sighed softly and nestled closer, her pale skin a marked contrast to his own honey color.

A sound from the room below distracted him. Louis paused, wondering if the alley cat Brigette fed had somehow gotten into the house. He was about to investigate when his lover wrapped her long, slender leg around his and edged closer to his side. She nibbled his earlobe, stroking the fires of his newly awakened manhood. He was about to turn her on her backside and bury himself in her silken heat when the door flew open.

Sound exploded through the peaceful silence.

Louis's heart nearly burst as two men dressed entirely in black burst into the room. Their faces were covered with camouflage paint. Twin submachine guns were aimed at him and Brigette.

Terror froze Louis's throat muscles as he struggled upright. Brigette grabbed a sheet and held it against her bare breasts and screamed. Her cry was silenced by a popping sound. Blood soaked through the sheet as the woman he loved toppled forward. Louis choked back a strangled cry of grief and horror.

Before he could react, or reach out to the beautiful French woman, he was dragged naked from the bed. Fighting as best he could, he kicked and shoved. Pain exploded against the side of his jaw as he was hit with the butt of the machine gun. Blood filled his mouth, and he gagged and spat out a broken tooth. The two men worked silently, binding his hands behind his back.

"What do you want?" he pleaded, first in French and then in English and German.

They didn't answer.

"Please," he begged as they dragged him down the stairs. Each man had hold of one elbow, and the top of his feet slapped noisily against the stairs. "My father will pay you anything you ask."

The taller of the two men smiled. His teeth gleamed white, and his eyes filled with hate. Sick laughter broke the eerie silence. "Yes, we know."

The infamous Christmas tree was decorated. Cain stood back to examine their efforts, then shook his head. It was the sorriest-looking tree he'd ever seen.

"What?" Linette asked defensively. They'd spent the better part of the afternoon stringing popcorn and cranberries. Patty and John's two children, Mark and Philip, had constructed long paper chains out of strips of colored paper, chattering excitedly and generally eating him out of house and home.

The two boys had returned to their place, and Cain

and Linette were left alone once more. But Cain couldn't stop studying the Christmas tree. No matter which way he looked at it, it was by far the ugliest thing he'd ever seen.

"The star's crooked," he announced, dragging a dining room chair across the living room carpet. Standing on the cushioned seat, he adjusted the aluminum star he'd cut from cardboard and covered with foil.

"There?" he asked, attempting to judge if he'd done any good. He glanced down at Linette. "Is it straight now?"

"It's exactly right." Linette sagged onto the chair and stretched out her legs. Her arms dangled over the sides. "It's the most gorgeous tree I've ever seen," she said with a sigh of appreciation.

Briefly Cain wondered if she was looking at the same tree he was.

"It would have been better if I'd remembered to buy ornaments." Frankly, it hadn't occurred to him how he intended to decorate a Christmas tree. Never having put up one before, he hadn't given the matter a second thought.

Vaguely, in the back of his mind, he recalled a Christmas when his mother had been alive. Cain couldn't have been any more than three or four. He didn't remember Santa Claus or opening gifts, or any of the traditional things usually associated with the holiday. What he did recall was the sound of his mother singing to him and the lights of the Christmas tree. Like a miser, he'd clung to that memory, one of a few that he had of his mother.

"I like the tree just the way it is," Linette insisted.

A loud knock sounded against the door, and a moment later Patty stuck her head in from the kitchen. "I'm not interrupting anything, am I?"

"No," Cain assured her, and leaped down from the chair.

"Wow." A grin brightened Patty's pretty blue eyes. "That's some tree." Doing her best to disguise a smile, she held out a plate of decorated gingerbread men. "I figured you two deserved this for keeping my boys occupied."

Cain helped himself to a cookie. Frankly, he'd enjoyed himself with those two hooligans. The boys had been a little in awe of him and eager to please. Cain had met the two Stamp children only once, a year or so earlier, and they'd stayed close to their mother's skirts. He'd never thought much about kids. He wasn't sure he knew how to act around them.

Linette hadn't seemed to have a problem, so he'd followed her example. He talked to them as he would anyone, no matter what their age. Before he quite knew how it happened, he was sitting on the rug with them, stringing cranberries with a fat sewing needle.

"You've got a fine pair of boys," Cain said.

"Thank you." Patty smiled.

"How about some coffee?" Linette offered.

Patty nodded. "That sounds great."

Linette poured coffee and carried the mugs into the living room on a tray. Cain took it from her and set it on the table.

"Actually . . . " Patty began, rubbing her palms together slowly, and Cain noticed the way her eyes refused to meet his. "I've come to ask a favor."

"Sure," Linette said automatically.

Cain knew better than to agree to anything without knowing what it was.

All three sat around the dining room table. Patty's small hands cupped the coffee mug. "Every year on Christmas Eve, John dresses up in a Santa costume and delivers presents to the boys."

Cain could tell what was coming.

"But Mark's in first grade this year, and he told me he doesn't believe in Santa anymore. He's just a little boy, and he wants to believe. The thing is, he'll recognize John. I don't want to carry this Santa thing too far, but I hate to disappoint Philip. He's only five, and he believes Santa's coming Christmas Eve to bring him a train set and cowboy boots."

"You want Cain to dress up like Santa?" Linette asked.

Patty turned wide, hope-filled eyes to Cain and nodded.

Cain raised both hands and shook his head. "I'm really sorry, Patty, but I'm no good at that sort of thing."

"Sure you are," Linette countered swiftly. "You were great with the boys earlier."

Cain ignored her. "I wouldn't know what to say."

Once more it was Linette who protested. "All you need is a few ho-ho-ho's every now and again. Anyone can do that."

Cain cast her a look he hoped would silence her. After the death-defying search for the perfect Christmas tree, he should have known better.

"The costume probably won't fit," he suggested next. Heaven knew he was taller and bigger than John.

"It's one size fits all," Patty said a little sheepishly. "It was a little big on John, so I imagine you'll fit into it just fine."

"I'm sure you're right," Linette said confidently, as if this were a done deal.

Both women turned to him with a look that said if he were any kind of a man, he'd leap at the opportunity to do this one small thing. Cain wasn't about to let a couple of women gang up on him. He refused to give in to the pressure. He had a well-established conscience, and he sure as hell wasn't going to apologize for not making a complete ass of himself dressed in a red suit.

"I'm sorry, Patty," he said firmly, "but I'm not your man."

Linette stepped back to examine Cain in the bright red suit and fake beard. "You're so cute."

Cain cursed under his breath and caught part of Santa's whiskers between his lips. He spat out the fake hair. "No pictures."

"I promised, didn't I?" She'd batted her pretty eyes at him, and he was lost. Apparently there was no end to the ways he was willing to be made a fool for her. Even now he wasn't quite sure how it'd happened.

One minute he'd declared there was no possible way he'd agree to dress up as Santa. The next thing he knew, he was standing in front of a mirror with a pillow strapped to his belly.

What truly frightened him was the easy way in which Linette had gotten him from an out-of-the-question no and into this ridiculous-looking suit. What Tim Mallory and the others would say if they saw him didn't bear thinking about.

Linette adjusted the wide black belt about his middle. "Your cheeks could use a little color."

Cain knew better than to grumble, otherwise he was likely to get another mouthful of beard. He yanked the thing from his face. "You aren't putting any of that stuff women stick on their faces on me."

She gave him an indignant look. "I wasn't going to suggest any such thing."

"Good." He released the beard, and the elastic snapped it back into place.

"You're being a good sport about all this."

Linette didn't know the half of it. He glanced at his reflection in the mirror, and once he got over the shock of seeing himself, he figured he made a halfway decent-looking Santa.

Planting his hands on his belly, he practiced laughing jovially. Not bad, he decided. He tried again, laughing deeper this time.

"How's that sound?" he asked Linette.

"Santa couldn't do any better himself."

Cain studied his reflection once more. Linette was right about the lack of color in his cheeks. He remembered hearing something about Santa's face being bright. He pinched his cheeks hard enough to cause his eyes to water, but the red drained away as quickly as it came.

"I suppose we should go downstairs and wait for the signal," Linette suggested.

Patty was supposed to turn on the porch light when they were ready for Cain's appearance.

"All right," he agreed.

Downstairs, Cain stopped to look at himself in the

mirror once more. "Linette," he said seriously, "could you come here a moment?"

"Sure."

He sat on the sofa and when she approached gripped her around the waist and brought her into his lap. She gave a small, startled cry, then laughed.

"And what is it you'd like for Christmas, little girl?" he asked, and for good measure added a couple of ho-ho-ho's.

"It feels so good to laugh again, to celebrate life and not death. I can't think of a thing I need more than what I already have." Her eyes filled with such warmth and happiness that Cain was forced to look away.

He felt as if his well-ordered life were slowly beginning to come undone, not unlike the Christmas presents he'd soon be delivering. Soon it would be too late. It almost was now. He knew what it felt like to hold Linette, to taste her. To feel her silky-smooth skin beneath his fingertips. She was like a madness that had taken hold of his senses.

Neither spoke, and emotion thickened the air until it demanded all Cain's effort to continue breathing. He marveled at the beauty of the woman in his lap. Her laughter was like music.

He'd kissed her twice now but had avoided anything more, promising himself he wouldn't, couldn't get physically involved with her. Despite his good intentions, he noticed the way her breasts tightened beneath the white silk blouse. Her nipples seemed to stab through the thin material like gold-embossed invitations.

Cain's breath burned in his chest. Slowly he removed the stocking cap and fake beard and set them aside. He wove his fingers into Linette's dark hair and directed her mouth down to his. His kiss was gentle, mainly because he feared what would happen if he kissed her the way he wanted.

Linette's lips parted, and with a groan of surrender he thrust his tongue inside. Her own shyly met his with soft, welcoming parleys. Her nipples, hard and hot, seared holes straight through his chest.

All Cain knew was that if he didn't touch her soon, he'd die. His good intentions swooshed down the drain. All the silent vows he'd made about not laying a hand on her vanished.

When he dared to look at her, he discovered her eyes were filled with longings that, he feared, mirrored his own. He raised his hands to her blouse and fumbled with the buttons, his fingers trembling so badly that he could barely unfasten the tiny openings. Linette kissed his jaw, then brushed his hands aside and completed the task. After pulling the blouse free of her waist, she reached behind and unfastened her bra.

Cain stopped breathing entirely as her breasts sprang free of the confining material. He lifted each one and felt a shiver run through her. He lowered his mouth to one pouting nipple, and she moaned even before his mouth closed over it. He sucked at the pouting peak so strongly, her back arched and she clasped her hands against his head and held him to her. It wasn't enough to satisfy either of them for long. Linette writhed atop him, her soft derriere creating a torture all its own.

"Linette," he said, gasping, dragging himself away from her bounty. He kissed both puckering nipples once and then, with a supreme act of will, closed her front. "Someone's coming."

She gasped and flew off his lap as if she'd sat on a hornet's nest. She made it into the bathroom just in time to close the door before John walked boldly into the living room. Cain reached for the cap and beard.

"What are you doing here?" John demanded. "The porch light's been on for a good ten minutes."

"Sorry," Cain managed, hoping that if John guessed what had delayed him, he'd be kind enough not to mention it. "I got distracted."

"Say, you look great." John slapped him companionably across the back. "How'd you manage to get your cheeks so red? Man, you're damn good at this sort of thing, aren't you?"

Cain glanced over his shoulder as he walked out of the house to find Linette peeking out from behind the bathroom door. She beamed him a wide smile and blew him a kiss.

There was a limit to what he was willing to do to please this woman. He should tell her, just so she'd know.

A half hour later he learned exactly how much he was willing to do for Linette.

"Church," Cain repeated, nearly choking on a hot buttered rum. He sat with Linette in John and Patty Stamp's living room. His stint as ol' St. Nick had gone amazingly well.

Mark and Philip were busy with their new toys, and Cain was about to suggest he and Linette return to the main house. If the truth be known, he was far more interested in picking up where they'd left off before John's untimely arrival.

"What a wonderful idea!" Linette leaped on Patty's

suggestion as if the woman were handing out gold coins. "I didn't dare hope there would be church services anywhere close by."

"It's an old country church. You probably saw the white steeple when you drove in."

"We didn't," Cain inserted, hoping Linette would pick up on his decided lack of enthusiasm for this latest adventure.

She didn't.

"Well, it's there," Patty said, casting him a snide look. She turned her attention back to Linette. "Every Christmas Eve John gets the old sleigh ready and we ride to church in it. I look forward to the sleigh ride every year."

Linette scooted to the edge of her seat, her enthusiasm bubbling over.

"I'm sure there wouldn't be enough room for the two of us," Cain said confidently. He'd seen that old sleigh stored in the barn a hundred times. There was barely room for the Stamps, let alone two others.

"We'll make room," John insisted. "It's the least we can do to thank you, if you get my drift." To emphasize his point, he nodded toward the two boys.

Cain got John's drift all right, but this wasn't the reward he was looking to collect.

"Could we?" Linette eyes were liquid with a tender kind of wanting. It simply wasn't in Cain to disappoint her. Hell and damnation. This evening wasn't going anything like he wanted.

All right, all right, he revised mentally, perhaps a trip to church was for the best. If he returned to the house with Linette and touched her again, he wouldn't be able to stop with a few deep kisses, and he knew it.

Before either of them had an opportunity to think through what they were doing, he'd be making love to her. Once wouldn't be near enough to satisfy him, either. It would mushroom from there into something completely out of his control.

Cain couldn't allow that to happen.

In the beginning he'd needed Linette's softness as an absolution of who he was and the things he'd done. In a matter of days it had gone far beyond that. His entire body ached for her. This was the kind of ache that a cold shower wasn't likely to help. He needed her, warm and willing, beneath him.

"Sure, we can attend church services," Cain said, offering John and Patty a weak smile. He remembered the last time his figure had darkened a church door. He must have been around fifteen, he guessed, and in love with the Baptist preacher's daughter.

An hour later, just before nine, they all climbed into the horse-drawn sleigh. Fat, glistening snowflakes drifted down from a dark, moonless sky. Linette settled next to him, and he wrapped his arm around her shoulder. Because there was no place else for him to sit, five-year-old Philip was nestled in Cain's lap.

Patty and Mark sat across from them, and John sat on the narrow seat up front, guiding the horses.

Philip's head was bobbing. The five-year-old was exhausted, but too proud to admit it. The lad pressed his head against Cain's chest and promptly fell asleep. For a moment Cain suspected something might be physically wrong with his heart. It actually ached. He hurt for the child he was never allowed to be, for the son he never planned to sire. For a simple life in the country that would never be his.

Just then, softly at first, the sound barely above a whisper, Linette started to sing "Silent Night." Her soprano voice was hauntingly beautiful. Soon Patty's voice blended in two-part harmony with Linette's. In all his life, Cain had never heard the old carol sung more beautifully.

By the time they arrived at the church, the parking lot was crowded. A number of other ranchers had arrived in sleighs as well.

He handed Philip, who was fast asleep, to Linette, climbed down, and then helped Patty and Mark down, while John dealt with the horses. When he looked up to assist Linette, he hesitated. Seeing her with a sleeping child in her arms produced that funny ache in his heart once again. Only this time it hit him harder, stronger.

Godalmighty, what was he doing? The question was there, but not the answer. He didn't belong in church any more than he belonged with this woman. The uncomfortable feeling refused to leave. Talk about a fish out of water. He was a killer. He had no business walking inside a church with these good people.

The thundering music from a pipe organ swelled through the old church. They sang a number of favorite Christmas carols. Cain hadn't sung in years. At first he mouthed along, not wanting Linette to think he couldn't sing. Gradually, as the music infected his spirit, his voice blended with the others.

Before he realized what had happened, Cain relaxed. The preacher, a silver-haired man around sixty, with a voice a sports announcer would envy, gave a short message about love and peace and goodwill toward all mankind. Heady stuff, if you dared to believe such matters were possible in this day and age of hate and war.

But then there'd been hate and war nearly two thousand years earlier, Cain realized.

At the end of the service, tapered candles were passed out to everyone in the congregation. The lights were turned out, and darkness settled over them. Then the first candle was lit. Its warm glow spread like a beacon through the bleak night. Then the pastor lit the candle of the first person in each row, and they in turn passed the flame from one to the other until the entire church glowed with light.

The service closed with the singing of "Silent Night." Cain couldn't participate for the hard knot that gripped his throat. He didn't want to ruin this moment, standing in this country church with Linette at his side.

For the first time in years he felt almost whole. Almost good. Almost clean.

Unfortunately, it didn't last. Within an hour of returning home, Cain was reminded of exactly who and what he was.

One moment Linette was sound asleep and the next she was awake. It took her a couple of seconds to remember where she was, then another moment to realize Cain was with her. His face was only a few inches from her own.

"Cain?" she whispered.

The moonlight reflecting off the freshly fallen snow revealed his taut features. The look in his eyes was wild, almost primitive. She could feel every breath he drew and see his pulse throb at the base of his throat.

"Is something wrong?" she asked in a whisper, and knew without his answering that there was.

He shook his head, denying everything. "I need to kiss you."

It never occurred to her to ask what he was doing in her bedroom in the middle of the night. It never occurred to her to refuse his request. She raised her arms and linked them around his neck, and smiled up at him.

"Did anyone ever tell you you're too trusting?" he said as he lowered his mouth to hers.

Linette experienced the familiar, hot excitement as his lips settled over hers. It was as it had been in the beginning for them. A coming home, a renewal of life. One touch and the desperate loneliness she'd lived with since Michael's death eased.

They were staring at each other in the golden glow of moonlight, when Linette realized something was different about Cain. Gone was the man who'd dressed up as Santa in order to surprise two small boys. Gone was the man who'd sat next to her in a sleigh, holding a sleeping child in his arms.

She didn't recognize this Cain. Then again, perhaps she did. This was the man she'd met at Nancy and Rob's Christmas party, the one who took her out to dinner and asked her about her life while freezing her out of his.

Confused and a bit dazed, she attempted to gather her scattered senses. Cain would never hurt her, never take what she wasn't willing to give.

She lovingly stroked the side of his neck and kissed the underside of his jaw. He released his breath slowly, in a barely audible rush.

"Can you tell me what's—"

"No." He answered her question before she had a

chance to fully ask it. He kissed her again with a hunger that left them both gasping for breath. When he lifted his head from hers, she could read the desire in his eyes. She could feel his arousal as well.

He seemed to get a grip on himself, and he gently folded back the blankets. His hands found her breasts, and he lifted his eyes to hers. "May I? One last time?"

She nodded, although she wasn't completely sure she understood what he sought. Slowly he lowered his head to her breasts, licking each nipple to a heated peak until it was all Linette could do not to ask him to take her in his mouth.

He fulfilled her unspoken request and tightly fit his lips over her nipple and sucked. A shaft of intense pleasure shot through her. Instinctively she arched her back.

He rolled onto his side and held her against him with one hand. He slid his free hand over her stomach, past the elastic of her silk-lined bottoms. He hesitated, seeming to wait for some sign from her. Linette gave it by parting her thighs. He lowered his hand. The intimate contact caused her to suck in a deep breath and bite down on her lower lip.

He was kissing her again, deeply, hungrily. All at once he stopped and broke away from her, rolling onto his back. His chest heaved, and he groaned from between clenched teeth.

Linette was undergoing some heavy breathing of her own. First and foremost she wanted to know why he'd stopped. It was just beginning to get interesting.

"Cain?"

It took another moment or two for him to compose himself. He sat up and gently kissed her forehead. "I'm sorry." He rubbed a hand down his face. "I shouldn't be here. It would have been better if I'd left you a note."

"A note?"

"I have to go."

She didn't understand. "Go?"

"I got a call, for a mission."

"Mission? But it's Christmas."

"I know. I've already talked to John. He'll drive you to the airport in the morning. I've arranged for your flight back to San Francisco."

By the time Linette could sit up, he'd made it across the room and was walking out the door. "Cain?"

He paused but didn't turn around.

"When will I see you again?"

His shoulders tensed. "You won't." With that he closed the door.

Linette fell back against the pillow, fighting a hundred conflicting emotions. She had one thing to say for Cain McClellan. He had a hell of a way of saying good-bye.

6

Francine Holden loved her family. Loved spending the Christmas holidays with them. Loved smothering all ten of her nieces and nephews with a heart full of love and a bounty of attention.

But it wasn't the holiday season or the gifts collected under the brightly decorated Christmas tree that occupied Francine's thoughts this year.

It was her patient, Tim Mallory.

"I swear life gets better every year." Her grizzly bear of a father wrapped his massive arms around his wife of thirty-two years and planted a noisy kiss on the side of Martha Holden's neck.

"I never understood why a woman as talented and beautiful as your mother married a man like me," Chuck Holden told his daughter.

Francine smiled and pulled down the spices from the oak rack and took them to her mother. Martha's hands were buried in a thick ceramic bowl filled with moistened bread cubes.

"It's times like this that I ask myself the same question," Francine's mother said with a teasing smile. "In case you hadn't noticed, I'm about to stuff this turkey."

"All right, all right," her father said, and laughed. "A man knows when he's not wanted."

Her father walked out of the large family kitchen, leaving the door to swing in his wake. Francine found herself alone with her mother for the first time that day.

"How are things going with your new patient?" Martha asked conversationally as Francine added an extra dash of rubbed sage to the dressing.

Francine hadn't been able to stop thinking about Tim Mallory, especially now, knowing he was spending Christmas Day alone. Rarely had she met a man more bullheaded and irritating. Rarely had she met a man who haunted her thoughts more.

His leg was responding well to the exercises and physical therapy, but mentally, despite her best efforts, she hadn't been able to reach him. It was as if he'd erected a concrete wall between the two of them.

Francine felt as if all she'd done in the last week was continually butt her head against the full force of his stubborn male pride.

"Things aren't going so well."

Francine felt her mother studying her. "Why not?"

"I've only been working with him a few days."

"But . . ."

Francine shouldn't be surprised by how well her mother knew her. "But I don't expect it to get much better. Not unless something happens.

"He doesn't trust me, doesn't want anything to do with me. He'd rather I left him alone." She'd spent several sleepless nights mulling over the problem with Tim Mallory and had found no solutions.

"Tell me about him," her mother prompted.

"His name's Tim Mallory." She gathered her thoughts together, making a mental assessment. Tim was a large, burly man, not unlike her own father, but the resemblance and just about everything else stopped there.

His anger spilled over like a spitting, bubbling cauldron, the heat of it driving nearly everyone away.

"How old is he?" her mother asked next.

"Thirty-five, I believe."

"Car accident?"

Francine shook her head. "He stepped on a land mine." The injury would have killed almost anyone else, she suspected. She had a few other suspicions as well, mainly that Tim Mallory wished he had died that day.

"A land mine?"

"He's a mercenary."

"A mercenary." This bit of information gave her mother pause.

"He's not like what you'd expect." It surprised Francine how quickly she came to Tim's defense. "He's acting like a wounded animal now because he's in pain."

"And you're the one inflicting it."

"Yes." But Tim's agony was far more than physical; the mental anguish outweighed anything else.

"Are his loved ones with him for Christmas?"

Francine shook her head. "He's alone."

"Alone?"

"He's never mentioned any family." Nor had Cain McClellan said anything to indicate Tim had one.

"Why, that's terrible. No one should be alone on Christmas."

Francine didn't have the heart to tell her mother that she suspected Tim Mallory preferred it that way.

Her mother didn't mention Tim again until after the huge dinner had been served. As Francine cleared off the table, she noticed Martha busily working at the kitchen counter.

"What are you doing, Mom?" Francine asked, joining her mother.

"I'm making up a dinner plate for your friend, Mr. Mallory."

"Mom, trust me, he isn't my friend."

Her mother nodded profoundly. "Maybe that's the problem, Francine. It seems to me a man with no family is in need of a friend. This may be the way to reach him. It's worth a try, isn't it?"

Her mother, with her warm, generous heart, couldn't bear the thought of anyone spending Christmas without being surrounded by loved ones and good friends. Martha didn't understand about men like Tim Mallory. Didn't understand the last thing he'd do was allow Francine into the fog of his pain. From what she knew of Tim, he'd rather starve than eat the dinner she delivered.

"I want you to take this dinner plate to him, and stay and visit until he's finished eating."

Francine knew better than to argue, especially when her mother wore a look that said she wasn't going to listen to reason.

"Take some sugar cookies and fruitcake with you," Martha called to Francine on her way out the door. Her mother added a paper plate full of homemade goodies to Francine's growing stack. "Make sure he understands you're his friend."

"I will," she promised, but doubted that she'd make it much beyond the front door.

By the time she parked her car in Tim's driveway, Francine was convinced she was making a terrible mistake. She walked up the porch steps with little enthusiasm and rang the doorbell. When no one answered, she got out the key Cain McClellan had given her and let herself into the house.

Stark silence greeted her. Her own family home was filled with the sound of children's laughter and the scent of mincemeat and holly.

"Who's there?" Tim's gruff voice called out from the family room, at the far end of the house.

Francine was grateful to realize he wasn't holed up in the bedroom. "It's me," she called, following the sound of his voice. She found him in the wheelchair in front of the big-screen television set, watching a football game. Probably the same one her father and brothers had been vehemently discussing earlier.

Mallory frowned when she walked into the room. "What are you doing here?" He stared at her with a decided lack of welcome.

She should have given more thought to what she intended to say, Francine mused, too late. Tim Mallory wasn't likely to believe she just happened to be in the neighborhood.

"I thought I'd stop in and see how you were doing."

She set both plates on the kitchen counter behind him.

His voice was gruff and unfriendly. "I don't need your pity."

"Good. I'm not offering it."

"Then what are you offering?" He swiveled the wheelchair around and glared at her menacingly.

Francine sat on the ottoman so they'd be at eye level. She studied her palms, debating what she might possibly say to reach him. The man was as obstinate as they came.

"I want to help you," she began slowly, her voice low and uncertain, "but I can't because you won't let me. I was hoping that if we sat down and talked, you might be more comfortable with me."

He looked away from her and back to the television screen. Apparently that was his answer, the same answer he'd been giving her all week. The same answer he'd been shouting at the world since his accident. He was shutting her and everyone else out as effectively as if he slammed a door closed. He didn't want her there, didn't want her anywhere close to him. Physically or mentally.

What her patient didn't understand was that Francine wasn't willing to accept this response. It was going to take a whole lot more than diverting his attention to persuade her to walk out that door.

She walked over to the coffee table, reached for the remote control, and turned off the football game. Then she deliberately set the controller out of Tim's reach.

His eyes followed her movements. His gaze told her it wouldn't take much more for his anger to explode. "We can do this the easy way," she said without emotion, "or we can do this the hard way. The choice is yours."

"Everything in my life has come hard, and it isn't going to change with you, sweetheart." A bitter smile twisted his lips.

She hated the way he said "sweetheart." In no way could it be construed as a term of affection. He made it sound like a four-letter word, as if saying it left an acrid taste in his mouth.

"Oh, that's smart," she muttered sarcastically. "In other words, you go out of your way to make life difficult."

He didn't answer, but then she hadn't expected he would.

"Just go," he ventured after a moment of uncomfortable silence.

"That would be much too easy." She sat back on the overstuffed chair and stretched her long legs onto the ottoman. Crossing her arms, she set her lips in the same stubborn, prim way her mother had so often.

"Just how long do you intend to plant yourself in my house?" he asked gruffly.

"As long as it takes to get you to walk again."

He snickered. "Neither of us is going to live that long."

So that was it. He didn't believe it was possible, couldn't see past the pain and the frustration. The light at the end of the tunnel was an oncoming freight train and not the hope she'd worked so hard to instill in him.

Tim had plunged himself into a cave of despair, crawled through the mire of pessimism, and was waiting for her to give up on him the way everyone else had. With the exception of Cain McClellan. She wouldn't, only he didn't know that. Not yet.

"You're going to walk, Tim Mallory, come hell or high

water, and you can count on that because I'm not going to allow you to waste the rest of your life feeling sorry for yourself."

Tim's hands tightened into fists. He clenched his teeth so tight, his jaw went white. Francine guessed that the control on his temper was precarious at best.

"So that's it," he said in a voice best described as a growl. "You want me to walk. You need me to walk. Because if I do, it's a feather in your professional cap. You can't allow me to ruin your perfect record. Can't allow me to smear your lily white reputation."

Francine knew this probably wasn't the moment to laugh, but she couldn't help herself. She giggled.

Tim cursed and wheeled away from her. There wasn't any place he could go that she couldn't follow. He must have figured she was just the type to go after him because he suddenly rotated back around. "Did it ever occur to you that I might not want to walk again?"

"Frankly, no," she returned smoothly. "You want it so damn much you can taste it. You want it so much you're scared spitless. You're more frightened now than you've been at any other time of your life because if you dare to think it's possible, then it won't happen."

"Who the hell do you think you are, Sigmund Freud?"

"Tim," she said, allowing her voice to soften significantly. "I've been a physical therapist for a long time. You aren't so different from the others I've worked with over the years. There's no shame in fear. No disgrace in pain. If anything, it's a common denominator."

The fierce light in his eyes brightened.

"I can help, if you'll let me." She scooted to the edge of the cushioned chair and prayed some of what she'd said made sense in that stubborn head of his. "Listen, Tim—"

"No one calls me Tim," he said.

"No one calls me 'sweetheart,'" she countered without reproach.

He gave a snickering laugh. "I can see why. What did McClellan do, search for the ugliest therapist he could find?"

His verbal attack was so brutal and unexpected that it left Francine reeling. She'd underestimated his ability to find her weakest point and charge full speed ahead.

It shouldn't hurt this much. She should be used to it by now. Tim Mallory was only saying what others thought, only saying what she knew to be true.

But it did hurt. Like hell. For several excruciating moments she waited for the pain to fade.

"Oh, so now we're going to get nasty and personal," she said, faking a small laugh. "I have news for you, Tim Mallory. If you think insults are going to send me running, you're wrong. I'm not going to give up on you, even if you've given up on yourself. I'm here for the long haul."

Fire leaped into his eyes. "We'll see about that."

"Yes, we will," she countered, unwilling to budge so much as an inch. But then, neither was he.

Bouncing from one airport to the next wasn't the way Linette had expected to spend Christmas Day. She'd envisioned a turkey roasting in the oven, music on the stereo, and sitting in front of the fireplace with Cain.

Airline food, crying babies, and short-tempered

vacationers wasn't her idea of Christmas, but she refused to surrender to self-pity.

Christmas for the last two years had been strained with memories of Michael and her personal struggles with grief. Major on the majors, Michael had once told her. She'd dug her nails into a rock and hung on until the holidays were over.

Her time with Cain, although cut short, had been a reprieve. She couldn't help wondering where he was, what he was doing, couldn't help worrying. Just a little. Even when she knew he wouldn't want her to fret.

The first thing she'd done when she'd arrived at the airport was to buy every newspaper she could get her hands on. She tore through the pages, hoping to find some clue from world events what might prompt the army to call for Cain in the middle of the night.

Political unrest was everywhere, but she could find nothing to indicate the reason Cain had been obligated to leave so suddenly. But then, she realized, whatever had happened wasn't likely to be made public. Yet.

His abrupt departure had come at her from left field. He couldn't possibly have meant what he'd said about not seeing her again. She was convinced of that.

Surely he wouldn't have touched her and kissed her the way he had if that was his intention. It simply wasn't possible, and she refused to believe it.

The plane landed in San Francisco late that afternoon. the sky was dark, the weather gloomy. The gaily decorated Christmas tree in the center of the terminal sagged to one side, and the poinsettias had lost several red leaves. The tree looked the way Linette felt.

As she made her way to the luggage carousel, she

noticed a man standing off to one side, scanning the crowd, holding up a piece of cardboard with her name printed on it.

"I'm Linette Collins," she said, not sure what to expect.

"The limousine's waiting outside."

"The limo? I didn't order one."

"You didn't." He looked perplexed and reached inside his black suit jacket, pulling out a sheet of paper. "The job order and payment came in early this morning from Cain McClellan." He looked at her expectantly.

"I see," she murmured, and smiled softly to herself.

She'd hear from Cain again. Linette was willing to stake just about anything on it. Otherwise he would have let her find her own way home.

Francine arrived bright and early the morning following Christmas. She found Greg in the kitchen, nursing a cup of coffee, looking as if he weren't quite awake yet. As a morning person, Francine was the type who woke up with a song in her heart and a smile on her lips. True, she petered out in the early evening and was generally in bed before ten, but that had never bothered her. She wasn't the sort to have much of a night life anyway.

"Good morning," she greeted Greg cheerfully. Francine was especially happy this morning, encouraged by her meeting with her patient the day before. At least each knew where the other stood.

Tim Mallory didn't know the meaning of the word *stubborn* until he'd locked horns with her. Although he hadn't given her any reason to believe she'd reached him, she felt as if their little talk had helped clear the air.

"How was your Christmas?" she asked conversationally, and took a mug out of the cupboard. She poured herself a cup of coffee, savoring the first sip.

"Great. I think the beastmaster had company."

"How's that?" It didn't immediately occur to her that Greg was referring to her as Tim's company.

"There were two dirty plates. It looks like someone brought him dinner. Apparently he enjoyed whatever it was, except for the fruitcake."

"He ate?" Francine couldn't conceal her delight. She'd assumed he'd toss the two plates in the garbage before he'd stoop to accepting her peace offering.

Greg eyed her suspiciously. "It was you?"

"I stopped by, yes." She stirred a teaspoon of sugar into her mug, avoiding eye contact.

"Hey, don't tell me you're falling for this guy." Greg sounded concerned.

"Don't worry," she said, and raised her right hand. "A therapist knows better than to fall in love with her patient. It can cause all kinds of problems."

"Good. You're too nice a person to get hurt."

"Speaking of the great and mighty one, how's Tim this morning?"

"So it's Tim now?" Greg closed his eyes and slowly shook his head.

"All right, how's Mr. Mallory?"

Greg continued to study her with a worried frown. "About the same."

"Great," she said, and set aside the coffee mug. "I'll have him ready for you in an hour."

"I'll be there."

Carrying her bag with her, Francine made her way

down the hallway to the back bedroom. She knocked once and let herself into the room. To her surprise, Tim was sitting up, dressed and ready.

"Morning," she said as if nothing were out of the ordinary.

"I don't want you to get any ideas," Tim said gruffly.

"About what?"

"About me being awake and ready this morning. I couldn't sleep, so I figured I might as well wait for you." He reached for the alarm clock. "You're five minutes late."

"Sorry." She managed to swallow a smile, knowing he wouldn't appreciate her finding his behavior humorous. Actually, she was ecstatic, but she dared not let him know that.

"See that it doesn't happen again. Knowing McClellan, he's probably paying you top dollar for this."

"He had to," she told him. "You'd already scared off every therapist in a three-state radius." She reached inside her bag for the cream, applied it to her hands, and started working his calf muscles.

"I don't suppose I'd be lucky enough for you to quit voluntarily." Although he said the words, the antagonism and fighting conviction were missing.

She paused in her manipulations to smile up at him. "I'm not leaving, come hell or high water. That's one thing you can lay odds on, Tim Mallory. I've never quit on a patient yet."

"Maybe you should start." He sucked in his breath at a stab of pain. The fact that he was willing to acknowledge the sharp discomfort was another sign her visit had done some good.

"Remember," she told him in gentle tones, "there's no shame in pain."

"And damn little glory," he shot back heatedly.

"That'll come later, when you're standing on your own and walking."

"With a walker." He grimaced, and she wasn't sure if it was caused by her manipulations or the thought of being dependent upon assistance to move about.

"You'll need the walker for a time," she agreed. "But not for long."

"Sure, then I graduate to a cane for the rest of my life."

"A cane beats the hell out of a wheelchair."

He didn't respond with a biting comment, which was another bit of encouragement. Francine felt like singing.

It seemed Tim didn't have anything more to say. He submitted to the exercise with ill grace, which wasn't a whole lot more than what he'd been doing the week previously. She talked to him as she warmed up his muscles for the more strenuous exercises. His silence didn't dissuade her.

She chatted on about Christmas with her family and told him about her nieces and nephews. Not that she thought he was paying attention. She hoped that the sound of her voice would help put him at ease.

"Do you come from a large family?"

His question caught her unprepared. She feared he was being sarcastic and that by answering, she was stepping onto a rifle range where he could fire insults.

"In number or in size?" she returned in an effort to minimize any damage he planned to inflict.

"Number," he returned, seemingly surprised by her question.

"I have three younger brothers. All married."

"And you?" He asked the question from between gritted teeth.

"Am I married? No."

"Divorced?"

"I've never been married."

"Why not?"

"It's none of your damn business."

He laughed as if he found her answer amusing. "Which means no one's ever asked you."

Francine could feel the heat crawling up her neck. She'd walk out of this room before she'd admit to the truth of that. "What about you?" The best defense was a good offense. At least that was what her father had claimed. But now that she thought about it, he might have been referring to football.

"What about me? Am I married? Hardly."

"Which means every woman you ever asked turned you down."

"No," he said in what easily could have been mistaken for a friendly tone, if she didn't know better. "It means I've never asked. I haven't been so much as tempted. It'll be a cold day in hell before I consider marriage."

"I see," Francine said smugly. "You're the love 'em and leave 'em type."

"You got that right."

Their conversation was followed by a companionable silence.

"You date much?" Tim asked her out of the blue.

"Some." Damn little if the truth be known, but she wasn't about to tell him that. "What makes you ask?"

"No reason."

After the warm-up exercises, Greg arrived and readied Tim for the more strenuous session in the swimming pool. He was crabby and exhausted by the time she finished. She knew he'd eat a good lunch and sleep a portion of the afternoon. But she wasn't through with him for the day. Not by a long shot.

All Louis St. Cyr felt was pain. His jaw throbbed where the butt of the gun had been slammed against his face. Part of a tooth was missing, and every time he drew in a deep breath a stab of agony shot through him. He didn't dare move his jaw, and he suspected it was broken.

He hadn't a clue where he was. His kidnappers had taken him for a long drive. The minute they'd arrived, he'd been shoved inside a dark closet. Twice a day one of the two men opened the door and thrust in some food and water. Louis had drunk the water, not caring about the pain in his jaw or his molar. After two days he'd attempted to eat something and found he couldn't.

He lay on the closet floor and tried not to think about what was happening to him. He tried not to think about Brigette. Instead he closed his eyes and remembered his mother. If he could make himself focus his thoughts on her, the pain wasn't nearly as bad.

He thought about a blue dress she'd worn when he was a young boy. He'd loved the shade against her whiskey-colored skin and the way her skirt had billowed out at her hips when she whirled around.

Louis had asked her to spin for him so he could see the skirts twirl, then he'd laughed and laughed. The sound of his boyhood amusement filled his ears now.

Louis recalled the time he'd been sick with chicken pox and his mother had sat by his bedside and read him to sleep. His younger sister, Anne, had been ill at the same time.

Louis missed Anne.

He didn't want to die. Not like this. Like an animal trapped in a cage.

Tears shimmered in his eyes. He wanted his mother. He wanted his family.

He heard voices on the other side of the locked door. Strange new ones, talking in a language he didn't recognize. They were deciding his fate, and he couldn't understand what they were saying.

A sob swelled in his chest, and he choked off a cry of anguish. He'd be damned if he was going to let those bastards see him cry.

But then he was already damned.

He must have blacked out because the next thing he knew he was being jerked out of the closet. With little care to his injuries, he was slammed against a wall.

An involuntary moan escaped his lips. He bit it off as soon as he could, refusing to give his captors the satisfaction of knowing the pain they'd caused.

The lights blinded him. It demanded every ounce of strength he possessed to remain upright. Someone shouted at him angrily, but he didn't understand what they said. And even if he had, he wouldn't have followed their instructions.

Someone grabbed him by the shoulders and pulled him upright. Louis hadn't realized he'd slid down the wall. He opened one eye long enough to see the submachine gun aimed at him.

So this was how it was to end. He was to be shot like a criminal before a firing squad.

He squared his shoulders, praying death would come quickly and that he could face it with dignity. He wouldn't grovel. Wouldn't plead for mercy.

He was a St. Cyr and would do his family proud. He pictured his father's strong, proud face in his mind and clung to the memory of his mother and young sister. He prayed God would mercifully claim his soul.

A grinding, softly discordant sound followed.

Curious, Louis St. Cyr squinted into the bright lights. Only then did he realize they weren't going to shoot him.

His captors had taken his picture.

7

"*You'll come for New Year's,* won't you?"
Michael's mother pressed Linette. "We haven't seen you
in far too long." Then, as if she needed to dole out additional incentive, Janet Collins, added, "We missed seeing
you on Christmas." The guilt was being tossed Linette's
way at breakneck speed.

Sighing inwardly, Linette closed her eyes, wishing she
were the kind of person who could refuse graciously and
not feel bad afterward. The last thing she wanted was
stress between her and Michael's family.

If only she could invent something that sounded
believable. Her hand tightened around the telephone
receiver. Bonnie was watching her out of the corner of
her eye, waiting for Linette to make a decision.

"How was your Christmas?" Janet continued when
Linette didn't answer immediately.

"Wonderful." The two days preceding the holiday had

been filled with happiness. The vivid memory of trekking through the snow and cutting down the Christmas tree with Cain would stay with her a long time. The snowy ride in the sleigh with the Stamp family, singing Christmas carols in two-part harmony with Patty, warmed her heart still. As did the Christmas Eve church service with Cain standing at her side, her hand clasped firmly in his.

"I'm pleased you had such a good time with your . . . friend," Janet continued, and then added with a labored sigh, "Christmas just didn't seem right without you. I do hope you'll come for New Year's. You will, won't you?"

"Ah, perhaps I could make it for dinner."

"That would be perfect. I thought we'd eat around three."

"I'll see you then," Linette said, and after a few parting words of farewell, she replaced the telephone receiver. She didn't dare look at Bonnie, already feeling her employee's censure.

"So you gave in to the pressure," Bonnie said.

"I couldn't think of any way to say no."

"You might have said you had other plans."

"Yes, but I don't. Not really. Michael's parents are dear people, and they mean well. It's just that they continue to play this 'let's pretend' game."

"It's easier than having to deal with the loss of a son, isn't it?"

"I suppose. To hear them speak, it's as if Michael is away on an extended trip and will return at any moment, so they dare not change a thing until that happens."

"And when you're with them, they want you to play along," Bonnie added as if she'd met Michael's family herself.

"Exactly."

Linette walked over to the rack of knitting books and straightened them, mulling over the conversation with Janet Collins.

"How are Michael's parents going to deal with it when you start dating again?"

"I don't know." Judging from their reaction when she changed her plans for Christmas, Linette didn't think they were going to handle it well. "He was their only son."

"Is this bit of news significant?"

"Not really. It just explains why they've clung to me."

"What they want," Bonnie said in that gentle yet cautious way of hers, "is for you to become a living memorial to their dead son."

"You can't be sure of that," Linette chastised, although she was beginning to suspect her friend was right.

"Perhaps I'm way off base," Bonnie agreed, "but it's an educated guess. Think about what's been happening the last two years with you and your in-laws. If you were to fall in love and remarry, they wouldn't be able to continue pretending Michael's alive. It would mean having to face the bitter truth that the son they loved and cherished is forever gone."

The truth of Bonnie's words tolled in her ears like a church bell on Easter morning. Her friend was right, and Linette knew it.

"The longer you continue to play along," Bonnie added, "the more difficult it will be for you *and them* to move forward in life."

Until Linette had met Cain, the charade the Collinses

continued to play hadn't seemed pressing or important. Linette had gone along, hoping the time would come when they'd be ready to face the reality of Michael's passing. Linette realized now that she'd done them both a disservice. Instead of helping each other through the grieving process, they'd hindered one another. What surprised Linette was how blind she'd been to the truth.

"I think it's time to clear the air," Linette said bravely.

"Good girl." Bonnie gave her an affectionate hug.

Linette gave the meeting with her in-laws a good deal of thought over the next few days. On New Year's Day she arrived at their house shortly before three. She carried a wicker basket filled with fresh rolls she'd baked that morning. She was dreading this dinner and the confrontation that was sure to arise.

"Linette." Jake, her kind-hearted father-in-law, answered the door and immediately pulled her into his embrace. His hug was filled with warmth and affection. "We're so pleased you could make it."

Janet walked out of the kitchen, smiling broadly. "My dear, you are lovelier every time I see you." She kissed Linette's cheek and then leaned back as if to get a better look at her. "You're looking a little pale."

"I'm fine."

"Your timing couldn't be better. I've just finished setting the table."

A look at the three place settings told Linette her sister-in-law and family wouldn't be joining them. Now that Linette thought about it, she wasn't sure Nancy had spent Christmas with her parents, either.

When the meal was ready the three of them gathered around the table. "Nancy and I had lunch right before

Christmas," Linette said conversationally. "She told me her good news. You must be thrilled."

"Of course we're are," Janet said in a way that caused Linette to glance at her mother-in-law.

"They were here for Christmas, weren't they?" Linette asked. She'd made the assumption that Nancy would be joining her parents as she had in years passed.

"No," Jake answered, his eyes revealing his hurt.

"Unfortunately Nancy and I had a bit of a misunderstanding," Janet said, busying herself by buttering a roll. She took inordinate care in doing so, Linette noticed, spreading the butter evenly over the surface of the roll.

"It's nothing serious," her father-in-law said quickly. "Of course we couldn't be more pleased about having another grandchild."

All at once it was as if a thick fog had cleared in Linette's mind. "The misunderstanding was over Michael, wasn't it?" Nancy hadn't said anything to Linette about a disagreement with her mother, nor would she. But her sister-in-law's eagerness to match her up with another man told Linette everything she needed to know.

"Don't you worry your pretty little head about Nancy," Jake said hurriedly. "I swear this is the best ham we've had since last Easter." He directed the comment to his wife in a blatant effort to change the subject.

"How was Christmas?" Linette asked, seeking a way to put the conversation back on an even keel while she digested what she'd learned.

"Lonely," Janet supplied with a beleaguered look. "We missed you. I have to tell you, Linette, both Jake and I were worried sick about you. When we learned that you barely knew this young man . . . why, anything could have become of you."

"I met Cain through Rob and Nancy."

"As I understand it, this man was a high school friend of Rob's, and the two of them haven't seen each other in several years. There's no saying what kind of person he is now."

"You were angry with Nancy because she introduced me to Cain." Knowing she had been the reason for the rift between mother and daughter greatly saddened Linette.

"And when we didn't hear from you right after Christmas, we didn't know what to think."

This was an additional serving of guilt, dished up with a look meant to instill shame.

"I have a thriving business, you know," Linette said in explanation, although that had little or nothing to do with the reasons she hadn't contacted her in-laws.

"We understand how busy you've been." Jake had always been the peacemaker in the family. Linette noticed that he seemed to be growing uncomfortable with the nuances of their dinner conversation.

"I only hope you won't be seeing this young man again," Janet said without emotion as she reached for the molded gelatin salad.

Linette frowned. "Why would you wish for that?"

Janet blinked. "Because of Michael, of course."

"Michael has been dead for over two years."

Her mother-in-law paled slightly. "I realize that, dear, but by the same token, you're vulnerable just yet. Two years is no time whatsoever to grieve over the loss of a husband. Anyone could step in and take advantage of your tender heart. Jacob and I feel strongly that there should be someone to look out for your best interests. Someone who loves you and can guide you during these difficult days."

To hear her mother-in-law speak, it sounded as if Michael had passed on only recently and Linette had been a child bride.

"It's been two years," she said a second time. "I'm perfectly capable of looking out for my own life and my own interests. I appreciate your kindness and your concern, but I prefer to make my own decisions."

Jake nodded, but Janet's gaze clashed with Linette's. "How do you think Michael feels, knowing you took off with a man you barely know?"

"Michael doesn't feel," Linette responded, and her voice trembled.

"But Michael knows. Don't think he doesn't know what you did." Janet's voice elevated with disapproval.

"And what did I do?" Linette asked calmly.

"It's done and over with now," Jake inserted, glancing from one woman to the other. "Let's put it all behind us. Janet tells me she made pecan pie for dessert." This remark was directed to Linette.

"Michael's favorite," Linette whispered. Janet would bake pecan pie for Linette until her dying day and not know her daughter-in-law didn't like pecans.

"We all love pecan pie," Janet said stiffly.

"It isn't one of my favorites."

"Don't be ridiculous," Janet flared, her eyes flashing with resentment. "You love pecan pie."

"If I eat the pie and tell you how good it is, then it's almost like Michael being here, isn't it?" Linette suggested softly.

Janet ignored her and looked across the table at her husband. "All these years and never once does she tell me she doesn't like pecan pie. You'd think she'd have said something before now." Janet slid her knife across the sliced ham with enough force to mark the plate.

"What you're really angry about is that I spent Christmas with Cain McClellan." Her appetite gone, Linette set her napkin beside her plate.

"I'll tell you this much," Janet said in arctic tones, "I would never have believed you were the kind of young woman who'd travel with a man you'd only met once. Heaven only knows what went on between you two."

"Janet, please," her husband warned softly. "Linette is with us now. Let's forget all about Christmas."

"God knows what she did to disgrace Michael's memory."

"Janet," her father-in-law pleaded once more, "drop it, please."

"No," the older woman snapped. "Let's clear the air once and for all." She turned her attention to Linette. "If you're going to remain our daughter-in-law, if you're going to honor the memory of our son, your husband, then we simply can't have you behaving in such an undignified, tasteless manner."

"I see," Linette said. The vehemence of her mother-in-law's words felt like a cold slap. "In other words, you don't want me to see other men."

"Of course we want you to date again," Jake insisted in a hurried effort to smooth the waters.

"But only after the appropriate time for mourning," Janet added, her voice not as impassioned as it had been earlier. "Michael has only been gone two short years."

"I'm ready to date again," she said. It would be a disservice to mislead them, especially now. Scooting back her chair, Linette stood. "I love you both so much," she said, pressing her hands against the side of the table. "It hurts to know that I've disappointed you. I loved Michael with everything there was in me to love. And he loved me. I know that he wouldn't have wanted me to spend the rest of my life as a living memorial to him."

"All we're asking—"

"All you're asking," Linette said, cutting off her mother-in-law, "is for me to pretend Michael isn't really gone. I can't do that anymore. I won't be involved in this charade any longer."

"I think you've said enough." Janet slapped her linen napkin down beside her plate.

"Maybe it would be better if we discussed this at another time," Jake suggested with a pained expression. "We certainly didn't want for our time together to—"

"Can't you see what Linette's done?" Janet demanded of her husband. "If you look at her, you can see it in her eyes. She's disgraced Michael's memory. She's pushed him out of her life. It makes me wonder if she ever really loved him."

Linette knew she couldn't stand to listen to much more of this. She hurriedly found her jacket and moved toward the front door. Looking back, she found Jake standing behind his wife, who remained sitting at the dining room table.

His hands were on Janet's shoulders as he attempted to comfort her. He glanced up, and Linette saw that his tired eyes had filled with tears. Her own were fast welling with emotion.

"Good-bye," Linette said sadly. Unless matters changed, she doubted that she'd ever be back.

Cain was beginning to feel the faint stirring of faith that Louis St. Cyr might be alive. His family had recently received a photograph of the youth. He didn't look to be in good shape, but it was proof that he was alive. Or had been within the last week.

The boy's family had wept with joy at the sight of their son, despite his condition. It was the first bit of encouragement they'd been given following the ransom demand. Unfortunately there was no hope of fulfilling the requirements. If the kidnappers had asked for money, they might have been able to work out a deal, but the terrorists weren't interested in cash. The ransom note had been delivered four days earlier, demanding the release of three political prisoners.

What the kidnappers didn't know was that the day of the kidnapping, the three prisoners had been extradited to the United States for a long list of offenses. A senator who was aware of the situation had recommended that Louis St. Cyr Sr. contact Cain. News of the extradition had been kept out of the media. If it were released, Louis junior would be as good as dead.

The problem now was finding out where the terrorists were holding the teenager. The best information Cain had been given had led him to a series of dead ends. Once Deliverance Company knew St. Cyr's whereabouts, the strategy for the rescue mission could be planned. But finding the youth was proving to be highly difficult.

The boy's parents were frantic with worry. From what Cain understood, the mother was on sedatives. Deliverance Company was doing what they could, but it seemed like damn little.

Exhausted, Cain made his way into the back bedroom. He hadn't slept in over twenty hours. He was past sleepy, past tired. He'd reached his limit of endurance and knew it.

As he shrugged off his clothes and turned back the sheets, Cain knew with his resistance this low, he wouldn't be able to keep thoughts of Linette out of his mind. He closed his eyes and waited for her to come.

As his head settled against the thick pillow mattress, she appeared in his mind's eye. It took him a moment to realize she was standing on the porch outside his Montana house.

It was dusk, and she was dressed in moonbeams. Light shimmered around her, drawing his attention, causing his heart to swell with a longing so intense, it was painful.

Silently he called out to her. In slow motion she whirled around, and when she saw it was Cain, she broke into a wide smile. With wings at her heels, her arms open, she raced down the steps and rushed toward him. Her arms were as wide as her heart. As wide as the love she had to offer him.

Just before she reached him, she vanished.

Cain knew this was because he'd vowed he wouldn't be seeing her again. Nor would he allow her to mess up his mind while he was on a mission. Too many lives depended on his having a cool head and a steady hand. The potential to hurt others with a single slip, a single lapse, was all the warning he needed.

So he dreamed of her, and even then certain restrictions applied. She would always remain out of his reach.

Fantasizing about Linette was a compromise Cain had made with himself. He'd banished all thoughts of her from his daytime activities but lowered the mental gates of his resistance at night.

She visited him often. Cain wondered if it were possible for any woman to be as beautiful as Linette was in his sleep-induced memories. He wondered if any woman could be as giving, as loving, or as charming as he remembered Linette. It didn't seem possible.

Caught between the lure of sleep and the cold reality of this world, Cain tried to think about the nineteen-year-old boy he was attempting to find and rescue. The photo image of the youth flashed in and out of his mind, refusing to stay.

It was as if Linette had stepped forward and insisted this was her time with him. If he was going to dwell on business, then he could do it while he was awake. This time was hers, and she'd been waiting impatiently for him to join her.

Rolling onto his side, Cain gave his mind free rein to take him where it would. After a moment he found Linette in her apartment. He scanned the room until he located the cardboard star he'd made for the top of their Christmas tree. She'd placed the aluminum-covered ornament on the fireplace mantel as if it were a valuable piece of artwork.

A peace settled over Cain like a warm blanket in the coldest part of winter. A tranquillity he could give no name.

Linette hadn't forgotten him, either. It was a fantasy,

he tried to tell himself, conscious enough to filter out what was real and what wasn't.

He hadn't a clue of what had become of that ridiculous-looking star he'd crafted. Why he should feel the least bit of anything to think Linette had brought it back with her was beyond his comprehension.

Nevertheless, he could feel the pressing worries of the day leave him. His shoulders relaxed, and the tight muscles in his neck slackened. All at once he was free to walk into the waiting arms of slumber.

At the knocking sound, he bolted upright out of a dead sleep. "Come in." He wiped a hand down his face in an effort to clear his thoughts. Once asleep, he was a man who rarely dreamed. Over the course of his life, he recalled only a handful of times he'd remembered his dreams. But this night he remembered. All too well.

"It's Jack." The communications expert for Deliverance Company walked into the bedroom. "You asked me to come for you if there was any news."

"Is there?"

"We think so."

"Give me two minutes to get dressed."

"You got it."

Cain sat on the edge of the mattress and gathered his wits. The dream continued to plague him. Normally he would have shrugged off something like this, but this particular dream involved Linette. The details of it were as vivid as if he'd been living it. She was in a hospital waiting room, pacing and filled with nervous energy. He didn't know whom she was there to see or what the problem was. All he'd felt was the overwhelming urge to take her in his arms and comfort her.

He needed coffee. Needed to tuck the woman who dominated his dreams back into the locked mental compartment. Needed a clear head in order to deal with the problem of rescuing Louis St. Cyr. Before it was too late, if it wasn't already.

"Morning," Murphy said when Cain appeared.

"What have you got?"

"Good news," Murphy said, grinning widely. "We've located the house outside of Paris where they're keeping the kid."

"And the bad news?" There was always the alternative to go along with anything positive.

"It's going to be a bitch to get him out."

"So what's new?" Rescues rarely came easy, no matter how well planned.

"His captors are a group of fanatics with plenty of sympathizers holed up with them. They're armed to the teeth, and would welcome any excuse to kill the kid."

"Sounds like just the sort of mission we specialize in," Cain said with a grin, and slapped Murphy across the back. "Call Bailey and Stan. We've got work to do. While you're at it, get us the first available flight to Paris."

Already Cain could feel the adrenaline pumping. Deliverance Company was about to do what they did best. If good luck and the fates were with them, there was a chance they could save this poor kid's ass.

8

Francine knew Tim was well past the point of being tired, and still he pushed himself. He insisted they stay in the pool and go through the series of exercises one last time, driving himself, and her, to the brink of exhaustion.

Francine had been ready to get out of the swimming pool forty minutes earlier.

"Enough," she insisted. "If you work too hard, you'll damage the muscles." For a moment she feared Tim was going to ignore her.

His shoulders heaved with the effort of his exertion. He swam to the far end of the pool, nodded and lowered his head as he caught his breath.

"I'll call for Greg," she said, ready to walk up the steps and out of the pale blue water.

"No." Tim reached for her arms and stopped her. He was sitting on the third step from the top, the water lapping about his shoulders. "Not yet."

"But you're exhausted."

"I know. I won't do any more exercises today. Just stay with me a couple of minutes until I get my wind back."

"All right." She sat on the step beside him. They'd been working for most of the afternoon. The progress her patient had made in the past two weeks astonished her.

She hadn't thought it possible for a man to make such a complete turnaround in attitude. Francine had the impression Tim still didn't like her, still didn't want her around. He tolerated her company, but most important, he respected her and acknowledged that it was through her efforts he would walk again.

If there was one thing she'd accomplished with Tim Mallory, it had been hope. Somehow she'd managed to get it through that thick skull of his that he would walk again.

When she arrived first thing in the morning, he generally acknowledged her cheerful greeting with a grunt. It didn't trouble her. A grunt was worth a thousand demands that she leave him alone.

Francine knew the workouts in the pool were the ones that drained her patient the most. But his energy level increased daily. His progress was nothing sort of phenomenal. The fact that he was taking an active role in his recovery thrilled her and gave her more hope than the physical improvements she witnessed.

"Are you ready yet?" she asked.

"No," he said gruffly. He looked away from her. "Listen, there's something I've been meaning to say." His voice wasn't any less brusque, but Francine could tell that he wasn't angry. If anything, she read a certain hesitancy in him.

"Yes?"

"I'm not much good at this sort of thing." He paused and cleared his throat.

Francine wasn't sure what to make of this. "Not good at this?"

"Apologies," he muttered thickly.

"You don't owe me an apology."

"The hell I don't," he said, and raked a hand through his thick wet hair. "I said some nasty things to you when we first started working together. Things I regret now. I want you to know I didn't mean what I said about you being unattractive."

The room went quiet. Even the water in the pool seemed to go still. A tightness gripped Francine's throat. "It doesn't matter. It's long forgotten." She attempted to stand, but he took hold of her arm.

"There's more." His curt tone was back.

"More?" Francine looked away, not wanting to see his expression or have him read hers. This discussion embarrassed her acutely. Tim hadn't insulted her with anything she didn't already know. Her body wasn't going to be mistaken for that of a model. Nor had she been graced in the looks department. Her features were too blunt for that. Too round. She was large boned, and she'd learned long before that men liked their women small and delicate. The fact that she could bench press more weight than most men wasn't something a fragile male ego could handle.

Tim's hand caught her by the chin, and he turned her face toward his. His deep, dark eyes met hers. "I was wrong about you from the first. You're really quite lovely."

She was about to tell him it was time they left, when he kissed her. The action stunned her so much that the words were trapped in her throat, forever lost.

The kiss was gentle, a delicate pressing of his mouth over hers. Francine wouldn't have guessed that Tim was capable of such tenderness. She trembled and raised her hands to his bare chest in order to shove him away and tell him how inappropriate it was for them to be doing this.

Not only was it inappropriate, it was wrong. The cardinal rule with a therapist was never to become romantically involved with a patient. But he caught her hands in his and continued, and soon she was fully involved in the kiss herself.

After a moment, he drew back. Francine lowered her gaze, but she could feel him study her. He seemed as surprised by what he'd done as she was.

Neither spoke. Francine didn't know what to say, and she strongly suspected Tim was fast thinking of an excuse. Something that would assure them both that it had been a fluke, not to be repeated or mentioned hereafter.

His eyes lingered on her face, until she was certain her cheeks were red enough to be mistaken for cooked lobster.

"You're an incredible woman." His voice was as rough as moonshine.

Francine knew she had to escape before she found herself believing what he said. She swallowed, and her heart, her silly, romantic heart, seemed to stick in her throat. What she needed now was some witty comment that would lighten the mood and remind them that what they were doing would only lead to problems. Instead her throat felt as if it had been stuffed with a whole apple and her eyes were filled with tears.

He wiped the moisture from her cheek, and before she could object, he kissed her again. This time it was much different. Much better. Much deeper. Much more intense.

He parted her lips with his tongue and penetrated her mouth. Francine moaned and trembled. She was afraid, almost desperately so, but not because Tim frightened her. Never that. He tempted her, and she couldn't give in to that fascination.

He deepened the kiss and sent his tongue in search of hers. She moved her own forward hesitantly until it touched his, then swiftly withdrew it in a panic. A moment later he sought her out again, and she allowed him to find her for another shy taste.

By the time he broke off the kiss, Francine's heart thundered in her ears. Her eyes remained closed and her head fell forward. She'd been kissed, but never quite like this.

"I've been wanting to do that all week," Tim whispered, smoothing the hair from her face.

"I should go."

"No," he said roughly, insistently. "Not now. We've only gotten started."

She lifted her questioning eyes to his. "What do you mean?"

"Mean?" He laughed lightly and kissed her gently. "What else could I mean? I'm dying to make love to you, woman. Don't tell me you haven't noticed. It's been downright embarrassing."

"What?" It was all Francine could do not to leap out of the water right then. As a matter of fact, she hadn't noticed, hadn't thought of him in those terms. Nor would she.

"Come on, sweetheart, there isn't any reason to play coy with me. It isn't necessary. We're both adults, and I want you, and if the way you kissed me back is any indication, you're just as hot for me."

She stared at him as if he were speaking in a foreign language.

"I've been a long time without a woman, so the first few bouts are going to be hot and fast. Just be patient and I promise to make it up to you later."

Francine was struck dumb. She glared at him and blinked several times before she found the strength to pull herself free of his embrace. Although her knees were weak, she managed to step out of the water.

"Is something wrong?" Tim asked.

She reached for her towel and wiped the moisture from her face. "I don't know what led you to think I'd be willing to share a bed with you, Tim Mallory, but frankly, I'm not interested."

Her refusal must have come as something of a shock, because he looked at her as if he were sure he hadn't heard her right. "The hell you aren't," he said after an awkward moment.

"When I go to bed with a man, it'll be for reasons other than the ones you gave me. You want a body to relieve your physical frustration. Any woman would do. Any body. I just happen to be convenient."

"You're as hot for me as I am for you."

Francine didn't have an answer to that because she

feared it was true. "Look at me, Tim," she said, "really look. Do you think that because I'm not svelte and beautiful that I'd be willing to settle for anything less than a man who loves me?"

His gaze narrowed suspiciously, and then he groaned and wiped a hand down his face. "You're a virgin, aren't you?" He muttered several curses as if her lack of experience were some great detriment. Some great deficiency on her part.

Francine pressed her lips together firmly. Hell would freeze over before she gave him the satisfaction of knowing he'd hurt her.

"I'll send for Greg," she said on her way out.

Linette stepped into the foyer of her apartment building and unlocked her mail slot. She anxiously sorted through the envelopes. She hadn't heard from Cain, and although she repeatedly told herself it didn't matter, it did.

She was beginning to believe he'd meant what he said. That he wouldn't be seeing her again. No matter how hard she tried, she couldn't make herself believe what they'd shared hadn't been something very special. He was special.

Cain had gifted her with the precious promise of the future. Until they'd met, she hadn't been able to look beyond a single day. She had no dreams. Cain had proven that in the two years since she'd lost Michael, she hadn't lost her heart. She could feel again. Could respond to a man's touch.

Apparently she had been nothing more than a passing fancy to him.

Linette let herself into the apartment, tossed the mail onto the kitchen counter, and slipped out of her pumps. She was about to survey her cupboard for dinner ideas when the doorbell chimed. A quick check in the peephole revealed her sister-in-law.

"Nancy," Linette said happily, unlocking the door. "This is a pleasant surprise. Come in." She'd meant to call Nancy all week, but with one thing or another, she hadn't gotten around to it. If the truth be known, she had delayed putting off the call for fear Nancy would ask her about Cain. And she just wasn't sure what to say.

"How are you feeling?" Linette asked.

Nancy peeled off her coat and collapsed onto the overstuffed sofa. She tucked her feet beneath her and settled in as if she meant to stay a good long while. "Dreadful. I've spent the last week with my head poised above the toilet."

"Flu?"

Nancy shook her head. "Morning sickness."

"Can I get you something? Tea? Coffee? Water?"

"Nothing, thanks."

Linette sank onto the chair opposite her sister-in-law. "I've been meaning to call all week. I had dinner with your parents on New Year's."

Nancy's gaze shifted away from Linette. "They aren't happy with me just now."

"I know."

"You know?"

"I'm afraid they aren't exactly overjoyed with me, either. As you're probably aware, they didn't think it was a good idea for me to spend Christmas with Cain."

Nancy flattened her hand against her chest. "I was

responsible for the two of you meeting, and my parents . . . well, mostly it was Mom, seemed to think I'd dishonored Michael's memory by introducing you to Cain."

"So I heard. I didn't realize what was happening with Mom and Dad," Linette said softly. "I knew that they found dealing with Michael's death difficult, and they were more comfortable ignoring the fact he'd died. But it's gone beyond that now."

"I've been tempted to say something to you for more than a year now," Nancy murmured, "but it's difficult, and I didn't want to do anything to ruin our relationship, especially when the one with my parents was becoming more and more strained."

"They don't want me to date. I didn't realize that or the reason why until I met Cain. They feel threatened and afraid. I can understand that, but at the same time I can't live my life in order to please them."

Nancy looked worried. "You're seeing Cain, then? You never said anything about him when you returned from Montana, and I didn't want to pry."

Linette clenched her hands together, wanting to disguise her disappointment and not sure if she could. "I haven't heard from him."

Her sister-in-law released a heavy sigh. Her shoulders sagged, and she closed her eyes momentarily. "That might be for the best. You don't know how concerned I've been. I've been so afraid you would fall for him."

Linette didn't understand. It was Nancy who'd worked so hard playing the role of matchmaker, eager to introduce her to Cain. As it happened, they'd met on their own. "You'd rather I didn't see Cain again? But why?"

Linette shifted positions, looking decidedly uncomfortable. "Rob and I were talking last night, and I was saying how disappointed I was that you hadn't called and told me how everything went over Christmas. I made some pithy comment about how nice it would be if the two of you fell in love. Then I said something along the lines that it might be difficult for the two of you, being that Cain's in the military and all. Long-distance relationships can be tricky."

"I think you might be right." Having Cain in the military certainly hadn't helped matters thus far. Linette was left hanging, waiting to hear from him. At the same time she wasn't sure he would contact her.

"I was afraid something like this was going to happen," Nancy said, breaking into her thoughts.

"You don't like Cain?" Linette didn't understand.

"I don't know him well enough to like or dislike him. But after what Rob told me, I regret ever suggesting the two of you meet."

"What Rob told you?"

"Yes, last night out of the blue, my dear husband drops this bombshell. Cain isn't in the military. He's—"

"Of course he is," Linette interrupted. "He was called away on a mission early Christmas morning. He didn't want to leave any more than I wanted to see him go."

Nancy's features tightened. "Rob told me Cain McClellan is a mercenary. Rob assumed I knew, and I told him I didn't and that I didn't think you did, either. He suggested we get together and talk."

Mercenary. The word echoed in Linette's ears like a giant gong, but instead of fading, the sound grew louder and louder, more and more deafening.

"Linette?"

It took an instant for her to realize that Nancy was speaking to her. "In other words, he's a hired killer," she said slowly.

"Yes. I'm sorry, so sorry. I feel like such a fool."

Linette forced herself to give Nancy a reassuring smile. "You didn't know."

"But I should have questioned Rob more thoroughly before I suggested introducing you two. I don't think Cain's a bad person, don't misunderstand me. It's just that . . . well, you've already lost one husband, and you don't need to get involved with a man in a high-risk occupation like his."

"You're right, I don't." Linette's fingernails dug painfully into her palms. If there was one single thing she had learned during Michael's illness, it was how very precious life is. She couldn't bear the thought of anyone wasting a gift of such value.

"What upsets me most is the big stink I made with my parents. They asked me all these questions about Cain, looking for one small thing to discredit him. Mom was furious with me and Rob, and when I learned what he was, Linette, I can't tell you how upset I've been. Thank God she never found out."

"There's nothing to worry about. No harm done."

"You're sure?" she asked with a heavy sigh. "I can't tell you how guilty I've felt over all this."

"Don't," Linette insisted. If she was angry with anyone, it was with Cain. He'd clearly misled her, clearly chosen to let her believe he was in the service. She knew why. Had she known the truth, she would never have agreed to travel to Montana with him. Would never have become involved with him.

"I hope this doesn't mean you're going to be gunshy," Nancy continued, then smiled. "No pun intended. Cain's just one man, and if you were attracted to him, then there are bound to be others, don't you think?"

"Of course." But Linette wasn't interested in anyone else. In time she would be willing to try dating again, but not soon. As it was, she felt like a yo-yo on one of those around-the-world spins. Her emotions had been looped around almost full circle. A feeling of emptiness swamped her.

She knew what Cain had told her before he'd left was true: he wouldn't be contacting her again. He couldn't risk involving his heart any more than she could allow herself to care for a man who'd built his life around death and destruction.

"I'd better go," Nancy said after a moment. "I hate being the bearer of bad news."

"I don't want you to feel guilty over this," Linette said, handing Nancy her coat.

"I can't help it. I'm my mother's daughter. I cut my baby teeth on guilt. Little happens in this world that I can't find a reason to accept some of the blame."

Linette laughed, and the two women hugged. "Don't look so worried," she said, and unlocked her front door.

"But I am. You're going to be all right, aren't you?"

"Of course."

Nancy hesitated, and Linette knew her sister-in-law wished there was something she could do or say to set matters right. Nancy, however, had already paid a hefty price. She'd stood her ground against her parents on Linette's behalf. That hadn't been easy and had helped pave the way for her confrontation with the Collinses later.

After Nancy had gone, Linette sat on the sofa, suddenly cold. She wrapped a hand-knit blanket around her shoulders. In the worst part of Michael's illness she'd sat in exactly this position, with this same autumn-colored afghan tucked about her like a security blanket.

She'd needed it then. She needed it now.

The force of the explosion knocked Cain onto his belly. His breath gushed from his lungs as the wind was knocked out of him. He lay there in intense pain, too stunned to move.

What the bloody hell had happened? The only thing he could think was that the explosives had gone off too soon. It wasn't supposed to go like this.

The explosion had been planned as a diversion. Unfortunately, the only ones it had distracted were the men of Deliverance Company. Not a single man was in position. The whole mission had literally blown up in their faces.

They weren't ready. This was a hell of a way to announce their arrival. If the terrorists holding Louis St. Cyr had any brains, and they must have, they'd quickly figured out this was a rescue attempt gone awry.

Instinct took over, and Cain leaped to his feet and ran around the side of the building, dodging the rapid fire of a machine gun. Out of the corner of his eyes he saw Jack and Murphy crash through the underbrush to join him. Jack literally hurled himself behind the building, cursing as he slammed onto his stomach. Murphy followed.

"It's too soon," Jack said as though Cain hadn't figured that much out himself.

As far as Cain could see, they had two choices. Ignore the fact that all their careful arrangements had gone up in smoke and go in after the kid.

Or get out alive, while they could.

One thing was certain—if they turned tail now, the kid was a goner. For all Cain knew, the teenager might already be dead. There were no guarantees he'd survived one moment beyond having his photo taken. He'd been held hostage for nearly three weeks as it was. The odds of his surviving the first few minutes following the explosion were slim to none.

"We're going in," Cain decided.

His men followed without hesitation.

He was the first one through the door. The first one to fire his weapon, spitting death at a faceless enemy. The first one to see just how big a disaster they'd walked into.

One man fell and then another. Bullets whistled past Cain, hitting the wall directly behind him. He fell to the ground and rolled, firing as he twisted. If they were going to kill him, he sure as hell wasn't going to make an easy target.

It had been almost a month now that Francine had been working with Tim, and in all that time she hadn't dreaded a morning more than this one.

She wasn't sure she could look Tim in the eye. Wasn't sure she could pretend he hadn't touched her, hadn't kissed her, hadn't told her he wanted to make love to her. At first she was tempted to call in sick and arrange for a substitute, but that was a coward's way out. Sooner or later she was going to have to face her patient again.

The way she figured it, she'd prefer to get this over with as quickly as possible.

After some deliberation, Francine decided she was going to walk into his bedroom the way she always did. She would greet him the same way she did every morning and pray to high heaven he didn't mention what had happened in the pool.

"Good luck with the beastmaster," Greg told her when she let herself into the house. "He's in one bear of a mood."

Francine was afraid of that, but prepared. She walked down the hallway to his bedroom, feeling very much like Marie Antoinette facing the guillotine.

She knocked lightly, and after squaring her shoulders and gathering her composure, she let herself into the bedroom. "Good morning," she said as if nothing had changed between them. It hadn't, because she wouldn't allow it.

Tim was sitting in his wheelchair, dressed and ready. He raised his head expectantly when she walked inside. He seemed surprised to see her.

"Morning," he murmured. "I didn't know if you'd be here."

"Why not?" Which was a ridiculous question, and one she immediately regretted. "We have work to do," she said, not giving him the opportunity to answer.

"I expect you want me to apologize," he said in the same gruff-affectionate tone he often used with her. "If you do, then you've got a long wait."

"The only thing I expect of you, Tim Mallory, is for you to walk again. It's the reason I was hired, and by all that's holy that's what I intend to see happen."

"I have a vested interest in walking myself."

"Good," she answered, relieved. "Then we're on the same wavelength."

"What about yesterday?" His gaze held hers.

Her cheeks felt hot, but she ignored the ready way in which her body betrayed her. "What about it?"

"I suppose you want to forget about it."

"I . . . think that would be best."

"Fine," he said, but he didn't sound pleased.

"Good."

"When will I start walking again?" he demanded with thick impatience.

"We need to take this one step at a time, no pun intended. First we've got to get your leg strong enough to support your weight. For the last month I've been working at building up your muscle strength. You're gaining weight and getting stronger every day, but we have a ways to go."

"When can I stand?"

It was true that he'd gained weight, but he remained weak, and she hated to take any chances. Physically he could handle a setback, but emotionally . . . she wasn't so sure. Thus far everything had been going along smoothly.

"You think you're ready now?" she asked.

"I was ready last week." A hint of a smile touched the edges of his mouth.

Francine couldn't keep from smiling herself. "All right, big boy, let's see what you can do."

She started out with the rubdown, the way she did every morning, massaging his muscles, warming them up for the more strenuous work out that would follow.

He was sprawled across the top of his mattress as she kneaded the thick muscles of his injured leg. She worked hard, preoccupied with the task.

"You aren't talking," Tim muttered.

"Not talking?"

"You're usually a regular chatty Cathy. In the beginning I would have sold my soul to shut you up, but I've grown accustomed to your prattle."

It was true Francine generally made a point of chatting to put him at ease. But all at once she didn't seem to have anything to say. She wasn't entirely sure what she'd been telling him all these weeks.

"It's your turn to entertain me," she suggested.

"Me, talk? I'm not much good at that sort of thing."

"I'm all out of stories."

"Tell me about the time your brother locked you out of the bathroom and then jumped down the laundry chute so you couldn't get ready for your date."

"I was all of sixteen, and fighting mad."

"And this was the night of your first real date," he said, filling in the details for her. "You had to answer the front door with hot curlers dangling from your forehead, and it was your date, fifteen minutes early."

"So you think that's funny, do you?" She swatted him playfully across the butt.

"Ouch."

"Listen, big boy, you don't know what pain is until I'm finished with you."

Tim chuckled, and to the best of her knowledge it was the first time Francine could remember hearing him laugh. It surprised her to realize how much she liked him. As he was being slowly freed of his disability, she was seeing more and more of the man he'd been before the accident. The more she saw, the better she liked him.

A knock against the door was followed by Greg, letting himself into the bedroom. He was carrying the portable phone.

"It's McClellan," Tim's attendant told her patient.

"Thank God." Tim sighed with relief, and Greg handed him the receiver.

"Do you want me to leave?" Francine asked.

He shook his head.

Although Francine could hear only one side of the conversation, it was clear that Cain had been out on some kind of mission. At first Tim seemed worried, but he became more and more relieved as the conversation continued.

"He wants to talk to you," Tim said when he'd finished. He handed Francine the phone.

"This is Francine Holden," she said, although an introduction wasn't necessary.

"How's the patient?" Cain's voice sounded as if it were coming from the bottom of a deep well. She wasn't sure if it was from a poor connection or the distance.

"Cranky. Stubborn. Impatient. Better."

"I like the last part best. It seems he thinks he's ready to stand."

"We'll see. If matters progress the way they have, it's possible for him to be walking within another month."

Her prediction was met with stark silence. "I don't believe it," Cain said after a tense moment. "I didn't dare believe it would happen."

That had been Tim's mistake as well. He didn't dare

to believe it, either. "Wait until you see the changes in him."

"I have to be in San Francisco next week," Cain announced. "I'll be by the house to see this amazing transformation myself. I didn't think it was possible. Thank you, Francine."

"Don't thank me yet." It was much too soon for that. They had a long way to go and almost all of it was uphill.

When she was finished, she handed the telephone back to Greg, who was waiting outside the door. Tim's attendant left, and she returned to his bedside.

"They did it," Tim said, sounding jubilant.

"Did it?"

"Rescued some poor kid who was being held as a political prisoner. Cain said everything that could go wrong did, but they managed to pull it off. The teenager's back with his family, and Deliverance Company is taking an all-expenses-paid trip to the Bahamas, recuperating in the sunshine."

"Was anyone hurt?"

"Only minor injuries." Tim clenched his fist. "Damn, but I wish I'd been there. I'd give my eyeteeth to be in the thick of it again. They could have used me, too."

"It appears to me," Francine said stiffly, "that you've been in the thick of one too many missions as it is."

"Hey, don't go all soft on me. Fighting is what I do best. In case you haven't noticed, I'm damn good at it."

"I can tell," she muttered sarcastically.

Tim was silent for a moment. "If I didn't know better, I might think you actually cared."

"What I care about is seeing you whole and healthy, but I'll tell you right now, I'm not working this hard for you to go off like some white knight to get yourself shot up again."

Tim slapped his hands together. "You do care!"

"I don't," she said in what was a blatant lie. And Tim knew it.

"You know," he said, sounding almost gleeful, "I just might grow on you. I wouldn't be a bad lover, you know. Fact is, I've never had any complaints. We could have some good times, you and me. Some real good times. What do you say, Francine?" He waited for a response, and she answered him with a blistering look. Tim burst out laughing.

"I don't think you're the least bit amusing."

"I wasn't trying to be. I'm dead serious."

"Tim, please, don't."

"Has anyone ever told you how expressive your face is?"

"I think you're ready for the pool."

"I'm ready all right." He jiggled his eyebrows. "And after a few kisses you'd be ready, too."

"Would you stop?" she demanded, sterner this time. She didn't know how to react to his teasing. He seemed bent on making her blush, on seducing her with words.

"You know what I wish?" he said, rolling onto his good side and elevating his head with his elbow. "Just once I'd like for you to wear one of those swimsuits with a zipper up the front."

"That is the most ridiculous thing you've ever said to me, Tim Mallory."

"Just once."

"Exactly why would you care what style of suit I wear?"

"Because, my sexy Amazon, I'd take great delight in opening that zipper."

Her face filled with raging color.

Tim laughed boisterously. "My guess is you've got a pair of the most beautiful breasts I'm ever going to find. Someday you're going to show them to me, and then I'm going to show you how a man satisfies a woman."

He was saying these things just to fluster her, just to disconcert her. "Unless you stop right this minute, I'm walking out and calling for a replacement."

"No, you won't," he said confidently.

Francine seethed inwardly. "What makes you so certain?"

"Because," he said, smiling with a grin that would rival that of the Cheshire cat, "you're crazy about me. Only you don't know it yet."

9

It was one of those winter evenings that Linette referred to as a Sherlock Holmes night, when San Francisco and the Bay Area were shrouded in a thick fog. Linette closed up the shop for the day, tired and lonely. Bonnie had left an hour earlier, leaving her to an endless stack of paperwork. Now she was ready to head home.

The lights along the pier glowed as through a lacy veil as she ambled along, mentally listing chores. The cashmere yarn a customer had ordered had arrived, and she'd forgotten to have Bonnie phone her. She needed to pick up stamps in the morning. Her dry cleaning was ready.

As she came to the end of the pier, Linette hesitated. There, silhouetted against the fog, against the glow of a fading lamp, stood Cain. He was waiting for her, his hands buried deep inside his pockets.

"Hello," he said.

Linette's throat closed up on her. She wasn't prepared for this, hadn't believed it would be necessary to prepare herself. Cain had assured her she wouldn't see him again.

It had taken her far longer than necessary to accept the truth of this. Far longer to accept the reasons why.

"I figured I owed you an explanation."

Still she didn't move, didn't speak.

"Can I buy you dinner?" He glanced down the waterfront to the restaurant they'd gone into when they'd first met.

"I have an appointment," she said when she found her voice.

"A date?" His eyes narrowed with the question.

"No, an appointment."

He looked as if he weren't sure he should believe her.

"I do volunteer work at City Hospital two nights a week, counseling families of cancer patients."

It took him a moment to digest this information. "How long before you need to be at the hospital?"

She checked her watch, hardly able to believe that they were having this civilized discussion. It was all she could do not to scream at him for deceiving her, for the cruel way in which he'd said good-bye.

By all that was right, she should ask him to get the hell out of her life. She'd been perfectly content until he'd come along. All right, not *perfectly content,* but close to it. By all that was right, she should tell him that. Unfortunately, it demanded every ounce of self-control she possessed not to hurl herself into his arms.

"I'm due at the hospital in forty minutes."

"That's time enough." He motioned toward the restaurant. "Will you have a drink with me, Linette?"

"Why didn't you tell me you were a mercenary?" she demanded.

"Would you have come to Montana with me if you'd known?"

"No."

"That's why."

"Was having me with you that important?"

He waited a moment before answering. "Yes."

Linette closed her eyes, fighting the urge to go to him. She didn't know what had brought him back to San Francisco. Didn't want to know, because she was afraid he'd returned for her.

"All right," Cain admitted with a sigh. "It was selfish of me, I'll admit that. If you're looking for an excuse to hate me, then you've got one."

"I don't hate you."

"That's the problem," he said roughly. "Maybe you should."

He held out one arm to her, and without hesitation Linette walked into his embrace.

Cain's eyes slowly drifted closed. He'd dreamed of this moment for weeks. Of holding her against him, of savoring her softness. He was tired of fighting a battle he couldn't win. Tired of pretending he was strong when he wasn't. Tired of waiting. He rubbed his jaw against the softness of her hair and breathed in the fresh scent of her.

Linette buried herself in his embrace and inadvertently moved against the tender flesh of his injury. Cain swallowed an involuntary moan.

"You're hurt?" Linette abruptly moved away from

him, which produced an even greater pain for him. He'd waited too long for this moment to have it cut short.

"A flesh wound," he said, making light of the pain. He held out his good arm to her once more, but she ignored the unspoken invitation.

"How'd it happen?" she pleaded, and then shook her head. "I don't want to know. Don't tell me. I don't think I could bear it."

Bright tears glistened in her eyes. She struggled to hide the emotion from him as if this weakness embarrassed her. Her tears had a curious effect upon Cain. A curious need reached deep inside him and tightened like a clenched fist.

"It's nothing," he said, longing to reassure her enough to bring her back into his arms. "Come on, let's go have that drink."

She hesitated but didn't protest when he reached for her hand. He cupped her fingers around his elbow, which was an excuse to have her close. It felt right to have her there. Powerfully right.

Instead of going inside the restaurant the way they had previously, Cain stepped up to the fish and chips stand and ordered two beers. When he turned around, he found Linette had taken a seat at one of the brightly colored picnic tables situated next to the stand. Fog swirled around the area, muting the lights.

Cain handed her the Styrofoam cup and sat across the table from her. The simple pleasure of studying her, watching her expression, fed his need.

Keeping her head lowered, she asked in what appeared to be a casual tone, "So what brings you to San Francisco this time?"

He could have lied, could have made up a song-and-dance about some business venture. Mallory was a convenient excuse, and he could have told her about the two-hour meeting with his friend. He hadn't openly lied to her yet, didn't plan on sugar-coating the truth, even at the risk of her anger.

The stark truth was that he hadn't taken the first available flight out of the Bahamas because of Tim Mallory. He'd returned to the Bay Area because he couldn't stay away from Linette another minute.

"I came to see you."

Her eyes drifted closed, and she whispered, "I wish you hadn't."

This woman wasn't good for his ego, Cain could see that. He wasn't keen to play the role of the fool.

"We don't have to decide anything right now," he said. "Let me take you to dinner tomorrow night and we can talk this out."

"I can't."

She was making this damned difficult. "Another appointment?"

"No, a date."

Cain felt as if he'd been sucker punched. Years of training enabled him to conceal his reaction.

"I can't believe this," Linette muttered, and her hand fussed nervously with her purse clasp. "You misled me. You eluded the truth, knowing how I'd feel about a man who kills for a living. You said I wouldn't see you again, and then bingo, you pop back into my life just when I've accepted a blind date."

A blind date. Cain felt better. Mildly better. But then she could date a hundred men at one time and it wouldn't be any of his damn business. He had no claim on her.

He'd been involved with other women over the years. Several of them had had an active social life when he was away. It had never troubled him. Why should it now? He wasn't looking for someone to sit by a window and wait for his return. What came as an emotional blow was how possessive he felt toward Linette.

"Then of course you should go on your date." She'd never know what it cost him to make that suggestion. The thought of another man holding her, another man kissing her, another man making love to her, was enough to set his teeth on edge. Yet he sat across from her as if he hadn't a care in the world, when in reality he was damn near having a stroke.

The silence was tense. Linette was the one who broke it.

"How were you hurt?" The words came quickly, as if she regretted the need to know.

He could make up something to satisfy her curiosity but didn't. "A rescue effort."

"You were on a mission."

Generally Cain didn't relay the details of his assignments. He would make an exception with Linette, mainly because he felt he owed her that much. "Terrorists kidnapped a nineteen-year-old boy, the son of an important man. We found where they were keeping him."

"The teenager? What happened to him?"

"He's alive. He's recuperating at home with his family."

"Did anyone else get hurt?"

"Yes," Cain said, unwilling to disguise the truth again. "Four men were killed."

She took a moment to digest this information. "Any of your men?"

He shook his head. They'd been fortunate. He'd come away with the worst of it, two cracked ribs and a bullet that had grazed his side. A couple of inches in the other direction and he would have lost a kidney. And would not be sitting across from Linette now.

"How long will you be in town?"

"A few more days."

"Then where will you go next?"

"Florida. I have a compound there for training purposes."

"So you have another mission?"

"Not right away." Clearly she didn't understand that his assignments were never planned in advance. He was often called, as he had been early Christmas morning, without warning. Desperate voices in desperate situations. Lives depended on his quick response. It had been hell leaving her that day, but Linette didn't know that.

She glanced at her watch.

Cain could take a hint. "I'll walk you to your car."

The four-block trek passed with lengthy lapses in their conversation. Neither seemed to know what to say. This meeting had gone badly. She'd already learned what he'd come to tell her.

When they arrived at her car, she turned to him, her keys in her hand. Cain held himself stiffly away from her, knowing she was about to ask him not to contact her again. He didn't blame her.

Taking matters into his own hands, Cain reached for her. She came without resistance. Not even a token one.

They exchanged a slow, sweet kiss. Then, like the gathering turbulent winds of a storm, the kiss changed. Their need for each other grew more urgent, deep and desperate. If this was the last time she would see him, then Cain was determined she would remember him. If she was going to date someone else, he wanted the imprint of his kisses on her lips.

Linette broke away, her shoulders heaving. "Why did you have to come back?" she asked.

"I couldn't stay away."

She was the one who kissed him, being careful of his injury. She pulled aside his coat and flattened her hand against the bandage. Her touch was gentle and caring.

"You're going to be killed someday," she whispered, and bit into her lower lip.

He tried to make light of her fears. "We all have to die sooner or later."

She shook her head. "I couldn't bear to bury another man I love."

Cain realized he was asking a good deal of this woman. He couldn't be anything less than fair. "If you want me to leave you, I will. I'll never contact you again. All you need do is ask."

Her silence encouraged him. He kissed the underside of her jaw, nibbled at her earlobe, and rubbed his hand down the small of her back. This was crazy, and they both knew it. Forbidden fruit was sweeter by far. No woman had ever been sweeter.

The words to send him out of her life never came.

"I'll pick you up Saturday," he said between deep, lingering kisses, his heart pounding with triumph. For the first time Cain could remember there was music in his soul, and all because a beautiful young widow had agreed to have dinner with him.

Tim Mallory had never been more glad to see anyone than Cain McClellan. Cain had arrived the day before, and the two men had talked nonstop for hours. Then Cain had made some weak excuse Mallory didn't understand and left. Frankly Mallory wondered what was so all-fired important.

If he didn't know better, Mallory would think a woman was responsible. But in all the years he'd known Cain, he'd never seen his boss lose his head over a woman.

Although Mallory remained self-conscious about having to use the walker, it felt so damn good to be in an upright position that he didn't care. He gladly accepted the imposition of a metal contraption since it meant he could stand.

Walking was another matter. Thus far all he'd managed to do was shuffle about awkwardly, but Mallory had never been prouder than the moment he'd first placed one foot in front of the other. An Olympic gold medal winner couldn't have been more pleased with himself.

Naturally Mallory griped long and loud about the walker to Francine. But only because he derived a good deal of pleasure in complaining when she was around; also it kept both of them on their toes.

Thinking about his physical therapist produced a small smile. In the beginning, Mallory had viewed her as a hard-ass bully. Even now he couldn't picture Francine as any angel in white.

He enjoyed baiting her, enjoyed watching the color

creep into her face. Other than the one time he'd kissed her, there'd been no sexual contact between them, but not because of any lack of effort on his part. The woman had a backbone of iron. He should know, since he'd suffered a head-on collision with that stubborn pride of hers on more than one occasion.

Mallory had never told her how furious he'd been Christmas Day when she'd dropped by uninvited. He had to hand it to her, though, she'd given as good as she'd taken. Not until later that day did he realize how alive he felt. After spending the majority of eighteen months on his backside, to have the blood pumping through his veins again felt damn good.

"I can't believe the progress you've made since I last saw you," Cain said. He'd arrived shortly after Mallory's morning workout in the pool and was staying for lunch. Mallory was grateful to see his friend, but frankly he was going to miss having lunch with his feisty therapist.

"I have to tell you, it feels good to be standing," Mallory said in response to Cain's comment. "I won't be needing the walker much longer."

"You most certainly will be needing that walker," Francine announced, leaning against the doorjamb, her arms folded. "Just because everything's progressing quickly doesn't mean you're going to be walking all on your own by next week."

She'd changed out of her swimsuit and back into the basic uniform she favored. Damp tendrils of hair framed her face. Tim drank in the sight of her, wondering how he could have ever thought of her as unattractive. It was true, she wasn't a classic beauty, but then the Miss America types never had appealed to him.

She was Francine. Stubborn. Demanding. Spunky. And one hundred percent woman.

His therapist might think his ultimate goal was to walk again, but she was wrong. Somehow, some way, he was going to get this sexy Amazon beauty into bed with him. Mallory spent a good portion of each night planning just that.

Greg delivered their lunches. Soup, salad, and a couple of thick sandwiches. Mallory was hungry. An appetite was something novel. Food hadn't appealed to him for months. He wasn't sure when it had happened. Sometime around Christmas, he guessed. About the time Francine had waltzed into his disgruntled life.

"Didn't I tell you you'd be back with Deliverance Company someday?" Cain said, looking too damn smug to suit Mallory.

"Yeah, but it'll never be the same." There would always be limitations now. He wouldn't be able to do all he had before the accident. One thing was sure, he refused to be a weak link on the team's chain.

"There's plenty you can do."

Mallory frowned. "I want to be in the field."

"Fine, I'll put you in the field."

Francine stepped into the room, her eyes flashing. "What do you mean, you'll put him in the field?"

"Mallory says he wants to be in on a mission, then I say he's in."

"No, he isn't." Francine circled the table like a shark closing in on dinner. Mallory had seen her like this often enough to know when to keep his mouth shut. He knew to bide his time and wait until he had the advantage before tackling her when she was in this frame of mind.

"If you think I've worked this hard with this man just so you can haul his sorry butt out on some crazy soldier-boy escapade and get hurt again, then I suggest you rethink your game plan."

Cain's jaw sagged open. Few dared to cross Cain McClellan. It did Mallory's heart good for his boss to get a taste of the sheer brute stubbornness he'd faced in the last few months.

"You can trust me, Francine," Cain said with admirable restraint. "I'm not going to put Mallory in a position where he'll be hurt."

"If that's the case, then kindly explain how he nearly lost his leg." She folded her arms and shifted her weight to one foot with ill-concealed impatience.

"Perhaps I should clear this up," Mallory suggested.

"Stay out of it," Francine snapped.

"I'll handle this," Cain insisted.

The two glared at each other while Mallory calmly ate his sandwich. If the truth be known, it was all he could do to keep from laughing.

Cain left without explanation early that same evening, and Mallory was disappointed. He'd counted on the two of them talking over old times and sharing a couple of drinks. Being with Cain filled him with eagerness to return to Florida and the good friends he'd left behind.

After he'd first been injured, Mallory had spurned their efforts to help him. He regretted that now. Regretted the things he'd said and his childish behavior.

Thinking Cain was going to be around for the evening, Mallory had given Greg the night off as well. Now, with both Greg and Cain out of his hair, he was left to his own devices for dinner.

He mulled over his options. He could order out and have it delivered. Or he could cook something himself. Not an impossible task. Actually he welcomed the freedom to move about the kitchen. Before the accident he'd cooked the majority of his own meals. The idea of tackling this simple project appealed to him.

After checking out the freezer, he decided upon a thick T-bone steak. Two thick T-bone steaks. Why not? After the afternoon workout with Francine he deserved a reward.

He was fumbling around the kitchen, shocked by how quickly his energy left him, when the doorbell rang. Before he could do anything but wonder who it could be, Francine flew into the room like a small tornado.

"We need to talk," she said, her eyes snapping.

He stared at her for a moment, wondering what burr she had up her butt, when she apparently noticed he was standing in front of the stove with a steak dangling from his hand.

"Exactly what are you doing?" she demanded. Not waiting for him to answer, she whirled around as if looking for something. "Where's Greg?"

"I gave him the night off."

"And your friend, although I'm using that term loosely?"

"Hell if I know where he went. He left about an hour ago."

"He left you?" She made it sound as if Cain McClellan should be strung up from the nearest tree.

"I don't need a baby-sitter, Francine."

"Then kindly explain what you're doing with that steak. And what's that?"

Mallory looked at the cast-iron skillet, surprised by her question. "A frying pan."

"I know that much. What have you got in it?"

"Salt. You sprinkle a teaspoon or so on the bottom, turn it up on high, and sear the steak. That way the meat doesn't stick to the pan."

She shook her head as if this were the most ridiculous thing she'd ever heard. "What were you planning to cook other than that T-bone?"

"I hadn't given it much thought."

"Sit down," she ordered.

Actually Mallory was more than ready to do exactly that. "You're getting bossy in your old age, aren't you?"

"Do you want dinner or not?"

"You cooking?"

"Yup. Any objections?"

He felt like whistling. "None. I like my steak rare."

"How rare?"

He thought about it a minute. "So rare a good vet would have that cow back on its feet."

Francine laughed softly.

Mallory made his way to the table and sank onto the chair. Not until then did he notice the therapist was wearing something other than her uniform. She had on jeans and a cable-knit sweater the color of winter wheat. The sweater did an admirable job of showing off her ample breasts. Other than when they were in the swimming pool, he hadn't paid much attention to her breasts. They were nice and full, just the way he liked. He'd told her that once and damn near got his head bit off.

This was one hell of a woman, only she hadn't figured it out yet. He just prayed he was around when she did.

"Do you always wear your hair in a braid?" he asked.

"Yes." She was busy at the stove.

"Why?" Tim watched her remove the pan from the burner and set it aside. Not exactly a promising start if she was cooking his dinner.

"It keeps the hair out of my face."

He should have suspected it was something as utilitarian as that. "I don't mean to question your obvious culinary skill, but exactly what are you doing?"

Francine turned about, a surprised look on her face. "Cooking dinner, what else? I thought you should have something other than protein. There's a couple of potatoes in here I was going to slice up and fry, and while I was at it I'll grill a few onions. I'll fix a salad, too."

She opened the refrigerator and bent forward, searching through the contents of the vegetable bin. This particular view of her soft derriere was something Tim had never seen, and it surprised him by how incredibly sexy he found this woman.

"How about gunslinger's sauce?"

The question came out of left field. "I beg your pardon?"

"You'll like it, I promise. It's flavored with whiskey."

"Yeah, but what do I put it on?"

She straightened and turned around. "Your steak, of course."

"Naturally," he echoed with mild sarcasm. "What else are you cooking up? Boot Hill broccoli?"

She laughed, and the sound of her amusement caused him to smile. Holding a carrot in her hand, she waved it at him. "We're still going to have that talk."

"Anything you say, dahlin', only feed me first."

She blinked at the endearment and quickly reverted

to the task of salad making. "I'm not your dahlin', your sweetheart, or anything else."

"Yes, but with a little sweet talk you could be."

She grated the carrot as if she intended to puree the thing. "If you continue in this vein, I'll walk right out that door."

"And leave me here half starved?"

"Yes."

Mallory didn't doubt she would, either. "All right, I'll be good."

She continued slicing tomatoes and tossing those with the lettuce, and Mallory continued studying her. Damn, but he liked her. Francine was his equal in every way. In all his years, he'd never met a woman like her.

Finished with the salad, she set it in the middle of the table. Recognizing this as an opportune moment, Tim caught her around the waist. "Take your hair out of the braid," he said.

She blinked down at him as if he'd spoken in Greek, then braced her hands over his, although she didn't shove them aside. "Why?"

"Because I want to see you with your hair down." Not waiting for her to refuse, he reached behind her back until he found the end of the French braid and released the clasp. The long, thick strands sprang free, almost bouncing in their eagerness to comply with his wish.

"Tim, please," she whispered. "I don't think this is a good idea."

"Sit," he ordered. He wanted to look at her without getting a crick in his neck. With his good leg he dragged a chair away from the table and gently eased her onto it.

She kept her eyes lowered, refusing to look at him. "I wish you wouldn't," she whispered.

"That's too bad." He splayed his fingers through the soft blond hair, draping the abundance over her shoulders. Leaning back on his chair, he studied the effect. His heart caught in his throat at the beauty he found her to be. How could he have been so blind? Francine Holden literally took his breath away.

"I better slice the potatoes."

Mallory edged his chair closer to hers. "Don't leave," he said, weaving his fingers through her hair and using it to urge her mouth toward his.

"I . . . I thought you were hungry."

"I'm famished," he whispered just before his mouth settled on hers.

Mallory was convinced neither one of them had anticipated the explosion of fire and need that would erupt between them. He'd intended to go slow and easy, introduce her gradually to his touch, coax and soothe her as he would before riding a feisty mare. But the minute she welcomed his kiss, encouraged his touch, Mallory was lost.

His lack of control surprised even him. He kissed her long and hard a number of times. Instead of appeasing his appetite, it increased a need for more of her. He reached inside her sweater, half expecting her to stop him. Encouraged that she'd allowed this small invasion, he cupped her breasts in his palms. He groaned as her nipples tightened and seemed to grow hot beneath the manipulations of his fingers. With a decided lack of finesse, he reached behind her and undid the clasp. The damn thing wasn't the least bit cooperative, and he was tempted to tear the obstinate slip of lace, and would have, if it hadn't freed her lush breasts just then.

Her bounty spilled from the confines of her bra. Godalmighty, she felt good. The need to make love to her was so intense, it was painful. It seemed every part of his body throbbed. All he could think about was getting Francine into his bed. And fast. He wanted her nipples in his mouth and her legs wrapped around his waist. With exquisite anticipation, he yearned to fill her beautiful body with his. Never in all his life had he needed a woman more.

Not any woman, either. He needed Francine. Mallory didn't know much about love. But he knew a hell of a lot about sex. What he felt for her was an off-balance configuration of both, he decided. At the moment the scales tipped toward sexual satisfaction, but not at the expense of hurting her.

Mallory needed Francine. The pounding in his loins was evidence enough of the physical desire he suffered, but it was the emotional craving he didn't understand. Didn't know how to appease.

He wanted her with him. At the end of the day when she walked out the door, he immediately calculated how many hours would pass before he'd be with her again. She dominated his thoughts. The monotony of many a long, torturous night passed while he filled his head with thoughts of her.

"Tim . . ."

All she said was his name, but the way she said it, low and sensual, warm and wanting, caused his body to tighten. He felt lost, and she was the home he'd never had. The love he'd never secured.

He struggled now, breathing hard in an effort to regain some semblance of control. He reminded himself she was a virgin. He couldn't allow himself to forget that. Nor could he make love to her for the first time on the kitchen floor. But God only knew how long it would take him to drag his way into the bedroom with that cursed walker.

He eased her closer and bent forward and nuzzled his face between her breasts. Sliding his mouth to one side, he took her hardened nipple between his lips and sucked deeply. Francine nearly came off the chair. She moaned and clamped her arms around his head.

He continued to suckle her breasts, then gradually reduced the pressure. "Go to my bedroom," he instructed her, kissing the underside of her jaw.

"Your bedroom," she repeated as if she were a robot.

"Wait for me there."

"But . . . "

"Please, Francine, just this once do as I ask."

"Should I . . . do you want me to undress?"

"Yes."

Reluctantly she moved away from him. Her parting word as she rushed from the room was, "Hurry."

Mallory didn't need any such inducement. He had his shirt off even before he was upright. His hands gripped hold of the walker, and he raised himself out of the chair, using the contraption for leverage. He wasn't looking at any watch, but he suspected he made record time, shuffling his way down the long hallway.

His bedroom door was closed, but it would take a hell of a lot more than a little thing like a door to stand between him and Francine.

He walked inside, not surprised that she'd left the light off. Actually he preferred that they made love in the dark. Although Francine was intimately familiar with his body, Mallory found himself self-conscious. This was different.

He closed the door, and the room became pitch black. Slowly, he made his way to the bed.

"Tim, before we make love, don't you think we should talk?"

"Later," he promised gently. He appreciated her fears, but he wasn't going to destroy this time with a lot of foolish chit-chat. As it was, he felt as if he were about to explode.

Awkwardly he climbed into the bed next to her. Unfortunately there was barely room for the two of them in the hospital bed. Holding Francine close, he kissed her slowly, sensually, and felt a heady rush of desire at her ready response.

She'd done as he asked and removed her clothes. Mallory took several moments to run his hands down the silky-smooth texture of her skin. Soon she'd sheathe him inside her. Soon she'd find her release, as he would his.

The problem Mallory hadn't anticipated was exactly how they were going to accomplish this. He hadn't made love to a woman since his accident and feared he was incapable of the traditional missionary position. Nor was he sure his injured hip and thigh would support her weight if he positioned her over him.

Rolling onto his good side, he pressed her body flush against his. Her breasts snuggled against his torso, her nipples hard and hot. He lifted her leg and eased it over his scarred hip. She was as hot and ready as he was himself.

"What about . . . you know?" Francine said.

Mallory could hear the self-consciousness creep into her voice. *You know?* He didn't.

"What about what?" he asked, hiding his eagerness as best he could and suspecting he did a damn poor job of it.

"Birth control." Her tone was hesitant and unsure, her words barely audible.

In all his adult life, Mallory had never been so desperate for a woman that he'd forgotten something this important. Worse, he realized he didn't have anything with which to protect her.

"I don't have anything here," he confessed.

"Oh."

As much as he wanted to make love to Francine, he couldn't do this, couldn't love her and then worry that his seed had taken shelter inside her generous body.

"It doesn't matter," she whispered hesitantly.

"Unfortunately, it does," he said between gritted teeth, and reached for the lamp on the stand next to the bed. "The last thing I want is to create another bastard."

10

Cain had never wooed a woman. Frankly, he wasn't sure how to go about it. When he arrived outside Linette's apartment Saturday evening, he hoped he'd covered all the bases. Flowers. Chocolates. Chilled champagne.

To be on the safe side he brought along a fresh bouquet of flowers. Roses, carnations, yellow lilies, and a few other blossoms he couldn't name. It was the biggest bouquet he could find, and it had cost him plenty. But he would have gladly paid ten times that fifty bucks if it would help his cause with Linette.

The box of chocolates was an ultrarich French variety, and the champagne was Dom Pérignon.

With his arms full, Cain had a difficult time ringing the bell. Linette opened the door and smiled when she saw him. Funny what a little thing like a smile could do, Cain mused. One tiny one from her, and he would have gladly trekked up three flights of stairs on his knees. She wore a pretty blue dress and was so strikingly lovely that for an embarrassing moment he couldn't take his eyes off her.

"I came bearing gifts," he said finally, and stepped inside. His first thought was to set everything aside and drag her into his arms. Surely one small kiss wasn't too much to ask. He didn't, however, for fear he'd upset their evening. He dared not risk offending her.

"I'm a little early," he said apologetically.

"I am, too," she said, taking the flowers out of his arms and carrying them into the kitchen. Standing next to her sink, she closed her eyes and buried her nose in their scent. "They're beautiful. Thank you."

Cain set the frilly box of candy and the bottle of champagne on the countertop while Linette reached in the cupboard below and brought out a vase. She filled it with water and carefully arranged the bouquet inside it. When she finished, she set it in the center of the dining room table.

"Our reservations aren't for another hour," he told her. "Would you like me to open the wine?"

"Please." She retrieved two flutes from the china hutch while Cain manipulated the top off the champagne bottle. The popping sound shattered the silence.

"I've never tasted Dom Pérignon before," she said, smiling up at him. "From what I understand it's very expensive."

"It's not too bad." Hell would freeze over before he'd admit it was the most expensive wine he'd ever purchased.

Cain filled the two glasses. "Shall we drink to us?"

She bit into her lower lip, then nodded. "To us," she said with a gentle smile. Cain touched the rim of his glass against hers.

They each sampled the wine.

"So," he said, walking into the living room and taking a seat. He leaned back casually against the thick cushion. "How'd your blind date go?" He hadn't intended to start off their evening with an interrogation of her evening, but a stomach-twisting bout of curiosity got the best of him.

He'd spent the majority of the night before wrestling demons, thinking about Linette dining, laughing, and enjoying the company of another man. It wasn't something he looked forward to repeating any time soon.

Linette laughed softly. "You don't want to know."

"Sure I do." He'd feel a thousand times better if the blind date had turned out to be a horror story. They could laugh together over what one was obligated to do for well-meaning friends. He might even relate a couple of fiascos of his own just so she'd feel better.

"His name is Charles Garner."

She wasn't immediately forthcoming with details, so Cain helped her along a little. "What's he do for a living?" She seemed to be studying the champagne bubbles.

"He's an attorney."

"Divorced?" Already Cain had him pictured as a greedy son of a bitch. To his way of thinking, a fair portion of lawyers were known charlatans. At least the ones he'd been in contact with over the years were.

"No. His wife died of leukemia. The same rare type that killed Michael."

This was beginning to sound less promising. "So the

two of you had a lot to talk about," Cain commented with less enthusiasm.

"Yes, only we didn't talk about leukemia. Neither one of us wanted to dredge up the pain of the past."

"I see." If Cain understood her correctly, she was telling him the two had formed this automatic kinship, born out of their shared experiences.

"Charles is probably one of the nicest men I've ever met. He's gentle and sweet, determined to be a good father to his two children."

"So there're children involved?" This didn't bode well, either. Cain recalled how much Linette wanted a family. This man came complete, a package deal, something Cain could never offer her.

"Charles has two boys. Jesse's seven and has bright red freckles and Steve's five and as cute as a bug's ear."

Already she knew their names. Cain could fast see that the flowers, candy, and champagne weren't going to cut it. At the rate this conversation was going, human sacrifice wouldn't, either.

To listen to Linette speak, it was as if she'd found the perfect match. Mr. Impeccable was everything Cain wasn't and would never be. Her blind date could offer her the security she needed. Something she sure as hell wasn't going to get with him.

"He sounds wonderful," Cain said with a sorry lack of enthusiasm.

"Charles is."

If Cain had a lick of sense, he'd set aside the wine-glass, reach for his coat, and walk out now. Instead he was a glutton for punishment. "When will you be seeing him again?"

It seemed to take an inordinate amount of time for her to answer. "I won't be."

Cain's head snapped up so fast, he heard a bone in his neck pop. "You won't?"

"No." The admission came soft and low.

"Why wouldn't you? This guy sounds ideal for you."

Linette rolled the stem of the glassware between her palms. "It wouldn't be fair to Charles."

"Not fair?"

"To accept another date would mislead him into thinking we could have a relationship."

"You don't want a relationship with Charles?"

"No." She raised her head so that her eyes slammed into his. Her beautiful, expressive gaze snapped with irritation.

"The whole time I was with Charles, all I could think about was you," she said, her lips pinched as if it cost her a good deal to admit this. "He took me to a fabulous, ultraexpensive restaurant, and instead of enjoying myself the way I should have, all I could think about was how much I'd rather be with you. What have you done to me, Cain McClellan?"

Cain had no answers to give her. Although he had several questions of his own.

"I was thoroughly miserable the entire night," she admitted, and then added on a spirited note, "Don't you dare smile, either."

"I'm not smiling."

"You most certainly are. I shouldn't have told you about Charles. I'm sorry now I did."

"I'm very pleased you did." He set aside his champagne glass, reached for her crystal flute, and placed it on the coffee table. Then he lifted her fingers to his mouth and kissed the tip of each one. "I have a few complaints of my own about you, Widow Collins." His lips moved over the inside of her wrist, his tongue making slow circles over her smooth skin. "You've haunted my dreams from the moment we met. It's because of you I'm here in San Francisco when I promised myself I'd never see you again."

"That's another thing I want to discuss with you."

He noted the irritation had left her voice. Draping one of her arms over his shoulder, he reached for her free hand, then repeated the procedure of kissing her fingers, turning over her hand and exposing her wrist to his mouth. Then he moved his tongue over the inside curve of her elbow and placed her unresisting arm on his shoulder. Her wrists dangled behind his neck.

"I don't think it's a good idea for you to kiss me," she said, her voice reedy and thin. Her resistance would be token at best, Cain guessed.

"Why not?" His heart clamored loudly in his ears, the way it always did when she was this close. His thumb and finger lifted her chin so that she was forced to meet his eyes.

"Because every time you do . . . " The words trembled reluctantly from her lips. She paused.

"Yes," he coaxed.

She shook her head, refusing to say more.

"Because every time we kiss," he repeated, and then finished the statement for her, "you want me to make love to you."

She pulled away from him immediately; her arms slid

from his shoulders and fell free. The truth of his words burned in her eyes.

"How do you think I know this?" he asked her gently. "It's because I want the same thing."

"I can't . . . I won't become sexually involved with you."

"I know that, too. It's far better that we don't make love." There was danger in emotional commitment. Danger in allowing himself to become accustomed to her softness. This woman was deadly. He'd known that from the first. Yet he defied the danger again and again by seeking her out.

Cain hadn't a clue where this relationship would lead. Didn't know anything beyond the complicated realization that he couldn't stay away from her.

Francine gladly accepted the shopping date with her mother. She'd been looking for an excuse to casually talk about her relationship with Tim. Martha Holden was both mother and friend to Francine. There were several important questions she needed answered, but she didn't want to be obvious about her reasons for wanting to know.

They met at the Embarcadaro at Nordstrom. Who would have ever believed Francine would have the most important discussion of her life in women's lingerie? Certainly not her.

It all began naturally. "How long did you and Dad date before you were married?" Francine asked. As she recalled, at the time her mother had been an English literature major and her father an apprentice plumber.

Both families had been left shaking their heads in wonder at the explosive romance that developed between the two.

Francine's father was a burly giant, reaching nearly six feet six inches. Everything about him was big. His hands were monstrous, his feet so large they had to special order his shoes. Her mother, on the other hand, was a full foot and two inches shorter and a delicate soul who loved poetry, classical music, and English literature.

As fate would have it, Francine had favored her father's side of the family. She reached six feet by the time she was fourteen and was several inches taller than two of her own brothers.

"Your father and I met in September and married in October a year later," her mother answered.

Actually Francine knew this but wanted to ease into the discussion. "What attracted you to Dad?"

Martha Holden smiled softly and held a black lacy bra against her stomach. She looked straight ahead and into warm memories, Francine suspected.

"I was much too young to know about love," Martha Holden began. "He was such a bear of a man, even more so then, but his heart has always been big and gentle. Soon after we met, I saw him bend down and comfort a little boy who'd fallen off his bicycle. There was something so tender and caring in the way he talked to that child. I think it was then that I fell in love with him."

Francine made busy sorting through a rack of satin pajamas, her eyes avoiding her mother's. "Did you and Dad sleep together before the wedding?"

Her mother, who'd been busy checking bra sizes, hesitated. "No," she answered softly. "I realize that isn't what you expected to hear. Not in this day and age, not then, either, for that matter. We met during the sixties, in the age of free love, when AIDS and the like wasn't a consideration."

"I admire your restraint," Francine said, sorry now she'd brought up the subject, which was far more personal than anything she'd asked previously. "It must have been difficult being so much in love."

"Congratulate your father, then. If it had been up to me, we would have lived together two months before the wedding. He was the one who insisted we wait. Trust me, Francine, I did everything I knew to break his resolve, but your father wanted things right for me."

"Are you glad you waited?"

Martha laughed. "Yes, but not for the reasons you're thinking. You were born nine months to the day after the wedding. I don't think either of us anticipated me being so fertile."

Francine was certain her cheeks had turned crimson. She'd come very close to testing her own fertility with Tim. Hoping her mother didn't notice her red cheeks, she picked out a pair of pajamas, a new bra, and some bikini underwear and paid the cashier.

"How's the patient coming along these days?" her mother asked, broaching the very subject Francine had hoped to avoid.

"Good. He's improving more every day."

Her mother tucked her arm in Francine's. "How long have you been in love with him?"

Francine felt like bursting into tears. She had hoped she hadn't been that obvious. The best answer she could give was a shrug. "He's a mercenary, Mother. Can you believe I could do something so stupid as to fall for a soldier of fortune? To complicate matters even more, he's a patient. Good therapists don't allow this sort of thing to happen."

"You're only human. Now stop being so hard on yourself!" She led Francine away from the lingerie department. "Come on, let's take a break and you can tell me all about what's been happening between you and Mr. Mallory."

Before long they were sitting across a table from each other.

"I'm so angry with Tim, I can barely work with him."

"Angry," her mother repeated. "I thought you said you were in love with him."

"I am. On Friday I learned that he's chomping at the bit to get back in the field with his cronies. The man's a crazed fool. He was nearly killed the last time. I didn't work this hard to watch him go off and get himself killed."

"Do you normally care what your patients do after therapy?" her mother asked.

"No," Francine answered softly.

"What did you expect him to do once he started walking again?"

"I don't know. I guess I didn't think about it. But I never believed, not for one moment, that he'd be fool enough to risk his life again."

"Have you—"

"Made love?" Francine finished for her. "No, but it was close. We . . . Tim didn't have a condom, and he refused to risk it. His mother wasn't married when she had him. Apparently he was tossed from one foster home to another."

"In other words, he was the one who put an end to it?"

Francine nodded but avoided meeting her mother's eyes.

"He must feel deeply about you, Francine. If he didn't, he wouldn't have cared about the risk, despite his own background. Why should he when he'll be gone shortly?"

" Afterward I thought about what happened."

"Yes," her mother coaxed.

"And I realized I went to bed with him for all the wrong reasons. I love him, yes, but in my heart that was only a small part of my wanting to make love."

"You thought it would keep him in San Francisco," her mother supplied for her.

Francine's head shot up. "That's exactly what I hoped, but I know now it would never have worked. Every day Tim drives himself harder and harder with one goal in mind. He's eager to get back to Florida. Get back with his friends."

"In other words, he's eager to leave you."

"Yes."

"Let him go, Francine."

"You make it sound so easy. I know what you're going to say—if it's meant to be, he'll come back. I wish it were that simple, but it isn't."

"What can you do to hold him here?"

Francine had already given this matter a good deal of thought. "Nothing."

Her mother patted her hand gently.

"It isn't fair. This is the first time in my life that I've ever been in love. There hasn't been another man I ever loved like this. He may be the only one I ever will."

"Perhaps."

However painful, Francine was grateful her mother didn't try to convince her otherwise. It had taken her nearly thirty-one years to fall in love the first time. She'd be over sixty if she had to wait that long again.

All at once Francine had the incredible urge to laugh. It started out as a soft giggle, then gained in intensity until she was nearly doubled over.

"Francine?" Her mother was looking at her strangely.

"Monday morning when I arrived at the house," she said between breaths, "Tim had a case of condoms delivered."

"I beg your pardon?"

Francine wiped the moisture from her cheeks. Leaning toward her mother, she lowered her voice. "Tim had one hundred and forty-four condoms brought to the house just in case we found ourselves in similar circumstances. I swear he has them planted in every room. There's even an ashtray full of condoms by the pool."

"I think I could grow to like your Mr. Mallory."

"That's the problem, Mom, he isn't mine."

"Don't give up just yet," her mother said softly. "Life has a way of working matters out for the best. If you lose him, then that was the way it was meant to be. My guess is that he knows less about love than most men. He's as perplexed about the whole thing as you are. Give him time."

Francine mulled over her mother's words of wisdom that night. The following morning she arrived at Tim's house at her usual time. Her job was nearly finished now. At the rate her patient was progressing, he'd be able to walk, with the aid of a cane, inside of a month.

His progress thus far was nothing sort of phenomenal. Nothing short of a miracle.

Tim was sitting up in bed, waiting for her.

"Morning," she greeted him, setting her bag on the chair. His gaze followed her every move, the same way it had for weeks. It was all she could do not to ask him to stop watching her.

"Morning," he returned, sounding downright chipper. "I gave Greg the night off," he said, and waited as if he expected her to respond.

"So?"

"So, I thought I'd invite you over for dinner." He jiggled his eyebrows suggestively.

"Who's cooking?" she was foolish enough to ask.

"We both will be if everything goes the way I'm planning."

"Tim, please."

"That's what you'll be saying all right."

Francine swore his grin stretched from ear to ear. "Is everything one big joke to you?" she demanded.

"No." He reached out and caught her hand, bringing her closer to the edge of the mattress. "Come on, sweetheart, there's no need to be shy about this. I'm crazy about you, and it's apparent you feel the same way about me. Why pretend otherwise?"

Francine closed her eyes, unable to offer a suitable argument.

"I can understand you not wanting to fool around during work hours. I've tried to respect that the last couple of days, but I have to tell you, honey, it's damn hard. Fact is, you may or may not have noticed, it's a *big and hard* problem."

"What about Cain?" She couldn't believe she was seriously contemplating doing this.

"No problem. He's been gone every evening as it is. If you want, I'll ask him to stay away."

A strained silence passed.

"This is highly unethical."

"Irresponsible on both our parts," Tim added softly.

"Foolish in the extreme."

"Crazy."

Francine smiled and whispered, "I bought lacy underwear the other day."

Tim groaned. "Don't tell me you have it on now."

"I do."

His eyes slammed closed, and his fingers tightened around hers. "Six o'clock. Salad, steak, and champagne," he said.

"What's for dessert?"

Tim grinned as if he were absolutely delighted she'd asked. "You and me, my love. You and me."

"Have you got a minute?" Mallory asked Cain early that same afternoon. Cain was reading the morning paper at the kitchen table when his friend joined him.

"Sure." He wasn't scheduled to meet Linette until after six. He'd gotten two tickets to the symphony as a surprise, knowing how much she'd enjoy it. In a thousand lifetimes he never would have believed he'd willingly sit through a bunch of men and women in tuxedos playing musical instruments. He liked songs with words.

"I've been meaning to talk to you, too," Cain said, setting aside the newspaper. He didn't know what was going on between Mallory and the therapist, but apparently it was more than met the eye.

"I need a small favor," Mallory said, looking a bit sheepish.

"You've got it."

"Would you mind staying away for the night?"

"Staying away?"

Tim heaved a deep sigh. "If you must know, I'm going to have company."

"For the night?"

"For the whole night."

Cain studied his friend carefully. "Is this someone I know?"

"Yeah," Tim answered defensively. "It's Francine."

This was what Cain feared. "Do you think that's wise?"

"I didn't ask your opinion, McClellan. I don't give a shit if it's wise or not. She's coming."

"If it's a woman you want, I can arrange—"

"There's only one woman who interests me." His words were packed with irritation.

After meeting Linette, Cain knew the feeling. He'd bumped heads with Mallory's therapist once already, and he'd strongly suspected then a romance was brewing between the two. What he didn't know was his friend's feelings toward Francine.

"All right, you got it," he said. "I'll spend the night in a hotel."

"I appreciate it." Tim said, and then waited before asking, "You wanted to talk to me about something?"

"Yeah." Now, however, he wasn't sure. "It has to do with Francine."

"What about her?" Mallory's whole posture was defensive, and Cain wished he'd chosen his time more carefully.

"I'm not going to give you advice, if that's what you're thinking."

"I appreciate that."

"But . . ."

Mallory grinned. "Somehow I thought there was going to be a 'but' in this."

"I just want to warn you that a woman can really screw up your head." He was one to talk! He'd been following Linette around like a calf after its mother from the moment he'd arrived in town.

"We've both seen it happen," Mallory commented.

"You're coming back to Deliverance Company?"

Mallory's shoulders went back with surprise. "Of course."

"You aren't going to let some woman change your mind?"

"Hell, no."

Cain relaxed and reached for the newspaper once more. "Good. You had me worried there."

The calls didn't always come in the middle of the night. No sooner had Cain finished speaking with Mallory than the phone rang. The crazy part was, Cain didn't give a thought to the fact that he was being called back to work. The first thing that went through his head was that he wouldn't be able to take Linette to the symphony after all.

An hour earlier he'd issued unwanted advice to

Mallory when he should have been saying it to himself. Linette had him twisted in such tight knots, within a matter of days he'd forgotten who he was.

Cain listened as Murphy outlined the details of the case. This time it was a cultural attaché being held political prisoner. In Central America. Jungle. Heat. Death.

When Cain finished with the call, he immediately dialed the airlines and scheduled his flight to Florida. The mission would be planned from there. Two of his men were flying in from other parts of the country. They'd rendezvous first thing in the morning and leave together from there.

But first, before he did anything more, Cain had to talk to Linette. He dreaded this moment more than anything he could remember in a long while. He dreaded it more than he had leaving her at Christmas.

Linette looked surprised when he arrived at Wild and Wooly, and her eyes brightened with pleasure. But something about him must have told her why he'd come, because he watched the happiness quickly drain away.

"You're leaving?"

He nodded.

She said something to Bonnie and walked into the back room.

Cain followed her. He found her sitting, her back against the wall, her hands clasped in her lap. When she looked up, he noted that her eyes were bright.

Cain's heart constricted as he knelt down in front of her and cupped her hands in both of his.

"Where?" she asked in a whisper.

"Central America."

"What happened?"

"A man. A good man with a wife and family was taken hostage by a faction looking to pressure the government. He's an American."

"Then why don't we send in the army or something?"

What she was really asking, Cain realized, was why he was the one who had to go.

"They can't do that."

"But why?" she pressed, and Cain realized she was trembling. She freed one hand and stroked the side of his face. "Why?" she repeated.

"It's long and involved. The United States government doesn't negotiate with terrorists. I'm not entirely sure I can answer the wheres and whys myself. All I know is that Deliverance Company has been contacted."

She lowered her head. "Do you have to go?"

"Yes, Linette. This is what I do."

"What about your broken ribs?"

"They're healed enough."

"But—"

He stopped her by gently pressing his finger against her lips. "I'm leaving. My flight takes off in less than two hours. I came because I wanted to tell you myself." He kissed her bunched up fingers, wishing with everything inside him that he could calm her fears. "This is who I am. I'm good, baby, real good. Don't worry, all right?"

"When will you be back?"

"I don't know. Someday soon."

"You won't take any unnecessary chances, will you?"

"I'm not going to do anything stupid."

"There isn't any chance you'll be killed, is there?"

Cain closed his eyes and wished he could lie to her. "I can't make that promise."

Her trembling increased. "I know," she said.

11

Paul Curnyn was going to die. Not once had he doubted the certainty of his fate. The only question that remained unanswered was how and when.

Bound and gagged, beaten and bloody, he steeled himself against the pain that throbbed through his back and legs. The sound of his own screams echoed in his ears.

He closed his eyes and felt tears burning for release. He silently damned his captors for reducing him to this level of weakness. He couldn't deal with much more of the pain. Couldn't keep from screaming. If they continued to torture him, he wouldn't have the strength to keep from begging them to stop. He prayed his family would never know how much he'd suffered.

His family.

Paul's mind focused on his wife, Delores, and his two children. Jennifer and Sean. He wished now he'd been a better husband and father. Wished now he'd cared less about making a name for himself at the State Department and more about his family. He prayed his children would remember him.

Paul tensed as one of his captors approached him. Out of the corner of his eye, he saw the man remove his revolver from a leather holster and point it at Paul's temple. The steel barrel felt cold and evil against his skin.

A flurry of Spanish erupted between the men. The one who held the gun shouted the loudest. The dialect was one Paul wasn't fluent enough with to fully understand. What words he was able to translate sent chills of terror scooting down his spine.

Paul heard the gun hammer pull back and closed his eyes.

It would have been easier, Francine decided, if she and Tim hadn't planned their lovemaking. It felt cold and calculating to know in advance what they were about to do. Worse to know why she was doing it. He hadn't declared his love, only his need, but her reasons for coming weren't any more sterling. If she satisfied him in bed, then maybe, just maybe, he wouldn't be so eager to leave her.

Francine swallowed tightly. She felt like an emotional wreck. Over the years she'd heard from her friends and read in a variety of accounts that the first time a woman made love could be painful. She didn't fear the pain as much as she worried about disappointing Tim with her complete lack of expertise. She must be some kind of idiot to think that she could hold a man with her sexual favors when she was a virgin.

By the time she stood outside the house, Francine's stomach was queasy. She breathed deeply several times in an effort to calm her fractured nerves. Then she painted a bright smile on her face, opened the door, and walked inside, carrying her overnight bag with her.

"Anyone home?" she called out cheerfully.

"In here."

Tim was waiting for her in the kitchen. One thing was sure, she was in no mood to eat anything. All she could think about was getting this ordeal over with as quickly as possible.

"Hi," she said, unable to meet his eyes. She'd worn her hair down, the way he liked it, and wished now she hadn't. It kept falling over her shoulder and getting in the way.

"So you decided to come after all." He didn't sound particularly delighted to see her.

"Yeah."

"I hope you're hungry. I sent Greg out for Chinese, and he brought back enough food to feed an army."

"I . . . I don't have much of an appetite yet."

"Me either."

Francine chanced her first look in his direction. Tim was sitting at the table with an atlas spread open. Apparently he'd developed a sudden interest in Central America.

"Greg's gone?" she asking, glancing around.

"I told him to get lost for the night."

Not exactly a delicate way to announce Tim was expecting company.

"That kid's getting to be a real smart-ass. Seems he felt the need to lecture me about you."

"He knows about us?" The question slipped out before she could censor it.

Tim's laughter lacked any real amusement. "Cain figured it out, too. I haven't exactly had much of a social life lately. You're the only woman who's been around in the last year and a half. Neither man is blind or stupid."

"I suppose it only makes sense they'd know."

"Were you planning on hiding it from them?"

"No." But by the same token she wasn't exactly planning on holding a symposium on their relationship, either. "What did Greg have to say?"

"That you were a fool for getting involved with me."

"He should have told me that, not you." Although to be fair, he had warned her.

Tim muttered something under his breath and then said, "I suspect Greg's half in love with you himself."

"Greg?" Francine didn't believe it for a moment.

"So you're not hungry?"

"No."

"Me either," he confessed. He closed the atlas, but Francine noticed the way his gaze lingered over the volume cover.

They sat in silence, and it seemed neither one of them knew what to say next.

"I suppose we should get at it, then."

Get at it certainly didn't leave a lot of room for romance.

"I suppose we should," she answered, stiffening. Tim wasn't teasing her the way he had before, taking delight in making her blush. Nor did he appear to be overly eager to make love when the suggestion had dominated every word and action for weeks.

"Why don't you go in the bedroom and get undressed," he suggested.

Francine expanded her lungs with a giant breath. "I don't think that's a good idea."

"Not a good idea?" His eyes shot to hers. "Why not?"

"This isn't working," she whispered, more to herself than to Tim, amazed that she'd managed to come this far.

Tim leaned back on his chair and studied the ceiling tile. "All right," he said, and released his breath forcefully. "I apologize. My mind's been on other things. Cain's gone."

Francine didn't understand. "It was my understanding that you were going to ask him to leave."

"I mean gone as in he's been called away on a mission," he explained.

"A mission." It made perfect sense to Francine now. Tim longed to be with his friend on some field of death rather than stuck in San Francisco with her. If she'd ever needed a reminder that he would dally with her, use her, and then callously leave her, she had it now.

Tim glanced at his watch. "He'll land in Florida in a couple of hours. Murphy's there, and Jack and Bailey are flying in this evening. My guess is they'll land in Tehuantepec by tomorrow afternoon."

Francine had never heard of the place, but if the atlas

was any indication, it was situated somewhere in Central America.

"Timing is everything in these cases. For all we know, that poor bastard could already be dead." Agitated, Tim flexed and unflexed his hands.

Francine scooted back the seat, stood, and reached for her bag.

Tim looked over at her. "Where are you going?"

"Home."

He frowned. "Why? Listen, I know our night hasn't gotten off to a good start, but that doesn't mean we can't have some fun together."

Francine held up her hand while she waited for her thoughts to sort themselves out. "On second thought, I don't think our making love is such a good idea after all."

Tim reached for his walker and pulled himself upright. "What do you mean?" he asked. His eyes were grave and dark. Disappointed.

"I meant exactly what I said. You're looking for a good-time girl. Someone to take your mind off your boredom for the next couple of weeks before you head back to your friends."

Tim's frown darkened to a glower. "What you're really saying is you've changed your mind."

Francine wasn't going to argue the point with him. "Yes."

"Come on, sweetheart, we got off to a bad start, but that doesn't mean we have to call the whole thing off. You want me as much as I want you."

He brought up another point she couldn't argue. "The only thing you have to offer me is a few weeks of casual sex. I thought that would be enough, but I see now that it isn't. I'm sorry to disappoint you, but I need more than you're willing to offer."

He closed his eyes as if calling upon a nameless god for patience. "What's wrong? Do you need me to pretty it up with a few flowery words? Fine. I can do that. You'll get what you need, and I'll get what I need. It isn't such a bad deal."

"I'd be a fool to turn you down."

He smiled for the first time. "Exactly."

"No thanks." She felt considerably foolish. It might have worked if he hadn't been drooling over some atlas. It was a vivid reminder of exactly who and what he was. A vivid reminder of what she was willing to become.

"No thanks," he repeated sarcastically. "Listen, sweetheart, you've apparently got some hair up your butt about sex all of a sudden. It's a perfectly natural human function. There's no need to mess it up with a bunch of other emotions. I've always called a spade a spade and admired you for doing the same. Don't disappoint me now."

"I don't want you to leave," she said in a rush. "You don't need to be a soldier. You could do anything, be anything at all. You don't have to—"

"So that's it," Tim said, his face tightening with irritation. "You seem to think you can use that body of yours for leverage to wrap me around your little finger. I got news for you. It ain't going to work. Go ahead and walk out that door," he challenged, and pointed the way out to her.

Francine's hand tightened around the handle of the overnight bag before she turned away from him.

"But before you leave, you'd best think about the real reasons you're going."

"I don't need you to tell me why," she snapped.

"That's not the way I see it. You're backing down because you're chicken. You're afraid, so own up to it. Because this bull about me insulting you is a crock of shit."

"All right," she said, turning back to face him. "You hit the nail on the head. I'm afraid." And she was. She was scared spitless that she was giving her heart to a man who would love her one night and forget her name the next. Afraid he would forever mark her life and then calmly walk out of it.

"There's no need to be afraid." His words were soft and full of inducement. "Let me love you, Francine. Let me show you what it can be like between us. If you still want to leave afterward, then fine, you can go. Just don't walk out now. We've only just begun, sweetheart."

Francine battled back a flood of tears.

"Come on," he coaxed once more. "Let's sit down and have dinner. That's all I'm asking. It's a shame for all this food to go to waste." He gestured to the table behind him. "We've come this far. Let's not turn back now."

Francine wavered. Dear sweet heaven, what was the matter with her? Never once in all her life had she thought of herself as weak. Tim made her that way, and she hated it. She'd suffer more than a few regrets if she gave in to him now. On the other hand, she'd be left wondering the rest of her life what it would have been like with him. God help her, she loved him.

Francine walked over to him and stood in front of the walker. She crouched down and set her small suitcase on the floor, then wrapped her arms around Tim's torso. His eyes brightened with anticipation as she kissed him.

His mouth opened to hers, taking advantage of her generosity. With his one free hand, he wove his fingers into her hair and kissed her with a hunger and need that left her clinging and weak in the knees.

"This is more like it," he said, and brought her lips back to his. He kissed her twice more, each kiss more potent than the previous one. They were both left trembling with desire.

"You've got far too many clothes on," he said, his voice little more than a whisper. "Now go to my room, strip, and wait for me. We've got all night for me to appease those fears. But you never know, it might take longer." He released her slowly, as if it demanded every ounce of will he possessed to do so. "I only hope one case of condoms is enough."

Francine stepped back, took a moment to catch her breath, and then pressed her hand to his cheek. "Goodbye, Tim Mallory, and thank you."

His eyes widened as if she'd slapped him. "Good-bye?"

She reached for her bag and literally ran for the door. She feared if he said one word more, she wouldn't have the strength to leave him. And leave him she must, for her own peace of mind.

Two days later Greg phoned Francine at home.

"Hello, Greg," she said, immediately regretting not contacting him herself. She owed Greg more than the brief letter of resignation she'd had delivered to the house.

"How are you?"

"Great." A lie, but the truth would only depress him.

"The beastmaster got your letter."

"I should have stopped in and said good-bye to you. I'm sorry, Greg."

"No problem. Listen, this isn't any of my business, but I want to make sure that Mr. Mallory . . . I want to be sure he didn't hurt you."

Francine braced her forehead against the kitchen wall. "Of course not, what makes you ask that?"

Greg hesitated. "No reason. It's just that . . . well, never mind. It isn't important. He's gone, you know."

"Tim's left San Francisco?" She straightened in shock.

"Yeah, he had me book the first available flight to Miami as soon as he read your letter."

"I see."

"I hope that list of instructions you gave him wasn't important. He crushed it up into a ball and threw it across the room."

"He'll be fine," Francine assured Tim's assistant. She would be, too, in time.

"I can't tell you how much I've enjoyed this last month," Charles Garner told Linette. He'd unexpectedly stopped off at the shop and stayed until closing time.

He was a striking-looking man, Linette thought, kind and good-natured. But he didn't make her heart zing the way Cain did. She didn't spend time with him and then wonder how long it would be before she saw him again. But none of that mattered, she reminded herself.

Linette had made the painful decision not to see Cain again. He'd been in Central America five weeks now. These silent days without him had been some of the most agonizing of her life.

It would have helped if he'd contacted her in some way. She hadn't heard so much as a word from him. Not even a postcard. For all she knew, he could be dead. Each day of not knowing was hell. The fears ate her alive. The interminable waiting. Was he hurt? Dying? Had he forgotten her completely?

Linette tried not to worry about Cain. Tried not to think of him in some foreign jungle, hurting, perhaps dying. Tried not to think of standing over the grave of another man she'd loved and buried.

The first week after he'd left had been the worst. She rarely slept, and when she did, her dreams were filled with horror scenes involving Cain. She lost five pounds in eight days, weight she couldn't afford to shed.

Bonnie was the one who sat her down and talked some sense into her. It seemed crystal clear when her friend said it. Cain was a mercenary. Fighting and killing was his profession. Either accept him as he was or break off the relationship. It was one or the other.

Afterward Linette knew what she had to do. As painful as it was, she realized Cain wasn't going to change. She also realized she couldn't accept living with the risks he took. She wanted to tell him, only there hadn't been any word from him.

He wouldn't catch her off guard this time, she vowed. If he showed up unexpectedly the way he had before, she'd be prepared. What she intended to tell him was all planned out.

She wouldn't allow her heart to take control next time. No matter how glad she was to see him. No matter how light-headed and dizzy the sight of him made her.

"How are the boys?" she asked Charles, determined to keep her mind off Cain.

"Great," the attorney answered. They were standing outside her yarn shop, and he took the key out of her hand and locked up for her. "They loved it that we went roller-skating with them. They like you, Linette."

"I like them, too."

Charles smiled as he handed her back her key chain. "I thought we might get together next weekend. The boys have been hounding me to take them kite flying. No better month than March for that. I thought we'd go down to Golden Gate Park and give it a shot. Are you game?"

"Sure, that sounds like fun."

"Later, I'll arrange for a sitter for the boys and take you out for a night on the town. I thought we'd start with dinner and then take in a play. I understand *The Phantom of the Opera*'s in town. Getting tickets shouldn't be too much of a problem."

"It might be. Why don't I cook something up at your place, and we can rent a couple of videos? The boys can help with dinner. They did a great job cooking the spaghetti last week, remember?" Linette enjoyed her time with Charles's young sons immensely. The two youngsters had helped ease the sting of missing Cain far more than her dates with their father.

Charles hesitated. "You still think about Cain, don't you?"

Linette lowered her eyes and nodded. "I'm sorry, Charles, really I am."

"I take it you haven't heard from him?"

"Not a word." Nor did she have an address where she could write him.

"Once he does contact you, then you can put the relationship to rest. It's over. You know it, but he doesn't."

Linette bit into her lower lip and nodded.

"You're sure this is what you want?" Charles asked, studying her. He was far more understanding about her relationship with Cain than she'd expected him to be. He'd talked to her about it on several occasions, and he'd helped her realize how futile linking her life with Cain's would be.

"This is what I want," she said quickly—perhaps too quickly, because Charles frowned and reached for her hand, clasping it firmly in his own.

"You can't tie your life up in a dead-end relationship. There's no future in loving a mercenary."

"I know all that." She didn't need Charles to tell her what she'd struggled so painfully to acknowledge herself. Loving Cain was like living in an earthquake zone. He was going to be killed. Sometime. Somewhere. Some day soon. Without notice. Kill or be killed.

"We'll have dinner out, then?" Charles coaxed. "And the play?"

"All right," she agreed, wishing she could dredge up more enthusiasm for the outing.

Charles had a good heart. The problem was that Linette found him dull. She sincerely hoped Cain hadn't ruined her for other men.

He walked her to her car and kissed her cheek. "I'll pick you up around ten Saturday morning."

"I'll be ready."

When she arrived back at her apartment, Linette forced herself to cook dinner. After dining on a frozen entree she'd cooked in her microwave, she took a long hot bath and climbed into bed. She read for a while, then turned off the light. To her surprise, she felt herself drifting off to sleep almost immediately.

The sound of the phone caught her in the middle of a dream. She lifted her head from the pillow and glanced at the clock. Realizing it was the phone and not her alarm, she lifted the receiver and pressed it to her ear. She hadn't a clue who would phone her at two in the morning.

"Hello," she said, still half asleep. Her eyes were closed and her voice sounded drugged.

"Linette."

The connection wasn't good. Static buzzed and hissed over the wires.

"Linette, it's Cain."

Her eyes flew open then, and her heart kicked into double time. "Cain?" she cried, and sitting upright, she grabbed hold of the telephone receiver with both hands. "Where are you?"

"Some hellhole of a town in Central America. You'd think a country this size would know what a pay phone was. Never mind that. How are you?"

His voice faded in and out. "Fine," she said, louder this time. "What about you?"

"I'm fine. Don't sound so worried."

"Did you find . . . " She wanted to ask him about the

American he'd told her about, the one who'd been kid-napped, but static erupted on the line.

"We found him. He was dead."

"Oh, no."

"Listen, I don't know how much longer this line will last."

"Cain, please, I need to talk to you." She was shouting, frantic for him to listen to her.

More static, this time so loud and discordant, Linette was forced to hold the phone away from her ear.

"Cain," she cried, afraid the line had been disconnected.

"Can you hear me?" His voice faded again.

"Only a little."

"I'm flying directly from here to San Francisco. I should land—"

"No," she cried. This wasn't how she intended to tell him, but she couldn't have him rush to her, believing she'd be waiting for him with open arms. For the thousandth time she cursed herself for not having the strength to tell him face-to-face before he'd left.

Static again.

"Linette?"

"I didn't know if you were alive or dead," she said, angry now.

"I know, baby, I'm sorry. Dear Lord, I've missed you. I promise to make it up to you."

"Don't come," she shouted. "Stay away from me. Please, just stay away. I don't want to see you again."

"You don't mean that."

"I do. I'm dating Charles now. It's over between us, understand?"

"Linette—"

The phone went dead. Linette stared at the phone, not knowing if Cain had hung up on her or if the connection had been cut. It didn't matter. She'd said all she wanted.

Slowly she replaced the receiver. Her hands trembled as she brushed the hair out of her face. Lying back down, she gathered the blankets around her and hugged the spare pillow, burying her face in its softness.

It was over.

"Another beer?" Mallory asked Cain.

"Sure. You buying?"

"Yeah." Mallory raised his hand to attract the bartender's attention. It was a seedy place in a bad part of town, where the music was slow and the women fast. Frankly, Mallory didn't care about either. As long as the beer was cold he didn't give a damn.

"You haven't had much to say," Mallory commented. He noticed Cain had been withdrawn ever since he'd returned from the last mission.

"You don't seem to be much of a conversationalist yourself."

"I've got an excuse."

"Excuse?"

"I'm walking, aren't I? It takes a lot of concentration to put one foot in front of the other."

Cain smiled, but the amusement didn't reach his eyes.

The bartender set two bottles of beer on the counter. Mallory paid him, and the old guy drifted down to the other end of the long bar to talk to the cocktail waitress. Mallory glanced at the buxom blonde, and his stomach clenched. With a few minor changes—all right, major changes—in her appearance the woman could have been Francine.

Mallory didn't want to think about the therapist. Instead he turned to his friend. "Tell me about Paul Curnyn."

"There isn't much to say. My guess is that he was killed the first couple of days after he was kidnapped."

"Did they torture him?"

"It looked that way."

"The bastards."

"My sentiments exactly," Cain muttered. He raised the beer bottle to his lips and hesitated when the cocktail waitress came into view.

Mallory watched as the blonde's gaze connected with Cain's. He'd seen the look before.

"You've got an admirer," Mallory whispered. "You interested?"

"Maybe." Cain tipped the beer bottle and took a deep swallow. "If I don't want her, maybe I could talk her into trying her luck with you."

Mallory laughed. "I'll do my own talking."

"You interested?"

Mallory had to think about that. It had been a good long while since he'd had a woman. He should be frothing at the mouth, but he wasn't. It was all he could do to pretend.

"You can have her."

Cain turned and studied him. "Does this have anything to do with Francine Holden?"

"No," Mallory snapped. "It doesn't have a damn thing to do with anything."

Cain's eyebrows arched. "What happened between the two of you, anyway?"

Mallory sighed and rubbed his jaw. "If you must know, not a damn thing."

"But I thought—"

"It didn't happen."

"Why not?"

Mallory slapped his beer bottle onto the surface of the bar with enough force for it to make a loud clanking sound. Both the bartender and the cocktail waitress stared at him.

"She went off on the fact I wasn't offering her a gold ring and a house with a white picket fence." He paused and frowned. "I'm telling you right now, this is the last time I have anything to do with a virgin."

"So you won't be seeing her again?"

Mallory downed half his beer. "Hell will freeze over first."

Cain was silent for several moments. "Women are nothing but trouble."

"Ain't that the truth." Cain wasn't going to get an argument out of him.

Mallory studied his friend closely. Something was troubling McClellan, and had been ever since he'd returned from Tehuantepec. Whatever it was, Cain had kept it to himself.

"Are you sure you don't want the waitress?" Tim asked. She wasn't half bad looking, and with his eyes closed he could pretend she was Francine. One thing was certain, he had to find some way to ease the ache in his loins.

"I'm sure," Cain answered after what seemed a long time.

"Maybe we're being hasty here. We're both healthy, strong American men with time on our hands and a pocket full of coins going to waste. She looks like the type who wouldn't mind letting us both sample her wares."

Cain laughed softly. "Sorry, I'm not interested."

As a matter of fact, neither was Mallory.

12

"*I don't know what your* problem is, Mallory, but whatever it is, fix it. I'm not taking any more of your bullshit." With that Jack Keller slammed out of the office.

Cain stood up and walked over to the door. Mallory sat at a desk in the room across the hallway from Cain's. He crumpled up the sheet of paper and tossed it toward the wastepaper basket. His aim was off, and the paper fell to the floor. Apparently Mallory had lost his touch, because several bunched-up papers circled the garbage container.

For two months Cain had stood by silently and watched what was happening to his old friend. He felt useless to help. Mallory was bored and restless, cranky and uncommunicative. Each man in Deliverance Company had wrangled with him over one point or another in the last few weeks.

Cain made it a policy not to become involved in squabbles between his men, unless they interfered with their work. Thus far, all Mallory had accomplished was to make himself the least popular team member. It was almost as if he wanted to give Cain an excuse to fire him.

Until now, Cain had been patient, perhaps more than he should have been. He knew the source of the mercenary's trouble was a certain physical therapist. Cain had given his friend extra slack, but unfortunately Mallory had used it to fashion a noose around his own throat. Something had to be said, and unfortunately he was the one who'd have to say it.

He'd bide his time, Cain decided, closing his office door and returning to his desk, wait until Mallory's temper had cooled, and then they'd sit down and clear the air, man to man.

Problem was, he admitted as he took his seat, he could appreciate Mallory's problem since he suffered a similar fate himself.

It had been three months since he'd last seen Linette. He'd spent countless hours convincing himself to stay out of her life. The problem was he was a selfish bastard. He derived damn little satisfaction from being noble. Damn little consolation for stepping aside so she could date Mr. Perfect Attorney and smother a couple of motherless boys with a heart full of attention.

As it was, he wasted far too much time thinking about Linette. He wasn't a man who knew much about love. For most of his life he thought himself incapable of the emotion. Now he wasn't so sure.

Linette didn't want to see him again. She'd begged

him to leave her alone. Cain had no option but to comply. He couldn't love her and bring worry and pain into her life. She'd suffered enough.

In reviewing his time with her, however brief, he sought some way to thank her, some way of letting her know that in his own way he cared deeply for her. If the emotion had a name, it was probably love, although he found it difficult to admit that even to himself.

The answer came to him one afternoon as he looked through the papers in his safety deposit box. Soon afterward he contacted his attorney and had his will changed.

When he died, Linette Collins would become a wealthy woman. Cain had invested his money wisely. Other than the Montana cattle ranch, he owned several apartment buildings, plus a house in the Caribbean. With the aid of a financial adviser, he'd accumulated a fortune in stocks and bonds.

Money meant little or nothing to him. As a young man it had been everything. No longer. If he believed Linette would accept it, Cain would give everything to her now. He didn't need anything. Except her, and she was lost to him.

A knock sounded. Mallory opened the door and stuck in his head. "Have you got a minute?"

"Sure." Cain gestured toward a vacant chair.

Mallory came into the office, closed the door, and ambled toward him. He limped, but it was barely noticeable.

A team of surgeons had told Cain that Mallory's chances of walking again were less than fifty-fifty. If the injured man did manage to walk, he'd require the assistance of either a walker or a cane.

Mallory, with Francine Holden's help, required neither.

He sank onto the chair across from Cain. Although Mallory's health had vastly improved in the last six months, he was discontented. His color was good and he'd regained his strength, but he was as listless and unhappy as he'd been when confined to a wheelchair.

"You have something on your mind?" Cain asked.

Mallory snickered. "You might say that. It seems I've been something of a bastard lately."

"Seems that way." Cain wasn't going to lie. "Do you want to talk about it?"

Mallory leaned back on the chair and rubbed his eyes. "I'm not sure it'll do any good."

"Give it a shot," Cain advised.

Mallory straightened, leaned forward, and pressed his elbows to his knees. "I've lost it."

"Lost what?"

"Whatever it was that made me a good soldier. I thought once I returned to the compound with you and the others it would all come back. At first I assumed it was because I was gunshy, but it's more than that. A hell of a lot more.

"When it comes right down to it, I don't want to do this anymore. My heart's just not in it."

Cain's first instinct was to argue. Mallory hadn't given himself near enough time. He'd been back to the compound for less than two months, not nearly enough time to make this kind of drastic decision.

Cain would have put up a hell of a debate if Mallory hadn't used the word *heart*. *My heart's just not in it.* Mallory's heart, Cain strongly suspected, was back in San Francisco with a feisty physical therapist.

"What are you going to do with yourself?" Cain asked, and restrained himself from reminding Mallory that he had yet to participate in a mission. One good rescue could change everything. Then again, involving Mallory in a mission, with his current attitude, might jeopardize them all.

"I don't know what I'll do. At least I haven't made a firm decision."

"But you've been thinking about it."

"Some," Mallory admitted hesitantly. "Several years back I bought a ten-acre spread on Vashon Island in Washington State. It's a beautiful piece of property on a hill overlooking Puget Sound. The only way off the island is by boat or plane, so it has a rustic appeal. You might think I'm going a little crazy, but I've been toying with the idea of raising llamas."

"Llamas?" Cain swallowed his surprise. "You mean those South American creatures with long necks? Don't they look like a sheep on stilts?" Mallory playing nursemaid to a bunch of cantankerous billy goat types! The picture just didn't fit.

Mallory chuckled. "Those are the ones. I've served my time, Cain. I always said I'd soldier until I got tired of it. I never thought it'd happen, but it has. I want out."

Cain had always been uncomfortable with sentiment. He didn't want to lose Mallory. They'd been friends, damn good friends. Mallory had covered his backside on more than one occasion. But caring deeply about someone, whether it was Mallory or Linette, meant giving that person the freedom to walk away. It seemed he was going to be asked to do it a second time in as many months.

"You can't tell me the others will be sorry to see me go," Mallory said with a soft, mocking laugh.

"I'll be sorry," Cain admitted hoarsely. "When do you intend to leave?"

"If you have no objection, I'd like to go as soon as I can arrange a flight."

Reluctantly Cain nodded. He stood, walked around his desk, and offered Mallory his hand. The other man stood, gripped Cain's shoulders, and hugged him tight.

Neither spoke for several moments. Cain sat back down at his desk, unwilling to watch another person walk out of his life. Unwilling to say good-bye again.

"One thing more," Mallory said when he reached the door.

"Anything."

"I never thanked you for saving my sorry ass. I owe you, McClellan. Someday I might be able to repay the favor."

It was another one of those days when nothing seemed to go right. Francine's car had been stopped in heavy traffic because of an accident a mile away. Although she'd given herself plenty of time, there was nothing she could do but sit and wait as the frustrating minutes ticked endlessly by. Just when the road cleared and cars started to move again, she heard the distinctive thump-thump-thump of her wheel.

She had a flat tire.

By the time she'd arrived for the interview, she was thirty minutes late and so flustered she was sure the agency would never hire her. She didn't blame them.

Her mother had told her that if it was meant to be, Tim would return to her. In two months it hadn't happened. As for the decision she'd made not to sleep with him, well, she'd vacillated back and forth on that. One day she regretted having cheated herself out of the experience. The next day, like clockwork, she was convinced beyond any doubt that she'd made a prudent choice. If she'd given her body to Tim, she would have set herself up for a lose-lose situation. She'd done the smart thing.

Depending on the day, she was either a frustrated virgin or a wise and discerning woman.

Today she was a little of both. She was thirty-one years old and sick to death of waiting for her life to start. Sick to death of well-meaning friends and family smothering her with advice. So she was looking to make a change. A new job, a new city, a new circle of friends.

Her mother claimed she sought a geographical cure, and Francine suspected her parent was right. But a cure was a cure, and she was desperate.

The doorbell rang, and Francine cast an irritated glance in the direction of her living room. Word had circulated among her brothers about her imminent move. Twice now one of her younger siblings had made an effort to persuade her to stay in California.

After the rotten day she'd had, Francine didn't have the patience to sit through yet another "don't do anything rash" lecture.

She was all prepared to make some flimsy excuse—washing her hair or something equally stupid—when she opened the door.

She didn't get the chance. Her mouth froze in a half-open position. Her heart stopped cold, then jolted back, beating hard and quick.

Tim Mallory stood on the other side of the screen door, bigger than life. He was taller than she remembered and as handsome as the devil himself.

His eyes met hers, as daring and reckless as his smile.

"Tim." His name was little more than a wisp of breath. For one desperate moment she was convinced he was a figment of her imagination. Until he spoke.

"Hello, sweetheart."

"No one calls me that," she reminded him emotionally.

"I do," he told her. "I intend to for the rest of our lives." With that he opened the screen door and with a rough groan hauled her into his arms.

Francine buried her face in his neck and wrapped her arms tightly around him. His breath fell unevenly against the side of her face, as if he'd traveled a long way to reach her. As if a knot of emotion had blocked his lungs from breathing properly.

If there were words to be spoken, it wouldn't happen then. The pure, unadulterated pleasure of holding each other took precedence.

Francine didn't know how long they clung to one another. When her head cleared enough for her to think, she asked, "What are you doing here?"

"I'll explain later," he said tenderly. She felt his gaze like a warm caress and knew he intended to kiss her.

She intended to let him. Smiling up at him, she noticed how dark his eyes were and how full of promise.

"I'm serious. What are you—"

His mouth brushed hers.

It was a struggle not to surrender then and there.

Surely he wouldn't be so cruel as to walk back into her life only to leave again.

"We've already been through this once before. Don't play with me, Tim Mallory."

His mouth was poised over hers, and just before he claimed her lips, he whispered, "Ah, sweetheart, that's exactly what I intend to do, for a very long time."

Her resolve melted away.

Tim led her to the sofa and sat her down, then joined her.

"Can we talk now?" she asked.

"In a minute," he promised. He wrapped his arms around her and directed her mouth back to his. While his lips worked over hers, he pulled her blouse free and expertly unfastened the small buttons. He freed her breasts and moaned when they spilled into his waiting hands.

"Tim." Her protest was weak.

"Let me look at you," he said. "You have such beautiful breasts. I've dreamed of this, Francine, of watching your eyes when I touch them." His thumb made its way across her nipples, and he smiled as they pebbled into tight knots.

"This is all fine and dandy, but—"

"You want to know my intentions."

It was an old-fashioned way of putting it, but basically he had it right. "Yes." She swallowed tightly. "Are you here on some mission? Here today, gone tomorrow?"

"Something like that."

Her heart sank like a concrete brick. "I see. And you thought you'd drop by with your case of condoms and put them to good use while you're in town. No use letting them go to waste, is there, when you can seduce me into giving you what you want?"

His grin was as broad as the Grand Canyon. "We're going to use that case, dahlin'. Every last one of them."

This was the classic example of how dangerous love could be. He knew how empty she'd felt, how she'd suffered the last weeks without him. He was all too aware of her loneliness.

She covered her face with her hands. "Just go, Tim Mallory."

"Go?" He sounded shocked.

"Yes. Before I throw you out." She'd be roasted over a barbecue before she'd allow this man to toy with her heart one more time.

He looked confused and uncertain, then laughed and said, "You and what army?"

She didn't have an answer for him.

"It's going to take a hell of a lot more than a threat to keep me away from you. I made a mistake leaving you the first time. I'm not going to repeat it."

"A mistake?"

"I've come to finish what we started," he told her.

"So you think you can sweet-talk me into your bed."

"I'm sure as hell gonna try," he said, grinning broadly once more.

"Tell me one good reason why I should let you make love to me," she said, crossing her arms, steeling herself.

His eyes glinted as if he looked forward to the challenge. "I'm crazy about you."

Francine laughed without humor. "My current patient is crazy about me, too, but I wouldn't sleep with him."

"Him?" Tim's eyes narrowed.

"His name's Peter McWilliams, and he's eight."

Tim leaned back and braced his ankle over his knee. "You're right. Being crazy doesn't count." He inhaled a deep breath as though this would aid the thinking process. "I could tell you I loved you." He exhaled in a long-drawn-out breath. "All right, if you must know, I do love you."

"Just how much do you know about love?"

"You mean I have to bring references?"

"Don't be ridiculous."

He tipped back his head. "How do I love you?" He pointed his index finger toward the ceiling. "Let me count the ways. One. I'm here, aren't I? Two. I love you enough to resign my position from Deliverance Company. Three . . . " He paused and studied her. "I hoped one and two would convince you."

Her heart started to pound faster, but she wasn't sure yet if she should trust him. "Resign from Deliverance Company? For how long?" she asked, her voice barely above a whisper.

"Forever. But there's a condition."

"Condition?"

"Yeah. Soldiering's the only thing I know. If I'm going to give it up, then I'm going to need something to keep my hands occupied." He pointedly examined her breasts.

"Tim!"

His laugh was full and rowdy. "Look. Even your nipples are blushing."

Embarrassed, Francine quickly adjusted her clothing.

"I believe I have the answer."

Once again her heart filled with eager anticipation.

"Llamas."

Her shoulders sank, and so did her spirits.

"Believe it or not, I'm fairly good at this sort of thing. I've got a green thumb and a certain way with animals. It seems to me that if I'm going to take on this project, it wouldn't hurt to throw in a wife and a couple of babies."

Francine wondered if she dared believe what she heard. "A wife?"

"Only one."

"That's a smart idea."

"I could always move to one of the Arab countries and take on two or three. However, the wife I have in mind is sure to demand all my time and attention."

"Are you toying with me again?" she asked, not sure she could bear it if he was.

The teasing light left his eyes. "No, Francine." He reached for her hand and clasped it between his own much larger ones.

"I've never asked a woman to marry me before. I'm not entirely sure how these things are done." He scooted off the sofa and knelt down on one knee in front of her. Slowly he raised his eyes to meet hers. "I love you, Francine Holden. There's nothing I want more than you in my life. Would you do me the supreme honor of being my wife?"

She would have answered him with words if her throat hadn't been suddenly blocked shut. Instead she nodded repeatedly.

"Is that a yes?"

"Yes." The lone word squeezed through the tightness in her throat, high-pitched and discordant.

As if he were looking for something, Tim patted his

pockets. Francine was sure he was searching for a ring. "You bought me a ring?" she asked, so excited that it was difficult to think coherently.

His eyes grew big and round. "I was supposed to buy you a ring? I have the feeling a wife is going to be expensive."

"No, it doesn't matter," she was quick to assure him, sorry now that she'd said anything.

"As it happens, I do have one with me." Having said that, he withdrew from his coat pocket the most exquisite solitaire diamond she'd ever seen. "I hope it fits. I don't think Cracker Jack will size it."

Francine hugged his head. Tim buried his face between her breasts. "A man could get used to this." Unexpectedly he pushed her back against the sofa and kissed her with a desire so hot, it sizzled.

"When are you going to make love to me, Tim Mallory?" she whispered, and spread a row of nibbling kisses along the underside of his jaw. "Might I suggest right now?"

Tim tensed, inhaled sharply, and raised his head. "Don't ask me why I feel it's important, but if you don't object, I'd like to wait until after we're married."

After weeks of chasing her, teasing her, tempting her into his bed, he wanted to wait until after the wedding! "You're joking?"

He shook his head. "I want everything to be right for you, Francine."

She remembered what her mother had told her about her father, and she nodded. If she'd ever needed confirmation that he did indeed love her, this was it.

"We've waited this long. What's another few days?"

"A few days?" she cried. "Why, that's impossible—" She stopped abruptly. Only a fool would argue with a man she loved when he wanted to marry her. "Then again, I might be able to arrange it."

"Good." He wrapped his arms around her waist. "Don't take time buying a trousseau, either. You won't be needing many clothes."

Francine threw back her head and laughed. "Llamas?" she questioned.

"Llamas," he repeated, "and a couple of kids, the human variety."

Something wasn't right. Cain could feel it in his bones as clearly now as the day Mallory stepped on the land mine. The threat of danger swirled around him, clinging to his skin in the humid jungle heat. The thick foliage crawled with vermin and fear.

Word had come a week earlier that Carl Lindman, a captured CEO from a major American conglomerate, would be transported that afternoon from one location to another. The informant had been reliable before, but that didn't mean Cain trusted him. The man would sell his children for a snort of cocaine.

Cain and his men had carefully planned the ambush, and Deliverance Company were positioned in several key locations.

The waiting was always hard, especially in the jungle heat. Nervous. Ready. Uncomfortable. It was times like these, when the minutes dragged and the humidity clung to him like a second skin, that Cain fought to banish the image of a beautiful young widow from his thoughts. She was a world away from him, a world that consisted of more than just time and distance.

The distinct whopping sound of an approaching helicopter could be heard faintly in the distance. Cain and his men were camouflaged by brush and verdant growth, so there was virtually no chance the men aboard the helicopter would see them.

The sound of the chopper intensified to deafening proportions. After surveying the area, the pilot settled into the clearing as gently as if a mother were tucking her infant in a bassinet.

Two men toting Uzis leapt onto the jungle floor, their weapons poised and ready. Their gazes scanned the area, looking for anything out of the ordinary.

The two were sloppy, Cain noticed, and was grateful.

The team of men scheduled to rendezvous with the chopper wouldn't be coming. But these guys didn't know that.

Lindman was half dragged, half shoved out of the chopper. It was for this moment that Cain and his men had been waiting.

Another man climbed out of the chopper. He was clean, suave, and clearly disgruntled by the delay. Cain didn't recognize him, but that pretty face of his could have been displayed on a boy-toy calendar.

When Cain gave the signal, his men rose from their positions and attacked. Weapons were fired in rapid succession. The rat-a-tat sounds burst into the serenity of the jungle.

The CEO, not understanding what was happening, hunched his shoulders and whirled around like a top. Cain screamed for the man to hit the ground. The sound of his voice must have reached through Lindman's panic because the CEO dropped face first to the jungle floor.

However, in instructing Lindman, Cain gave away his position. The two men with the Uzis, protected now by the belly of the chopper, trained their weapons on him. The ground around Cain was sprayed with bullets.

Cain returned the fire, rolling over and over, the roar of his own weapon bursting like firecrackers in his ears. He took out the first soldier and heard Pretty Boy scream. Murphy got the second.

The blades picked up speed slowly. Pretty Boy leapt inside, firing crazily as he went. As soon as he was on board, the chopper lifted from the ground. Elevated no more than a few feet, the gunman scanned the ground with the tip of his weapon, looking for his captive. If Cain didn't act fast, Lindman would soon be dead.

Rearing back on his haunches and siting his weapon, Cain fired into the opening of the helicopter. His first shot went wild.

Distracted by the sudden burst of gunfire, Pretty Boy lifted his weapon and fired at Cain.

The bullet hit him. The force of it propelled him backward, knocking him to the ground. Blood gushed down his face and soaked through his clothes. Cain felt nothing. No pain. No stinging. No fear.

The chopper was gone, and Cain stared into the deep blue sky. He placed his hand over his head and felt the blood pump against his palm.

"McClellan." Murphy was at his side. "Take it easy, man. Take it easy. You're going to be all right."

"Holy shit." This was Jack, ever eloquent. He certainly had a way with words.

"He's going to be fine." Murphy again, with a complete lack of conviction.

Bailey was the last one to arrive with Unit One, the first-aid bag. Not that there was anything anyone would be able to do.

"You're going to make it," Murphy assured him again.

"Liar," Cain murmured, and closed his eyes. He was going to die out here in this godforsaken jungle. He didn't want the last thing he saw to be the anxious faces of his friends.

Instead he concentrated on Linette. He pictured her standing on the end of the pier at Fisherman's Wharf, the wind tousling her hair, her eyes bright as she smiled at him. He could almost hear the sound of her laughter, and he found it more lovely than a song.

He coughed, and pain seared through him like a white-hot poker. His breathing became shallow and difficult, and it seemed that his heart labored with each beat.

"Cain." The voice sounded as if it came from the inside of a tunnel.

He struggled to open his eyes but couldn't make them do anything more than flutter. "Linette," he said.

"He's asking for someone."

"Lynn Something or other? Who's that?"

"Hell if I know."

Consciousness began to fade, but Cain hadn't the strength to cling to it. He hadn't the will to fight any longer. Hadn't any reason to live.

Linette was busy baking chocolate-chip cookies for Jesse and Steve's visit when her doorbell chimed. She checked her watch, thinking it might be Charles. If so, he was several hours early.

She opened the door to one of the largest men she could ever remember seeing. He must have stood six five and had shoulders as broad as a Mack truck. Although he was large, she didn't find him intimidating. He appeared equally curious about her and seemed to be trying to place her. He didn't say anything for a couple of moments.

"Can I help you?" she asked.

"Are you Linette Collins?"

"Yes."

"You don't know me. My name's Tim Mallory, and I'm a friend of Cain McClellan."

Linette could think of only one reason one of Cain's men would come to visit her. Something had happened to Cain.

"Please come in," she said, and realized her voice trembled.

Tim stepped inside her living room, holding himself stiffly.

"Would you like to sit down?" She gestured toward the davenport.

"Thank you."

They both sat, one across from the other. Both nervous and struggling to hide it. Tim planted his hands on his knees and cleared his throat. "I hope I'm not intruding."

"No," she said nervously. "Not at all." Then, gathering her courage, she continued, speaking so fast that the words ran together. "What's happened to Cain?"

Tim lowered his head.

"Is he dead? Please, just tell me if he's dead."

"I'm sorry, ma'am. I shouldn't have come here like this without warning. It's just that Murphy and the others didn't know about you. Apparently Cain never mentioned you."

"How'd you find me?"

"Cain left instructions that if anything ever happened to him, you were to be contacted. Your name and address are listed in his will. He must have had it revised recently.

"Keller found a copy of it in the mail when he arrived back from South America."

The room swayed. "Oh, dear God."

"Ma'am? . . . Ma'am, are you all right? . . . Damn, I knew I should've brought Francine with me."

13

"*Can I get you anything?* Water?" The big man leapt to his feet and headed toward the kitchen.

A terrible tightness gripped her chest and heart. "How did it happen?" she asked, her voice a thin, emotionless thread of sound.

"During a rescue." Tim held a half-filled glass in his hand. A wide swath of water followed him out from the kitchen.

Linette closed her eyes and bit into her lower lip.

"Do you want me to get you something more? Aspirin?" Mallory suggested awkwardly. "I really should have brought my fiancée. As you can see, I'm not much good at this sort of thing."

"I'll be fine," Linette whispered in an effort to relieve his distress.

"I knew you'd be upset. I figured you'd want to know. Cain would want you to know. He listed you as his beneficiary. It's obvious he holds strong feelings for you." Cain's friend wiped his face. "Francine suggested I come and tell you personally rather than have someone phone."

"I appreciate your letting me know."

"If you want, I can make arrangements for someone to meet you in Grenada."

"Grenada?"

"That's where Cain is now. The backup medical team stabilized him in Venezuela—"

Linette's eyes flew open. "Stabilized him?"

Mallory nodded. "They were able to med-evac him to Grenada. Be assured he's getting absolutely the best medical attention available. Of course, he's listed in critical condition, and has been for several days, but—"

"He's alive?" Had her ears deceived her? Linette feared she was so desperate to believe Cain had survived that her mind was playing her for a fool.

"Yes, of course he's alive. You thought . . . you mean to say you thought he was dead? Hell, I'm sorry. I guess I was trying so hard to protect you from the bad news that I led you to think worse."

"But his will . . . "

"That's where we got your name and address. Murphy said Cain whispered your name just before he lost consciousness. When he called to tell me Cain'd been shot, he asked if I knew anything about you."

"I see."

"Believe me, I couldn't be more sorry."

She shook her head, her relief so great that it was all she could do not to hurl herself into his arms and thank him. "I assumed he was dead."

"No wonder, me talking about wills and all."

"What happened?" she asked in a rush, all at once, needing to know. She felt euphoric and struggled to hold back the sudden need to laugh. The sudden need to cry.

"Not being there myself, I can't really say. When I talked to Murphy and Jack, they only gave me sketchy details, other than . . . "

"Yes," she coaxed.

"They said Cain put himself in the line of fire in order to save someone else."

Cain close to death. Cain dying alone in a foreign hospital. All at once Linette was tired. Tired of pretending she didn't love him. Tired of fearing the worst. Tired of insulating her heart.

"You can arrange a flight for me to Grenada," she said, her voice gaining conviction. "When?"

"There's one leaving this evening."

"I'll take it."

"How'd it go?" Francine met Tim at the front door of her parents' house. He'd been nervous about meeting Linette Collins and telling her of Cain's mishap.

Tim pulled her into his arms and kissed her. "I wish you'd gone with me," he said. "I'm afraid I made everything sound much worse than it is."

"Sound worse? It doesn't get much worse than this. From what Murphy said, Cain's holding on to his life by a thread."

"He'll live," Tim said with such confidence that Francine eased her head back to meet his eyes.

"How can you be so sure?"

"He's made it this far, hasn't he?"

"Yes, but that's no guarantee." Although Tim had trouble expressing his emotions, Francine knew he was thoroughly shaken by Cain's injury. She feared he was painting a rosy picture in his mind of his friend's condition rather than dealing with harsh reality.

"Linette's flying into Grenada this evening. She'll give him the incentive he needs to stay alive," Tim said matter-of-factly.

Francine walked into the kitchen and poured herself a glass of iced tea. She noticed when she lifted the pitcher that her hand shook. She set it down with a clunk and closed her eyes before voicing the concerns that plagued her. "Are you sorry you weren't with him when it happened?" she asked, doing her best to keep her voice even and detached. "Do you think if you'd been there, things might have turned out differently?"

Tim stepped behind her and cupped her shoulders, his touch gentle and reassuring. "I don't have any regrets, if that's what you're asking me. That portion of my life is over. I'll never go back to soldiering."

Francine trembled with relief. "Don't say it if you don't mean it. That would be even more cruel than to marry me and then leave me."

Tenderly he kissed the side of her neck. "I wouldn't have asked you to be my wife if I wasn't sure about this."

The kitchen door opened and Francine's mother walked into the room, her arms full with two bags of groceries.

"Timothy Mallory, what are you doing here?" she demanded. "Tradition says you're not supposed to see the bride the day of the wedding."

"But the ceremony isn't for hours yet," he protested as if staying away from Francine were too much to ask of him. "You can't expect me to wait that long."

"Of course I do. Shoo. We've got a million things to do before this evening." Martha Holden all but booted him out of the room.

Tim cast Francine a pleading glance on his way out the door.

"Really, Mom," she protested on his behalf. "Don't you think you're going to extremes?"

"Perhaps. But that's my prerogative as his future mother-in-law. I take my duty as mother of the bride seriously." She laughed, her eyes gleaming with pride and happiness.

"You like Tim, don't you?"

"You love him. That's enough for me, but as it happens, I find him endearing. He reminds me a good deal of your father years ago. He's got that same brash nature, with an appreciation for the mischievous. You're going to be happy with this man, Francine. I couldn't have chosen a husband better suited to you had I gone out and searched myself."

Francine unloaded the first grocery sack. "I love him so much. I've been so afraid, ever since Murphy phoned with the news about Cain McClellan."

"Afraid?"

Francine nodded. "I worried that Tim would somehow feel responsible for what happened. That his being there might have changed everything."

"So that was what you were talking about when I interrupted you."

"I was afraid to bring up the subject until now, then I

decided I had to know. If Tim did feel that way, I don't know what I would have done."

"Does he?" her mother asked gently.

Francine shook her head. "He assured me that part of his life is over. He means it, Mom. He really means it. I'm not a passing fancy to him, he honestly loves me."

"He had the chance to learn that on his own," her mother said gently. "He's confident in his decision. But he might not have been that way had you pressured him into not going back to Florida. My heart ached for you when he left."

"But he came back, Mom, and this time he's going to stay."

Knowing Tim was truly hers went through her mind as Francine walked down the aisle on her father's arm later that evening.

The wedding was a simple affair, held in the church Francine had attended from the time she was a toddler. Her immediate family was there, along with several aunts, uncles, cousins, and longtime family friends. It amazed Francine that her mother had been able to arrange a wedding on such short notice.

Her wedding gown was made of antique white satin with a lace-and-pearl overlay. When she first saw Tim in his black tuxedo with tails, she didn't recognize him. But when he winked and pointed to the jacket pocket, she knew it could be no other. He'd carried a condom with him to his own wedding.

Francine was sure her face turned a bright, fire-engine red.

When they spoke their vows, Tim's voice boomed proudly as he pledged his life to hers. Apparently he felt he needed to convince her family of his sincerity by shouting out his promises. Francine's own voice trembled with emotion and love.

The reception followed in the church hall. Her sisters-in-law stood ready to serve the cake and punch. The lace-covered table was stacked with an array of beautifully wrapped gifts. Francine was touched by such an abundant display of generosity, and Tim, too, repeatedly asked if all those gifts could possibly be for them.

"How soon can we escape?" her husband asked out of the corner of his mouth.

They'd barely arrived, and the reception line was just now getting started.

"Not yet," she whispered, flustered by his question.

"This condom is burning a hole in my pocket," he said as Francine's eighty-year-old great-aunt approached. Fortunately Aunt Emma was hard of hearing.

"Tim!" Francine said.

"It's the truth," he muttered.

"I'm eager, too," she assured him, and introduced him to Aunt Emma.

It didn't take long for her family and friends to progress through the line. Afterward, Francine hurried the cake-cutting ceremony.

Before she knew where the time had gone, they'd arrived at the hotel. Tim carried her into the plush suite at the St. Francis in the heart of San Francisco. Instead of putting her down after crossing the threshold, as she expected, he went into each of the three rooms, giving her a walking tour. Only he was the one who did the walking.

He made her feel that she weighed no more than a

bird, and she fretted about his bad leg. He silenced her worries with one deep kiss.

He had a bottle of French champagne on ice, and after laying her on top of the king-size mattress, he expertly opened the bottle.

He poured them each a glass, insisted she drink from his goblet, and when some dribbled down her chin, licked it from her face. His mouth trailed the slim column of her neck, dipping at the hollow of her throat.

Francine rolled back her head and sighed. Already she felt dizzy, and it wasn't from her one sip of champagne, either.

"Tim."

"Humm?"

"Make love to me."

"I am."

"I mean really make love to me."

He paused and lifted his head to look her in the eye. "You mean you're ready now?"

She laughed softly. "In case you hadn't noticed, I've been ready for weeks."

"But what about dinner? I thought we'd order room service."

"We will," she promised, so much in love with her husband, she felt as if she were about to burst. "But later. Okay?"

He stood and shucked off his suit jacket so fast, it was still in the air by the time he'd pulled the shirt over his head. He carelessly flung the shirt aside. As if he'd been too long away from her, he knelt on the edge of the mattress and kissed her once more. If he feared she was about to change her mind, he had no reason to worry.

One kiss, and in that time she felt seduced and wooed and deeply cherished. Francine opened her mouth to him and kissed him back, using her tongue as a blatant invitation for more intimacies.

Tim's breath caught as if he'd been taken by surprise. His tongue probed deeply, swirling, mating with hers in a ritual as old as man himself. He broke off the kiss roughly and centered his attention on her neck, blazing a trail of hot kisses over her throat and back to the scented hollow.

"I intended to go much slower than this," he whispered, and Francine could hear the apprehension in his voice.

"Next time we'll go slow," she promised. She sat up and lifted her hands behind her back in an effort to unfasten the row of pearl buttons that stretched down the length of the wedding dress. Her hair, which she'd wore unplaited, continued to get in the way.

Tim walked on his knees across the mattress to assist her. Francine held her hair up and out of the way.

"I didn't know virgins were this red hot."

"Do you want me to be shy and retiring?"

"No," he muttered, cursing under his breath at the difficulty the buttons gave him. "This damned dress is worse than a chastity belt."

Francine giggled and reached for her wineglass, sipping champagne. "Want me to help you undress?" she asked.

"Not when it's going to take the two of us all night to get you out of this contraption."

Francine couldn't remember a time she'd been happier. "We can cut it off me."

He cursed again. "It might come to that."

He made progress, but it was agonizingly slow.

"I could always lift my skirts and let you have your way with me." With that she sighed dramatically.

"The hell we will. I want you naked and beneath me. I've waited too damn long to get you in that position to be outsmarted by a blasted wedding dress. Who designed this thing, anyway? The Sisters of Perpetual Frustration?"

Francine smiled, and as he freed the bodice, she worked her arms free and peeled off the upper half. When he'd progressed sufficiently, she stood and slipped the material over her hips, letting the gown pool at her feet.

When she looked up, she found Tim staring at her.

"Is something wrong?" she asked.

"I had no idea a woman wore so many underthings. Are these going to be as difficult to remove?"

"Not at all." She proved it by stripping them off one by one with what she hoped was a maddening lack of haste. It gave her a certain pleasure to watch her husband's eyes widen with admiration.

Until she'd met Tim, Francine had always been self-conscious of her body. She was tall and thick waisted and built more like a lumberjack than a beauty queen. Yet Tim made her feel delicate and beautiful.

His eyes feasted on her. When she'd finished, he reached for her and took her back to the bed. She stood before him while he sat at the edge of the mattress. A slow smile brightened his features.

"How is it a woman so beautiful would ever marry a man like me?"

"You're just lucky, I guess," she told him, and reached for this man who was her husband.

Cain felt as if he were lost in a tunnel of pain. Drugged pain. The agony was there, but not the white-hot, searing agony he'd experienced soon after being wounded. This pain was chilling. As cold as a grave.

The drugs smothered the worst of it. He didn't fight it—he hadn't the strength. Instead he waited impatiently for the angel of death to arrive. The will to resist was gone, the will to live tenuous.

"Cain?"

Linette's voice came to him on a cloud, sounding ethereal, celestial. An angel of life when he'd expected the Grim Reaper to come swooping down to claim his soul.

He struggled to open his eyes but discovered he hadn't the strength. Linette, here? It wasn't possible. Perhaps he was already dead and didn't realize it. But if that were the case, he didn't understand why he should continue to hurt this way. Was this hell, to be trapped within earshot of the woman he loved? Already he'd been cursed never to hold her or love her again. He was sentenced to hear her call to him from another world and helpless to respond. Cursed to love her until his heart felt as if it would burst wide open and be unable to give her the assurance of his caring.

Perhaps this was all some part of a drug-induced dream. He must be dreaming, and yet . . . and yet, he felt her hand pressed over his, heard her soft voice, trembling with anxiety.

He'd never mentioned Linette to any of the men of Deliverance Company. Not even Mallory. He'd wanted to protect her from who he was and what he did. She was honest and pure, and he didn't want to taint her goodness.

"Oh, Cain," Linette said breathily. She must be close, because he could feel her soft breath fan his face. "Listen carefully, my darling. I love you. I'm here."

With every ounce of strength he possessed, Cain tried to respond, but the effort quickly drained what reservoir of energy he possessed.

"I'm praying," Linette continued, her voice trembling with emotion, "that you'll feel my love for you. Feel it, Cain. Let it be your shelter."

His shelter.

It was as if he'd walked out of the freezing cold into a room with a fire burning in the fireplace.

"I'm sorry, miss, you'll have to leave now."

The authoritative female voice sounded from behind Linette. Cain tried to protest but once more found it impossible to so much as flutter his eyelids.

"So soon?" Linette protested.

"I'm sorry," the other woman said, sounding sympathetic. "But you can only spend five minutes every hour with your friend. Those are the rules."

To hell with the rules! Cain screamed in his mind. He needed Linette.

"I'll be back," Linette promised. Her lips brushed his brow, and her fingers squeezed his. "Just remember what I said," she whispered in parting. "Let my love be your shelter."

A crushing pain filled his chest when she walked away.

The agony was familiar. This was what it had felt without love in his life. This emptiness. This loneliness.

Before he was aware of time passing, Linette was back.

"Hello, my darling," she whispered. She spoke to him in soothing tones, and he felt it again—the warmth he'd experienced when she'd first arrived. It was as though a heated blanket had been wrapped about his shoulders. Around his heart.

"I met your friends," she whispered. "They love you, too."

If he'd had the strength, Cain would have laughed out loud. He'd never thought of Murphy as the loving type. He was well aware his men respected him. Leave it to a woman to confuse regard with love.

"I'll be back soon," Linette promised.

He heard her footsteps against the floor as she walked out of the room. This time the warmth didn't go with her. It stayed, and for the first time since he'd been shot Cain realized he was going to live.

He knew this with a certainty he didn't question.

Linette was with him.

Linette loved him. He had a reason to fight.

14

Cain's men didn't like her. In the beginning, Linette thought it might have been her imagination, but the resentment was far too real to ignore. At times it seemed to come at her in waves, as though she were responsible for what had happened to their leader, their friend.

The man called Murphy was the worst. He acted as if she were an intruder. He made it plain that he didn't want her at the hospital. She could feel his indignation every time she returned from her hourly five minutes with Cain. Murphy seemed to believe he should be the one to linger at Cain's bedside. Yet when Linette had offered to let him visit Cain instead of her, he'd gruffly insisted she be the one.

"How's Cain doing?" Jack Keller asked when she stepped back into the waiting area. She'd been in Grenada a week now. In that time Cain had revealed only a few visible signs of improvement. Linette cele-brated each one. The doctors weren't making predic-tions on his chances of survival. They claimed Cain had hung on far longer than the experts had anticipated. If anyone would break the record, it would be he.

Those brief five-minute sessions with Cain drained Linette's energy. It was as if he demanded every ounce of strength she possessed, as though her being with him were what gave him the energy to live.

She frequently returned to the waiting area exhausted and literally collapsed onto the chair. More often than not, Murphy, Keller, or one of the other men would be waiting for her, eager for word of Cain's condition.

Although he hadn't spoken, Cain knew she was there. He'd squeezed her hand the day before, the action so weak that Linette had nearly wept. First with joy and relief and then with despair that he'd stepped so close to death's door—that she'd come so close to losing him.

"Cain's better, I think," she answered Keller's ques-tion. Of the men of Deliverance Company whom she'd met, Linette liked Keller the best. He was a no-nonsense sort of person, a little rough around the edges, with a hard-as-tacks exterior, but he cared deeply about Cain.

Keller—she never had learned any of the men's first names—was a pacer. In the week she'd been in Grenada, Linette had watched the gruff-looking man make deep grooves in the carpet with his constant pacing.

Murphy was the dark, silent type. Exactly why he didn't want her in Grenada Linette couldn't fathom. It was as if she were trespassing over territory he consid-ered sacred.

"You think Cain's better?" Murphy's low voice mocked her. He looked her way, and his gaze narrowed with dislike he didn't bother to disguise.

"Have I done something to offend you?" Linette asked. She hated confrontation, avoided it whenever possible, but she'd had about all she could take of this man's attitude.

"Not me, you haven't," Murphy returned.

"Who, then?"

"Cain."

"Cain?" Linette felt at a loss to understand this sullen man. "How have I hurt Cain?" If they were going to keep tabs, she could name a few infractions he'd committed against her, beginning with concealing the truth about himself.

"You messed up his head," Murphy said, glaring at her. "We all knew something wasn't right with Cain, and hasn't been for months. What we should have guessed was that it involved a woman."

"You can't blame me for what happened to Cain."

"You messed up his thinking," Murphy shot back. "Cain was willing to sacrifice his life, and now I know why. He couldn't think straight anymore."

Linette found she was shaking—not because of what Murphy told her; she'd guessed as much herself—but because she was tired and worried and afraid. Afraid what he said was true, that Cain had taken unnecessary chances because his mind had been on her instead of the mission.

"Lay off her," Keller snarled at Murphy. "Can't you see she's had about all she can take already?"

"See what I mean?" Murphy flared. "We barely know

her, and already she's causing dissension between us. Women are nothing but trouble."

"You didn't have to tell me about Cain," Linette said, fast losing her patience. "I'd never have known if Tim Mallory hadn't contacted me."

"Mallory's a prime example of what a woman can do to ruin a decent fighting man."

"I beg your pardon?"

"It's true," Murphy insisted. "Mallory used to be one of us. He was as good a man as any I've known, then he had to go and fall in love. Look what's happened to him since." He rammed his fingers through his short hair and pinched his lips as if to bite back a curse.

"Within a week of his return to Deliverance Company, there wasn't a one of us could bear the sight of him. He was rude, cantankerous, and miserable, and all because of a woman."

Linette briefly remembered Tim Mallory mentioning his fiancée.

"From what I understand, Mallory's got a ring looped through his nose and is being led around some pasture in Washington State. Mallory married. I never thought I'd see the day."

"I heard he was raising llamas," Keller inserted, shaking his head in wonder.

"Llamas?" Murphy cried. From the way he said it, one would have thought his cohort had desecrated a national monument. The mercenary slapped his hands against his thighs. "I rest my case."

"It's not fair to blame Linette for what happened to Cain," Keller mumbled, not sounding any too sure.

"You're damn right I blame her." Murphy tossed

Linette another of his menacing looks. "Now that I think about it, Cain hasn't been himself for a good long time. Next thing we know, he'll be applying for a regular job just so he can keep his sweetie-pie happy.' Women and mercenaries simply don't mix."

"The nurse told me she thinks Cain's made a turn for the better since Linette's arrival." It was Keller again, looking slightly embarrassed at Murphy's accusations.

"Who's to say that Linette had anything to do with it?" Murphy argued. "Cain's got the best medical team in the world working on him. You might credit the doctors."

"He was as good as dead, and we both know it."

The two men faced off, glaring at each other. "I say it was Linette," Keller returned heatedly.

"Please, don't," Linette pleaded. She placed herself between the two of them. Each man was several inches taller than she. Linette braced her hands against their chests, feeling a little like Samson between two giant pillars. Samson without hair, weakened and blind.

"The last thing you should be doing is fighting," she told them, struggling to remain calm herself.

"Then leave," Murphy told her.

"No," she returned evenly, although her heart was in turmoil.

"She has every right to stay if she wants," Keller insisted. "Cain needs her."

"The hell he does. Deliverance Company is Cain's life. He doesn't need anything more than that."

What Murphy said was true. The message had been delivered by Cain personally months earlier. "All right. All right, I'll leave," she said, shocking both men.

They diverted their attention to her. Keller's eyes

were filled with what looked like disappointment, and Murphy's shone with intense satisfaction. He'd gotten what he wanted.

"But in my own time," she amended. "When I'm sure Cain will recover."

She'd leave, she decided, when her heart had the strength to walk away from him. Again. But this would be the last time.

"When?" The question came from Murphy and was no surprise.

"Soon," she promised.

"Not soon enough," Murphy muttered, then turned and walked away.

Cain sensed a difference in Linette. She was gentle and encouraging as always, yet it felt as if she were miles away emotionally. She'd erected a roadblock between the two of them. It wasn't what she said or how she behaved; it was mental, and it confused the hell out of him.

The effort demanded to open his mouth was beyond comprehension. Saying her name proved to be a test of sheer physical endurance. The lone word worked its way up his throat, catching on emotion and gratitude.

"L-in—ette."

"Cain?" Her voice elevated with joy. "I'm here." She lifted his hand to her lips and kissed his knuckles repeatedly. He felt moisture against the back of his hand and knew she wept silently.

He wanted to tell her so many things and struggled valiantly to remain conscious. No longer did the cold plague him. He was warm and comfortable and within minutes fighting the lull of sleep.

Days blended one into the other with barely a notice. Cain was able to calculate the time by which nurse was on duty. The older nurse with white hair and angel eyes worked the graveyard shift. The pert brunette was with him from three to eleven. One named Hazel who arrived early in his day. Days of the week were more difficult to figure.

None of it mattered as long as Linette was with him. Each day was a gift to be cherished.

Then, when he'd mastered the ability to remain conscious for more than three or four minutes at a time, Linette left him. It might have taken him some time to realize she was gone if it hadn't been for Murphy.

"Where's Linette?" he asked his friend.

"Gone."

Cain felt as though someone had knifed him. "Gone?"

"You don't need her."

"What made her go?" Cain demanded, his voice shockingly weak.

"She has responsibilities. It's better this way, don't you think?"

Cain rolled his head to one side, unwilling to answer. Better for whom? Him? Not likely. It would have been a kindness to let him die rather than nurse him back from the brink of death and then doom him to a fate of loneliness.

He hadn't asked her to come, Cain reminded himself. He wasn't entirely sure who had told her he'd been injured. Mallory, most likely, but how he ever found out about her, Cain couldn't guess.

"You don't need her," Murphy went on to say.

Once more Cain didn't respond.

"There's nothing like a woman to screw up a man's thinking. I'm right, aren't I?"

Cain forced a nod. He might was well admit the truth. Murphy was right. He'd proved he could make it without Linette, and she sure as hell didn't need the likes of him.

"She's beautiful." Linette sat in Nancy's living room and gently cradled her sister-in-law's newborn baby daughter in her arms. A wealth of emotion filled her as she studied this perfect child. "Welcome, little Michelle," she whispered, her voice soft and low.

"We named her after Michael," Nancy said, studying Linette. Home from the hospital for only two days, the other woman looked fabulous. "You don't mind, do you?"

"Michael would be so pleased and proud," Linette whispered. "He'd consider it a great honor. I do, too." It came to Linette then how freely she could speak of her dead husband these days. Generally when his name cropped up, she experienced a sudden, crushing sense of loss. She wasn't sure when this had changed, but she was grateful.

With her index finger, Linette outlined Michelle's plump, pink face. The infant smelled of baby powder and summer and was precious beyond words. The love Linette experienced for this new life flooded her heart.

"Mom and Dad came to visit me while I was in the hospital," Nancy said casually, but it seemed to Linette that her sister-in-law was studying her, waiting for some response.

"I imagine they were thrilled to death with Michelle." Linette knew Nancy's relationship with her parents had been strained since the Christmas holidays. She hoped that this birth in their family would bridge their differences.

"They were very pleased we named her after Michael." Linette nodded. That much was understood.

"They asked about you," Nancy said. "They wanted to know if you were still involved with Cain."

"What did you tell them?" It grieved Linette that her last meeting with Michael's parents had ended so badly.

"I thought you were dating Charles Garner, but when I called to tell you about the baby, Bonnie told me you were on some Caribbean island, and that Cain McClellan had been badly injured."

"I was with Cain," she admitted reluctantly. "It didn't look like he was going to live."

"I see."

Perhaps Nancy did. At their last conversation, Linette had claimed it was over between her and Cain and that she was dating someone else.

Charles. If she were suffering regrets, it was over her brief relationship with the attorney. She hadn't phoned him since her return, and she wouldn't now. Their last conversation had gone poorly. She'd tried to explain why she was leaving for Grenada so abruptly. She'd told him about Cain's injuries and that it was a matter of life and death.

Charles had grown cold and angry and insisted she stay in San Francisco. Linette had never seen this side of him and pointed out that he had no right to demand anything of her. He'd called her a fool, and perhaps she was, but then so be it. She refused to allow him to make decisions for her.

Later, when she'd had time to think over their heated conversation, Linette decided it was best not to see Charles again. Clearly he expected more from her than she was willing to give.

"What about Charles?" Nancy asked, disrupting Linette's thoughts.

Linette answered with a short shake of her head.

"But I thought you liked him?"

"I was crazy about his boys," Linette admitted, and experienced a deep twinge of regret. "Unfortunately their father isn't nearly as appealing."

"What about Cain?" The question was low, as if Nancy were afraid of asking. "Oh, Linette, I've been so worried about you."

"There's no need. I sincerely doubt that I'll be seeing Cain again, either."

"But you'd like to?"

Linette didn't need long to think over her reply. "Yes."

"How can you say that, knowing what he does?"

Linette laughed softly and pressed her lips against the sleeping infant's brow. "I suppose I should have learned my lesson a long time ago," she admitted, but it was all wishful thinking, and she knew it. She expected never to see Cain again, but that didn't mean she would stop loving him.

The doorbell chimed. Eight-year-old Christopher darted across the living room carpet as if he expected to find Santa Claus on the other side. Before Nancy could stand or Linette could place Michelle inside the ruffle-laden bassinet, Christopher had thrown open the door.

"Grandma," the boy cried with delight.

"How's the big brother doing?" Jake Collins asked, ruffling Christopher's hair.

"I hope you don't mind us dropping by unexpectedly like this," Janet said, walking into the room. She hesitated, looking uncertain when she saw Linette.

"Hello, Janet," Linette greeted them, wanting to put her mother-in-law at ease.

"Hello, Linette." Michael's mother's voice stiffened, and she glanced toward her husband as if she weren't sure what she should do next.

"It's good to see you again," Jake said, and walked over to study his newest grandchild. "Isn't she the most beautiful baby you've ever seen?"

"Daddy, I think you might be considered prejudiced!" Nancy chided him.

"She's the most beautiful little girl in the world to me," her father protested. "The spitting image of you at that age."

Janet sat down across the room from Linette. "How are you feeling, Nancy?"

"Absolutely wonderful."

"She had the baby naturally, you know." This comment was directed with pride at Linette.

"No, I didn't. Congratulations, Nancy."

"I couldn't have done it without Rob. He was a great coach, and the difference between Christopher's birth and Michelle's is like night and day. I feel great."

"Would you like to hold Michelle?" Linette asked Janet.

Janet smiled and nodded.

Careful, so as not to disturb the baby, Linette stood and gently placed the tiny bundle in Michael's mother's arms. It seemed the austere features softened when she received her granddaughter.

"If this keeps up much longer, Michelle will expect to be held all the time," Nancy protested, but without conviction.

"I'll hold her whenever you need," Janet volunteered, and cooed at the infant. "That's my job. What good is it to be a grandmother if I can't spoil my grandchildren?"

Christopher found it imperative to show his grandfather something in his room, and soon afterward Nancy went to place the freshly washed diapers in the dryer. Unexpectedly, Linette was left alone with Janet.

The silence was heavy between them. Linette worked to formulate the words to show her regret over their last meeting, but before she could begin, Janet spoke.

"I'm pleased we have this opportunity alone," she said, her voice barely above a whisper. "I've done a good deal of thinking in the months since January. I don't agree with everything you said, but I concede that you might have a point." She lowered her head slightly. "Losing Michael, well . . . you of all people can appreciate how difficult it was. Although it's been nearly three years now . . . " She hesitated and bit into her lower lip. "I loved my son. . . . "

"I loved him, too," Linette said gently. She walked across the room and sat on the sofa next to Janet. She'd forgotten how small her mother-in-law was and looped her arm around her fragile shoulders.

"You don't know how many times I've thought about

you in the past several months," Janet said. "Jake and I've missed you terribly. When Michael died we felt we still had you, and then . . . There's no need to rehash our disagreement, but since New Year's Day, Jake and I've had a number of talks, and he's helped me realize how wrong I've been. I had no right to expect you to dedicate your life to Michael's memory."

"I regret our disagreement, too," Linette said, and gently squeezed her mother-in-law's shoulders.

"I didn't mean what I said about doubting your love for Michael. You were the best thing that ever happened to my son. He told me that himself just before he died. You seemed so strong, and it was far easier to lean on your strength, yours and Jake's, than accept the fact my son was forever gone from me."

Linette hadn't felt strong, especially in the first few weeks and months following Michael's passing. She didn't now.

"I know that you're dating other men these days, and I've accepted that you'll probably remarry. Both Jake and I want you to be happy, Linette. You deserve that much."

"Thank you." Her words teetered with emotion.

"I know I don't have any right to ask this of you, but when you do remarry, would you allow Jake and me to be grandparents to your children?"

"Oh, Janet." Tears filled Linette's eyes, and she found it impossible to speak for the lump in her throat.

"I promise you that I won't pretend the children are yours and Michael's family. It's just that Jake and I have come to think of you as our daughter. We love you, Linette, and are truly sorry for the way we behaved."

"I think my children would be fortunate to have you and Jake as their grandparents." A husband and family seemed impossible just then, and Janet's words produced a soft ache. She longed for a child. Holding Michelle was both a joy and a trial.

"For weeks I've been promising Jake I'd phone you. My heart nearly stopped when I saw you with Nancy, but I knew it was time to make amends. Long past time."

"I'm pleased we talked." She drew in a deep breath at the emotion that hovered so close to the surface. "Michael was blessed to have you and Jake for parents, and I feel the same way to have you as my in-laws."

"I still miss him."

"I know," Linette whispered. "I do, too, but it won't hurt as much with time. I'll never stop loving Michael, but I don't desperately cling to my memories of him. They're a part of me now. Some of the happiest days of my life were spent with him. I'm content now. My frustration and anger are gone, and the pain isn't as sharp. For the first time in more years than I can remember, I'm looking forward to the future."

A tear ran down the side of Janet's face. "I am, too."

As best they could, with Nancy's infant daughter between them, the two women hugged. That was how Nancy found them—hugging, laughing, and weeping.

"Hey, you two. If you're going to have a party, the least you could do is invite me."

15

Francine saw the dust rising from the driveway long before the car came into view. Standing on the
back porch, she wrapped her coat about her and pressed
her hand against the small of her back. The other hand
rested on her stomach, which protruded between the
coat's opening. With three months left before her baby
was due, she couldn't imagine getting any bigger.
Already it was difficult to climb in and out of a chair and
do the things she was accustomed to.

"We've got company," she called out to Tim, who was
working with Bubba, the most cantankerous of the llamas they owned.

"I'm not expecting anyone," Tim answered. She noted
that he didn't take his eyes off Bubba, and with good reason. He'd learned his lesson the first time.

"I'm not expecting anyone, either."

"Do you recognize the car?"

"No," she called back. The vehicle slowed as it rounded the last curve and pulled into the yard.

Tim stepped out of the corral, removed his hat, and wiped his brow with the back of his forearm.

"It's Cain McClellan," Francine announced excitedly, and hurried down the steps—"hurried" being the operative word. Francine didn't move all that speedily these days.

Tim moved to the car, and after Cain climbed out, the two men shook hands, then hugged briefly, slapping each other several times across the back.

"This is a pleasant surprise," Tim said.

"I just happened to be in the neighborhood," Cain said.

Francine watched, smiling, as the two men laughed at the blatant lie. Vashon Island was its own neighborhood. It had taken some getting used to, living her life according to a ferry schedule. Tim worried about her delivering the baby, but she was confident they'd have plenty of time to get to a hospital.

Cain's gaze scanned Francine and lingered at her abdomen. "I see you two have been busy."

Tim chuckled. "As best we can figure, I got her pregnant on our wedding night." His eyes connected with Francine's. "It's something of a family tradition."

"How are you, Cain?" Francine asked. She knew Tim and his friend frequently exchanged letters and talked occasionally on the phone, but this was the first she'd heard of Cain traveling.

"Much better, thanks."

"Come inside. There's no need to talk out here in the cold." Francine led the way into the family-size kitchen.

She assembled a pot of coffee while the two men pulled out chairs and sat themselves down at the round oak table.

"You're a sight for sore eyes," Tim said, studying his friend. "Damn, but it's good to see you."

"It's good to be here," Cain returned.

"How's everyone?"

Francine watched her husband, looking for any tell-tale signs that he missed his former life. They rarely discussed Deliverance Company. When she questioned him about the missions, he was tight-lipped. It was as if that part of his life were over and he had to struggle to remember what it was he'd done before they'd been married.

Although she was crazy in love with Tim, Francine couldn't help wondering about the adjustment in both their lives. It hadn't been easy for either one of them. They were both independent people with strong personalities. In addition, Francine missed her family dreadfully. The little things about island living continued to irritate her, but she was learning.

Tim seemed to have made the transition effortlessly, but there were times when she wondered. As she did now. Her fear was that Cain had returned to talk Tim into going back for one last mission. The very thought caused her blood to run cold.

"Murphy, Keller, and Jack all send their best. They're doing great."

"And you?" Tim asked.

"I'm getting stronger every day."

"I'm glad to hear it."

Francine poured coffee into three mugs and carried

two over to the table. Tim snaked his arm around her waist and held her against his side. "We've been married six months now, and I swear I still get horny every time I look at her."

"Tim!" Francine dared not look at Cain. Her cheeks burned with embarrassment.

Tim laughed and, after bouncing a kiss off her tummy, released her. Francine brought her coffee to the table and joined the two men. She studied Cain and realized how thin and pale he was. From what she understood, he was lucky to be alive.

"I'm thinking of selling Deliverance Company," Cain announced out of the blue.

Francine tensed, thinking Cain was giving Tim first crack at buying the business. Tim must have assumed the same thing, because his eyes found hers. It wasn't necessary to voice her objection. One look assured her that her fears were unsubstantiated.

Tim reached for her hand and laced his fingers through hers. "If you're offering it to me—"

"I'm not." Cain cut in. "At this point, Murphy's the one most interested, but I haven't completely made up my mind. I wanted to talk to the two of you first."

Tim and Francine looked at each other. "Us?" Tim asked, clearly puzzled.

"I wanted to see for myself if you were as happy as Mallory implies in his letters. I'll admit that when I learned you two were marrying, I didn't give the union much of a chance. I know Mallory too well. I wasn't sure he was the type to settle down and raise llamas."

"The hell I'm not," Tim protested.

"You've proved me wrong," Cain said, and he looked

pleased to admit the fault. "You've beaten the odds all to hell. It gives me hope."

"What would you do without Deliverance Company?" Tim asked.

"I'm not sure yet," Cain said after a short hesitation. "I'd probably move to Montana. I've got a spread there, but what I know about cattle ranching would fit inside the eye of a needle."

"You learn fast," Tim said, "trust me. Cattle can't be all that different from llamas. Besides, don't you have the world's best foreman? I remember you bragging about him a couple of years back."

"John Stamp and his family are the salt of the earth."

"Are you going to wait to see if you get some nibbles on Deliverance Company before you make up your mind?" Francine asked.

"No," Cain said, surprising them both. "Everything depends on a certain woman who owns a yarn shop. If she hasn't already decided she never wants to see me again."

"Linette?" Francine guessed.

Cain nodded. "I can't give her one good reason to marry me."

"She won't need any reasons," Francine said with unshakable confidence. "I didn't when I married Tim. Loving him was enough, and Linette loves you."

Cain certainly hoped what Francine said was true, and that Linette still loved him. It had been over six months since he'd last seen her. A whole lot could have changed in that time.

Cain arrived in San Francisco and checked into a hotel room. Slipping the room key into his pocket, he sat on the side of the mattress and closed his eyes. He'd thought about this day, lived for this day, for months.

He checked his watch, debating if he should phone her first. After a moment he decided it would be harder for her to close the door in his face than to hang up on him.

He caught a cab to her apartment building and took the stairs. A year earlier he'd raced up the three flights, taking two and three steps at a time. This year he walked up one step at a time and was shaky and weak before he reached the third floor. If Linette did agree to marry him, she should know she wasn't getting any bargain.

Straightening his shoulders, he pushed the doorbell and waited. An eternity passed before he heard the lock turn. The door opened, and all at once she was there. They stared at each other, breathless and stunned.

Cain didn't think she could be any more beautiful than the way he remembered her. But she was. She wore a winter rose silk dress, and her hair was pulled back from her face and held in place with pearl-edged combs.

She whispered, "Cain."

"Hello, Linette."

As if unaware of what she was doing, she raised her hands to his face and gently flattened them against his cheeks. Her touch was light and uncertain.

He briefly closed his eyes and smiled. "I'm real," he assured her.

All at once she was crying. Of all the responses Cain had anticipated, he hadn't thought she'd break down and weep. He held her against him. Once they were inside her apartment, he closed the door with his foot.

Cain felt as if he'd die if he didn't kiss her soon. He brought her close to him, and it was like stumbling through the gate of paradise. His heart swelled with a love so strong, so potent, he feared it couldn't withstand the pressure.

Sobbing, her tears moistening his face, Linette kissed him again and again and again as if she couldn't get enough of him.

It was that which broke him. Cain's arms tightened around her waist, and he lifted her from the floor. All the weeks of lying in the hospital, of dreaming of this moment, praying she still loved him, that he still had a chance with her. He'd been to hell and back, and he'd gladly retrace his steps if it meant he hadn't lost her.

"I love you," he chanted between long, deep, desperate kisses. "Marry me, Linette." He hadn't meant to propose like this, first thing. He'd thought long and hard about how he planned to ask her.

She lifted her face from his and stared down on him as if afraid she hadn't heard him correctly.

"You heard me right," he said. "I'm asking you to be my wife."

"What about—"

"I'm selling it to Murphy."

"You're sure?"

He smiled and nodded. "Positive."

The doorbell chimed, and Linette sighed and braced her forehead against his shoulder.

"Who's that?" Cain asked.

It took her a long moment to answer. "A . . . friend."

"Male or female?"

Again Linette hesitated. "Male."

Cain didn't have a single reason to be jealous. Linette's eager kisses convinced him she loved him. Nevertheless the green monster ate at Cain's confidence like a hungry rabbit devouring fresh garden lettuce.

The doorbell chimed again, and Cain stopped her from answering. "Is it that attorney you were seeing earlier in the year?"

"No. His name's Phil." She bit into her lower lip and moved toward the door. As if reading his thoughts, she offered Cain a weak smile. "He's just a friend."

A tall, attractive man stepped into the apartment, looking bright and cheerful. His gaze immediately connected with Cain's and narrowed. The laughter drained from his eyes.

"Hello," Cain said, and held out his hand. "It seems we have a bit of a problem."

"Phil Duncan, meet Cain McClellan," Linette murmured.

As Cain moved forward to exchange handshakes with Linette's date, he noticed how flustered she looked. It would have been better if he'd phoned first, he realized now, instead of placing her in this awkward position.

"Linette's mentioned you before," Phil said thoughtfully, and following the brief introduction, he sat on the sofa. It seemed to Cain that the other man went to lengths to make himself comfortable, or at least give the appearance of being so. "How long are you in town for this time?"

The censure was too thick to ignore. "As long as Linette will have me. I've asked her to be my wife."

His words were met with a strained silence. Then, "She'd be crazy to accept." Phil looked to Linette for a response. "You haven't, have you?"

"Not yet," Cain answered on her behalf, and sat across from the other man. He was on the edge of the cushion, and their eyes were level. It was a matter of male pride, but Cain didn't want her answering to anyone but him.

"Linette?" Phil looked directly at her, waiting. She was the only one left standing, and frankly Cain wished she'd sit down.

"I . . . I . . . " She hesitated. "I have a few questions I need Cain to answer first."

"Great, ask away," Phil instructed, showing enthusiasm. He leaned forward and pressed his elbows to his knees. "While we're at it, let me throw my hat in the ring."

"Throw your hat in the ring?" Linette echoed, frowning.

"Right. We've been dating how long now? Three, four months?"

Linette opened and closed her mouth before casting Cain an apologetic look.

"Four. Actually, now that I think about it, it's closer to five," Phil answered for her.

Cain hadn't expected her to keep a silent vigil awaiting his return, but it pricked at his pride that she had gotten involved with another man so soon after her return from Grenada.

"We were friends a long time before we ever started dating, isn't that right?"

"Yes," Linette admitted reluctantly.

"I'm not willing to do the gentlemanly thing and step

aside because you're infatuated with your soldier friend here. He's moved in and out of your life like a bad storm for the last year."

"I'm here to stay," Cain said forcefully. It was apparent that buddy boy wasn't going to surrender without a fight. What the man apparently didn't realize was that when it came to war, Cain was the expert. He'd make mincemeat of Phil Duncan in seconds.

But at what price? Cain asked himself. He studied the other man and found him to be clean-cut, successful from the looks of him, a decent sort. As much as it irked him, Cain experienced a grudging respect for Linette's *friend*.

"I'd like to marry Linette as well," Phil announced. Silence fell like a butcher's cleaver into the middle of the room.

"Phil." Looking shocked, Linette pressed the tips of her fingers to her lips.

"Exactly how long have you two known each other?"

Cain directed the question to Linette, but it was Phil who answered. "Long enough. I was a friend of Michael's."

"I see," Cain murmured.

"Phil and Laura are . . . were good friends of ours," Linette explained.

"Our divorce was final this summer," Phil went on to explain in that nonchalant way of his. He spoke of the end of his marriage as he would report the stock market averages, revealing little emotion.

It certainly hadn't taken good ol' Phil long to seek out greener pastures, Cain noted.

"It's apparent I can give Linette what's important in

life," the other man went on to say. "Love, security, and a solid future." Leaning back, balancing his ankle on his knee, Duncan appeared cocky and sure of himself. "What is it you intend to offer her?"

Cain weighed his response carefully, knowing it could well sway her decision. "My heart. Children. As for the future, it doesn't come with any guarantees. Linette's probably more aware of that than either of us. So I can't and won't predict what could happen there."

Buddy boy frowned. "Frankly, that doesn't sound like much."

"It isn't," Cain agreed readily enough. "All I can offer her is my love. It's taken me nearly twelve months to figure out what I should have recognized from the first. I need her. You're right, I'm no prize. Linette would be a fool to marry me and move to some cattle ranch with a man who doesn't know a bloody thing about being a rancher."

"We'd live in Montana?" she asked.

He nodded.

"Children?" This word quivered as it left her lips.

"As many as you want, but you should realize I don't know any more about being a husband and a father than I do about ranching."

"You'll learn," she said confidently, and then frowned. "What about Deliverance Company? You're through with fighting?"

"Never again."

Linette laughed softly and kissed Phil Duncan on the cheek. "You really ought to take up acting, Phil. You gave an Academy Award performance. Thank you."

"Who said I was acting?"

"Laura might take exception to your becoming a bigamist."

Cain frowned and looked from one to the other. "What's going on here? I thought you said you were divorced."

The other man grinned broadly. "I lied, but you know what they say about love and war. I figured this was as good a way as any to have you spell out your intentions."

Frankly Cain didn't appreciate Phil's efforts and told him so with a menacing look.

"Be good to her, McClellan, she deserves a man who appreciates her."

This was exactly what Cain intended to do. "I will," he promised.

Phil stood and addressed Linette. "I suppose this means you won't be joining Laura and me for dinner?"

Linette laughed and nodded. "You'll forgive me?"

Phil answered her with a dramatic sigh. "I suppose. Just make sure we get an invitation to the wedding, understand?"

"You've got it," Cain promised. The men shook hands a second time, and Phil left shortly afterward.

No sooner had the door closed than Linette was back in Cain's embrace. "Did you mean what you said about children?"

"Every word."

"How soon can we be married?" Linette wanted to know. She asked this as if she were afraid he would change his mind. Quickly she added, "Soon, I hope. I've waited a long time for this moment."

"I'm not going to change my mind." He felt as though her love would heal him faster than any doctor. The emotional wounds had marked him far more intensely than the physical ones.

His arms linked around her waist, Cain pulled her close. "We can apply for the license first thing in the morning. Where would you like to spend our honeymoon?"

A twinkle came into her eyes as she lifted her mouth to his. "Bed."

Nancy and Rob agreed to stand up for them, and Linette was grateful for their love and friendship. If it hadn't been for her brother- and sister-in-law, Linette would never have met Cain McClellan.

Linette knew Nancy had her doubts. Perhaps Rob did, too, but neither voiced them. It was hard for Nancy to hold her tongue. All Linette wanted was for her former sister-in-law to be happy for her. Marrying Cain was what she wanted, what she'd dreamed would happen. She might be a fool, but she was grabbing this opportunity for happiness with both hands and holding on as though her life depended on it.

Bonnie was a godsend in the days before the wedding. Linette swore she was more nervous as a bride the second time than she had been with Michael.

When the time arrived, the church was filled with a party of nearly fifty people. Her own family and Michael's parents were there. Linette was touched to find that Cain's foreman and wife, John and Patty Stamp, had flown in for the ceremony from Cain's cattle ranch in Montana.

Linette held a bouquet of pink rosebuds and proudly took her place next to Cain at the altar. In her heart she recognized that she would be content to spend the next fifty years beside this man. Love was like that.

Following the short reception, they left in Cain's vehicle, heading north.

"Where are we going?" she asked, her head resting against his shoulder.

"To bed," Cain teased, and kissed the crown of her head. "That was where you said you wanted to spend our honeymoon, but you omitted saying exactly where that would be, so I took matters into my own hands."

"Frankly, I wouldn't care if it was on the moon as long as I could be with you."

"Wife," Cain said, as if testing the word on his tongue. "It has a nice sound to it."

"Trust me, so does husband."

For a long time they rode in silence, content to be close to each other, eager to be closer and more intimate. After a while Linette traced her fingertips down the side of his face and over the rigid line of his jaw. She swore Cain stopped breathing.

Linette experienced a rush of love at the sensual power she had over him. No more than a moment passed before he captured her hand and entwined his fingers with hers.

"You're making it difficult to concentrate on driving."

"How far do we have to go yet?"

"Too damn far if you continue touching me."

"I was hoping on doing more than that."

"So was I." He mumbled something more under his breath that she didn't understand. "Fifty miles," he said. "I promise to make it worth the wait."

"I should hope so," she said, loving the freedom to

be close to him. She placed her hand on his thigh and gently dug her nails into the hard muscle of his leg.

"Linette," he said between his teeth. "You're playing with fire."

She laughed softly. "Fire always did intrigue me."

Cain pulled off to the side of the road, and the tires spat up dirt and gravel. He set the car into park and reached for her. Linette barely had time to recover before his mouth swooped down on hers. He kissed her deep and hard, his hands expertly finding their way to her breasts, cupping them in his palms.

Her nipples beaded instantly under the manipulation of his fingers, and she moaned softly.

"Do you have a clue of how difficult it's been not to make love to you these last few days?" he asked, trailing kisses along the side of her neck.

"Yes." She knew exactly how hard it had been on them both, but she felt cherished and adored that he'd insisted they wait until after the wedding. She loved him all the more for his patience.

He kissed her again slowly, with restraint, using his tongue to show her what he'd like to be doing to her body. What he would soon be doing.

When he dragged his mouth from hers, he rested his chin on the top of her head. "Much more of this and we could be arrested."

Linette smiled softly to herself. "The way I feel right now, it would almost be worth it."

Cain drove fifteen miles over the speed limit for the rest of the trip, then stopped in a small seaside town. Apparently he was familiar with the area because he drove directly to a house perched against a windswept hillside that overlooked the Pacific Ocean.

"Is anyone home?" Linette asked, noticing the light shining from inside the huge house.

"I certainly hope not," was all Cain would say. He helped her out of the car, lifted the suitcase from the trunk, and led the way up a brick-lined pathway. "This place belongs to a friend of mine."

"Have I met him?"

"No. Fact is, until just a few days ago, I hadn't talked to him in over ten years. He told me that if I ever needed a retreat, I should give him a call. I phoned last week."

"Ten years, and he still remembered you?"

"He remembered. I saved his life." After digging the key out of his side pocket, Cain inserted it into the lock and pushed open the door. He propped the suitcases against the door to hold it open and then effortlessly lifted Linette into his arms. Their eyes met, and he smiled meaningfully.

Linette linked her arms around his neck as he carried her over the threshold. They kissed long and passionately. The wind howled behind them, and reluctantly Cain set her feet back on the floor and dealt with the luggage.

While he was tucking away their suitcases in the back bedroom, Linette explored the house. Huge picture windows looked out over the churning Pacific Ocean, but night blocked out the majority of the view.

Hearing movement behind her, Linette turned to discover Cain standing on the opposite side of the room. His hands were buried in his pants pockets.

"I imagine the view's lovely in daylight," he said.

If Linette hadn't known better, she would have thought her husband of less than four hours was nervous.

"I'm sure it is."

"Are you hungry?" he asked, glancing toward the kitchen. "The refrigerator's stocked with enough food to last us a week or longer."

"I'm famished."

"Great." Cain moved eagerly toward the other room. "I'll see to dinner."

"My appetite isn't for food, Cain McClellan," she chided him, her voice low and breathless. "It's being your wife that strongly appeals to me." Anxious herself, Linette could have sworn her heart beat like cymbals crashing against each other.

Cain smiled, and Linette was certain she'd never seen a man look more relieved. "I wondered how I was going to manage to sit through a meal and not ravish you." He ate up the distance between them in two giant strides. He reached for her and brought her into his arms.

Cain swore he'd never known pleasure this profound. Over the course of their wedding night, they'd made love twice. Linette had wept when she'd viewed the thick, still pink scars that marked his body. Not wanting anything to distract her, he'd turned out the light.

Cain glanced toward the digital clock on the nightstand. It was almost four. Dawn was hours away yet. Linette breathed evenly and snuggled up against his side. He urged her head onto his shoulder, and she draped her hand over his abdomen. In that moment Cain would have rather died than move.

He'd never experienced contentment like this. Physically he was sated, but it was his emotions that he found himself analyzing. So this was what it meant to love someone so much that it brought a physical ache just thinking about it. So this was what it meant to give your heart completely to another.

Cain had been afraid. He'd been terrified commitment to Linette would mean surrendering a part of himself. He'd been wrong, very wrong. Only now did he realize how deeply he'd cheated himself in the last year. In loving Linette, he'd realized he was the receiver. Her love had made him whole. Her tenderness had wiped away the pain of a bitter childhood, the need to prove himself, the drive to gain the attention and approval of an alcoholic father—a man incapable of giving either. A father long dead and long buried.

"What time is it?" Linette asked in a husky whisper.

"You're awake?"

"Not really. I'm just curious about the time." She remained exactly as she was, her ear pressed over his heart, her arm draped over his middle.

Cain grinned. "About four."

"You couldn't sleep?"

"I woke up."

She started to pull away. "You're not accustomed to sleeping with anyone, and I—"

"No," he interrupted, stopping her. "Don't move."

Linette went still. "So you are accustomed to sleeping with someone?"

He chuckled. "No. You sound jealous."

"Should I be?"

He weighed his words carefully. Heaven would vouch he was no saint. Never had been and probably never would be. "There hasn't been another woman from the moment I met you."

Linette's body relaxed against his. "I love you, Cain McClellan."

He closed his eyes and kissed the crown of her head. "And I love you." He stroked her bare back and was surprised at the ready way his body fired to life. His one concern before he'd asked Linette to marry him had been his health. The doctors had claimed it would take a good deal of time to recover from the gunshot wound. It embarrassed him to inquire about his sexual stamina, but his questions had been greeted with professional ease. The doctor didn't know for certain, but he speculated that in light of Cain's injuries, his physical endurance would be limited.

His physician, however, wasn't married to Linette. To Cain's relief and delight, he discovered his recovery time from lovemaking was amazingly quick.

His hand descended lower and cupped her bare buttock. "Linette?" he quizzed softly.

"Humm?"

"Just how asleep are you?"

He felt her smile against his bare chest. "What makes you ask?"

"I don't know," he hedged. "Idle curiosity, I guess, and the fact I can't seem to keep my hands off you."

"I like your hands on me," she assured him. Edging upward, she slid her glorious body over him, tantalizing him until she located his earlobe and caught it between her teeth.

Two could play that game, Cain decided, and rolled his head to one side to capture her nipple between his lips. His hands bunched her breasts, and he slid his moist mouth between the two extended nipples, creating a moist, slick trail between the peaks. He paid equal attention to the two and smiled in gratitude when he realized Linette had gone still.

"I love your breasts," Cain told her before capturing one and sucking deep and hard.

Linette squirmed. "I love what you do to them," she said in a husky whisper.

Cain eased his hand between her thighs. She parted her legs to grant him easy access and eased her weight onto her side. Cain rolled so that they were facing each other.

"I . . . we just, I mean . . ."

"Sh-h," he said, and lifted her leg and placed it over his hip, urging the lower half of her body closer to his rigid staff, which throbbed in readiness.

Linette rolled her head back and sighed as he linked their bodies. Cain swallowed a deep moan. It wasn't supposed to be this good. Pressing his hand against the side of her hip, he braced himself against the onslaught to pleasure. He moved without the haste and urgency that had ruled their previous lovemaking.

"Cain," Linette pleaded, raising her hips, silently demanding that he make love to her.

His hands stilled her efforts. When he spoke, his voice revealed the effort it demanded not to give in to her command. "Not this time," he whispered, panting for control. "We're going to do this slow."

"I can't wait." She writhed mindlessly against him,

clenching his shoulders as she worked the lower half of her body against him.

Cain found he couldn't wait, either. He possessed her with a love and tenderness unlike anything he had experienced with other women. She carried him to paradise and back, until he was convinced he would have gladly died right then and there. It might have been hours or only minutes, Cain could only speculate, before he floated back to earth.

Linette lay beside him quietly, cradled close against his long, muscled length. Their legs were entwined, their arms wrapped around each other. Cain brushed a kiss across her cheek. Her eyes were closed, and she smiled dreamily.

"A woman could become accustomed to this kind of attention," she whispered.

Cain grinned. "I wonder when I'm going to have time to learn about cattle ranching. I'd much rather spend time in bed with you."

Linette smiled lazily. "You'll learn. We both will."

Cain understood what she was saying. This was a change of lifestyle for them both. They'd relinquished the past and grabbed hold of the future without looking back, without regrets. At least not yet. Linette had sold her knitting shop to Bonnie. She hadn't said much about letting go of the business, but Cain recognized the sacrifice it had entailed. Wild and Wooly had given her purpose following Michael's death. She'd funneled her energy into the business. The shop represented the life she'd built stone upon stone, one day at a time, after losing her first husband. Yet she'd freely relinquished this part of herself in order to marry him. It had been no small sacrifice.

o   o   o

She was the prettiest woman in the cantina, and Jack Keller swore she'd been watching him from the moment he'd arrived. He'd come to quench his thirst, but if a saucy señorita was interested in adding a bit of spice to his afternoon, Jack wasn't opposed. He didn't have anything better to do with his time. Killing an hour or two in bed was just the tonic he needed, he mused.

Murphy had sent him on assignment to this godforsaken stinkhole. If Cain had been the one issuing the orders, he wouldn't have minded, but this was Murphy. It didn't seem right to be taking orders from anyone other than Cain.

As far as Jack was concerned, the new owner of Deliverance Company had a lot to learn. It would be a long time before Murphy was the caliber of leader Cain McClellan had been.

Cain married. Mallory, too. Disgusted, Jack shook his head. It didn't sit right with him or the other team members. What was this world coming to, when two of the best fighting men he'd ever known allowed themselves to fall into the worst trap of all? Marriage.

This new lifestyle was inconsistent with everything Jack knew about his colleagues. He couldn't speak for the others, but he was hoping that after a few months of pandering to a wife, Cain would come to his senses and return to Deliverance Company. This was where he belonged. Try as he might, he couldn't picture Cain with a ring through his nose.

Jack took a deep swallow of the cold beer and wiped

the back of his hand across his mouth. Carrying the chipped mug with him, he strolled over to where the young lady sat.

"Care if I join you?" he asked her in Spanish.

She fluttered her eyelashes and shrugged one delicate shoulder. "Feel free," she responded.

Jack pulled out a chair, twisted it around, and straddled it. He took another drink of his beer and called for the bartender and ordered two more, one for him and the other for the girl.

"You got a name?" she asked.

"Yeah," he teased. "What about you?"

"Zita."

"Pretty name for a pretty lady." That had to be the oldest line in the book, but one look told him she wasn't interested in his wit.

"Thank you."

The bartender delivered two more mugs, and Jack paid him. Zita reached across the table for the beer, and Jack noticed that she bent low to be sure he received an ample view of her wares. Her breasts were large and lush, the size of cantaloupes. Jack wished more women were inclined to wear blouses with elastic necklines. It made access to their breasts easier than fiddling with all those silly buttons.

"How much?" he asked, getting to the point. There was no need to be coy. He knew what she was.

She cast him a hot look. "You insult me."

He laughed, and wanting her to think he didn't have much time, he checked his watch. "I doubt anyone's capable of offending you."

Keep your pants zipped. That was something Cain had

said often enough and loud enough. Only Cain wasn't running the show any longer, Murphy was.

"Another time, then," Jack said, setting aside his beer.

"Wait," Zita said quickly, and slipped her hand across his thigh, her long nails digging into the hard muscle there. "Don't go. Not yet."

Jack cast her a half smile. "Then give me a reason to stay."

She slid her hand slightly forward toward his crotch and splayed her fingers like a cat flexing its claws. "I'm very good," she said under her breath.

"I believe you." Already Jack could feel the hot blood racing through his veins.

"I don't come cheap."

"I didn't think you did."

"I have a place with a clean bed close by."

He hid a smile. "That's a plus."

"You'll pay me first?"

Jack hesitated. "Half now. Half later."

She grinned and nodded. "Follow me."

Jack stood and followed the woman out of the cantina. Her hips swayed as she hurried across the courtyard. "Hey," Jack said, calling after her, "what's the hurry?"

"No hurry," she assured him, placing a hand on her hip and tossing him a slow, sexual smile.

Impatient to sample her wares, Jack caught her by the shoulder and turned into a nearby alley. Her back was against a wall as she looked up at him with deep chocolate eyes. Slowly Jack lowered his mouth to hers. She tasted of warm beer and passion. He could live without the stale taste of beer, but the passion excited him.

Entwining his fingers in her thick dark hair, he kissed her again.

She squirmed against him. "Not here," she said, pushing against him.

"Why not?" He looked around, and not seeing anyone close, he reached under her skirt and slid his hand over her bare buttocks.

"My house is very close," she promised.

The way Jack was feeling just then, "very close" wasn't near enough. Rarely had he been this hot for a woman, but it had been a good long while since he'd given in to his baser needs. Apparently too long.

"Please, Señor," she pleaded softly.

Jack dragged a cooling breath through his lungs. "All right," he mumbled.

She relaxed against him and kissed him long and hard. Then, taking him by the hand, she led him down a narrow side street. Jack was in too much of a rush to notice much about which way they were headed. He was fairly certain he'd find his way back to the cantina without a problem.

Smiling up at him, she unlocked the door and threw it open. Once more Jack reached for her, turned her into his arms, and kissed her lustily. His hands were on her breasts as he eased her through the doorway. His intention was to steer her toward the bedroom and have his way with her. Heaven would testify she was willing enough.

Jack opened his eyes, and it felt as if the breath had been knocked out of him. There, sitting at the rough wood table, was a man, eating casually with one hand. In the other was a pistol pointed directly at Jack's heart.

"Welcome to hell, Jack Keller," he said with a sick laugh, licking the fingertips of his free hand. "You don't remember me, do you?"

Jack backed away from Zita, his blood turning cold. He did recognize the other man. The last time he'd seen this gunman, the desperado had been standing in the belly of a helicopter with his weapon trained on Cain McClellan.

"Trust me. Before the day is over, you will remember everything," the man said. "You will curse God that your friend didn't die the first time."

16

"If you're going to be a real cowboy, I suspect I should teach you the code," John Stamp said casually to Cain.

"Code?" Cain shifted his weight atop the large sorrel and studied the rolling snow-covered hillside, hoping to familiarize himself with the landscape.

"To the best of my knowledge it's nothing that's formally written down. It's a way of thinking and acting. You'd pick it up sooner or later."

"Be easier if you told me outright, wouldn't it?" Cain commented. He'd been working with John every day for the past three weeks, harder, he swore, than he'd ever worked in his life. Each night he returned to Linette with his head crammed full of things he'd learned about his land and his herd of cattle, his head buzzing with the certainty he could work this land for the next fifty years and still be a greenhorn.

"I believe you've already figured out how important it is to close gates."

Cain snickered at the memory of his first day riding with John. "I've got that one down pat."

"Good."

"Also, it's not a good idea to keep someone waiting for you."

Cain eyed the foreman speculatively. "You told the women that? I swear it takes five minutes longer after Linette claims she's ready to leave."

"So the honeymoon's over, is it?" John said teasingly.

Actually it wasn't. Cain had adjusted with little trouble to married life, which surprised him. He'd expected they'd need to adapt more to each other's ways than they had. Naturally, being crazy in love helped. As for the honeymoon part, he felt as frisky as someone fifteen years his junior. Cain had never considered himself especially oversexed, but that had changed since his marriage. It amazed him how frequently he needed his wife.

"What's so funny?" John asked.

"Nothing," Cain said, his hands tightening around the sorrel's reins. "Go on with your list, I'm listening."

John seemed to require a few moments to think. "If Linette hasn't said anything yet, she will. Remember to remove your spurs before going into the house."

"The slang for spurs is 'can openers'?" Cain had heard one of the other hired men say something along those lines recently.

"You got it."

Cain had soon learned that cowboys had their own lingo. He was picking up a few words here and there, but there were several he hadn't quite figured out. The day before, he'd heard Pete, a wiry fellow in his early fifties, talk about a gelding who was cut proud. Cain still hadn't figured out what that meant. Ah, well, he'd learn soon enough.

"Anything more?"

"Plenty," John assured him. "This one's important. Don't ever cuss out another man's dog."

"You make it sound like writing a check without any money in the bank."

"It's worse than that."

"They throw you in jail for bouncing checks."

"You don't want to know what happens to someone who cusses out a neighbor's dog. You can say what you will about his wife, but leave his dog alone."

That wouldn't hold true with Cain, but he didn't want to be teased about being a newlywed, so he kept his mouth closed. Glancing at his watch, he calculated how long it'd be before they'd head back to the house.

The day before, he'd arrived home just as Linette was taking a loaf of freshly baked bread out of the oven, and the earthy scent of yeast had filled the house. Her eyes had lit up when she'd seen him, and his heart had done a little flip-flop just knowing she was his. Cain had never suspected life could be this good.

"Another thing," John said, cutting into Cain's musings. "Always drink upstream from the herd."

Cain chuckled. "I suppose the next thing you're going to tell me is that a horse in the barn is worth two in the bush."

John rubbed his hand down the side of his face as if testing to see whether he needed a shave or not. "You're learning, McClellan. Won't be long now before the creak's out of your saddle."

Linette hummed as she polished the cherrywood end table. Soon she was meeting Patty Stamp and the two were driving into town. Generally they made the drive only once a month, and the men tagged along, but this trip was special. Something Cain didn't know about. A surprise of sorts, although it shouldn't have been.

Linette suspected she was pregnant.

She didn't want to say anything until she was positive. The test kit Patty Stamp had provided read positive, but Linette wouldn't believe it until she heard it directly from the physician himself.

Other than missing her period, she suffered none of the obvious symptoms heard about. No morning sickness. Nor was she overly tired. Perhaps it was too soon. They'd been married less than six weeks. From what she'd heard, it wasn't supposed to be this easy.

The sound of an approaching vehicle prompted Linette to set aside her dusting rag and look out the front window. A large oversize pickup barreled down the driveway.

Thinking something must be wrong, Linette reached for her jacket and stepped onto the porch. She wrapped her arms around her to ward off the cold wind, which howled like a stray calf.

Her heart staggered at the sight of Murphy, Cain's former colleague, who leapt down from the cab. He stood with his feet braced apart as if he expected to do battle with her.

"Where's Cain?" he asked, and the wind howled louder behind him.

"On the range."

"Can you reach him?"

A chill raced up Linette's arms. "Would you care to come inside? We may have had our differences in the past, but that isn't any reason to stand here in the cold and shout at each other."

He nodded once, giving the impression he was lowering his standards to do as she requested. Linette gritted her teeth to keep from saying it didn't hurt her any to leave him outside to freeze if that was what he wanted. To her credit, she managed to swallow the sarcastic comment.

Murphy took the porch steps two at a time. "How long will it take to reach Cain?" he demanded.

Linette ignored the command in his voice. The mercenary might be accustomed to issuing orders and having them obeyed, but she wasn't one of his men.

"Would you care for some coffee?" she asked instead.

Murphy glared at her. "I asked about Cain."

"And I asked if you'd like some coffee."

"I don't want coffee, I need to talk to Cain," he said with a decided lack of patience.

"All right." Linette left him and headed for the kitchen but was saved the effort of contacting her husband. Just then Cain walked in the back door, looking dusty, tired, and so damn loving that it was all she could do to keep herself from running into his arms.

"You're early," she said, forcing a smile.

"Yup." He devoured the short distance between them and took her into his arms. He kissed her before she could tell him about Murphy. Once her husband's mouth was over hers, it demanded every ounce of will she possessed to remember the other man herself.

"How about taking a shower with me?" he whispered close to her ear.

"Cain—"

"How long has it been since we last made love?" he asked, then answered the question himself. "Too long." He kissed her so thoroughly, she felt her knees would go out from under her.

"Cain—"

"I believe she's trying to tell you I'm here," Murphy said from the kitchen doorway. One hand held open the door and the other was braced against his hip, his eyes disapproving.

"Murphy." Cain stepped away from Linette, and the two men exchanged hearty handshakes. "What the hell are you doing here?"

"We've got a problem."

Linette noticed the reference to "we" even if Cain didn't. Her husband had promised her his warring days were over. He'd given her his word of honor. Never again, he'd said.

Linette forced herself to relax. She was leaping to conclusions. Just because Murphy showed up unexpectedly and announced he was in trouble, even if he had prefaced the problem with "we," that didn't mean Cain would become involved.

"What's wrong?" By tacit agreement the two men moved to the kitchen table. Linette took down three mugs and poured them each a cup of coffee. Unwilling to be excluded from the conversation, she pulled out a chair and sat next to Cain.

Murphy hesitated when Linette sat down.

"You can speak freely," Cain assured him.

Murphy began, "Does the name Enrique mean anything to you?"

Cain frowned. "Just the one name?"

Murphy nodded.

"Should I know it?"

"He was the man who shot you."

"Ah, yes. Pretty Boy." He wasn't someone Cain was likely to forget, Linette suspected, although she wasn't sure he'd ever known the other man's name.

"He's back in action," Murphy said, and his mouth thinned just saying the words.

"Another CEO this time?"

As Linette watched her husband, a knot began to form in the lower part of her stomach. His eyes lit up, and a half smile touched his lips.

"No. This time he's got Jack."

"Jack Keller?"

Murphy nodded.

Cain frowned fiercely. "What the hell does he want from Jack?"

"I don't know."

"Has he demanded a ransom?"

"That's the funny part. He hasn't asked for a dime."

"You're sure Jack's alive?"

"No."

"What are your plans?"

"Rescue Jack if I can, then kill Enrique. Either way the bastard's taken his last man. The problem is I'm going to need help."

Linette stiffened. The two men talked about life and

death with stark indifference as if neither was of any real consequence.

She wanted to stand up and shout at them to look at themselves, to listen to what they said, to really listen. It might have been her imagination, but it seemed to Linette that Cain, the man she loved, the man she shared a bed with each night, the man who was the father of the child she suspected she carried, became a stranger to her. His heart grew hard and cold before her very eyes.

"When are you leaving?" Cain asked.

"Within the week." The other man's eyes held Cain's. "I want you with me."

Cain hesitated and looked to Linette.

"You promised me never again," she whispered, her voice sounding scratchy and weak.

"This is Jack," Murphy exploded, and stood. "If it wasn't for Jack, Cain wouldn't be here now. None of us would be. Jack's a good man. He doesn't deserve to die friendless. You know damn good and well that if the situation was reversed, he'd be the first one to volunteer to go in after you."

Still Cain hesitated. "Let me talk to Linette."

Murphy glared at her, then turned and walked out of the kitchen, leaving the door to swing in his wake.

For a long moment neither spoke. Linette knew what Cain wanted. He was waiting for her to absolve him from his promise. Waiting for her to tell him that these were extenuating circumstances and it only made sense that he be the one to rescue his buddy.

Linette, however, wasn't willing to be that generous.

"Honey?"

"It doesn't matter what I say. You'll do what you want anyway."

"It does matter," Cain insisted.

"We haven't been married two months and already you've got an excuse to go back into the field."

"This isn't like any other operation. This is for a friend, a man I've worked with for years. This sort of thing has never happened before. It won't again."

"You promised me before we were married that you wouldn't go back."

Cain forcefully expelled a sigh. "Under normal circumstances I wouldn't. But this is for Jack. I owe him my life."

Linette closed her eyes. It might have been paranoid of her, but she wondered if Murphy had his own agenda as far as Cain was concerned. She wouldn't put it past the mercenary to bring Cain back into Deliverance Company little by little.

"Why does it have to be you?" she asked.

"Because I'm good. Jack's chances are better if I'm the one heading the mission. Sweetheart, Jack's a friend, a good friend. And Enrique's the bastard who shot me."

"In other words you want to go?"

It took Cain a long time to answer. "Yes."

Something died inside of Linette.

If it hadn't been for the gunshot wound and his close brush with death, Cain would have been content to leave matters between them as they were. His injuries had reminded him of his mortality. He was lucky to be alive, and given a second chance, he wanted to make the most of it. For a time he'd managed to convince himself he could change his stripes.

"What about your other promises?" she asked, staring straight ahead. She discovered she couldn't look at him and focused instead on an inanimate object on the counter.

"What promises?"

"Love, cherish, the vows we spoke in church. Do you want me to absolve you from those as well?"

"Linette," Cain said on the tail end of a sigh that revealed his exasperation with her. "You're making more out of this than necessary. A friend of mine is in trouble. He needs help, and I'm in a position to rescue him. It doesn't mean I'm going back to Deliverance Company."

"What is it you want from me?"

"I was hoping we could talk about this sensibly."

"You're looking for me to release you from your promise. Admit it, Cain. Be honest enough to own up to the truth."

"All right, if that's what you want me to say, then I will. You're right, I did promise you I wouldn't go back into the field, but then I didn't count on one of my best friends being taken captive, either."

There was a knock at the back door and Patty Stamp stepped into the kitchen. "You ready, Linette?" she asked cheerfully, then hesitated when she saw Cain. "Oh, sorry, I didn't mean to interrupt anything."

"You didn't," Linette said, forcing a smile. "Let me get my coat and purse and I'll be ready."

"I'll wait out in the car," Patty said.

"I'll only be a moment," Linette promised, and headed out of the kitchen.

"Linette." Exasperated, Cain called after her.

"Yes?" she answered lightly as if not understanding why he would delay her.

"What about Jack?"

"I'll tell you what, Cain. I'll leave the decision in your hands."

"No," he said forcefully. "I refuse to accept that."

"Then go," she said without emotion, "but don't kid yourself into thinking this is the last time. There'll always be a good reason. It'll always be just this one time. Always be someone else who needs you more than me."

"You're overreacting," he snapped.

"Maybe," she answered, "but I doubt it." She didn't wait for his answer. With tears blurring her vision, she hurriedly reached for her purse and jacket and raced outside.

Linette joined Patty on the front seat of the minivan and ran her glove-covered hand across her face. Patty glanced at her as if she weren't sure what she should do.

"I'm fine," Linette said with a shaky laugh.

"You don't look so good to me. Did you two have your first spat?"

"You could say that."

"Don't worry, everything will work itself out."

Linette couldn't help but wonder. Patty eased the car into drive and headed down the long dirt driveway that led to the main road.

"I didn't know you had company," Patty said when she spied Murphy's truck.

"It's a friend of Cain's."

"Don't you fret," Patty said a second time. "By the time you get home, Cain will be so pleased to see you, he'll want to kiss and make up soon enough."

"Cain won't be here."

"Nonsense. Where else would he be?"

"God only knows," she said chokingly.

Several hours later the physician had confirmed what a test kit and nature had already told her: Linette was pregnant. The certainty that Cain's child grew beneath her heart was what helped her through the long drive back to the ranch.

"Wait until Cain hears this," Patty said. "Boy, would I love to be a fly on the wall when he learns you're going to have a baby."

Linette knew Patty was trying to lift her spirits, but she didn't try to kid herself into thinking Cain would be waiting for her when she arrived home. Yet she couldn't help hoping.

It was dark by the time they arrived at the ranch.

"See, what did I tell you?" Patty said, sounding wise and smug. "Cain's home."

Murphy was there as well.

Patty dropped her off, and Linette walked in the back door off the kitchen. Cain and Murphy were sitting at the table, going over some papers.

Cain's eyes held hers. "Where'd you go?"

"Town," she said, going over to the oven to check on the roast she'd left slow cooking there. "I had some errands to run." She wouldn't tell him about the pregnancy now. She refused to use their child as a weapon.

"Murphy and I've been talking, and I've made up my mind. I'm going with him after Jack." He announced his decision as if he expected her to argue.

There was no fight left in her. "I figured you would."

"We leave at first light."

Her hand tightened around the pot holder, and she nodded.

That evening Cain and Murphy talked long after dinner. Linette finished the dishes, put a load of wash into the machine, and casually announced she was going up to bed.

"If I don't see you in the morning, Murphy," she said smoothly, "have a safe trip."

He eyed her as if he weren't sure he should believe her. "I'll do my damnedest."

"Take care of Cain for me." Her eyes held his for a lengthy moment before he nodded.

"Thank you," she said, and, turning, walked slowly up the stairs.

Linette was asleep when Cain joined her several hours later in the large king-size bed. She sighed when he started to nibble on her earlobe.

"Wake up, sleepyhead," he whispered, his voice low and seductive. His hand massaged her gently.

"Is it morning already?" Her eyes burned, and she felt as if she hadn't slept more than a hour. It seemed impossible that it was time to wake up.

"Don't worry. We've got four or five hours. But I didn't want to waste our last bit of time together sleeping," Cain told her, expertly unfastening the buttons to open the front of her pajamas.

"You want to talk?" she asked, and yawned loudly.

"No," he said, gently rolling her onto her back. "I want to make sure you miss me as much as I'm going to miss you." Already he'd eased his hand beneath the elastic of her pajama bottoms.

Her response to her husband was instinctive. He helped her out of her pajamas, then shucked off his own. She raised her hips off the mattress in order to meet his first thrust and then whimpered at the intense pleasure they were capable of giving each other.

"Baby, I promise—"

Linette stopped him. "Don't make me any more promises," she told him.

It was over almost before it started, their need was so great. They were both too exhausted to speak afterward, for which Linette was grateful. As a result Linette fell asleep tucked securely against her husband, his arms around her.

His kiss against the side of her neck woke her.

"Again?" she asked groggily, thinking he wanted to make love a second time, an occurrence that wasn't uncommon in the weeks since their marriage.

Cain chuckled and kissed her again. "I don't have time. Murphy and I are about to leave."

Linette eyes flew open and she sat up on the bed, her heart pounding hard and fast. "Already?" A glance at the clock radio told her it was barely three.

"We've got a flight to catch."

She nodded and swallowed against the constriction blocking her throat. It came to her to tell Cain that within a few short months he'd be a father, but it didn't seem right under these circumstances.

"I'll be back before you know it," he assured her.

Linette did her best to smile.

"Don't ever doubt my love for you," he said.

Murphy's shout came from below.

"I'll be there in a minute," Cain called back. He walked across the room, then hesitated as if he weren't certain yet he had the strength to leave her.

Linette cradled her arms around her middle. "Don't do anything stupid."

He stood in the doorway. "I won't."

Linette closed her eyes, unwilling for him to see how close she was to tears. "Good-bye."

"Good-bye."

She scooted back down into the warm blankets and waited for the man she'd married to calmly walk out of her life.

"What have you learned about Enrique?" Cain asked Matt Morrissey, the newest member of Deliverance Company.

"Nothing we didn't already know," Matt said.

"The girl? Zita, wasn't it?"

Matt nodded. "She says she'll only talk to you. My guess is that Enrique paid her handsomely to lure Jack into her place, and now she's looking for a handout from us as well. I doubt she'll be able to help us."

"You're sure of that?" The first communications from Enrique had been addressed to Cain, which was one of the reasons Murphy had initially contacted him at the ranch. Apparently the drug lord didn't know Cain had sold Deliverance Company. Cain was beginning to think there was more to the kidnapping than met the eye.

"I'm not sure of anything," Matt Morrissey said, "but she looks like the type who would gladly cut out her grandmother's liver for five extra dollars."

"You have her with you?"

"She's waiting outside."

"Bring her in." The information phase of this rescue wasn't going well. They'd expected a ransom or other demands long before now, which led to speculation that

Jack might no longer be alive. The prospect left those who knew and worked with Jack Keller depressed and short-tempered.

A few moments later Morrissey returned with a beautiful young woman with eyes as round and dark as a fawn's. "Hello," Cain greeted her in her mother language.

The woman eyed him without emotion. "You're Cain McClellan?" she asked.

Cain nodded.

"He wants you dead, you know?" She said this as if it gave her a good deal of pleasure to be the one to tell him the news.

"Many men want me dead."

"Enrique wants more than for you to die."

Cain yawned. He'd heard this and more from several men.

"You killed his favorite brother, and now he wants to return the favor."

"Jack isn't my brother."

"No, he is your friend." This was said smugly, as if she expected a reaction. She laughed then, and the eerie sound of it echoed against the bare walls. "You are a good friend to this Jack, aren't you?"

Cain's gaze narrowed, and he said nothing.

She laughed again and leaned forward, exposing her breasts. "Are my breasts as beautiful as your wife's?"

Cain discovered he was fast losing his patience. "What does Enrique want?" he demanded brusquely.

Dramatically she tossed her hands into the air. "Nothing. He has everything he needs. He wishes me to thank you for your quick response."

The woman spoke in riddles. Cain could think of

nothing more to ask her. Matt returned and took her away, and Murphy joined Cain shortly afterward.

"It makes no sense," Cain told his friend.

"What doesn't?" Murphy inquired. "Apparently I killed Enrique's brother and he's after revenge."

"That's why he has Jack."

"That's what he wants us to think, but I don't buy it. Jack's a friend, but he isn't my brother. I'd feel bad if anything happened to Jack, but it wouldn't change my life. Jack readily put his life on the line with every mission."

Cain was packing now, his mind working fast. "How many people know I'm married?"

Murphy shrugged as if he found the question of little consequence.

"Zita knows," Cain snapped. "Enrique knows."

"It isn't like you were planning on keeping it a secret, is it?"

"No, but if Pretty Boy was looking for revenge, just where do you think he'd start?" Cain couldn't believe how stupid he'd been. He'd walked right into Enrique's trap. The drug lord had lured him away from the ranch, away from Linette, with Jack's kidnapping.

"You don't think he'd actually do anything to Linette, do you?" Murphy asked.

"I've got to get to a phone."

It took them the better part of twenty minutes to make long-distance connections with the United States. The better part of Cain's sanity was lost in that time. He'd abandoned his wife and in doing so had set her in a death trap.

When he finally was able to reach the house, there was no answer.

"It may not be as bad as it looks," Murphy said, looking anxious himself. "According to my calculations, it's three in the afternoon. She might be outside. Try again in a couple of minutes."

"Mallory," Cain said next.

"But he's in Washington State," Murphy said, apparently not understanding.

Cain was well aware of exactly where Mallory lived. "If Enrique was looking for a brother to kill, Mallory's as close to me as any relative."

No one answered at Mallory's place, either.

In desperation Cain contacted John Stamp. "Where's Linette?" he asked when Patty answered the phone.

"Cain, is that you? Good grief, you sound like you're phoning from the moon."

"Where's Linette?" Cain pleaded a second time. "Patty, listen, it's very important that I speak to her immediately."

"I'm sorry, but I haven't seen her all day."

"Where is she?"

"Honestly, I don't know why you're so upset, but I don't have a clue where she might be. Funny, now that you mention it, but the truck's here, and I didn't see her leave. Are you sure there's no answer at the house?"

17

Mallory didn't venture far from the house these days. Francine was due to deliver their baby any time now, and frankly he didn't know how much more of this suspense he could take. When he'd first learned Francine was pregnant, Tim had been justifiably proud. It hadn't taken long for his seed to take root, and there was a certain amount of male pride associated with the speed with which he'd impregnated his wife.

Now that the baby was due, Mallory's thoughts were consumed with Francine's well-being. He'd wanted temporarily to move off Vashon Island, where only minimal health care was available. It seemed perfectly logical to him that they rent a hotel room close to the hospital to await the blessed event. But his stubborn wife would hear none of it.

Francine, who hadn't been delicate and small before the pregnancy, was as big as a house now, yet Mallory was convinced he'd never seen her look more beautiful. Her stomach protruded halfway into the next room, yet every move she made was marked with grace and poise. He marveled at her and not for the first time recognized that he was a damn lucky son of a bitch to have married this remarkable woman.

The other day he'd found her in the nursery, preparing the room for their child. He'd seen her fold a minute T-shirt and found it impossible to believe that any child of his would ever be so small.

His son or daughter. The significance of his as-yet-unborn child hadn't fully impacted Mallory. At first the baby was a something rather than a someone. They'd talked about the baby, but the reality of him or her hadn't struck home until Mallory had watched his child blossom and grow inside Francine's womb. This new life had stretched and explored its world, and Mallory had been amazed to have his child kick against his own hand.

Mallory was worried. He was a man who'd spent the better part of his adult life on a battlefield. Yet nothing had concerned him more than this young life he'd created with Francine.

His gaze followed his wife as she set their dinner on the table. He didn't want her to know how anxious and fretful he'd become. Yet it had become harder and harder to hide his distress.

"It really isn't necessary to watch my every move," Francine said, one hand braced against the small of her back. "Trust me, Tim, we'll have plenty of warning before Junior makes an appearance."

"I don't know why you won't listen to reason."

Francine smiled and her eyes brightened, and Mallory

swore he would love this woman on his dying day. "We'll
have plenty of time to get to the hospital, I promise you."

"The ferries—"

"Run every half hour. Now stop worrying and come to
the table. Dinner's ready."

Mallory set aside the evening newspaper and joined
his wife at the dining room table. He discovered as her
time drew near that he didn't have nearly as hearty an
appetite as usual. If this waiting went on much longer,
he'd be skin and bone.

"Would you stop," she snapped. "You'd think I was the
only woman in the world to be nine months pregnant."

Mallory reached across the table and squeezed her
hand. "As far as I'm concerned, you are." It was in his
mind to kiss her, but he decided against it. They hadn't
made love in three weeks, two days, and ten hours, not
that he was counting. The problem was, Mallory had
never desired his wife more. Kissing her just then was
more temptation than he could handle.

"Take heart. I talked to my mother this morning, and
she'll be here for two weeks following my release from
the hospital. You can relax and let Grandma take over."

Mallory didn't know how other husbands felt about
their mothers-in-law, but frankly, he was overjoyed that
Martha would be with them.

"Good," he said, and reached for the bread and butter. "But I still think we should be hiring a nurse or a
nanny or whatever it is other families do."

"We aren't going to need a nanny. We're going to
care for this baby ourselves. We'll take turns changing
diapers."

"Hey, just a minute," Mallory said, holding up his

right hand. "No one said anything to me about messy diapers."

"I'm saying it now. You wanted to be a father, remember?"

Mallory grinned. "As I recall, I was far more interested in the creative process."

The phone rang just then. Francine looked to him. "Let the answering machine get it," she pleaded. "You know how much I dislike having our dinner interrupted."

It was a small request, and Mallory agreed. "I doubt it's important."

They finished their meal, and as Mallory carried the dishes to the sink, he noticed Francine staring out the window above the kitchen sink.

"Something wrong?"

"The light's off inside the barn."

Mallory glanced out the window himself. A still, eerie darkness permeated the night.

"It'd be just like Bubba to use this as an excuse to raise all kinds of hell," Francine murmured.

The male llama had been a thorn in Mallory's side from the first. After months of working together, man and beast had a grudging respect for each other.

"You'd better see about getting the bulbs changed. Do you want me to come with you?"

"Every light's off," Mallory said, wondering what had blown the breaker. It wasn't likely that every light bulb had malfunctioned at the same time.

"I'll finish up here," Francine told him, and opened the dishwasher.

Mallory kissed her on the cheek on his way out the

door. Humming to himself, he made his way across the yard. His steps slowed. Tension filled the night air. It was almost as if he were on a mission again, and Cain McClellan were at his side. The hair on the back of his neck rose, and it wasn't from static electricity.

He was only a few steps away from the barn door when he heard Francine.

"Tim. Tim," she called, her voice filled with controlled fear.

Mallory whirled around to discover his wife standing on the porch steps, her arms cradling her grossly extended stomach. The light above the door illuminated her face. Her eyes were round and imploring.

Mallory swore his blood ran cold. "Is it the baby?"

"John," Cain said hurriedly into the telephone receiver. His plane was scheduled to depart in twenty minutes, but he was frantic to learn what he could of his wife's whereabouts. "Have you talked to Linette yet?"

"I can't say that I have. But don't you worry, I'm sure everything's fine. I've sent Patty over to the house to check up on her."

"No," Cain cried. "Don't send Patty there alone."

"I'm sorry, Cain, but I'm having trouble hearing you. There's a bunch of static on the line. Can you hear me?"

The irony of the situation was that his end of the telephone was as clear as Austrian church bells. Rarely had Cain felt more helpless. He'd spent the better part of two fruitless hours attempting to warn those closest to him that he suspected they were in grave danger.

Unable to talk to Mallory personally, Cain had been

forced to leave a cryptic message on his answering machine. This was his second, or was it his third call to the Stamps? He didn't remember any longer. The local sheriff had promised to send someone out to check on Linette, but that could be hours yet.

"John, listen to me, and listen carefully. Linette may be in danger. There's a man seeking revenge against me. He knows about Linette."

"Cain, listen, I apologize, but I still can't hear you. Your voice keeps fading in and out. From what I understand, you're worried about Linette."

"Yes!" Cain screamed. Worried was the understatement of the year.

"I'm sure everything's fine. By the way, I understand congratulations are in order."

"Congratulations?" He didn't know if his wife was alive or dead, and his foreman was issuing congratulations. It didn't seem possible that in this nightmare there might be news that was good.

"Patty went to the doctor with Linette. So you're going to be a father."

Cain felt the sudden need to sit down. Linette hadn't said a word. Hadn't so much as hinted at her condition, not even when she might have used the information to keep him from leaving with Murphy. He closed his eyes and braced his forehead against the wall.

"Patty gave her one of those home test kits, but Linette wanted a GYN to confirm her condition. You'll like Dr. Adams. He delivered both our boys."

"Find Linette," Cain shouted into the receiver. "Keep her safe. I'll be there as soon as I can."

"You haven't got a thing to worry about," John assured him. "Just relax and you'll be home before you know it."

"I'm sorry, I didn't mean to alarm everyone," Linette said, looking to John and Patty Stamp. The couple stood at the end of her bed, looking slightly embarrassed for having walked uninvited into the house.

"It's just that Cain phoned and said he was worried about you," John explained.

"Worried. Whatever for?"

"John couldn't make it out. Apparently the line was bad," Patty said. "Men . . . I doubt we'll ever understand them."

"I haven't felt good all day. I think I might be coming down with a case of the flu." Linette felt mildly guilty. The phone had been ringing off the hook all morning. She'd finally unplugged it in order to sleep without constant interruptions.

"You say Cain's been trying to reach me?"

"That's what he said. He's on his way home. I don't understand it myself, but he wants you to stay with us until he's back."

"That's ridiculous."

"He's probably concerned about your being pregnant," Patty offered.

"He doesn't know," Linette admitted sheepishly. "I didn't tell him."

John Stamp buried his hands in his jean pockets and shifted his weight from one leg to the other. "He knows now. I didn't realize you were keeping it a secret. I congratulated him when he phoned."

"He knows?" This left Linette to wonder if this was the reason Cain was rushing back to Montana.

"He didn't act surprised."

"He wouldn't," Patty muttered.

Linette understood why. No man would willingly admit to his hired help that he'd been left in the dark about his own wife's condition.

"Did he say when to expect him?"

John rotated the brim of his hat in his large hands. "I can't rightly say. He seemed far more concerned about you staying with the missus and me for the next couple of days."

"But that's ridiculous."

"It's what Cain wants."

"I'm not leaving this house, John Stamp, no matter what instructions my husband gave you. Not when I can barely lift my head off this pillow. I don't know what's gotten into Cain, but I assure you, I can take care of myself."

Still John hesitated. "You're sure about that?"

"Positive."

"Then so be it. Just be sure you let Cain know that the decision was yours. I've seen that man when he's upset, and I don't want to be on the receiving end of his temper."

"You won't be," Linette promised.

"How are you feeling now?" Patty asked.

"My stomach's queasy." Her head throbbed with a killer headache, and she alternated between sweats and chills.

"When was the last time you had anything to eat?" Patty asked.

Linette shook her head. She didn't remember. "Morning, I guess." Tea and dry toast. Neither had stayed down for long, but she wasn't sure if that could be attributed to the flu or to morning sickness.

"It might be a good idea if I stayed the night with her," Linette heard Patty suggest to her husband. "You and the boys can manage one night without me, can't you?"

"No problem," John assured her.

"Patty, that isn't necessary. All I do is sleep. You can check on me every four or five hours if you want, but there's no need for you to spend the night here."

"Nonsense. Don't deprive me of this night of peace and quiet. It'd be like a minivacation for me." Patty kissed her husband and shooed him out of the room ahead of her. "I'll be back before you know it," her friend told her.

Linette tried to smile, but her head hurt and she discovered she was sleepy again. She'd rest her eyes a few moments, she told herself, and be awake by the time Patty returned.

"What is it?" Mallory asked as he raced toward the house.

"I think it's time," Francine said. "I felt this sharp pain, and the next thing I knew my water broke."

"Okay," Mallory said, sounding calm and collected when he was anything but. "We'll phone the doctor, get your suitcase, and head for the hospital."

"You phone the doctor," Francine said. "There are a couple of items I still need to stick inside my suitcase."

Mallory froze on the top step. "You mean to tell me

that after nine months you still aren't ready for this baby?"

Francine smiled calmly and kissed the corner of his mouth. "Don't panic. Everything's going to work out just fine."

Panic was an adequate word to describe Mallory's brewing emotions. They'd been waiting for this moment for weeks, and now that their child's birth was imminent, Mallory wasn't sure he was mentally prepared for the ordeal. Already it felt as if his bad leg were about to go out on him. He tried to disguise his fear from Francine and doubted his playacting worked.

As calmly as possible, he walked over to the phone and picked up the receiver. He looked up and punched out the Seattle number, then realized there was no dial tone. To make sure he wasn't imagining things, he tapped the plunger several times. Nothing.

The flashing red light of the answering machine blinked on and off, reminding him the phone had been working only moments earlier. He hit the switch on the machine and was surprised to hear Cain's voice.

"Mallory . . . Cain here. Listen, I hate . . . alarmist, but . . . danger . . . lurking about. Don't . . . chances. Enrique . . . revenge. I'll explain everything . . . worried . . . take care."

Mallory rewound the tape and listened to it a second time. The connection was bad. One thing was certain, Cain wouldn't have left the message if he didn't believe Mallory and Francine were in danger.

That explained what had happened to the lights and the phone.

"Tim?" Francine stood just inside the doorway to his small office. "What's wrong?"

"The line's dead." He couldn't very well tell his wife, who was in the first stages of labor, that they didn't dare leave the house for fear of what they'd encounter outside their back door.

"Someone's out there," Francine said without emotion. "Someone who wants you dead."

Mallory frowned. This woman never ceased to amaze him. "How'd you know that?"

"I heard part of Cain's message. Who's Enrique?"

"The hell if I know." Mallory ran a hand down his face. "He wouldn't be the first man who wanted to see me six feet under. He probably won't be the last."

"What are we going to do?" Francine asked, and bit into her lower lip. He admired her for staying calm and wasn't sure there were many women with her coolness.

"Don't worry about a thing," Mallory said, hoping to reassure her.

All at once Francine sucked in her breath and widened her eyes.

"What is it?" he asked, hurrying toward her. He gripped her hands in his own, surprised at the strength with which she held on to him.

After a moment she relaxed and smiled up at him. "That, my darling husband, was a labor pain."

"How strong was it? Is this your first one? How far apart are they?" His heart was pounding so loud, it was sounding out taps in his ear.

"Slow down," Francine advised, her hands squeezing his. "I'm fine, and so is the baby. I got a bit frightened there when my water broke, but everything's going to be all right. What's our situation like?"

Mallory closed his eyes in an effort to calm his heart and his head. "I don't know. My guess is that we're being watched."

"Can we leave the house?"

"I don't know that yet."

"I'm going to lie down," Francine said without emotion. "More water leaks out every time I have a pain, and I don't think it's a good idea for me to be walking around so much."

Mallory nodded and, taking her by the elbow, escorted her into the master bedroom. He left the lights out and helped Francine onto the mattress.

After adjusting the pillow and bringing her a fresh supply of towels, he asked, "Can I get you anything more?"

"I'm fine."

Unfortunately Mallory couldn't say the same thing. He was a wreck. He didn't know who or what lurked outside his front door. His wife was in labor, and for all his medical experience in the field, he didn't know shit about delivering a baby.

His phone was out of order. As far as he could see, only one option was left open to him. He had to discover for himself exactly what danger awaited them before he brought Francine out of their house.

His camouflage gear was tucked away in a trunk in the attic. Using a flashlight, Mallory climbed the stairs to where his equipment was stored. He changed clothes quickly and smeared a mixture of black and green paint over his face.

"Tim?"

He heard Francine timid voice almost immediately. "I'm coming, sweetheart."

Francine gasped and levered herself on one elbow when she saw him. A smile softened her features. "Just what do you think you're doing?"

"I don't know," he said sarcastically. "It seemed like a good time to dress up for Halloween. What the hell do you think I'm doing?"

"Just where are you going?"

"Outside."

All at once she bit into her lower lip, closed her eyes, and breathed in deeply. She seemed to be counting silently, her head moving almost imperceptibly. "How long will you be gone?"

Mallory knelt down on the floor beside the mattress. "I don't know. Will you be all right alone for a few moments?"

"Of course." How confident she sounded, as if she gave birth once a week the way some women did the washing. "Just promise me one thing."

"You got it."

"Please be careful, Tim," she whispered, her hands resting over her rounded tummy. "I don't want to have to deliver this baby on my own."

"You haven't got a thing to worry about, sweetheart," he said with supreme confidence. When it came to fighting for money, Mallory had been one of the best, but this time it was his family. He was protecting his wife and their child; he'd be more than good.

He'd be lethal.

◦   ◦   ◦

"Are you feeling any better?" Patty asked Linette. She sat on the edge of the mattress and held a tray in her hand. Linette noted that her neighbor had been thoughtful enough to bring her soup. Chicken noodle, from the looks of it, along with several soda crackers.

Somehow Linette managed a weak smile. She felt worse now than earlier. "I don't know that I can eat anything."

"Give it a try. A couple of spoonfuls of soup and we'll see how your stomach handles that. Have you been drinking plenty of liquids?"

Linette closed her eyes. She'd barely gotten out of bed in two days.

"Don't answer that, I can tell that you haven't. Here," Patty said, setting a glass of water next to the bedstand. She stayed with Linette until she managed two pitiful mouthfuls of the soup, and then shook her head, unable to take more.

"Is there anything else I can get you?"

"No. I'm fine. Really. I'll rest and feel better by morning."

"I'm sure you will," Patty said, brushing the hair away from Linette's brow. "At least your fever's broken. That's a good sign."

"See, I'm already on the road to recovery."

Cain was on his way home. Linette wasn't sure how she felt about that. He'd broken his word. He'd walked out on her. Now he seemed to think that all he needed to do was come rushing back and everything would return to the way it had been before.

Wrong.

What Cain failed to realize was that if he had the

option to pick and choose which promises he opted to keep, then she did as well.

Although she'd sold Wild and Wooly to Bonnie, she still felt very much a part of the business. Bonnie was a wonderful manager, but for all her business finesse, the older woman didn't have the strong personal relationship with the customers that Linette had worked so hard to build. From what Bonnie wrote, several of her former clients had asked about Linette. Even more had inquired about the evening classes she'd once taught.

As much as she tried to tell herself otherwise, Linette missed San Francisco and her life there. She could understand the desire Cain felt to go back to Deliverance Company. Murphy had offered him the perfect reason.

She could understand, but she couldn't accept that he'd broken his word. He'd left her sitting at home, twiddling her thumbs, waiting like a dutiful wife for her husband's return.

Patty came back a few minutes later and removed the dinner tray. She carried a thick novel with her. "I can't tell you how long I've been waiting to read this book. I'm going to soak in a bubble bath until my skin shrivels up into tiny wrinkles. You'll call me if you need me, won't you?"

"I'm feeling much better already," Linette assured her friend. "Take your time and enjoy yourself."

"I will. I can't remember the last time I took a bath without little green army men camped along the edge of the tub. This is going to be pure heaven."

It might have been the soup or the fact she had company, Linette didn't know which, but she did feel better.

Sitting up in bed, she reached down and plugged in the phone. To her amazement it rang almost immediately.

"Hello," she said into the mouthpiece.

"Linette? It's Cain."

"Hello. Cain?" She wished she didn't sound so pleased to hear from him, but she was, despite everything.

"Are you all right? Is someone there with you?"

Her hand tightened around the receiver. "I'm perfectly fine. I don't need a keeper, you know."

"Who's with you?"

"Patty Stamp."

Cain's response sounded very much like a string of swear words.

"Where are you?" she asked.

"I just landed in Florida. Listen, babe, I don't know if John fully understands the situation."

"What about Jack?"

"He hasn't been found yet," he answered impatiently.

"Then what are you doing back in the States?" She closed her eyes, already knowing the answer to her questions. "Is it because I'm pregnant?"

"Where's John?" he asked, ignoring her words.

"His house, I suppose."

Again his response was followed by a list of words she'd never heard her husband use in her presence before. Linette frowned, not knowing what to think.

"Cain, what's wrong? Patty said the sheriff stopped by to check up on me."

"Nothing you need to worry about," he said in a tight, strained voice that said otherwise. "I was thinking maybe it would be a good idea if you visited Nancy for a few days."

"My sister-in-law, Nancy Lewis? Whatever for? Cain, there's something you're not telling me." She could hear the alarm in his voice, and if she read him right, it had little or nothing to do with her pregnancy.

"Linette, listen, I made a mistake in leaving you. Jack's capture was a setup to get me out of the country."

"A setup?"

"There's a man by the name of Enrique who wants me to suffer, and the way to hurt me is through the people I love. He's knows I'm married, and I'm afraid it won't take him long to discover you're alone at the ranch."

Linette sucked in her breath. "Oh, dear God."

"I've already hired a couple of men to watch the house for any unusual activity, but for the love of heaven, Linette, don't trust anyone. I made a mistake in not making John understand the seriousness of the situation, but I didn't want to alarm him. I don't have the luxury of that any longer."

"What do you want me to do?" Linette's hand was trembling so badly that it was difficult to keep hold of the telephone.

"You'll be safer with Nancy. Get there as soon as you can make the arrangements."

"What about you?"

"I can take care of myself," he assured her. "But damn it all to hell, Linette, I can do a better job of it if I'm not worried sick about you."

She stiffened at his words. "I apologize for being such a burden to you."

He swore again, this time with regret. "I couldn't live with myself if anything were ever to happen to you or the baby. You're my life. I was a fool to have ever left you. Trust me, this isn't a mistake I'll soon forget."

"I sincerely hope not," she told him.

"I don't want you to worry, you're safe for now."

A thought suddenly occurred to her. "But how will I know the bad guys from the good guys?"

"You won't, but then it's unlikely that you'll ever see either. Just get to San Francisco as soon as you can."

"But what if I'm followed?"

"You will be," he assured her.

"I mean by the wrong people," she insisted. "I don't want to put Nancy or her family in jeopardy."

"You won't, babe, I assure you. Just promise me you'll take care of yourself."

"I will. You too."

"I will. I will."

"And Cain?"

"Yes."

"Get that son of a bitch."

Her husband chuckled. "My thoughts exactly."

18

There were two men, Mallory decided. The first had positioned himself outside the barn, and the second was stationed behind a tree and was studying the house. Mallory didn't know how much time he had before they made their move. He wasn't sure how much time Francine had, either.

Cold fury tightened his muscles until he had to force himself to relax. He didn't have the luxury of venting his anger. Just yet. Soon, though. Soon enough these men would pay.

Try as he might, Mallory couldn't get Francine out of his mind. It was vital on any mission to clear his head of distractions. His wife, her body twisted with labor pains, was more than a minor distraction, however.

She'd attempted to disguise her fears, but Mallory had seen through her brave front. She was frightened. Hell, so was he.

Mallory worked his way around the outside of the barn, circling the first man, taking care to remain as silent as possible. Only he wasn't quiet enough.

Mallory stopped breathing when a shadowy figure emerged from the barn no more than ten feet from where he was standing. For one horrible moment he assumed there was another man he hadn't known about and he'd blithely walked into their trap. His heart beat in slow, irregular thuds for several seconds until he realized the figure wasn't that of a man.

It was Bubba, his cantankerous male llama, the bane of his existence.

Bubba had heard Mallory. Apparently the llama assumed that if Mallory was in the vicinity, it must be feeding time, whether the sun was out or not.

Mallory's attention went to the gunman positioned alongside the barn. The man, dressed in army fatigues, lifted his head and peered into the thick darkness like a wild beast testing the wind. After a moment he signaled to the second man, who zigzagged across the yard before joining him.

Mallory was a safe distance from the pair but close enough to pick up the majority of their conversation. Luckily he was fluent in Spanish and understood every word.

"What the hell's that? It looks like a horse," the gunman stated.

"It's a llama."

"A what?"

"A llama."

"What's it doing out here?"

"Hell if I know."

The second man checked his weapon. "Are they still inside the house?"

"The woman is."

"What about Mallory?"

The second man was silent for a moment, then, "He knows we're here. He's out here somewhere, watching, waiting."

"Let's get the woman. That'll flush him out."

The other man's soft laugh lacked humor. "Trust me, neither one of us would make it two steps inside that house."

After a bit more, the two separated. The first man returned to his post near the front of the barn.

Thinking all these visitors should pay him heed, Bubba followed the gunman at a leisurely pace. He stopped and craned his long, sleek neck over the fence, seeking a handout. At first the man ignored the beast, but Bubba, bless his miserable, black heart, didn't take kindly to being ignored.

He spat at him.

The gunman swore and wiped the slime from his face.

If circumstances had been any different, Mallory would have laughed outright. The hired killer whirled around and cursed the llama vehemently. This was the moment Mallory had been waiting for. Bubba had provided the distraction he needed.

Mallory slithered forward from his hiding place. For an instant all he could think about was Francine and his need to get back to her. All he could see was his wife, waiting inside the house, frightened and worried. His wife, giving birth to his child alone, not knowing if he'd return.

Deliberately he wiped her image from his mind. No longer was he a husband. No longer was he a soon-to-be father. For that moment he was a trained killer.

The first man went down without knowing what had hit him. Mallory ducked behind the side of the barn and waited for the second hired gun to realize something was amiss.

All around him was silence. The kind that broke through sound barriers and rocked men's souls. The kind that throbbed like a breathing, living beast. The waiting game was about to end.

Inside, Francine's nails dug into her thick comforter and she struggled not to cry out as a contraction twisted her body. Tim had been gone for hours. Time lost meaning. Between pains she prayed for his safety, knowing that if anything happened to him, the killers would come for her and the baby.

Francine tried not to think about what was happening outside the house. Every ounce of energy she possessed was tunneled into the birthing process.

The pains became stronger. She didn't know how much longer she could withstand the agony without crying out. Yet she dared not.

"It wasn't supposed to happen like this," she whispered to her unborn child. Her hand rested on her tightening abdomen, which she rubbed, wanting to reassure both her and her infant.

The labor pain came on slowly, working its way from the small of her back around her abdomen, growing in intensity.

"Tim," she pleaded into the dark silence between deep, even breaths. "Please, oh, please hurry."

Knowing she'd have two, possibly three minutes to rest between contractions, Francine closed her eyes and tried to relax. She tried desperately not to think about what was happening outside her home. Tried not to think if her husband was alive or dead.

She wasn't one to give in to panic, but she felt the emotion bubbling up inside her like fizz ready to explode from a pop bottle.

Another contraction arrived, this one more acute than the others. Francine bore it as best she could. By the time the pain receded, she tasted blood and knew her teeth had cut into her lip.

A door slammed, followed by the sound of running footsteps. Before she drew another breath, Tim was kneeling on the floor next to her. He gathered her in his arms and hugged her as if he wanted never to let her go.

"Are you all right?" she asked, brushing the hair from his face, looking for signs that he might have been hurt.

"Yes. Yes. Let's get you to the hospital."

"No," she said softly, gripping his large hand with both of hers. "It's too late for that now."

"Too late? What do you mean, it's too late?"

She loved the way his voice rose and cracked with a loving kind of hysteria.

"In case you didn't know, we're about to have a baby," she told him softly, her strength fading.

"I've known that for close to nine months. I was there in the beginning, remember?" He spoke fast, running the words together.

"I mean we're about to have a baby *soon*."

"How soon?" He was on his feet and backing away from her as if he suspected what she had was contagious.

"Within the hour, I'd guess. The pains are less than two minutes apart. I'm about to enter the second stage of labor." Briefly she closed her eyes, sensing his fear, facing her own. "I'm going to need your help."

Tim looked down on her as though he were tempted to turn and run. Again he knelt on the floor beside her and gripped her hands.

"Tell me what you want me to do."

She smiled up at him through her tears. "I love you, Tim Mallory."

"You must," he agreed, rolling up the sleeves of his camouflage shirt. "Otherwise you wouldn't be willing to go through this."

John Stamp carried Linette's suitcase out to the car and glanced about him suspiciously. "You're sure about driving out of here alone?" he asked as if he were looking for her to change her mind. He stood back, waiting for her reply.

"I'll be fine," Linette assured him. She didn't say it, but it was probably safer as well for John and the Stamp family that she left.

John looked to his wife as if seeking confirmation. Patty didn't seem any more confident than her husband. "This doesn't seem right to me," she said to her husband. "I don't see anyone out here who's going to protect you."

"Cain said I should go. Now stop worrying."

"I wish Cain had said something to *me*," John muttered.

"Is there a phone number where I can reach you?" Patty asked Linette.

Linette hesitated, uncertain she should give out Nancy's phone number. "I'm feeling much better now, don't fret. I'll give you a call once I'm settled." She opened the car door and slipped inside the driver's side. John held the door open, and it seemed to Linette that he was looking for an excuse to keep her.

"You promise to keep in touch?" Patty asked a second time, her voice slightly higher than normal.

Linette nodded. She reached for the door, and John released it reluctantly. He wrapped his arm around his wife's shoulder, and the pair stepped back as Linette started the engine. The driveway had never seemed so long as when she pulled out of the yard.

Once on the main road, Linette reached for the radio and turned on the local station. Anything to fill the silence. Anything to take her mind off who might be watching her every move.

She'd phoned early that morning and booked the first available flight to San Francisco. A call to Nancy and Rob had assured her of a warm welcome. Cain had promised to contact her in San Francisco to be sure she'd arrived safely.

A glance in her rearview mirror revealed a black luxury car coming behind her at a fast rate of speed. Her heart started to pound, but she forced herself to repeat Cain's reassurances. He'd promised her that she would never see either the good or the bad guys.

The car gained speed. Linette certainly hoped these folks were patient because it might be several miles before there was a chance to pass her on these twisty, curvy roads.

The sedan was practically on her bumper. Suspicious, Linette sped up. The other car increased its speed. Her nervousness mounted with every moment. At long last the car chose to go around her. Linette wondered at their wisdom. The edge of the road led to a steep embankment, and it made her nervous to look over the side. It had always bothered her to drive this stretch of road without guardrails.

The vehicle pulled alongside her, and Linette knew then that something was very wrong. The two men in the car were looking at her. The two cars were so close, their side panels touched.

Linette refused to give ground. There was none to give. Another two or three feet and she'd be forced over the embankment.

Her heart raced like an oil drill pumping out raw crude. Her fingers felt as if they were fused to the steering column.

So much for Cain's reassurances. This wasn't a silly game played by two overgrown teenagers. These men were attempting to kill her.

Adrenaline shot through Linette like liquid fire. The sedan slammed hard against the side of her vehicle, the hit jolting her. Linette screamed in terror at the sound of metal scraping against metal. Her hands gripped the steering wheel as firmly as she'd hold on to a life preserver in a sea storm.

The wheels on the right side of the car were off the road now, spitting up gravel and dirt. She'd lost ground, precious inches.

She realized she wasn't going to be able to save herself. She'd barely talked to Cain about their baby. She hadn't had the chance to tell her husband that she'd never been more pleased about anything. Her baby. She refused to allow these men to destroy her child.

From some reserve of strength and determination she hadn't known she possessed, Linette turned the car directly into the other vehicle. Sparks flew from the clash of steel. Again she was jarred; she felt her head whip to the side and slam against the window. Struggling to remain conscious, she decided she wasn't going to let them kill her without putting up a hell of a fight.

Her concentration was absorbed in staying on the road. In staying alive. All at once, without warning, she noticed a third vehicle headed straight toward her. A head-on collision was inevitable.

Everything happened in slow motion. Linette slammed on her brakes and instinctively raised her arms to protect her face. The instant her hands were off the steering wheel, the car veered to the right. Two wheels teetered on the ledge of the embankment before cata-pulting over.

Linette screamed as the car rolled again and again and again. Her cries reverberated inside the car, playing back to her as if from a Swiss mountainside.

Then she knew nothing.

It hurt to breathe. Jack Keller suspected he had four broken ribs and an equal number of broken, nailless fingers. This was what he got for being so stupid. He'd walked right into that trap. After all his years of training, he knew better than to do his thinking with his pecker.

His one good finger on his right hand tentatively investigated the extent of his injuries, and he felt one rib bone jutting out against his skin. He moaned softly. He tried to open his eyes, but both were swollen shut. What he did manage to see between the narrow sliver of light wasn't encouraging. It looked as if he were behind bars. How long he'd been there, he could only speculate. Too long.

He heard a pair of voices from the other side of the wall. One sounded vaguely familiar. Enrique's? No, he decided. He hadn't seen the drug lord in several days and had no wish to make the other man's acquaintance again.

Enrique had been full of questions about Cain. Jack had pretended not to know anything. His silence had cost him dearly. He'd talked plenty, but he hadn't told them anything they could use against Cain.

The faintly familiar voice drifted toward Jack a second time. If he didn't know better, he'd think it was Murphy. But even Murphy's accent was better than that.

It wasn't Murphy. It couldn't be. No one knew where Jack was. This stinkhole was too deep for him to ever be found. The way he figured, with his internal injuries, he wouldn't last much longer anyway.

He had regrets. Didn't everyone? He thought about his life. The turns in the road he'd taken, the choices he'd made. Good and bad. He would have preferred to live to a ripe old age and pass on with a loving family gathered around his bedside. Instead he was likely to die without anyone ever learning what had happened to him. He'd decided, early in his army career, to live by the sword. He expected to die by it. And he would.

Consciousness started to fade. Jack welcomed the oblivion.

A war seemed to be going on outside his door. Fitting, really, that he should go out surrounded by gunfire. The door burst open, and Jack feared Enrique's gorillas had come to torture him again.

"Jack."

It was Murphy.

"It's about time," he mumbled.

"Sweet Jesus, what have they done to you?"

Jack tried to smile. He knew he must look like shit. Well, that adequately described the way he felt.

"Never mind what you look like," Murphy said, chuckling. "You never were that good-looking anyway."

Tim wiped a cool cloth over Francine's face. "How are we doing?" he asked, and his voice shook slightly, as if he'd paid a heavy penalty for each of her contractions.

Her eyes remained closed, but she managed a weak smile. "So far so good." Her breathing was hard and labored. Giving birth was by far the most draining ordeal of her life.

A pain gripped her at the small of her back, and she whimpered, unable to disguise her agony as the contraction knotted her uterus, attempting to force the baby from her body. By the time the last of the pain had ebbed away, she was panting and weak.

"Can you see the baby's head?" she asked when she had her breath back.

Tim moved to the foot of the mattress. "Yes," he cried excitedly, sounding shocked and more than a little frightened. "The baby's almost here."

"I know," Francine whispered.

The time between contractions seemed like none at all. The next one gripped her body like a vise, and she had the strong urge to push. Her hands found and locked around the rails of the headboard as she bore down with all her might. The effort half lifted her from the bed.

"Good, sweetheart, good," Tim praised her.

After the next contraction, she felt the baby's head spill between her legs. Tim's gentle hands cradled their infant's tiny head. A mewling cry filled the room as their child drew its first breath.

"We have a son," Tim announced in a strangled voice that sounded nothing like his own.

Rising up on her elbows, Francine watched as her husband severed the umbilical cord and gently wrapped their freshly washed child in a soft, warm blanket. Tears fell unrestrained down her husband's cheeks as he gazed upon his son.

"A boy," he repeated, as if he didn't quite believe it even now. Taking exquisite care, he placed their child in Francine's waiting arms.

"He's beautiful," she whispered, weeping silently.

"It's little wonder when you're his mother."

Francine stared down at her son, completely enraptured by the pink, crinkly face topped with a crown of dark hair. Then she unwrapped the blanket to inspect his hands and feet, count his fingers and toes.

"I told you he was a boy," Tim said, as if she'd doubted his word.

"I love you, Tim Mallory," she whispered through her tears. She felt shaken by the enormity of the love that swept through her for her husband and for her baby. Never had she experienced anything so powerful.

Tim sat on the mattress and wrapped his arm around

her shoulders. "If you aren't partial to any name, I'd like to suggest one."

"Sure," she said, eager to hear his suggestion.

Tim smiled and gently kissed the crown of her head. "How about Bubba?"

19

Knowing Linette was safely on her way to San Francisco left Cain free to hunt down Enrique. He tracked the man deep into the heart of Central America.

He ended up in a known hangout of Enrique's, a cantina. Wearing a disguise, Cain pretended he was there to quench his thirst. Knowing it was best not to ask questions, he made himself comfortable and listened in on the conversations around him. Within a few hours Cain learned everything he needed to know. As he'd guessed, Enrique was in town. He left his killing to others—not that he didn't have the taste for it himself, but there were problems waiting for him in the States and he dared not take the chance of crossing the borders.

By nightfall Pretty Boy stopped by the cantina himself, his mood jubilant. Before long he had his arm around the waist of a lusty señorita, and it soon became apparent the two had matters other than conversation on their minds.

Cain watched Enrique closely from the shadowy corner in the back of the room. Pretty Boy was both careless and overconfident as he stood and followed the woman out of the bar.

One of his men looked up and called out in Spanish, "Hey, man. When you're through, I'll have a turn with her myself."

Enrique laughed, and his hand stroked the woman's slim buttocks. "Be patient, my friend," he said. "I have the feeling this may take a very long time."

His men booed, and in an effort to appease them, Enrique ordered a fresh round of drinks.

Cain left by means of the side door and made certain he wasn't being followed. By now Jack would have been rescued and Linette was safely tucked away with family. He followed the couple for several blocks.

"I understand you've been looking for me," Cain said, stepping close behind the other man.

Pretty Boy froze, then viciously pushed the woman away from him before he turned to face Cain. He swore violently, then smiled, revealing even white teeth in a humorless display.

Cain smiled in return, enjoying the advantage of surprise. "You're stupid," he told the other man, "to let yourself get caught like this. I would have thought better of you."

"I'm celebrating," Enrique told him, gesturing with his hand. "The news of your wife's death reached me this afternoon." He laughed sadistically. "Perhaps you should join her, McClellan." He pulled a gun from his pocket and fired the weapon in rapid succession.

Cain flung himself to the ground, shooting as he went

down. It was over within seconds. Enrique lay dead on the dusty street, his eyes staring blankly into the night sky.

Cain studied the man and felt no thrill in the death. No thrill in eliminating one who brought only suffering and heartache into the world.

A shout could be heard in the distance, and Cain made haste leaving town. He rendezvoused with Murphy an hour later.

"He's dead," Cain said without expression.

"Good." Murphy's eyes refused to meet Cain's. "Listen, I have some bad news. It's about Linette. You'd best get back to Montana fast."

The hours it took him to reach Montana were the longest of his life. Cain paced the hospital waiting room like a beast until an older couple glared at him, silently requesting that he stop.

The woman left the room, and minutes later a chaplain came into the area.

"Are you all right, son?" asked the minister, claiming the vacant chair next to Cain.

Cain looked over at the compassionate man, and his throat constricted. He wasn't anywhere close to being all right. Fear and anger festered inside him like a raging infection. Rarely had he tasted hate in such a bitter form.

"I'm fine," Cain said tightly, and clenched his fists so hard that the blood drained from his fingers. He stood then, because sitting for any length of time was impossible.

"Is there someone I can phone for you?"

"No one." Cain had sent both John and Patty Stamp home for fear his frustrations would spill over onto them. Neither deserved to receive the brunt of his anger.

The minister gently pressed his hand on Cain's shoulder. "The chapel's on the bottom floor if you change your mind. I'll be there until six this evening."

Cain nodded, eager for the man to leave him alone. The minister left, and Cain returned to the chair and buried his face in his hands. He hadn't slept in two nights. Hadn't been able to close his eyes without picturing Linette being pulled from the wreckage that had once been their car.

He could hear her screams of terror, feel her pain. The torment of those last moments hounded him like an evil spirit.

All this had happened to his wife because of him. Because of what he was and what he did.

A shuffle of footsteps attracted his attention, and Cain looked up to find Murphy standing just inside the doorway. He walked across the room and sat down next to Cain.

"Enrique's henchmen have been rounded up," he announced.

Cain regretted that he hadn't had the pleasure of killing the sons of bitches himself. "What about Jack?"

"He's been better."

"Is he going to make it all right?"

"Sure. Give him a month or two and he'll be good as new."

"I'm glad to hear it."

Murphy leaned forward and braced his elbows against his knees. "What about Linette?"

Pain tightened his chest, and Cain found he couldn't

answer. He shrugged. She'd been badly hurt, but it could have been much worse. He felt helpless to reach her, helpless to comfort her. The guilt of knowing he was the one responsible for what had happened ate at him like sharks in a feeding frenzy.

The two men sat side by side without speaking for the next hour. No sooner had Murphy left than Linette's physician stepped into the room.

Cain stood, his eyes connecting with the other man's. He instinctively squared his shoulders, dreading the worst.

"I'm sorry, but we couldn't save the baby. We did everything possible."

"My wife?"

"She's resting comfortably for now."

Cain's legs felt as if they'd gone out from under him, and he slumped onto the chair. The physician sat next to him, going over the extent of injuries. The prognosis for a complete recovery was excellent.

"When can I see her?"

"Soon. Let her sleep for now, that's what she needs most. Her body's been badly battered. The seat belt and air bag saved her, but the shock of losing the baby has taken its toll. I suggest you let her sleep."

Cain would have agreed to anything just then. "Fine. I'll be here."

A few more hours later Linette squinted against the bright light and rolled her head to one side. She discovered Cain sprawled on the red vinyl chair next to her hospital bed, asleep. His head drooped to one side and his arm dangled over the cushioned armrest, his knuckles brushing the polished floor.

She stared at her husband for several moments. The memory of everything that had happened flooded her mind. She'd lost the child. Nothing mattered but her baby. Not the men who'd attempted to murder her, not the fate of the occupants of the other vehicle. Nothing. Only the death of her child.

It was easier to close her eyes and sink back into a drug-induced sleep than deal with reality.

The next time Linette woke up, Cain was standing at her bedside, her hand cradled between both of his.

"Hello, honey," he whispered.

She blinked up at him, finding the lights inordinately bright. "The baby," she said. There was no question in her voice, only certainty.

His response seemed to require a long time. "There'll be other children," he said gently.

"I wanted this baby," she said, choking on a sob.

"I wanted this baby, too."

His words were meant to reassure her, but she felt no comfort, only pain, only grief, her old friends. After Michael's death, Linette had given up the hope of remarrying and having children. Then she'd met and married Cain, and it seemed that she'd been given a second chance at love and life. Now she realized it was only a second chance at grieving. A second chance of dealing with loss and pain.

Cain raised her hand to his face and pressed it against his cheek. "The sooner we get you home the better."

"Enrique?"

"Dead."

She bit into her lower lip, amazed at the amount of hate she felt for the dead man. "I hope he rots in hell."

"I don't think there's any question of that."

"The other people in the accident?"

"They weren't hurt. As for the men who ran you off the road, they're sitting in a jail cell, and I sincerely doubt that they'll see anything on this side of the bars for a good long while. It seems they're wanted for a long list of offenses."

"Good," she said without much enthusiasm. "What about the men you hired to protect me?"

"It doesn't matter, honey, nothing does but you getting well."

"Tell me," she said, louder this time, draining her strength.

Cain's eyes became dark and fierce. "Their bodies were found yesterday."

Linette closed her eyes. "Dear God."

"You don't need to worry. It's over now. Neither Enrique nor anyone else is ever going to hurt us again."

All this was more than Linette could take in at one time. She felt as though the world were caving in on her.

Physically Linette healed, but the emotional scars cut deep grooves into her heart. She grieved for the loss of her child the way she'd grieved for the husband who'd been taken in his prime. She had no energy, no will.

Cain was at her bedside every day. The room was crammed full of flowers, stuffed animals, gifts galore. Linette thanked him, but none of the trinkets he brought her meant a thing.

"Linette, please," he said the night before he was scheduled to take her home from the hospital. "What is it?"

She shook her head. The world felt gray and cold, and

even the warmth of Cain's love couldn't chase away the chill.

"Tell me." He squatted in front of her and gripped her hands in his. "I can make it right, whatever it is."

"You can't fix this," she said through her misery.

"I can't bear to see you so unhappy. Are you in pain?"

She shook her head. She was in pain yes, but not the kind that a kiss and a Band-Aid would cure. This agony was familiar, one she'd lived with those first weeks and months after losing Michael.

"What can I do to help you?"

Linette closed her eyes. "I want my baby."

Defeated, Cain buried his head in her lap.

Home offered little solace. Linette sat and stared into the distance. She ate only because it was easier to give in to Cain's urging than to argue. Each day she gained a little more strength, but she hadn't the will or the conviction to pull herself out of the lethargy that trapped her emotions.

At night Cain held her in his arms. He hadn't attempted to make love to her since the accident, in the beginning for practical reasons, later because she had no desire. It had died with their unborn child.

Their once active sex life came to a grinding halt. She shied away from his kisses, and soon he stopped offering them. Linette suspected Cain was losing patience with her, but she couldn't help herself.

Then one afternoon, about three months after the accident, when spring seemed to burst overnight onto the countryside, Cain came into the house for dinner.

"You'll never guess what I found this afternoon," he said conversationally, sitting down at the table and reaching for the bread. "A stray calf. It looks like her mother's dead. I brought her into the barn for the night."

"Her mother's dead?"

"John says this sort of thing is common. I'll bottle-feed her for a few days and then sell her at the auction."

After dinner dishes, Linette wandered out to the barn, thinking she'd find an adorable calf to pet. It might be fun to watch Cain feed it a bottle, she mused.

Instead of a cute, cuddly calf, Linette found a scroungy-looking thing leaning against the rail, its head drooping to the ground. It was ugly and filthy with cuts and mud caked all across its back side.

"You poor baby," Linette murmured.

Cain came out of the shed with a milk bottle, looking none too pleased to have to deal with a stray after a long day on the trail. "John said this should work."

"I'll do it," Linette found herself offering.

Cain looked at her as if he weren't sure he'd heard her correctly. "You're sure?"

Linette offered him a small smile and reached for the makeshift bottle. Although Cain made an excuse and left her, Linette knew he wasn't far away. More than likely he was waiting to come running when she called.

"Hello there, Funny Face," she said gently, moving into the pen where the calf waited. She patted her hand against the top of its head. Not having been around live-stock much, she wasn't sure what to expect.

She certainly didn't anticipate feeding a calf from an old milk bottle to be as easy as it turned out. Funny Face took to the improvised method as if born to it. She drank the last drop and then raised her ugly face to look at Linette with big brown eyes.

The following day, just before Cain had left with John Stamp, Linette asked, "What about the stray?"

Cain muttered something under his breath. "I forgot to feed her. Could you give her another bottle for me?"

She nodded, when that was what she'd wanted him to ask her all along. Why she should be so shy about it, she didn't know.

After the men were gone Linette wandered out to the barn. Funny Face rushed to the gate to greet her. For the next few days the calf mewled and came running the instant she caught sight of Linette.

Despite her depression, Linette found herself smiling at the ugly heifer. The calf wasn't so much interested in her as she was in the milk bottle.

After a week, when Funny Face had finished her morning feeding, Linette decided to give the heifer a long overdue bath. The entire back side of the stray was caked in thick, dark mud.

By the time she finished, Linette was convinced all she'd done was transfer the mud from Funny Face to herself. Cain found her like that, on her knees on the barn floor, brushing the snarls out of the calf's tangled hair, talking to the disgruntled stray in soothing tones.

"Don't you dare laugh at me, Cain McClellan," Linette warned. After wrestling with a stray calf for the last two hours, she was in no mood to be teased over her appearance.

"I have no intention of laughing at you," Cain said, letting himself into the gate. "If anything, I was thinking of kissing you."

"Kissing me . . . when I look like this?" Linette gazed down upon her mud-speckled shirt and water-soaked jeans. "Either you're desperate for a kiss or blind to my many faults."

"Both," he assured her.

Deliberately he removed the brush from her hand and set it aside. Then he gathered her in his arms and slowly, in painstaking inches, lowered his mouth to hers.

It had been weeks since he'd touched her this way. Weeks since she'd wanted him. But she desired him now with a strength that left her shaking.

Cain took her mouth fully, slanting his lips across hers, giving her his tongue. The hot rush of sensation took the starch out of Linette's knees, and she clung to him.

"You left me," she whispered, trembling. "You broke your word and left."

"I was wrong," he whispered huskily. "I'll never do it again."

"How can I believe you?"

Cain gently relaxed his hold on her. "I can't give you a single reason why you should. I've been so afraid I've ruined everything with my selfishness. It's because of me that we lost the baby. It's because of me that you were in the car accident. I don't know that I'll ever be able to forget that."

"It's over now."

"But it isn't," Cain said bitterly. "Each night I hold you in my arms and wonder if our lives will ever be the same again. If I were any kind of man, I'd release you, but I haven't got the courage to let you go. I need you too damn much."

"I need you, too."

"I'm asking for a second chance. God knows I don't

deserve it, but I've learned my lesson, honey. I discovered what Mallory did when he realized he was in love with Francine. I didn't have the heart for fighting anymore. I left it with you."

"You're sure this time?"

"Positive. There's nothing more I want in this life than to settle down on this ranch with you at my side. I like it. Even John's surprised by how well I've taken to managing a herd." He laced his hands together at the small of her back. "But it means nothing without you. Are you willing to give me a second chance?" He brushed his lips close to her ear. "I promise to make it worth your while."

Linette snuggled close into her husband. "I'm willing to put the past behind us." All at once the future looked clear and bright.

"Let's go inside," Cain said, breathing hard and fast.

"I'm a mess."

"You're the most beautiful woman in the world." He captured her lower lip between his teeth and sucked gently.

"Do you mean to have your way with me, Cain McClellan?"

"Without a doubt."

"It isn't even noon." She didn't know why she was putting up arguments when she was as eager for her husband as he was for her.

"I don't care what time it is."

"Eleven-fifteen."

Cain chuckled. "You know what they say about striking when the iron is hot." He kissed her again and it was wet and wild and Linette swore the two of them sizzled together.

Their mouths were fused together when Cain hoisted her into his arms and carried her across the barnyard and directly into the house.

"Take off your spurs," Linette cried as he started across her kitchen floor.

Muttering under his breath, Cain set her back on her feet and removed his spurs. Then, for no reason she could think of, he sat down and with some difficulty removed his cowboy boots as well.

"Anything else?" he asked.

Linette laughed. "Oh, yes, lots more."

Cain grinned and lifted her into his arms once again. He couldn't seem to make it more than two or three stair steps before he'd stop and kiss her. Their lips mated, and he used the time to unfasten another button of her western-style blouse. By the time they reached the top of the stairway, she was half naked, embarrassed someone might see her in her skimpy underwear.

"I need a bath," she protested.

"Later," he promised, and carried her into their bedroom. He laid her on the bed and stared down on her. His eyes were bright with need, bright with love.

"I've missed you so damn much," he whispered.

Linette helped him undress, her hands aggressively removing his clothes. His hips were taut and lean, and the evidence of exactly how much he'd missed her was all too evident.

Linette drew her husband on top of her, and wet, warm feelings of welcome erupted inside of her. He slid between her legs and with restrained savagery sank into her.

Linette cried out at the unexpected rush of pleasure.

Cain emitted a low, guttural sound. His hips began an immediate rhythm, the beat strong and steady. Linette followed his lead, her body surging up to meet his eager thrusts. It had been so long. She'd forgotten how good the lovemaking was between them, how good they were together.

She needed him now as never before, as she might possibly never need him again.

Her release came like an explosion. She cried out and whimpered and clung to him, crying and laughing both at once. Cain followed her shortly and seemed to share the same cataclysmic experience.

Cain's breathing was hard and fast as he lay sprawled across her. He was heavy, but she needed the heavy feel of him. Needed him. It felt good to say that, if only to herself.

Linette smiled up at her husband.

He smiled down on her, then kissed her long and sweetly with an uncharacteristic lack of haste. Tunneling his fingers through her hair, he raised his mouth a mere inch from hers.

"What changed?"

She knew what he was asking but wasn't sure she had the answer. "Funny Face needed me," was the only explanation she had to offer.

"Hell, woman, I've been walking around like a wounded calf for three months, and it didn't so much as faze you."

"We're going to be all right now," she said, brushing the hair from his temples. "Everything's going to be fine."

"I'll never leave you again," Cain promised, and he said the words as if speaking a solemn vow.

"I know." She became thoughtful, thinking of the men of Deliverance Company. "Murphy's not so bad, you know. He's just a poor misguided soul. What he really needs is a wife to straighten him out."

"Is that what you've done to me? Straightened me out?"

Linette had to think about that. Smiling, she shook her head. "No. All I had to do was love you."

Cain buried his face in her neck and linked their bodies. "Let me love you again."

"Yes," she whispered, placing her arms around his neck. Soon her body sang and her breathing stopped, only to start again in startled gasps of ecstasy. All that was necessary was love. She had the feeling it would be all they needed the rest of their lives.

Sooner Or Later

To my friends who love the smell of chlorine in the morning as much as I do.

Rachel Williams, Audrey Rugh, Lorraine Reece, Joyce Hudson, Leta Taylor, Marjorie Johnson, Debbie Noble, Mary Cammin, Maria Houston, Janet Hane, Sue Felix, Mark Ryan, Jessie Truax, Greg Northcutt, Bill Irvine, Per Johnson, and Kathy Davis for watching over us all.

ACKNOWLEDGMENTS

Every now and again a writer is challenged with a hero like Murphy. The man drove me bananas in *Someday Soon* and refused to leave me alone until I promised him his own book. I knew from the beginning that it would take a special woman to win this chauvinist's heart. Soon Letty was born in my mind. A woman of grit and faith. A woman with a mission. The story came, but I struggled with the title. Then on New Year's Eve my husband got tickets for us to see a sixties musical review. Among those playing was Gary Puckett. He came on stage and sang one of his earlier hits. The lyrics leaped out—*sooner or later love is gonna get you*. My husband assumed I was overcome with memories when I stood up and cheered, but my excitement was because I'd found the perfect title. *Sooner or Later*. Murphy had challenged the fates and by heaven love got him! I hope you'll come to love him, too.

My gratitude to those who lent a helping hand along the way. My editor, Carolyn Marino, for her blue pen and her insights. To Susan Wiggs for critiquing the manuscript for me. Irene Goodman, my agent, who either pats me on the shoulder or kicks me in the butt, depending on what I need most. As always to Wayne for twenty-seven years of love and support. I don't know of any writer who's been blessed with more loyal readers. Your letters have touched my heart.

Prologue

A woman's frantic scream pierced Luke Madden's slumber. He bolted upright and shook his head, hoping to clear the sleepy fog from his brain.

The rumors had been rampant for weeks, filled with threats of a military coup, but the Zarcero government was handling the situation competently. Less than a week ago, Luke had personally been assured by President Cartago that there was no need for concern.

The screech of rapid-fire gunshots was followed by shrieks of horror and outrage.

Luke threw back the lone sheet and reached for his pants. The hair on the back of his neck stood straight out as the sound of booted feet slapped on the boardwalk outside his window.

No sooner had he yanked up the zipper than his door slammed open. A crazy-eyed soldier toting an Uzi stormed into Luke's bedroom, screaming at him in hysterical Spanish, demanding that he join the others in the compound.

The first thought that flashed into Luke's mind was that he was going to die.

Away from home. Away from his twin sister.

In that split second, he realized how desperately he longed to live. A mental image of Rosita, the brown-eyed beauty he loved and planned to marry, filtered into his thoughts as he rushed to follow the guerrilla's orders.

Chaos greeted him outside. Frightened, desperate women huddled in a circle by the fountain, protecting their children. Frantically Luke searched for Rosita and was relieved when he found her with the other women.

The lifeless body of Ramón Hermosa lay sprawled in a pool of blood outside the chapel doors. Mowed down by hate. Murdered in the name of progress. The dead man's open eyes stared blankly into the night.

Ramón. *Dear God, not Ramón.* Anger surged through Luke like an electric current. The kind old man was no threat to anyone.

"What is it you want?" Luke cried out, clenching his fists.

Three men, all heavily armed, approached him. One slammed the butt of his rifle against Luke's shoulder, shoving him closer to the women. Intense pain spiraled down his arm.

"What do you want?" Luke repeated, ignoring the danger to himself.

The three men parted when an officer approached.

Hate gleamed in their commander's eyes as he studied Luke. Luke could feel the other man's loathing as keenly as he'd once felt Rosita's love.

"I understand you are a friend of our president," the commander spat out. Slowly a sinister, evil smile edged up the sides of his mouth. "Or should I say *former* president."

"This is a mission," Luke explained, gesturing toward the church. "I have nothing to do with politics."

"You should have thought of that before you made friends with José Cartago. You will pay dearly for that friendship, *Señor.* Very dearly indeed."

He removed a polished pistol from his holster and pointed it at Luke's head.

"No, for the love of God, *no!*" Rosita screamed, and raced across the grounds. Sobbing, she threw herself at the commander's feet. "Please, I beg of you in the name of the Virgin Mother, I plead with you not to do this."

But it was too late, Luke realized. He was a dead man.

1

"*I'm willing to pay you* for your services."

"Let me see if I understand you correctly," Murphy said, eyeing the prim and oh-so-proper postmistress who held his mail hostage. "You want *me* to accompany you to Zarcero?"

The woman was nuts, Murphy decided. There were no two ways about it. Letty Madden, postmistress of Boothill, Texas, was a prime candidate for the loony bin.

She looked up at him from behind her scarred oak desk in her private office, her brown eyes as dark as bittersweet chocolate. This female-in-distress performance might weaken another man's defenses, but not Murphy's. He had no intention of interrupting a well-deserved rest for some woman with an itch up her butt, seeking adventure.

His opinion of the opposite sex had never been high,

and since his friends Cain and Mallory had both married, his attitude was even worse. It'd take more than the fluttering of this postmistress's eyelashes for him to traipse through some jungle on a wild-goose chase.

"You don't understand," she insisted.

Murphy understood all right; he just didn't happen to be interested in the job. Besides, the postmistress wouldn't earn enough money in two lifetimes to afford him or the services of Deliverance Company.

"It's my brother," she continued, and bit into her trembling lower lip.

A nice touch, Murphy mused skeptically, but it wouldn't change his mind.

"He's a missionary."

She actually managed to look as though she were on the verge of weeping. She was good, Murphy gave her that much. Sincerity all but oozed from her pores.

"Since the Zarceran government collapsed, no one in the State Department or CIA can tell me what's happened to him. The phone lines are down, and now the United States has severed diplomatic relations. The people in the State Department won't even talk to me anymore. But I refuse to forget my brother."

"I can't help you." He didn't mean to be rude, or heartless, but he simply wasn't interested. He'd already told her as much three times, but she'd apparently opted not to believe him.

This was the first of several errors on her part. Murphy was a man who meant what he said. If her brother was stupid enough to plant himself in a country on the verge of political collapse, then he deserved what he got.

"Please," she added with a soft, breathless quality to her voice, "won't you reconsider?"

Murphy heaved an impatient sigh. The last thing he'd expected when he stopped off to retrieve his mail was to be cornered by one of Boothill's most virtuous citizens.

"You can help me," she insisted, her voice elevating with entreaty. "It's just that you won't. It isn't as if I'm asking you to do this out of the kindness of your heart!"

Good thing, because Murphy's nature didn't lean toward the charitable.

"I said I'd pay you, and I meant it. I realize a man of your expertise doesn't come cheap, and—"

"My expertise?" No one in Boothill knew what he did for a living, and that was the way he wanted it.

"You don't honestly think I don't know what you are, do you?" Her chin came up a notch, as if he'd insulted her intelligence. "I'm not stupid, Mr. Murphy. There are certain matters one cannot help but notice when sorting the mail. You're a soldier of fortune."

She said the words as though they made her mouth dirty. No doubt this lily white sister of a missionary had never sunk to such despicable levels before now. Murphy, lowlife that he was, loved it. He certainly didn't expect a decent, God-fearing woman like Letty Madden would encourage business dealings with the likes of him.

"I'll pay you," she offered again. "Anything you ask."

He snorted softly and purposely leveled his gaze at her breasts, wanting to shock her.

"I know all about Deliverance Company."

That caught Murphy's interest. "You do, do you?"

She stiffened. "Mr. Murphy, please, my brother is all I have. My parents . . . my father died four years ago and there's only Luke and me."

Murphy wasn't keen on delivering a few home truths, but it seemed necessary. "Listen, I'm sorry about your brother being in Zarcero. But nothing you say or do now is going to change the fact that the country's in chaos.

"If you're seeking my advice, then I'll give it. You'd be wasting your time, energy, and finances to look for your brother at this late date. The chances are he's been dead two weeks or more."

"No," she said with such vehemence that Murphy flinched. "Luke's my twin. I'd know if he were dead. I'd feel it here." She slapped her clenched fist over her heart, and her shoulders heaved with the strength of her conviction. "Believe me, Mr. Murphy, Luke's alive."

Murphy had no desire to argue with her. She could believe anything she damn well pleased, and if it comforted her to think her brother had survived the coup, so be it.

"Can I have my mail now?" he asked impatiently, and stretched out his arm.

Letty reluctantly handed him the few pieces. "Is there anything I can say or do to convince you to take on this assignment?" she asked, and boldly held his eyes.

"Not one damn thing." Now that he had what he'd come for, he turned and walked out the door. Before he left the post office, he glanced over his shoulder and experienced a twinge of regret when he saw her head bowed in defeat. He couldn't help feeling bad for her and her brother, but not enough that he'd sacrifice the first time he'd had free in months.

By the time Murphy arrived home twenty minutes later, his sympathy for the postmistress's plight had waned. He'd noticed her before, plenty of times. She was exactly the type of woman he avoided most. Those goody-goody, holier-than-thou ones were the worst.

Letty Madden was a pretty thing, or could be, if she'd ever stop apologizing for being a woman. She wore her long hair away from her face, as if pulling it tight enough against her head might erase any sign of wrinkles. The plain postal uniforms did nothing to enhance what nature had generously given her. If she wore any makeup, it would surprise him. She seemed downright afraid of her own femininity.

Murphy had no use for religion and even less use for women in general. Oh, they had their place, he'd be the first to admit, but that was generally atop a mattress, smelling of perfume and sex. He paid for their services and walked away free of any emotional entanglements.

He'd seen firsthand what a woman could do to mess up men's lives. In the last few years he'd lost his two best friends, and not to any bullet. No, the weapon that had ruined both Cain McClellan and Tim Mallory was far more deadly. Each had gotten hammered by the cockeyed emotion they called love.

At one time Deliverance Company had comprised

Cain, Mallory, Bailey, Jack Keller, and Murphy, a crack team of ex-military experts who'd pulled off some of the world's most daring rescue missions. But no more.

Murphy didn't need Cain or Mallory to teach him when it came to women. He'd learned everything he needed to know from his mother. The woman was both weak and pitiful. From the time he was ten, Murphy knew that he wanted nothing to do with the opposite sex. He may have only been a snot-nosed kid at the time, but his insight had served him well in the twenty-five years since.

Even Jack Keller, his best and most trusted friend, had been taken in by a woman's charms. His mistake had damn near cost him his life. Jack continued to carry the scars of his weakness, not that he'd learned his lesson, Murphy noted. Jack had come dangerously close to messing up more than one mission by not keeping his zipper closed. His friend had a weakness for a pretty face.

Murphy walked into his house ten miles outside of Boothill and slapped the mail on the kitchen counter. For all the hassle he'd gone through to get it, there wasn't anything more than a handful of bills and a few advertisements.

He opened the fridge, took out a cold beer, and headed for the porch.

The screen door slammed behind him as he slumped on the wicker chair and braced one booted foot against the post. The sun blared down hot and intense. Even the shimmering afternoon air seemed to protest the heat.

Boothill wasn't the end of the world, but a person could view it from there, and that suited Murphy just fine.

Smiling to himself, he took a long, deep swallow of the beer and wiped his forearm against his brow.

It didn't get any better than this.

2

Slim Watkins stepped into the post office at five minutes to five, right before closing time. The local rancher removed his hat and rotated the brim as he waited for Letty to acknowledge him.

She offered him a fragile smile and prayed he hadn't come to ask her to dinner. Her appetite had vanished when Murphy, her one last hope, had refused to help her. Not only was he not interested, but he'd barely given her a chance to tell him about Luke. Nor had he taken the time to hear her proposal. Letty didn't know what she was going to do now.

"Did you talk to him?" Slim asked anxiously. "The man you thought could help you?"

Slim was a decent, hardworking rancher. Although forty with one college-age son, he'd been Letty's most persistent suitor for the last couple of years. The pool of eligible young men had never been large in these parts and was fast evaporating.

"Letty?" he tried again when she didn't immediately respond.

"I talked to him."

"And?" Slim pressed. "Did he agree to accompany you to Zarcero?"

"No," she answered flatly.

A short, tense silence followed her announcement. "You aren't going alone, then, are you?"

"Of course I am," she insisted, irritated that he'd suggest otherwise. "I have to, don't you see? Luke's my brother."

"But I thought that man you talked to from the State Department advised you against making such a trip. He said there wasn't anything the United States could do if you got yourself in trouble."

"It doesn't matter what the State Department or anyone else advises me!" Letty cried. "I have to know what's happened to Luke. I don't have any other option. Luke would never leave me, and I refuse to abandon him."

The rancher lowered his head and slowly rotated the hat brim between his nimble fingers. "I'm going to worry about you, Letty, off in a foreign country, with no one there to protect you. You know I'd accompany you myself, but—"

"You have the ranch and your son. Billy might not live at home, but he still needs you."

Slim appeared relieved when she offered him a ready excuse.

"I'd go in a heartbeat if it wasn't for Billy."

Letty patted his forearm. "I know."

The rancher's eyes met hers. "How about dinner

tonight? I checked in at Rosie's and the special is Swiss steak. I know how you like Rosie's home cooking."

"Thanks, Slim, but not tonight," she said softly, knowing she was disappointing him. "I've got some thinking to do."

She had to find Luke. If she died in the process, so be it, but she refused to sit back and do nothing.

The house was dark but cool when Letty arrived home. She switched on the air conditioner and opened the top three buttons of her blouse, slipped off her shoes, and sat on the sofa. With her feet propped on the coffee table, she closed her eyes and let the cool air circulating the room revive her. A drop of perspiration slowly rolled from her neck toward the valley between her ample breasts. She pinched her lips, remembering how the mercenary's gaze had fallen to her breasts when she'd suggested paying him.

The man was dark and dangerous, and she'd been a fool to ask for his help. She should have known better, but she was desperate. He'd stood within inches of her, invading her space, filling up the tiny office with his presence. She could feel his heat, smell the uniquely masculine scent of him. The expression on his cold, dark face had been unreadable except when she'd offered to pay him. Then and only then had any expression leaked into his features, and he'd silently laughed at her.

Annoyed, she rose and in short order changed out of her uniform and into cotton pants and a sleeveless top. With a critical eye, she walked down the even rows of her herb garden, preferring to wait until the sun had set before she watered her precious plants.

Letty's grandmother, her namesake, had taught her about the medicinal properties of herbs. Letty had been an avid student until her grandmother's death when she was eleven. She'd grieved the death of Grammy more than she had the loss of her own mother.

Grammy had filled the shoes of Donna Madden soon after she'd abandoned her family and disappeared. Letty and Luke had only been five and far too young to comprehend what had happened. Over the course of years, rumors had reached Letty's tender ears about her mother's weaknesses. Stories of a woman addicted to alcohol and men.

After her mother's disappearance, their father, the local minister, had asked Grammy for help, so she'd moved in with the family.

Grammy was a grand southern woman who lacked neither grace nor charm. Whenever there was a death in the community, Grammy would visit the family home, stop the clocks, cover the mirrors with sheets, and place a cup of salt in the windowsill. More often than not Letty and Luke accompanied her on such trips. Letty never fully understood the purpose behind these rituals and didn't think to ask before Grammy's passing.

But when her father had laid his own mother to rest, Letty had raced home, and with tears streaming down her face, she'd reverently stopped the giant grandfather clock that tolled in the study and covered the bathroom mirror with a clean white sheet. Last, she'd dutifully set the salt in the kitchen window, then hurried back to the church, knowing her grandmother would have approved.

Letty had inherited her grandmother's green thumb, and her garden flourished year after year. She wasn't the healer her grandmother had been, but there were a number of home remedies she'd practiced on herself, her brother, and their father while he was alive.

The night before the news of the coup had reached Letty, she'd woken with her heart racing frantically, her head pounding. Instinctively she'd known something was terribly wrong with her twin. Many hours had passed before she'd heard that the government of Zarcero had fallen and guerrillas had taken over the capital. As the days progressed, news of atrocities committed against the people of Zarcero filled the television screen. Letty had watched in horror, praying her brother and his small, floundering group of followers had been spared.

The feeling that Luke was in trouble hadn't left Letty since that night. If anything, the sensation had intensified.

There was no help for it. She was going to Zarcero with or without help.

And it looked very much as if she'd be making the trip alone.

As luck would have it, two days later Murphy literally ran into Letty at the hardware store. He felt his backside bump against a soft, womanly figure and turned around, prepared to apologize. The words froze on his lips as his gaze slammed into Letty Madden's.

From her shocked expression, Murphy suspected their meeting had taken her by surprise as well.

"Good day, Mr. Murphy," she greeted him formally, as if they'd stumbled upon each other at a Sunday school picnic. Fat chance of that ever happening.

He nodded slightly and was ready to turn away when he noticed the contents of her shopping cart.

"I'm buying supplies for my trip into Zarcero," she informed him.

He picked up a flare and wondered if it was worth the effort to tell her that these were the last thing she was going to need.

"I thought flares might come in handy," she said, studying him.

Murphy tossed it back inside her cart. "Sure, if you want to alert the whole damn country that you've arrived."

"Oh, but I thought—" She stopped abruptly, clamping her mouth closed.

Murphy purchased what he needed and promptly left the store. At his best estimate Letty Madden would last fifteen minutes in Zarcero. If that.

He opened his truck door and was about to leave when she called out to him.

"Mr. Murphy . . . "

Groaning inwardly, Murphy climbed inside the cab. "What is it now?" he demanded, making sure she knew he resented the intrusion.

To her credit, she didn't cower the way some women would. "I won't keep you long." She stood on the sidewalk, looking uneasy but determined. The woman had mettle, he'd say that for her.

"When I approached you earlier, you didn't give me a chance to make my proposal."

"Any offer you could make wouldn't interest me." He didn't leave room for misunderstanding. Nothing she could propose would be enough to persuade him to join her in this suicide mission.

Her eyes held his. "I'm willing to pay you fifty thousand dollars to help me find my brother."

Murphy frowned, wondering where a woman like Letty Madden could come up with that kind of ready cash.

"My house is paid for, Mr. Murphy," she explained as though she'd read his mind. "It would be only a formality of signing a few papers at the bank for me to give you the cash in hand by tomorrow afternoon."

Damn it all, Murphy could feel himself weakening. It wasn't the money, either, but the woman. She was going to get herself killed for nothing.

He didn't figure he could stop her from going, but he wasn't going to encourage her. "There isn't enough money in the world to induce me to accompany you into Zarcero," he said smoothly, and started the ignition.

Her shoulders fell and she nodded, accepting his final word. "I apologize for detaining you. Have a good day, Mr. Murphy."

He didn't respond, merely put the truck in reverse and sped out of town, eager to make his escape.

"Damn fool woman," he muttered as he rode back to the house.

The light on his answering machine was blinking when Murphy walked into the kitchen. Only one person in the world outside of the good people of Boothill knew where he was: Jack Keller.

"How's the side?" Murphy asked when he reached his friend.

"It hurts like a son of a bitch," Jack muttered.

Murphy laughed. Jack had suffered two broken ribs from a confrontation with a runaway jeep during their last mission and had taken this time to recuperate in his condo. Jack preferred city life, but Murphy opted to stay away from people. The plains of Texas suited him just fine.

"I thought I'd check and see how things are going with you," Jack said.

If Murphy found any fault with his friend, it was that Jack was a social animal. The man simply didn't know how to relax. A week in Kansas City and Jack was bored, ready for new action.

"I'm fine," Murphy muttered. Damn, but he couldn't get that pesky Madden woman off his mind. Flares, she was buying flares to take into Zarcero. Talk about stupid.

Jack hesitated. "What's wrong?"

"Nothing," Murphy snapped.

"Well, something's troubling you. I can hear it in your voice."

Murphy didn't think it would do any harm to tell Jack about the postmistress. "I got a job offer," he said, and supplied the details.

"She's going to get herself killed," Jack announced flatly. Murphy didn't want to think about what would happen to Letty Madden when the rebel soldiers got hold of her. Odds were they'd torture her, rape her, and then take sadistic pleasure in killing her.

"What's she look like?" his friend asked next.

"What the hell does it matter?" Murphy barked. She was pretty and young, mid-twenties, by his estimate. Not that the guerrillas would care.

"Are you going to help her?"

Murphy's response was emphatic. "Not on your life."

"You know what it sounds like to me?" Jack said, and laughed lightly.

"I don't want to know."

"You need to get laid."

"What the hell?"

"You've been too long without a woman," Jack pronounced. "Otherwise this business with the postmistress wouldn't be bothering you so much. You've been living like a saint ever since you bought out Deliverance Company. Man, it's time to let down your hair and live a little."

"The last thing I need is a woman."

"Take my advice, Murphy, find yourself a hole-in-the-wall tavern, get good and drunk, and then let a woman take you home for the night. Trust me, you'll feel worlds better in the morning."

Sex was Jack's solution to everything. "My getting laid isn't going to stop the Madden dame from risking her damn fool neck," Murphy insisted.

"Maybe not, but you might not feel responsible for her death."

"I don't accept any responsibility for whatever happens to her."

Jack chuckled, that know-it-all laugh of his that caused Murphy's jaw to clench.

"What's so damn funny?"

"You," Jack returned evenly. "You're tempted to do it."

"The hell I am." It'd take a tornado to move him from his spread. He'd worked long and hard for this vacation, he deserved it, and he damn well was going to take it. He wasn't about to let an annoying postmistress interfere with his plans. If she was hell-bent on getting herself killed, it wasn't his problem.

"Admit it, Murphy, you want her."

"It's time we ended this conversation."

Murphy went to replace the telephone receiver when he heard Jack laugh and shout, "Call me when you get back from Zarcero."

"I'll rot in hell first," he muttered, satisfied.

The restlessness that plagued Murphy the rest of that day and all of the next refused to go away. He tried all the things that normally calmed his spirit. He worked on the truck, rode his stallion across his land, and sat on the porch with a beer and a good book until the sun set. Nothing worked.

Again and again he reminded himself that Letty Madden wasn't his responsibility. As far as he was concerned, the woman was on her own.

Normally Murphy wasn't a man overly burdened by conscience. No one in his profession could be. He lived by his own rules and his own code of honor.

He didn't want to become involved. But if the postmistress insisted on rescuing her brother, which was laughable when he thought about it, death would come as a blessing. Miss Sunday School Teacher viewed him as crude and vulgar, but he was a pussy-cat compared to the horror that awaited her in Zarcero.

There had to be a way to get her to listen to reason and at the same time absolve him of any guilt.

The idea of how to do both came to him the following afternoon.

Murphy whistled as he drove into town, his mood greatly improved. In a manner of speaking, he decided, Jack was responsible. Murphy parked his truck outside of the post office and made his way inside.

Letty was selling stamps to an older gentleman, but her gaze was immediately drawn to his. He noted the surprise and hope filter into her eyes as he sauntered over to his box. Her look didn't waver as he took his own sweet time removing his mail. When the post office was empty he approached Letty.

"May I help you?" she asked, clearly struggling to maintain a crisp, professional voice.

"Are you still intent on traveling to Zarcero?" he asked briskly.

"Of course. My flight into Hojancha is already booked. I leave in two days."

"I've had a change of heart," he said, leaning indolently against the counter.

Her relief was evident. "I thought . . . I hoped the money might influence you. I'll stop off at the bank this afternoon and make the arrangements. If you want, I'll give you half up front and half when we return."

"We'll talk about the money later. There are other, more pressing concerns we should discuss first."

She blinked and stared at him as if unsure she'd heard him correctly. "Such as?"

"No money will change hands until—"

"You want it in securities? That might take some time, and I'm not sure—"

"I said we'll discuss the financial arrangement later," he said impatiently, louder this time.

"What is it you want?"

"You're a virgin, aren't you?" He spoke slowly, letting his words sink into that thick, stubborn skull of hers.

Her eyes went incredibly round, and she swallowed uncomfortably. "That's none of your business."

Murphy laughed coarsely. "That tells me everything I need to know. I'll overlook your lack of experience. Generally I prefer a woman seasoned in the art of lovemaking."

She bristled. "Exactly what are you suggesting, Mr. Murphy?" She took two small steps away from him as if she feared contamination.

"A bargain."

Letty didn't say anything for a couple of moments, then swallowed hard and asked, "Exactly what kind of . . . 'bargain'?"

He smiled slowly and looked her over, allowing his gaze to linger over the fullness of her breasts and the subtle curve of her hips. He was sure to let his appreciation show in his eyes.

"One night. You and me together, all night. In exchange I'll accompany you into Zarcero."

Her eyes widened to such proportions that he struggled to keep from laughing outright. To say she hesitated would have been an understatement.

"It's a take-it-or-leave-it offer," he said. She'd leave it. There wasn't a single doubt in Murphy's mind. If she decided to tackle this project on her own, then she would leave him with a clean conscience. He'd laid his cards on the table. Either she agreed or not; it was up to her.

Satisfied, he turned to go. He made it all the way to the door before she stopped him.

"Shaun . . . Mr. Murphy," she called out to him in a voice that trembled.

Shaun. No one called him Shaun. Few even knew his given name. He didn't like the sound of it on her lips. Didn't like the way her lilting voice cried out to him.

Confident, he turned back.

She smiled weakly. "Would tomorrow evening be convenient?"

3

The man was mad. That was the only possible explanation, Letty decided, for what he'd asked—no, demanded—of her.

He'd guessed correctly that she was a virgin. Her experience with men had been limited to a few chaste kisses shared with Slim, which surprisingly she'd enjoyed. Her awakening sexuality made Letty uncomfortable and slightly afraid.

Although she'd been raised by her father and with Luke, Letty wasn't accustomed to men. The boys in her class had thought of her as bookish and mousy. Deep down, Letty feared she might be weak like her mother, and she couldn't bear the thought. For years she'd done everything she could to ignore the female part of herself.

In an effort to pull herself together emotionally and physically, Letty gripped the dresser drawer with both hands and took in several deep, calming breaths. She had no choice; she needed Murphy. For protection, for guidance. For survival.

Once she found Luke, she could be rid of the mercenary. If the price for his help cost Letty her virginity, so be it. She'd gladly pay that and a hell of a lot more if it meant saving her brother.

She'd close her eyes, grit her teeth, and bear the humiliation. It should be over soon enough.

When the doorbell chimed, Letty quickly surveyed the scene. The dinner table was set, a bottle of wine was on ice, and the steaks were ready to be grilled.

She squared her shoulders before opening the door. The soldier of fortune stood on the other side of the screen. He looked none too pleased for a man who was about to receive the most precious gift she had to give. He studied the full length of her.

She was well aware how she looked. She'd dressed as if the temperature dipped below freezing instead of soaring in the mid-nineties. Letty knew her features were pale. The blush she'd added to her cheeks had failed to disguise her pallor. Her long-sleeved blouse was buttoned all the way to her chin, and the collar seemed to have a choke hold around her neck. The full-length skirt swirled to her feet, not giving so much as a glimpse of her slim ankles.

Silently she held the screen door open for him. He wore fatigues, she noted, as if he were already in the jungle. When he walked into her house, she realized he towered a good six inches above her five-foot-five frame, dwarfing her. She didn't remember him being so large earlier.

His gaze moved past her to the dining room table, and he frowned.

"I thought we'd have dinner first," she suggested timidly, hating the way her voice trembled.

"As you wish."

Letty's hands felt clammy. She rubbed them together and made an effort at conversation. It soon became apparent that Murphy wasn't interested in small talk.

"If you'd open the wine bottle, I'll put the steaks on the barbecue," she said into the silence. "I imagine you like yours rare."

"Very rare."

Letty didn't know how she'd manage to down a single bite of her dinner, but she'd face that when the time came. Her heart was racing already, and she felt light-headed and dizzy, and they hadn't made it to the bedroom yet.

While he dealt with the wine bottle, she carried the meat outside. The heat was stifling, and sweat beaded on her upper lip.

Murphy appeared a couple of minutes later, bringing her a wineglass.

"Thank you, Shaun." She called him by his first name in an effort to ease some of the tension between them. Since they'd be traveling together for a number of days, it'd help if they came to some sort of agreement.

"Call me Murphy." His voice was low, gravelly, and unfriendly, setting the tone for this meeting.

"All right . . . Murphy." The T-bone steaks sizzled as she placed them on the hot grill.

He studied her. Every move she made. His eyes

were like those of a hawk, watching its prey, ready for just the precise moment to pounce.

"Smile," he ordered sharply.

Her head came up. "I beg your pardon?"

"You heard me; I asked you to smile. You look like you expect me to skewer and roast you over that barbecue any minute now." He mocked her with that cocky grin of his.

With a determined effort, she managed a half-hearted smile. "There, is that better?"

"A little, but not much."

Letty focused her attention on the meat and flipped both steaks.

"You're overplaying the martyr bit," he offered next.

Her fingers tightened around the spatula, but she didn't take the bait.

"What's the matter, Letty, are you afraid you might enjoy it? It can be a pleasurable experience if you let it," he added.

She stopped herself from responding. She'd agreed to his terms and came to him of her own free will, but she considered him a cold-blooded bastard. But then he was exactly what she'd need in Zarcero in order to find Luke and get them out of the country alive.

"That's it, isn't it?" Murphy demanded gleefully. "You're afraid you might enjoy it."

She couldn't keep quiet a second longer. "I sincerely doubt that," she blurted out, forcing her voice to remain even.

His laugh was low and mocking. "There are ways of

making you want me. Trust me, before I'm finished, you'll beg me to take you."

He moved closer, so close she could feel his breath against her temple. She stiffened. It was all she could do to keep from backing away from him. By the sheer force of her will, she managed to hold her ground.

"Do all men possess this colossal ego?" she challenged. "Or is it just you? Do you honestly believe you're so irresistible that I'll beg you to make love to me?" She made his claim sound ridiculous. "All I can say is that you've been listening to women you pay for this sort of enjoyment."

"Are you suggesting I'm not paying you?" he taunted.

Letty blanched.

"Don't worry about it, sweetheart. Comfort yourself any way you wish. If you want to tell yourself you're doing this for Luke, for God, for country, then feel free. If you've convinced yourself you're making a noble sacrifice of your virginity, that's all right by me, too. Make it easy on yourself, it's no skin off my nose." He tapped his finger against her nose, and involuntarily she flinched. The small display of weakness appeared to amuse him.

He trailed his index finger down the side of her face, then idly took a meandering route downward over her shoulder and lower to the crest of her breast. He paused, like a cat toying with a mouse, leaving her to suffer the anticipation of him circling her nipple. In that moment, Letty almost hated him.

"Tell yourself anything you want," he whispered

seductively, "if it'll make the lovemaking easier for you. But we both know the truth, don't we?"

"I don't know what you're talking about."

He laughed, but the sound was devoid of amusement. "You've been wanting to be rid of your virginity for a good long time now, haven't you?"

She sucked in her breath, desperately afraid he spoke the truth. "No," she denied vehemently.

Then, without reason, he backed away from her and sipped his wine. "It doesn't matter, you've got the perfect excuse. You're doing it for good ole Luke. Just don't be shocked when you learn he's already dead."

"Don't say that," she shouted. "I told you earlier, Luke's alive. I know he is, as surely as I live and breathe, my brother's alive. Why would I agree to this if he wasn't?"

"That's the real question, don't you think?" he asked calmly.

Shaking violently, Letty hurriedly dished the steaks onto a platter and carried them back inside the house. Murphy followed, closing the back door. It shut with an ominous clang.

Disguising her distress behind a smiling facade, she set the platter in the center of the table, then brought out two salad bowls from the refrigerator.

"You can sit down now," she said, and took her place at the far end of the table, as if this were a festive dinner party. She waited while he took his chair before removing the brightly colored linen napkin and setting it in her lap.

He reached for his fork. She reached for hers and waited for him to sample the salad.

"Everything in the salad came out of my garden," she said proudly. "The dressing is an old family recipe. I hope you enjoy it."

He didn't comment, which was just as well, Letty decided. She held her breath and waited until he'd finished the salad before finding the courage to sample her own. Murphy acted as if this were a contest on how fast one could consume a meal. He'd sliced into his steak before she'd had more than two bites of her salad.

Letty Madden had nerve. Murphy would say that for her. He'd done his damnedest to ridicule, mock, and intimidate her. Yet for all intents and purposes it looked as if she actually intended to follow through with their agreement.

Damn it all to hell, this wasn't the way it was supposed to happen. He'd fully expected the virgin to fold. Okay, so it was going to take more than a few idle threats. He was prepared for that as well.

While she nibbled at her dinner, he took the opportunity to eat the best damn meal he'd had in weeks. Generally he didn't fuss much with food. His freezer was stocked full of frozen entrées, and he wasn't opposed to one of those military food packs meant for the field now and again. But a steak, grilled over an open fire, why, that was too good to let pass.

"How . . . is everything?" she asked.

"Good." If she was looking for him to gush all over himself complimenting her, then she had a long wait. These delay tactics of hers would be good for only so long. He had to hand it to her; thus far her strategy had worked.

He hadn't anticipated her fixing dinner. The way he figured, he'd arrive and five minutes later he'd have her backside plastered against the mattress. It was a hell of a lot longer than any of those rebel soldiers would give her if they got their hands on her. The thought didn't comfort him.

He finished long before she did, stood, and carried his plate into the kitchen.

"You ready?" he asked, looking down the hallway toward what was sure to be her bedroom.

She paled, a good sign, he figured.

"I . . . haven't finished with my meal. I'll only take a minute. Have another glass of wine, if you want. There's plenty."

"No thanks."

He could almost see the dread settle over her. With a dignity reserved for those who could afford it, she placed the napkin on the table and stood. Her steps were weighted with reluctance.

She led him to her bedroom and turned abruptly to face him. "If you don't mind, I'd like to brush my teeth."

He hesitated, then shrugged. "Fine, but sooner or later you're going to have to make good on your promise." While he waited, he sat on the edge of the mattress and unlaced his boots.

She took a long white nightgown into the bathroom with her. Her steps were slow, as if she were royalty walking to the guillotine.

"Let your hair down," he instructed.

She hesitated, then nodded.

By the time she returned, Murphy had stripped out of his fatigues and was under the sheets, his back braced against the headboard. He locked his hands behind his head, his elbows jutting out on either side.

"Nice," he said, studying her, and he meant it. She resembled Little Bo Peep in her long white gown. All she lacked to complete the picture was a long wooden staff and a few lambs traipsing behind her.

Her dark brown hair flowed halfway down the middle of her back in gentle waves. Her feet were bare. If she was hoping the portrayal of a fairy-tale character would persuade him not to touch her, she was wrong.

"Move closer to the bed," he instructed.

"Are you nude?" Her eyes shifted away from his torso.

He grinned slowly. "What do you think?"

She dragged in a deep breath, stiffened, and closed her eyes.

"Are you ready to abandon your brother already?"

"No," she insisted shakily. "A deal's a deal. You can do with me whatever you want."

"I intend to," he said, leaving no room for doubt.

"You're a bastard."

He laughed. "So I've been told."

She glanced over her shoulder. "Would you mind if I turned off the light first?"

"Leave it on."

A look of panic came over her, and she dashed from the bedroom. Murphy resisted the urge to laugh outright. He hadn't so much as touched her and already she was racing for the hills. He loved it. The poor, dowdy virgin was deathly afraid of a naked man.

To his surprise, she returned a moment later with the wine. She drank directly from the bottle herself, dipping her head back and liberally downing the alcohol. Amazed, Murphy watched.

"Getting drunk won't help," he told her.

"Don't be so sure." She pressed the back of her hand against her lips and wiped away the moisture. "Is there anything you want me to do?"

"Plenty," he assured her, "but we'll get to that soon enough."

She crumpled onto the edge of the bed as if her legs would no longer hold her. The gown shifted in the front, exposing the swell of her breasts. Murphy was intrigued. She had beautiful breasts, lush and full.

Keller was right: he had been too long without a woman. Letty Madden was beginning to look damn good.

"Kiss me," he ordered.

Her eyes appeared enormous as her gaze settled on his mouth. She hesitated, gulped down another swallow of wine, and shifted toward him.

He took the bottle from her hand and set it on the nightstand. "I promise not to bite." He clasped her firmly about the waist and dragged her across the top of the mattress until her torso was pressed against his. Her eyes were huge, her face deathly pale, and she held his look, waiting. Worrying.

He eased forward slightly and touched her mouth with his. He wasn't a cruel man, and despite himself, he almost felt sorry for her.

She didn't resist, but she was as stiff as cardboard.

"Relax," he ordered impatiently.

"I'm trying."

"Try harder." Then, because he was angry with himself for being gentle with her, he captured her head between his hands and yanked her mouth to his. The least she owed him for all his trouble was a decent kiss, although he strongly suspected he'd need to tutor her.

Again she held herself stiff and unyielding. Repeatedly he moved his mouth over hers, less gently this time, molding her lips, shaping them with his own. He felt the peaks of her breasts and battled the growing excitement that threatened to overtake him. Giving himself over to the sensation, he hungrily claimed her lips.

"Open your mouth," he muttered.

"I don't understand, how—"

He took advantage of her doubts by slipping his tongue between her lips and sweeping her mouth. She squirmed, objecting to the invasion, and he let her, although her silk-covered breasts stroking his chest were a torment all their own. Again to her credit, she didn't pull away.

"Like that?" she whispered huskily when he'd finished.

She was doing just fine. More than fine. If they continued like this, soon there'd be no turning back. "Yeah," he mumbled, sounding breathless.

"This part's not so bad."

This wasn't working the way Murphy had planned. He kissed her again, and this time her tongue shyly

met his, welcoming his invasion. His breathing deepened, and he demanded more and more of her. To
his surprise she freely wrapped her arms around his
neck.

"You like this, do you?" He chuckled, wanting her
to believe he remained unaffected. He was grateful
for the blanket, which concealed his arousal. Her ability to excite him came as an unwelcome surprise. He
hadn't counted on the frumpy postmistress having
this strong an effect on him.

"What next?"

The only way his plan would work was if he made
this as unpleasant for her as possible. "Strip."

She blinked as if she hadn't heard him correctly.
"You want me to take off my nightgown?"

"That's what I said."

She looked toward the wall.

"Leave the light on," he insisted.

Ever so slowly, she climbed off the bed and stood
directly in front of him. She was nervous and embarrassed as she slowly unfastened the buttons, taking
her time with each one. Unfortunately she wasn't
aware how much her hesitation enhanced his anticipation. With her eyes tightly closed, she slipped the
material over one shoulder. She didn't seem to be
prepared for the slick fabric to slither down her body
and pool around her feet.

Murphy swallowed a gasp, shocked by her beauty.
She was magnificent. Her breasts rose full and proud,
her stomach was flat and smooth, and her hips were
wide and inviting. With her hands clenched at her
sides, she stood before him like a mythical goddess.

Kneeling on the mattress, he captured a nipple between his lips. She squeezed her eyes closed and whimpered softly as he continued to slide his moist tongue over her warm skin. She arched her back and bit into her lower lip.

Unable to wait any longer, he touched her breasts with his hands, bunching them together and squeezing them gently. Her nipples hardened beneath his touch, beading proudly. Her skin was soft, softer than anything he'd ever touched.

Nuzzling her neck with his lips, he ran his hands over her hips and buttocks, familiarizing himself with the silky feel of her. God help him, he'd never experienced anything quite like this, and he was the one with experience. Most of it had been with women far more practiced and skilled than this naive postmistress. Yet Murphy had rarely felt like this. Need clawed at his insides until it became a fierce kind of pain.

His finger touched the silky triangle of curls between the juncture of her thighs. She made a small sound.

"Open your legs for me." No longer did he sound like himself. His voice was husky with need.

"Please . . . let me turn off the light."

"No. Open your thighs," he said again, more forcefully this time.

"I can't."

He heard the anger in her voice, but it didn't sway him. Before another beat of his heart, she braced her feet a couple of inches apart.

"Very good," he praised her, and then, because he

wasn't sure what she expected him to do, he leaned forward and kissed her belly. Working his lips upward, he caught her nipple between his lips and sucked greedily. She swallowed a moan and he smiled to himself, pleased to note he wasn't the only one caught up in what they were doing.

He kissed her lips, subtly coaxing her responses, and then returned his mouth to her breasts. She gasped, and he took full advantage of her surprise to insert his finger inside her, delving between the soft folds of her femininity.

She tensed and started to struggle, but he braced his free hand against her waist.

"Relax," he whispered. "This isn't going to hurt."

Lightly he began to stroke her ultrasensitive flesh. It didn't take long before she was breathing hard.

"See? Didn't I tell you this would be good?"

Her eyes remained tightly shut. Murphy opened her legs farther apart with his hand and covered her mouth with his own.

His head spun and his control was close to snapping. Letty was soft and wet and on the verge of climaxing. She wasn't the only one deeply affected. Touching her like this was driving him wild.

His entire body was throbbing. Either they stopped right that minute or they raced full speed ahead. Murphy opened and closed his eyes in an effort to clear his thoughts. He felt as if he were sinking into a deep, dark pit.

It came to him then, what should have been abundantly clear from the first. Letty Madden wouldn't turn tail and run. Too much was at stake; she had no choice. She was his for the taking. Any hope of her backing out of their deal was lost, and frankly he was glad, because he wanted her. This stodgy, dull woman had turned the tables on him. He was so damned hot for her, he was close to losing it right then and there.

Not wasting any time, he caught her by the shoulders and brought her onto the mattress. Again he was amazed by her softness. She was smooth and sweet.

He kissed her, holding nothing back, then cursed under his breath when the room started to sway.

"What's wrong?" she asked.

"You. Me. Damn it, it's not supposed to be this good."

Fighting the need to rush, Murphy positioned himself between her legs, spreading them wide to accommodate his hips. When she felt his erection rubbing against her, she gasped and her eyes flew open.

"I'll go slow," he promised, forcing himself to remember she was a virgin.

"Murphy," she cried, "kiss me. It won't hurt so bad if you kiss me."

The room began to spin once more, only faster this time. He ignored the sensation and did as she asked, lowering his mouth to hers.

The kiss was wet and wild, as out of control as Murphy was starting to feel. The world began to tumble into a deep, dark precipice, taking him with it. He battled the sensation as long as he could.

He heard himself moan, felt Letty direct his mouth back to hers and kiss him. Damn, but she tasted good. All sweetness. The woman had given him one hell of a surprise.

He tried, God knew he tried. He reared back his head and pushed forward, but his aim was poor. He lowered his hand to his erection, to guide himself into her. She closed her eyes and turned her head, knowing there would be pain. He regretted bringing her pain. "I'll try not to hurt you," he whispered.

It was the last conscious thought Murphy remembered having.

The next time he opened his eyes, it was morning.

4

At *first light, Letty slipped* out of bed and dressed hurriedly. She dared not look Murphy in the eye for fear he'd know what she'd done. It had taken so long for the herb mixture to take effect that she'd begun to fear it never would. Since she hadn't concocted anything like that before, she wasn't entirely sure of its potency.

She'd thought—hoped, really—that there'd only be time for a few kisses and little else before he fell into a deep slumber.

She should have known he'd fight the effects. Instead he'd done far more than simply kiss her. Try as she might, she realized, she'd never forget her night with Murphy. She'd found pleasure in his arms, before and after.

In the middle of the night, she'd stirred to find herself trapped at his side. His arm was wrapped about her waist, her buttocks tightly tucked against his swollen manhood. By all that was decent, by all that was right she should have escaped him then and there. God forgive her, she hadn't. Even knowing what she did, Letty had closed her eyes and found a strange comfort and security in this mercenary's arms.

Before the herbs had taken effect, Murphy had mumbled that it wasn't supposed to happen this way. Once, he'd claimed it shouldn't be this good. The irony of the situation was that he'd voiced her own thoughts.

She felt that the kisses and the foreplay were something she'd need to endure in order for him to help her find Luke. The last thing she'd anticipated was pleasure. Her body had turned traitor on her. The warm sensation that had stolen over her had come as an unwelcome, unwanted surprise. Murphy was right, it shouldn't have been that good.

"What the hell happened?" he muttered from the other side of the bed.

"What do you mean?" she asked primly, fearing he'd guessed what she'd done.

He sat up and rubbed his face as if scrubbing awake his sleep-clogged mind. Letty was grateful to be completely dressed. She didn't trust him not to touch her again. Worse, she couldn't trust herself not to respond.

"Last night," he elaborated sourly.

"You know darn good and well what happened."

He glared at her, silent and knowing, as if reading her soul. Letty tensed, afraid he'd discovered the truth. The muscles along her shoulder blades tightened painfully.

Then he asked, "Did we . . . you know?"

It demanded every ounce of strength she possessed to look away. "I'd rather we didn't discuss last night."

"Like hell," he shouted, and then grimaced at the harsh sound of his own voice. "Just how much did I have to drink?" He reached for the wine bottle, and his brow folded into thick, irregular lines. "There was only this one bottle, wasn't there?"

"Our flight is scheduled to leave in four hours. I suggest we head for the airport as soon as you're dressed."

Her bags were already packed. She'd carefully considered each item. She had one suitcase, which she planned to leave in Hojancha, the country directly north of Zarcero. All she'd take into the country itself was a backpack. If they found Luke at the mission, they could be in and out in less than twenty-four hours. But if they had to break him out of some hellhole jail, it would take longer. How much longer, she didn't know.

"You're not going with me," Murphy announced coldly.

"Oh no, you don't," she said, furious that he would try to change their plans now. "We have a deal, one for which I've paid dearly. You can't modify the agreement now."

Despite his nakedness, he threw aside the sheets.

Letty's eyes widened at the sight of the hard muscles of his chest, his lean hips and powerful thighs.

He bore countless scars on his shoulders and stomach. The worst disfigurement was on his left shoulder and looked to have been a bullet wound. She battled back the tenderness that came over her at the sight of his scars. He wasn't the type of man who would appreciate her sympathy.

In him she viewed both strength and beauty. Letty

was mesmerized and embarrassed. She could feel the color creep up her neck and bleed into her cheeks.

Murphy chuckled and appeared to enjoy her discomfort. "Come now, don't you think it's a bit late for the outraged virgin bit? You've seen it all before." He reached for his pants, and his dog tags jingled as he dressed without displaying any uneasiness.

"I'm going with you." She wouldn't take no for an answer. Not when she'd come this far. Luke needed her, and despite what Murphy might think, so did he. In the last two years Letty had been to Zarcero three times. In addition, she was fluent in Spanish. She knew the country and was familiar with the cities and some roads. There were people she knew whom she could trust. Friends who would tell her about Luke, who would help her locate her brother.

"I agreed to find your precious brother for you, and I will," Murphy muttered testily. "I'll keep my word, but I work alone. The last thing I need is a woman tagging along with me."

"This is a fine time for you to tell me that," she cried, furious that he would try to pull this on her now. "We agreed that *you* would *accompany me* to Zarcero for a price. You collected your fee in bed with me last night. You can't change the agreement now."

The coldness in his eyes sliced her to the quick, but Letty didn't so much as flinch. "I'm going with or without you."

He swore. "I know what I'm doing," he shouted. "You'll slow me down."

"I'll help you."

He swore again, louder this time.

"I'm going to Zarcero to find my brother." Unwilling to debate the issue further, she slipped the backpack over her shoulder and carried her lone suitcase outside. His truck was parked behind her car.

She set the suitcase in the truck bed and climbed inside the cab, waiting for Murphy to appear.

It didn't take him long. He soon joined her, slammed the pickup door, swore again, then started the engine. Once on the road, he drove like a man bent on getting himself arrested.

Although he'd been more than willing to vocalize his opinions earlier, he didn't mutter a word during the ninety-minute drive to the airport.

For her part, Letty was filled with questions. Since they were flying into the country of Hojancha, she wanted to know how Murphy intended to get into Zarcero now that the borders had been closed. No traffic was allowed into or out of the country.

In the plane that flew from Houston, they were seated next to each other. His massive shoulders rubbed against hers. Once they were airborne, he removed a map from his carry-on bag. She wanted to volunteer what information she had, but it was apparent that he was in no mood to listen to her, so she said nothing.

Closing her eyes, Letty pressed her head against the window and silently prayed his sour mood would improve. This trip was going to be difficult enough without the two of them constantly at odds.

She didn't expect Murphy to be good company, but it would help if they could be civil to one another. She'd make the best of it, she decided, despite his attitude.

While pretending to be asleep, she studied him as she hadn't before. Her life and that of her brother rested in this man's hands. By no stretch of the imagination would she call him handsome. Everything about the man was intense. If she were to describe him—say, to Luke or one of her friends from church—she'd claim the mercenary possessed battered good looks. Nothing about him was gentle or soft. He was paid to kill, to inflict hate and death and pain upon others.

It came to her then, this contrast she'd discovered, this dark side he flaunted to the world. She'd experienced none of it during their night together. With her he'd been gentle and caring. With her he'd sought to give instead of take.

At first his words had been cruel and demeaning, but his hands and his mouth had displayed a fierce kind of tenderness that had rocked her very core. Shocked her. By the time he'd readied her for lovemaking and guided her onto the bed, she'd wanted him desperately.

It hurt her pride to admit that, but it was God's own truth. Had the herbs not taken effect at that precise moment, she would have given herself to him eagerly.

As it was, she'd been left feeling deeply disappointed and at the same time relieved. She'd been lucky for a woman who'd made a deal with the devil himself.

Damned lucky.

Murphy had made some stupid mistakes in his time, he realized, but this outdid them all. What he needed was to have his head examined. Now he was trapped.

He'd agreed to an assignment he fully considered to be a wild-goose chase. He didn't doubt for a minute Luke Madden's fate. The missionary was long dead.

Even now he didn't fully understand why he'd involved himself in this craziness. It wasn't often he misread people. His life depended on skill and intuition. He could have sworn the minute he went to touch his reticent virgin, she'd swoon. Either that or clench her principles against her plump breasts and run for high ground. It hadn't happened.

To be on the safe side, he'd come to her with a contingency plan. He was a soldier and well aware of the importance of strategy. On the rare possibility of her submitting to his lovemaking, Murphy had decided to leave her virginity intact and renegotiate their deal.

Instead he'd ended up taking her. He wasn't proud of the fact, but there was no going back now. He wasn't a weak man—unlike Jack Keller, who was often a victim of his own desires, especially those of the flesh. To Murphy's way of thinking, women were to be tolerated and used when the opportunity arose. Nothing more. Yet he'd fallen prey to his own physical desires and bedded Letty Madden.

Everytime he glanced her way, something he tried to avoid, he was left to wonder. For reasons he couldn't explain, his memory had gone patchy on him. He remembered everything that led up to the point when he'd actually committed the deed. It worried him.

It could have been the wine, or was it Letty herself he found so potent? Murphy wasn't sure he'd like the answer.

He found that reading her was damn near impossible. Each time he'd broached the subject of their lovemaking, she'd clammed up like an oyster hiding a pearl. God in heaven, he wished he could remember. Now, however, the deed was done, and he had no out. Because of his weakness he was stuck escorting Letty Madden into Zarcero.

The plane landed in Hojancha City at five that afternoon, Texas time. After clearing customs, which meant walking past a guard asleep at his desk, Murphy led the way into the busy terminal.

The inside of the airport had been uncomfortably warm, but the heat outside hit him like a sandblaster. It was like this for him the first few hours in the tropics. The heat, the stench, overpowered him. Depending on the time of day and the year, he sometimes found it difficult to breathe.

His clothes clung to him. Texas in summer wasn't exactly a Garden of Eden, but the tropics were something else. The heat could drain away a man's strength in a matter of hours. He glanced at Letty, wondering how she would adjust, and cursed under his breath at the thought of her tagging along after him through the jungle.

Letty scurried behind him, holding on to her luggage with both hands. Since she'd insisted on bringing along a suitcase, she could damn well carry it herself, Murphy decided.

"We'll be staying in a hotel for the night, won't we?"

"No." As far as he was concerned, the less she knew of his plans the better.

Murphy scanned the crowd, searching for Ramirez, his contact. Ramirez would deliver the weapons and put him in touch with men who'd provide him means across the border into Zarcero. No easy feat, according to what he'd learned. Both would be pricey. Not that he cared; he wasn't the one footing the bill.

"I'll need someplace safe where I can keep my suitcase."

"Did you bring along any valuables?" he asked, glancing over his shoulder. She was doing her best to keep pace with him and not succeeding.

"No, of course not."

At least she was smart enough not to carry cash. "What's inside?"

"Clothes for Luke and a few other medical supplies he might need."

Without hesitation, Murphy took the heavy suitcase out of her hand. He set it on the first available space he could find, flipped open the lock, and tossed a fresh set of clothes over his shoulder.

"What are you doing?" Letty shouted, scrambling to grab the shirt and slacks. Unfortunately a beggar reached them first.

"Murphy," she cried, her voice trembling with outrage.

He ignored her as he continued to discard the contents, including the medical supplies too bulky for her backpack. As far as he could see, there wasn't a damn thing either of them would need. Within seconds a crowd had gathered, scrambling for the clean clothes, creating a commotion behind him.

"You can't do that," Letty cried again. "Those things are for Luke."

She might have entered the fray herself if he hadn't

stuffed the empty suitcase into the closest trash can. Two toothless old men battled for that.

"Why . . . what about Luke?" Letty looked as if she were about to burst into tears.

"Let's get something straight right now," Murphy barked. "If you come into Zarcero with me, you do exactly what I say without question. The minute you contradict or argue with me, the whole deal's off. Understand?"

A rapid transformation came over her as she straightened her shoulders and nodded. "It would be crazy to pay you this ridiculous fee if I didn't bow to your expertise," she agreed, but glanced longingly at the clothes that had once belonged to her brother. "I'll trust you to supply whatever Luke needs when we locate him."

Murphy resisted the urge to remind her Luke was already dead. Far be it for him to burst her bubble. If she chose to believe her brother remained alive, it was her problem.

"We wait over there."

Together they crossed the street. Traffic buzzed past with little regard for safety. Rotting garbage was heaped up against the curb, the stench bad enough to make him want to gag. Murphy saw a rat crawl over it and wondered if Letty had seen it, too. As if she'd read his mind, she glanced at him and grimaced.

"You can wait in a clean hotel while I go into Zarcero if you want," he suggested, hoping she'd see the wisdom of his offer.

As he suspected she would, Letty rejected him with a hard shake of her head.

Murphy groaned inwardly. This was supposed to be his vacation, a little R & R before going back into the field. Instead he'd allowed himself to be outmaneuvered by the sister of a dead missionary. He just hoped Jack had the decency not to tell the others about the mess he'd gotten himself finagled into.

A jeep careened around the corner, and Murphy recognized Ramirez. He'd worked with the dark-skinned contact a couple of years earlier. Not only was Ramirez capable of providing the necessary supplies, his information was generally accurate.

The contact slammed on the brakes in front of the curb and smiled at Murphy, revealing a row of brown teeth. Without further delay, Murphy tossed his duffel bag into the back of the jeep and leaped into the front seat. Letty had a bit of difficulty and wasn't completely inside when Ramirez stepped on the gas and drove off. From his peripheral vision, Murphy saw Letty fall face first into the back, and he laughed silently. To her credit, she didn't cry out or complain, although he was certain her feathers had been ruffled.

"Who's the woman?" Ramirez asked in Spanish.

"No one important," he returned.

"What's she doing here?"

Murphy wasn't in the mood for long explanations. "You don't want to know."

Ramirez frowned. "Is she trouble?"

"No," he returned with a deep sigh, "just a royal pain in the ass."

5

Jack Keller played back the message on his answering machine twice, certain he'd missed something. It was Murphy's voice all right, but Keller had a difficult time believing what his friend was saying.

He'd done it. By heaven, Murphy had actually agreed to escort the do-gooder's sister into Zarcero. Keller wouldn't have believed it if he hadn't heard it with his own ears. His fellow mercenary didn't sound any too pleased about it, either. From the background noise, he must have phoned from the airport.

Ignoring the pain in his ribs, Keller sat back, folded his hands behind his head, and propped his feet on the ottoman. He couldn't help wondering what had brought on this bout of altruism. Jack grinned, knowing full well Murphy's feelings about this assignment. Either this postmistress had more money than God or she'd fed Murphy one hell of a line. But that didn't add up, either.

If this woman had that kind of wealth, she wouldn't be working for the post office. As for someone—particularly a woman—suckering Murphy into doing something he didn't want, well, Keller had yet to see that happen. Women weren't a big temptation for Murphy. He disapproved of any type of distraction. Murphy claimed he'd saved Jack's sorry ass more than once by keeping his pants zipped.

Unfortunately, Keller had learned his lesson the hard way. He'd been set up by a pretty señorita a couple of years back and damn near had the bejesus beat out of him as a result. It'd taken nearly six months for him to heal, and he'd carry the scars of that encounter all of his life. Since then he'd stringently followed Murphy's lead. A mission was a mission.

Kansas, however, was a different story. He liked to brag about his sexual exploits, and to be fair, he'd had his share of women. He'd never quite figured out what it was about him that attracted them. One look in the mirror confirmed he wasn't calendar material. He suspected it was his blue eyes. Women appeared to have a thing about blue eyes. Sinatra would testify to that. Brad Pitt, too.

For reasons he didn't want to examine too closely, Marcie Alexander came to mind. He'd been in town close to three weeks now and he'd yet to call on Marcie. Ever-welcoming Marcie. He could go six months or longer without contacting her, and the minute she saw him all was forgiven.

He couldn't remember where he'd met the blonde. Probably some bar. The hairdresser had a heart of pure gold. Unfortunately everyone knew it and took advantage of her generosity, Keller included. It shamed him when he thought about the way he'd used her over the years.

He'd arrive unannounced on her doorstep, and she'd take him in like a stray tomcat, feed him, pet him, make love to him, and expect damn little in return. Generally that was what she got.

She never questioned the lies he fed her, and there'd been some real doozies. Once she even bailed him out of jail. Now that he thought about it, he wasn't entirely sure he'd reimbursed her.

What he liked best about Marcie was that she never hassled him. Not with questions. Not with demands. She gave and he took. But then he figured he wasn't the only recipient of her generous nature. Marcie was the kind of woman a man used.

He'd been in town a while now, and he could have gotten laid every night of the week if he'd wanted. Trouble was, he didn't feel like paying for what most women would give away free. He'd never experienced much trouble convincing a lady to spread her thighs. What he didn't like was the expectation that went with it.

Just the other night he'd gone home with a stacked blonde, and after the usual tap dance to the bedroom, he'd spent the night. The next morning she'd asked if he'd fix her toilet for her. For the love of heaven, her toilet, and then she'd gotten all bent out of shape when he'd refused. Apparently she'd felt that since she'd pumped him dry, he owed her.

The more he thought about it, the more inclined he was to contact Marcie. He could use a little of her tender, loving care. She'd never been particularly beautiful, but what she lacked in looks was more than compensated for by her body. His mouth watered just thinking about her breasts. Lush and full, they were probably the finest specimens he'd ever laid eyes on, and he'd seen more than his fair share.

He loved it when they were in bed together and he'd be flat on his back and Marcie would lean over him. He'd play with her nipples, tease her unmercifully with his tongue until she'd whimper and whine. Only then would he give her what they both craved. Heaven almighty, the woman knew how to satisfy him, and she wasn't looking for him to work on her toilet afterward, either.

The decision made, Keller headed out the front door. If he timed it right, he'd arrive at Marcie's beauty shop before she closed down for the night.

By the time he started his car, Keller was wondering if he'd hold out long enough to make it over to her place. The way he felt right then, the chair in the lunch room in the back of the shop would suit him just fine.

Keller sighed with relief when he turned onto her street and saw Marcie's shop. A lot of things had changed in nine months, and he'd half feared she might have gone out of business.

He parked on the street, stopped off at the flower shop a couple of doors down, and picked up a bouquet of spring flowers. The roses were prettier, but a lot more expensive. Marcie wouldn't know the difference and certainly wouldn't care.

The bell above the door chimed when he entered

the shop. He was greeted with the faint acrid scent of perm solution. A young blond woman behind the counter eyed him with open curiosity.

"I'm looking for Marcie," he announced, flashing the girl an easy smile. His timing couldn't have been more perfect. There seemed to be a lull in business.

The girl ran her finger down the appointment book. "Are you scheduled?"

"I'm an old friend," Keller explained. "If she's in, I'd like to surprise her."

"She's here." The girl gestured with her head for him to go on back.

By then Keller was so eager, he nearly trotted to the rear of the shop. He pulled back the makeshift curtain and gifted Marcie with a smile potent enough to melt glacial ice.

"Hello, dahlin'."

She sat at the table, her feet propped up by a chair, eating popcorn. Her eyes widened with surprise mingled with delight when she saw who it was. "Johnny."

Another sin. Keller had never gotten around to telling her his name was Jack. What the hell, Johnny was close enough.

"You look fabulous." He told her that everytime he saw her, especially after a lengthy absence, only this time it was true. She'd done something different with her hair. It was shorter, curlier, blonder. He'd miss burying his hands into the thick, waist-deep length, but this style suited her much better.

She opened her mouth, but nothing came out.

He set the flowers on the table and reached for her,

lifting her out of the chair. Before she could protest, and he knew she wouldn't, he had her in his arms.

Her mouth was as sweet as he remembered. She tasted good, damn good. Better than anyone in a hell of a long time. She smelled faintly of lilacs instead of stale barroom smoke, as fresh and clean as summer itself.

One kiss didn't come anywhere close to satisfying him. Before she could tell him how much she'd missed him, he had her backed against the wall with his tongue halfway down her throat. She squirmed against him, her eagerness stroking his pride and his manhood. Soon he was so damned hard, his erection throbbed against the metal teeth of his zipper. This was even better than he expected. For the life of him, Keller couldn't remember why he'd waited so long to contact her.

"In a minute, baby," he whispered between deep kisses. He wanted to see and taste her breasts before he gave them what they both wanted.

He had three buttons of her pink uniform unfastened before he heard her.

"No, Johnny."

He was sure he'd misunderstood. "No?" He must be hearing things. Her body was telling him one thing and her lips another.

"It's been nine months since I last saw you."

"I told you before, baby, I travel for business."

She closed her eyes and breathed hard and heavy. "Then what's this?"

He slipped his hand inside her uniform and sighed audibly when he cupped her breast. Her nipple pearled instantly. "Pleasure, sweetheart, pure pleasure." He kissed her again before she could say anything more. When he finished, they were both breathing hard.

"This isn't such a good idea," she said. Again her body claimed it was the best idea either of them had had in a hell of a long time.

"I've missed you." To prove how much, he gripped her hand and placed it over his erection. "See?" he whispered.

"I don't think you heard me," she said, and it was clear she wanted him as much as he did her. "This isn't a good idea."

"Marcie, what's wrong?" He nuzzled her neck, sucking and licking, doing all the things she enjoyed most. At least he thought it was Marcie who enjoyed this kind of love play. Faces tended to blend together in his mind.

"I'm not the same person I was before."

Keller groaned and lifted his head reluctantly. "You got married?"

"No . . . ."

Relieved, he kissed her again, deeper this time, persuading her in ways words never would.

"Johnny . . ." She sounded as if she were about to weep.

"You're engaged?"

"No."

Kissing away her protests, he bunched her breasts with both hands. It took him far longer than it should have to realize there wasn't as much there as had been previously. Slowly he lifted his head, and his eyes found hers.

"I had breast reduction surgery." She answered the question before he could ask.

Personally Keller couldn't understand why she'd go and do anything so silly. He wanted to tell her that, but she started talking as if she intended never to stop.

"You can't flitter in and out of my life any longer. I've never been anything more than a convenience to you, Johnny. You're here one day and gone the next. You never let me know when you're coming or, worse, when you're leaving. The last time—" She stopped abruptly and seemed to strengthen her resolve before she said, "I refuse to be used any longer."

"Use you? Me? Honey, that's not true." He put on a hurt look, but that didn't seem to faze her.

"A bouquet of flowers isn't enough to make up for nine months of silence."

"But I've already explained—"

"You've barged in and out of my life for the last time," she said, cutting him off. "It'd be better for the both of us if you left now." Her eyes flashed with conviction.

"Fine, if that's the way you feel." He had half a mind to remind her there was plenty of what she gave away.

She lowered her head. "Good-bye, Johnny."

He turned around, intent on walking out the door, letting her think it was no skin off his nose. They'd had some fun together, could still, but she wasn't willing. So be it. He jerked back the cloth curtain and happened to glance back. Marcie stood with her shoulder braced against the door, her head lowered and her bottom lip trembling.

"Do I owe you any money?" he asked.

"No."

Hell if he could remember if he did or didn't. "Good-bye, Marcie," he said softly. With that he left the beauty salon.

An hour later he sat in a bar, feeling more than a little melancholy. He didn't know what the world was coming to these days. He hadn't had a cigarette in three years, but he needed one now. After downing the last of his beer, he walked outside.

A whore, dressed in leather pants and a halter top, leaned against the side of the building. Catching sight of him, she offered a coy smile.

"Looking for a good time, honey?" she asked.

It was a sad commentary that Keller had to think about the answer. Sure, he'd been after a good time, but he'd wanted it with Marcie.

"I don't know," he said, playing her game. "What are you offering?"

With her hand planted against the swell of her hips, she sidled toward him, her cherry lips easing into a sultry smile. "I'll give you anything your little heart desires," she whispered, then laughed softly, "and then some."

"What is this, a slow night?"

"You want it slow, you got it slow."

For the life of him, Keller couldn't dredge up the enthusiasm. All he could think about was Marcie and the feel of her as her sweet body had rubbed against him.

"Another time," he said.

"Hey, you're missing out on the best time of your life."

Keller doubted that. The best time had been nine months ago with Marcie. He wouldn't be any kind of man not to know she'd wanted him. Damn, he'd like to know what had gotten into her.

Marcie. By heaven, he'd have her again just as soon as he figured out a way to change her mind.

6

He was alive, although he wasn't sure why. After repeated interrogations and torture, Luke Madden would have welcomed anything that would relieve the agony of the past two weeks. Even death.

He tried to find a place in his heart to forgive the men who abused his body and tormented his soul. With regret, he admitted that forgiveness had become more of a struggle than dealing with the crippling pain.

From the look in the soldiers' eyes, Luke realized they found pleasure in his suffering. Pleasure in the power they held over him.

Once he figured out their game, he did his utmost to keep from crying out, refusing to give their demented souls the satisfaction they sought. Consequently they beat him harder, tortured him longer, in an effort to break his spirit and steal from him what remained of his dignity. That, too, along with everything else, lay in shambles at his feet. He had no will to continue.

Even now, Luke didn't understand the beatings. He was a missionary, a man of God. Despite evidence to the contrary, his captors believed his mission in Zarcero involved far more than preaching the gospel. They assumed he'd been a confidant of President Cartago. While it was true that he'd known and admired Zarcero's president, he'd never been an associate. From what Luke had gleaned, Cartago had managed to hide a large portion of the country's treasury before his death. Why his captors assumed he would know anything about that, Luke could only guess.

"Luke?" Rosita's voice came to him like a siren's song, soft and lilting, tender and healing.

With effort he raised his head from the thin mattress and tried to open his eyes, but they were swollen shut. After the interrogation, when the pain burned in his gut and racked his soul, he found comfort in thinking about Rosita. How beautiful she was, how gentle and kind.

"Rosita?" He prayed as he'd never prayed before that she hadn't been taken, and in the same breath, the same heartbeat, he thanked God for the one last opportunity to see her.

"I'm here. Don't fear, it's safe, no one knows."

"A guard . . . someone might find you."

"My uncle is a guard," she whispered. "He arranged it so I could see you."

The risk she took far outweighed any benefit. Luke

couldn't bear thinking about what would happen if she were discovered. His beautiful Rosita had risked her life for him.

Luke heard the key that opened the cell door.

"Oh, Luke, what have they done to you?" Emotion rocked her voice. How he wished he could have spared her this.

Luke knew that his swollen eyes were the least of his injuries. His figured that he had several broken ribs, along with any number of internal injuries. His fingernails had long since been ripped off, and he suspected a muscle in his leg had been torn.

Whispering in Spanish, Rosita gently brushed the hair from his brow, her fingers trembling with tenderness and love. He felt her anguish as keenly as his own.

With her arm supporting his neck, she elevated his head and pressed a cup to his lips. Luke drank thirstily, gratefully.

When he'd finished, she bent forward and whispered close to his ear, "We will free you soon. Hector and the others have a plan, and—"

"No, Rosita, no." He wouldn't survive much longer, of this he was certain. Another beating like the one that afternoon would surely kill him. He didn't understand even now why he was alive. The future held more pain; death would come as a welcome release, more of a friend than an enemy.

"Please, my love, be strong, hang on just a little longer," she whispered frantically.

"No." He refused to allow his friends to put their lives at risk in an effort to save him. "It's too late for me."

"No, you must be strong. Soon, very soon, you will be free."

"Rosita, I can't . . . forgive me, but no." With every ounce of strength he possessed, he pleaded with her.

He must have lost consciousness because the next thing he knew she was gone. Perhaps it had been a hallucination; he prayed it was. It would be far better that she not see him like this. His heart swelled with love and regret for the life they might have once shared. It was too late for them, much too late.

With thoughts of Rosita lingering in his mind, Luke felt weighted down with a great sadness. He hadn't the strength to continue or the will to go on. He prayed Rosita would forgive him. Rosita and his sister.

Thoughts of Letty crowded his head. They'd always been close, he and Letty. His death would devastate her, and for that he was truly sorry. He knew his twin as well as he knew his own heart. With that knowledge came the understanding that Letty wouldn't want him to suffer any longer.

7

Letty stood under the shade of a low-hung roof as the sun beat down upon the parched land like a giant hammer. Heat shimmered in the early afternoon, the sun so bright it nearly blinded her.

She was joined under the thatched roof by a young mother, who held an infant of about six months. The woman eyed Letty wearily and appeared to be waiting for one of the men arguing with Murphy on the other side of the road.

Letty focused her attention on Murphy and Ramirez while they haggled with the wiry, dark-skinned man and an older gentleman. Their raised, excited voices stirred the hot afternoon air. Letty could make out only an intermittent word, just enough to catch the gist of the disagreement, which had to do with money. Her Spanish was excellent, but the men all seemed to be talking at once, heatedly disagreeing with one another.

Murphy objected loudest. From what she could make out, the two men claimed that the danger had greatly increased and the price for guiding him and Letty across the Hojancha border into Zarcero had doubled.

Once, briefly, Ramirez glanced across the dirt road toward Letty, as if to let her know she was the real reason for their trouble. She stiffened her spine and glared right back, unwilling to let him intimidate her. Since she was the one financing this venture, he had no reason to complain.

From Murphy's stance, Letty could see he wasn't the least bit pleased with this turn of events. Not once did he look her way. She could have keeled over in a dead faint before he'd take the trouble to recognize her. If then.

Since they'd boarded the plane in Texas he'd gone out of his way to make it abundantly clear that he didn't want her with him. It went without saying that he considered her presence on this trip nothing but a damn nuisance.

Letty removed her hat and wiped the perspiration from her brow with the back of her forearm. The backpack cut into her shoulder blades and she shifted the thick straps, hoping to relieve the pressure. Her khaki shirt was drenched with sweat, but she'd die before she'd complain about the heat or anything else.

The previous night and a good portion of the morning had been spent being tossed about like a sack of potatoes in the back of Ramirez's jeep. She couldn't be sure what Murphy had told the other man, but she strongly suspected he'd offered him a bonus if he could find a way to be rid of her. The jeep's journey across Hojancha was worse than any carnival ride she'd taken.

When they'd arrived in this village, Murphy had ordered her out of the jeep like a drill sergeant talking to a raw recruit. Her legs had felt weak, but she'd managed to climb down.

When the wiry man and his friend arrived, Murphy had insisted she wait for him across the dirt roadway. It seemed to Letty that he could have used her help with the negotiations. But in an effort to keep the peace, she'd done as he asked without arguing. She did note, however, that Murphy was forced to rely on Ramirez more than once to translate for him. She could have done just as well.

Irritated and frustrated, Letty paced the shaded area and waited for the men to resolve the money issue. As far as she was concerned, it didn't matter what it cost. They had to get into Zarcero without being discovered.

A weak, pitiful cry cut into her thoughts. Letty turned to find the clean-scrubbed young mother attempting to comfort the infant in her arms by feeding her a bottle. A second frail sob racked the sick baby, and the woman's eyes filled with tears that she struggled to hold back.

Letty had been so caught up in her own troubles that she hadn't given the mother and child more than an indifferent glance.

"Is the baby ill?" Letty asked gently in Spanish.

The woman glanced up, her eyes riddled with worry and tears, but she didn't respond.

Letty pressed the back of her hand against the infant's forehead. The baby burned with fever.

The woman closed her arms more securely around her child and nodded.

Letty asked a number of questions and learned the other woman's name was Anna and the baby's Margherita.

Letty slipped the backpack off her shoulder and knelt on the dirt floor. Not knowing in what condition they'd find Luke, she'd brought along a variety of herb creams, tinctures, and ointments. Surely she could find something that would help reduce the baby's fever.

"I'm not a doctor," Letty explained as she drew out a small plastic bottle. She explained that the liquid had been made from Chinese honeysuckle, often called jin yin. "I know about herbs, and two small drops of this added to juice or sweetened water will help the baby's fever."

Anna's eyes widened as if she weren't sure she should trust Letty.

"You must reduce her fever," Letty implored, realizing she could offer Anna no reassurances. This woman knew nothing of her.

Weighing the decision carefully, Anna handed Letty her baby's bottle. Using an eye dropper, Letty added two tiny drops of the tincture to the water.

With a damp cloth, she moistened the infant's face and chest. Sitting side by side, the two women cooled the baby. Temporarily comfortable, the infant sucked her bottle dry.

"Ramón is Margherita's father," she said, glaring at the wiry fellow standing next to Murphy.

"Your husband?"

Quickly Anna lowered her eyes. "No." Her shoulders stiffened as she raised her head, her look strong and proud. "I came because I hoped Ramón would help me find a doctor for Margherita. When I told him I was pregnant, he said a baby was my responsibility, not his. I loved him. I gave my heart to a man with no soul." Leaning slightly closer, Anna gently pressed her hand over Letty's arm. "He is a man who makes many promises and delivers few. Learn from my mistake. Do not trust him."

Across the road, Murphy looked all the more disgruntled. Ramirez's face was red from arguing, and he shook his head repeatedly.

"I must get into Zarcero," Letty whispered, confiding in Anna.

Her face and eyes revealed her dismay. "No, señorita, Zarcero is a dangerous place for you and your man."

"My brother is there."

Anna's expressive face revealed her apprehension. "It isn't possible. The soldiers won't let you cross the border," she insisted.

"I know. Ramón was supposed to help us."

"Ramón?" Her dark eyes widened all the more, contrasting with the white peasant blouse and flowing skirt. "No," she said with conviction, and shook her head. "Do not put your faith in him, señorita."

"My brother is a good man," Letty returned. "He needs my help."

"A good person like you?" she asked, her hand gripping the tincture bottle.

Letty smiled. She wasn't as good as Luke, not nearly as generous or forgiving. He'd always been there for her, and she refused to abandon him now.

"Like my brother," she agreed meekly.

"I will help you," Anna promised.

"But how?"

Anna glanced over her shoulder and lowered her voice. "Wait here and I will bring my uncle."

"Your uncle?" In Zarcero, Letty had found, every citizen of the country seemed related in one way or another.

Anna smiled for the first time. "He is a man who knows many things."

She slipped away. Discouraged, Letty sat down in the dirt. No more than a minute had passed when Murphy, in a display of anger, stalked across the roadway. Slapping his hat against his thigh, Ramirez stormed to the jeep and drove off.

Joining Letty in the shade, Murphy slumped down next to her and draped his wrists over his knees. "I don't trust that son of a bitch. He'd sell his grandmother's liver without giving the matter a second thought."

"Ramón?" she asked casually.

He pinned her with his glare. "How'd you know his name?"

"How could I have missed it? You were arguing loud enough to alert the Canadian Mounties."

Murphy ran his hand along the back of his neck. "Getting into Zarcero isn't going to be any picnic."

"I didn't expect it would."

"Ramirez suggests we wait a couple of days. . . ."

"No," she responded emphatically, "we don't have that kind of time."

"Listen, I don't like this any better than you do. It's a pain in the ass, but we don't have a choice."

"I might have found someone who can help," she said.

If she hadn't garnered his full attention earlier, Letty had it now.

"What do you mean?"

"The young woman who was here earlier told me about her uncle. Apparently he has connections."

"An uncle? We're supposed to trust some girl's uncle?"

"I'd rather put my life in his hands than rely on your man. I'd like to remind you, I'm paying top dollar for your expertise. The next time we need someone, I suggest you check out their credentials."

To her surprise, Murphy tossed back his head and laughed out loud. "You want me to check their credentials? Now I know why I let you come along. For comic relief."

She ignored his humor, especially since it was at her expense.

Fifteen minutes later Anna returned with her uncle. The old man looked to be in his seventies. He was barely able to walk, his gait was slow and measured. A large straw hat shaded his face from the sun.

"I'm Carlos," he whispered in a voice that sounded surprisingly young. "I understand you are on an important mission?"

"Yes," Letty responded eagerly.

Murphy said nothing, but his eyes rounded with surprise when he realized she was fluent in Spanish.

"Come, my niece has been remiss in not offering you refreshments."

Encouraged, Letty stood and brushed the dirt from her backside.

The older gentleman's eyes bored into her. "Margherita is sleeping comfortably for the first time in two days."

Murphy scowled and glanced at Letty, not understanding. Letty didn't bother to enlighten him. If Murphy learned of her knowledge with herbs, he might put two and two together. It wouldn't take much for him to figure out the cause of his memory lapse.

Once inside the old man's dilapidated house, Carlos offered them canned juice. Before the old man could serve the refreshment, Murphy pulled him aside and started asking questions. Once again he ignored Letty as if she had no interest in the discussion.

The two men spoke in a low murmur. She noticed that Murphy did most of the talking. His body language told her that he found the terms to be more to his liking, and he nodded a couple of times.

Only once did he glance her way. He frowned before responding to Carlos's inquiry.

Letty was tired of being left out of the conversation, particularly one that pertained to her and rescuing Luke. She was strongly tempted to speak her mind, but soon the two men appeared to come to some agreement.

Carlos nodded and left, leaving Letty and Murphy alone in the tiny house.

"What's happening?" she asked.

"Carlos has a boat by the river. He's agreed to smuggle us into Zarcero himself. He's known and trusted, and even if he is stopped and questioned, the rebels aren't likely to search the boat." He hesitated and studied her as if seeing her with fresh eyes. "But if we are stopped, we need to be prepared. Do you know anything about guns?"

She swallowed uncomfortably. "Some." Damn little if the truth be known, but she was afraid to admit it.

"Well, you're about to get a crash course. If you're going into Zarcero, then you'd better damn well know how to take care of yourself."

"That's why I have you," she argued.

Apparently her answer didn't please him because he reached behind him and produced a deadly-looking handgun and laid it across his palm. "Either you learn how to fire this or you stay here and wait for me."

He walked out of the house, leaving her the option to follow him or sulk alone inside. Given no choice, she scurried after him. Murphy would like nothing better than to leave her behind.

Letty didn't know how long they walked; it seemed like forever. In reality, they'd probably gone a mile. The Hojancha countryside, like that of Zarcero, was unsurpassingly beautiful and variable. The air, cooler now, was soft and sweet as they traipsed across the parched grass.

By the time Murphy stopped, her legs ached and her breath stung her lungs, but she managed to keep up with his murderous pace.

Tucking a white piece of paper in the low-lying arms of a Cenizero tree, Murphy stated matter-of-factly, "We don't leave for Zarcero until you can fire a bullet into this."

"You've got to be joking."

One cold glance told her he wasn't.

"This isn't what I'm paying you for." She hated guns and couldn't imagine actually having to fire one, let alone kill another human being. She'd rather die herself.

Unfortunately Murphy gave her no option. It was either learn to handle the pistol or wait while he went into Zarcero for Luke.

"Give me the pistol," she demanded, determined to learn how to use it, just to spite Murphy.

8

The moon cast a reflective glow across the smooth waters of the Colon River, which separated Hojancha from Zarcero. Carlos's small engine echoed in the night like a rusty buzz saw. Letty wondered how it was that no one could hear their approach.

Hidden under the tarp, she lay tense and stiff after holding still for so many hours. Murphy, disguised in clothes borrowed from a native fisherman, sat next to Carlos in a boat little bigger than a dinghy. It amazed her that the vessel had been able to keep from sinking with the three of them, plus their supplies.

Letty would have liked to point out the unfairness of such an arrangement—her under the tarp, Murphy not—but she knew before she protested that it would do no good. When Murphy set his mind to something, it took an act of God to convince him otherwise.

In an effort to ward off the stench of rotting fish,

she alternately held her breath and closed her eyes, neither of which helped. She would have given just about anything to escape in the luxury of sleep. The night before she'd spent in the back of a jeep, being jostled around like a popcorn seed in hot grease. She could no more have slept during their road trip than leapt over the moon.

Murphy hadn't gotten any more rest than she, and she wondered how he fared. He gave no indication that it had affected him in any way, but for all she knew he might routinely go without sleep just to prove how tough he was.

"It isn't wise to take the woman with you," Letty heard Carlos say. She had to strain to hear Murphy's response.

"It isn't my choice."

"What is so important in Zarcero that you would risk your lives?"

"The less you know, old man, the better," Murphy returned without emotion.

The boat engine slowed to a crawl. "She is a good woman."

Murphy snorted.

In other circumstances Letty might have felt guilty for having duped Murphy into accompanying her to Zarcero, but not after his insulting proposition. As far as she was concerned, he got what he deserved.

It troubled her the way her mind continued to return, like a homing pigeon, to their lone night together. It had been a momentary lapse in judgment. She wasn't perfect, but she wasn't like her mother either, selling herself and her family for the pleasure she found in the arms of another man.

The episode wouldn't be repeated, of that she was confident.

The boat engine died completely, and Letty stirred beneath the tarp. Turning her face toward the narrow opening, she angled upward to catch a whiff of cool, fresh air.

"Are we there?" she whispered.

"I told you to keep quiet," Murphy answered impatiently.

"I want out from under here."

"All in good time." He pressed his booted foot against her rump. "Don't move a muscle, understand?"

"The area is said to be crawling with rebel troops," Carlos warned. "Stay off the main roads."

Not waiting another moment, fearing Murphy wasn't to be trusted not to leave her behind, Letty peeled back the tarp and sat upright. Even in the thick night, she felt Murphy's displeasure.

The rowboat butted gently against the bank.

Murphy grabbed Letty's upper arm and helped her to her feet. "Be as quiet as you can, understand?" he demanded.

"I wasn't planning to break into song."

Murphy leaped onto the riverbank and left Letty to make her own way out of the boat while he dealt with the equipment.

Carlos handed him the necessities collected from Ramirez earlier.

"Be very careful, my friends," Carlos warned before he made his way back to the helm and artfully steered the dinghy away from the bank. "I will search each night for the signal for your return."

"Thank you," Letty whispered back, and waved.

"Come on," Murphy urged, "remember what Carlos said."

The old man had said plenty, most of it in an effort to dissuade Letty from going into Zarcero. After a while she had paid little attention.

"Come on, we've got a long walk."

"I won't hold you up," she said, determined she'd keel over before she gave him the satisfaction. Carlos had given them the name of a friend, someone they could trust, who would put them up for the night.

After strapping the supplies onto his back, Murphy started walking. Letty hurriedly slung her backpack over her shoulder and followed. Neither spoke.

In other circumstances Letty would have paused to admire the heavens. A smattering of stars littered the night with tiny beacons of light. After the crushing heat of the day, the cool breeze came as a welcome relief.

Murphy didn't give her time to stargaze. She quickened her pace in order to keep up with him and was soon winded, but she didn't complain. Regulating her breathing, she kept her steps in line with his.

They rested once, and only then because Murphy thought he might have heard something. He held out his hand, pressed his finger to his lips, and stopped dead in his tracks. The moments seemed interminable. The night spoke to them in snippets of sounds. A bird's call echoed like crickets, or perhaps monkeys, and the breeze whispered through the thick foliage. Letty smelled orchids. The texture of this country her brother loved so dearly wrapped itself around her.

After what seemed a lifetime, they continued walk-

ing. It came to her that this was the first time she was
truly alone with Murphy. Her survival and that of her
brother rested squarely on his shoulders. The realization brought home the fact that she knew very little
about this man. Not much more than his name and
post office box. True, she'd sorted his mail for a number of years, such as it was. A few bills now and again,
magazines, most with a military orientation. What she
knew about him wouldn't fill an envelope, and yet
she'd trusted him with her life.

When the farmhouse Carlos had mentioned came
into sight, Letty sagged with relief. The straps from
the backpack dug into her shoulders, and her calves
ached from walking at Murphy's killing pace.

"Wait here," Murphy ordered in the imperious tone
he used with her. He guided her under the protection
of a large tree.

"Where are you going?" she asked.

"I can't and won't explain my motives everytime I
ask you to do something," he snapped. "I'll be back as
soon as I can."

She opened her mouth to argue and knew it would
be useless.

Carlos had already told them his cousin would see to
their needs. If it had been up to her, she would have
walked up to the farmer's front door, knocked politely,
and explained who she was. But not Murphy. He apparently felt it was necessary to break in like a criminal.

Unfortunately the moonlight wasn't bright enough
for her to see where he'd gone. The man all but disappeared into the shadows. Either that or she'd viewed
too many James Bond movies.

With her back braced against the tree trunk, Letty
sat. She must have drifted off to sleep, because the
next thing she knew, Murphy had returned.

"We'll spend the night in the barn," he whispered.

She rubbed the sleep from her face and nodded.
Anything with the word "sleep" in it appealed to her.

"There's a small catch."

She raised questioning eyes to him.

"We stay together."

She frowned, not understanding the problem since
she thought that was why she'd hired him.

"In other words, we sleep next to each other."

9

Men baffled and exasperated Marcie Alexander. She stood in the room in the back of her beauty shop and mulled over her life to this point.

For her first thirty-one years the only place she found herself capable of communicating with the opposite sex was in bed. Well, she was finished with that, finished with having her friends marry and start a family while she waited on the sidelines, and for what? To get passed over again and again.

She'd never had a problem attracting a man. At certain times in her life she'd dated three or four at a time. But instead of feeling wanted and charmed, she felt more like an air traffic controller.

Finding men had always been a snap, especially the needy kind. From the time she was sixteen and lost her virginity in the backseat of a car at a drive-in movie during *Raging Bull*, she'd maintained steady relationships with the opposite sex. Unfortunately her relationships rarely lasted more than a month or two at a stretch.

As the years progressed, Marcie had learned a painful lesson. Men flattered her, courted her, borrowed money from her—which they seldom repaid—and then promptly deserted her. The pattern rarely changed. She'd fallen in and out of love so often, it had all become a revolving door.

Men flocked to her. Mostly penniless ones with problems for her to solve. She specialized in rescue operations. For years she was convinced that all these poor, misunderstood men really needed was the love of a good woman.

In her search for a husband, Marcie had gone so far as to take out a loan in order for Danny, the man of the hour, to hire an attorney so he could get a divorce. It was understood that once he was free from his battle-ax of a wife, he'd marry her. It took Marcie two months to learn he'd never been married. The money had paid for a weekend in Vegas with another woman. It had taken her sixteen months to pay back the bank.

What hurt most was that a couple of her beauty school friends had been married twice. They'd already started families with two different men while Marcie had yet to snag even one husband.

Every time she saw another one of her friends with a baby and a doting husband, her heart ached. She wanted it all. A husband, a gentle, kind man who would love her to distraction. One man enough to keep her satisfied in life and in bed.

Heaven would testify that she'd done her best to

land herself a lifetime mate. But in her long, often tumultuous search, Marcie had met only one such candidate. Johnny.

She was crazy about him the minute she laid eyes on him in the Pour House, a local bar. Her mistake, she realized, was sleeping with him too soon. Way too soon.

He'd gone home with her on some phony excuse and, against her better judgment, stayed the night. Hard as she tried, Marcie couldn't make herself regret it. Sex with Johnny had been incredible. Probably the best of her entire life.

The following morning, after he'd left her, Marcie feared she'd never hear from him again. She'd nearly wept tears of joy when he showed up on her doorstep a month later. She'd already decided that, if given a second chance with him, she wouldn't make the same mistake. She'd been waiting all her life for a man like Johnny, and come hell or high water she was going to find a way to marry him.

Unfortunately Johnny made her weak, and before she'd realized what was happening, they were back in the bedroom again. This time he stayed the entire weekend. Nothing interrupted them. Not televised football. Not phone calls. Nothing. He didn't even want her to cook, had insisted on ordering out and paying for it himself. When he left her that time, Marcie was so completely exhausted she'd had to stay home from work for two days.

If ever there was a man capable of keeping her happy, it was Johnny. It went without saying that if she wanted to marry him, she'd need to play her cards right, and that meant careful planning.

She was well aware that becoming intimate before forging an emotional bond was a tactical error. Johnny had to want her for more than her body. Marcie knew it, yet she'd allowed herself to be manipulated right back into bed. Mainly because he was such an incredible lover.

As time progressed he stopped by more and more often, but rarely for longer than two or three days. Sometimes he'd show up unexpectedly at the shop and every now and again at her apartment. He wouldn't believe it if she told him, so she never did, but she hadn't been to bed with another man since they'd met.

In their times together, she noted that he rarely spoke about himself. But then they seldom talked other than superficially, which was fine. The trust would come in time. If she had to pick up snatches of his life here and there, that was okay with her, too. She was a patient woman.

What made Johnny special was that he proved to be an unselfish lover, inventive and generous. A fair portion of her previous lovers had been sexual brontosauruses. The type who considered lovemaking to consist of ripping off her clothes, throwing her down on the bed, completing the act while grunting as though in the midst of a cardiac arrest, then rolling over and promptly falling asleep.

The men Marcie had loved generally knew little about foreplay. This was where Johnny excelled. No one needed to tell her he was a rare breed. She'd been around long enough to appreciate a lover with a slow touch. One who titillated her verbally, who seduced her with words before he so much as kissed her.

It amazed Marcie how well he read her moods. There were times when she was too desperate for him to wade through the long, slow process of being undressed and adored as he stripped away each piece of clothing.

Johnny gauged her mood without her having to say a word. He'd smile, his mouth soft and sexy, then quickly dispense with the preliminaries. Before long he had her pinned against the wall, her skirt up around her waist. By the time he finished she was breathless and limp with satisfaction.

After she'd been seeing him fairly frequently, there'd been a lull. Several months passed without a word. At first she suspected he might be married. But having fallen into that trap before, she'd come to recognize the signs. Not Johnny. He was a free spirit, a salesman whose job often took him away for weeks on end.

It killed her not to question him, but if he wasn't willing to tell her of his own volition, then she didn't ask. To the best of her knowledge there was no faster way to get rid of a potential husband than to make demands on him. From her experience, if she mentioned the word "commitment," she might as well hold open the front door as he raced past. Mow a man down with questions and chances were the relationship wouldn't rebound.

Marcie had made far too many mistakes in her life to fall prey to those traps. She wanted Johnny and was willing to be patient.

After a lengthy silence, Marcie figured she'd lost him for good. That was when she'd taken a long hard look at her life. Frankly, she hadn't liked what she'd seen, so she'd made some basic changes. Cleaned up her act, so to speak.

The first thing she'd decided was that she wouldn't go to bed with a man again until there was a ring on her finger. When she'd first made the decision, it had sounded drastic even to her own ears. She'd enjoyed an active, healthy sex life from the time she was a teenager. But to her surprise, she found she rather enjoyed being celibate.

Clothes shopping took an entirely different slant. No longer did she judge an outfit by how sexy a man would find her or how seductive she looked. She purchased clothes that felt good, clothes that made her feel good about herself.

Once she looked at herself differently, she learned to view men by more than how much they needed her. She was no longer interested in rescue operations. The money and emotional energy she saved made her feel years younger.

She wanted to marry Johnny, but if she couldn't have him, then she had no option but to move on to greener pastures. So she'd gone on a campaign to find herself a husband. One who didn't frequent a bar.

A sign of exactly how serious she was came the day she applied for and received a library card. Because she hadn't paid nearly enough attention in school, her reading skills weren't what they should have been. She started out borrowing books on tape. That satisfied her for a while, but shortly afterward she progressed to reading the books by herself. Especially the self-help ones.

It wasn't long before she recognized that she was a woman who loved too much.

Too much. Too often. Too soon.

Now, just when she believed she was about to achieve her goal and meet someone decent, Johnny popped back into her life. Well, she wasn't the same woman he'd left behind. Besides, there was Clifford. She'd been dating him for two months, which was something of a record. It was certainly the longest time she'd gone out with a man without going to bed with him.

Clifford Cramden owned a plumbing company, played on the local softball team, and hadn't once asked for a loan. Well, he had run out of check blanks that once, but he'd repaid her promptly. He wasn't a bad kisser. Their petting had gotten heavy a couple of times, but he'd always put an end to the foreplay before it got out of hand. Only once had he suggested spending the night. Marcie had gently rejected the idea, and he hadn't pressed her. He wouldn't be any kind of man, she decided, if she didn't tempt him sexually.

They were at the point in their dating where Marcie felt free to talk about "their relationship." For the first time in her life, she was on first base, and she wasn't about to let a weekend fling with Johnny ruin that.

It sounded good when she reasoned it out. Johnny was in town briefly, looking for a good time, and she was a good-time girl. Or had been.

If ever a woman stood at the crossroads, it was Marcie. The minute Johnny had walked into her back room she'd seen the need flash in his eyes. Heaven help her, she'd wanted him too. That she'd been able to refuse him confirmed how much she'd changed.

Johnny would be back. Marcie would bet her last dollar on that. He wasn't used to losing, wasn't accustomed to not having what he wanted, when he wanted it. Next time, she suspected, he'd come with a whole lot more than a bouquet of cheap flowers.

"Marcie."

"In here," she answered, calling over her shoulder.

"Someone's come to see you."

Something in Samantha's voice alerted her that it wasn't one of her LOLs. Marcie worked wonders with older women's hair. Her little old ladies loved her, and she showered them with attention.

"Who?" she asked. She knew her schedule, and she was finished for the day. From the inflection in Samantha's voice, she guessed it was a man. Probably Johnny.

"Come and see."

She came out from the back, wiping her hands dry on a towel, praying for the strength to resist him. If ever a man could push her buttons, it was this salesman.

She saw the huge teddy bear first.

"Hi, sweetheart." Clifford's head appeared from behind the stuffed animal. His grin stretched wide.

"Clifford." Her relief was so great, she nearly succumbed to tears.

"Just a little something special so you'll know how much I love you."

10

He should be asleep, Murphy thought darkly. He would be, too, if the little hellion next to him hadn't irritated him to this extent.

Carlos's friend had generously put them up for the night, a risky proposition for a man who jeopardized his life doing a favor. After all, he and Letty were strangers, and this man owed them nothing, least of all his hospitality.

Murphy was the one who'd insisted they stay in the barn. From the look Miss Holier-Than-Thou had given the stall, one would think she'd expected him to locate a Hilton Hotel just for her comfort. Concierge level!

What irked him was that he was even in Zarcero. All he'd been looking for when he'd traveled to Texas was a little rest and relaxation. Instead he was risking his ass for a man already dead because this woman was convinced her brother was alive.

As best Murphy could figure it, there'd obviously

been a lapse in his sanity. He'd spent less than two days with Letty Madden and couldn't imagine enduring that many more.

Even asleep she irritated him. The pristine postmistress lived in fear that he'd take advantage of her. Well, Murphy had news for her. He'd rather become a monk than lay a finger on her.

Her problem, he decided, was that the woman didn't know what she wanted herself. Her mouth said one thing and her body another.

He doubted she'd be that forthright or honest about her own needs. She batted her eyes at him, moistened her lips, and tempted him beyond what any red-blooded man should be asked to endure.

One night with her had only created a need for more, but he wasn't game. This woman was trouble. Big trouble.

She'd have to strip naked and beg him to make love to her before he'd so much as touch her again. Even then, he'd need to think twice.

The outraged virgin could— He stopped. Letty was no longer a virgin. She'd surrendered that to him in exchange for his help.

Regret settled squarely, heavily, on his shoulders. Regret and guilt. He was uncomfortable with both emotions. Uncomfortable and unfamiliar.

Murphy wished to hell he could remember what had happened between them, but try as he might, the memory was lost.

Letty slept soundly at his side. They shared a common blanket, which she'd insisted they place on top of the straw instead of using it for warmth.

Her deep, even breathing lulled him into a state of semiwakefulness. With his hand tucked behind his head, he lay on his back and forced his body to relax.

It'd be light in another couple of hours. He'd prefer to travel at night. Both Carlos and Juan, the farmer, had warned him about guerrillas who roamed the countryside. Murphy wished he had the luxury of waiting, but he needed a vehicle and there wasn't exactly a used-car lot for him to choose from.

Without a means of transportation, it would take them several days to find their way into San Paulo, the capital. From what Letty had told him, Luke's mission was situated in Managna, less than ten miles outside of the capital.

San Paulo was located in the central part of the country, in a lush green valley. No matter which route he took, they had to get through the dense mountains.

His best chance, he decided, was to make his way into the nearest village and steal a jeep, preferably one from the army. Thievery didn't bother him while on an assignment, especially when he was able to abscond with the adversary's property.

Letty rolled from her back onto her side, facing him. Apparently she was cold, because she snuggled up against him tighter than a miser's budget. He was still figuring out how to ease himself away from her when she pressed her head against his shoulder, using him as a pillow.

With anyone else he might have shared his body's warmth, but he wasn't about to be accused of anything untoward with her. The woman was under the misconception that he lusted after her every minute of the day and night. Well, it'd be a cold day in hell before he'd give her that satisfaction.

Murphy squeezed his eyes closed, determined to ignore her close proximity. He'd partially succeeded when she moaned. He frowned, wondering if he'd imagined it.

Then she did it again, louder this time, as if she were in a great deal of pain. Murphy waited, unsure what he should do. Her head rolled from side to side, and a low, almost wailing sound slid from her lips.

"Letty," he whispered, not wanting to startle her awake. But he couldn't very well have her raise a commotion. A woman's scream had a way of echoing through the night. The last thing they needed was for her to send out an announcement of their arrival to a rebel outpost.

No sooner had the thought entered his head than Letty bolted upright and let loose with a bloodcurdling cry that roused the chickens and just about everything else.

Rarely had Murphy moved faster. He had her flipped onto her back with his hand planted over her mouth before another second passed.

Her frantic eyes flew open and met his in the dim moonlight. What happened next surprised him even more than her scream. She released a soft sob and wrapped her arms around his neck as if she intended never to let go. Next she buried her face in his neck and began to sob.

"Letty?" He'd experienced just about everything in his lifetime, but he hadn't a clue on how to comfort a crying woman. "What is it?"

"A dream." Her hold tightened, and she trembled in his arms.

"There's nothing to worry about—everything's fine," he said as matter-of-factly as he could.

"No. No, it isn't. My brother's in terrible pain."

He should have known the dream involved her brother. "It was a dream, Letty. You don't know what condition Luke's in."

"But I do. I saw him."

"Saw him?" The least he could do was humor her. Murphy didn't go for this so-called telepathy between her and Luke that she'd attempted to feed him. Something about a mental connection. Okay, so they were twins. But Luke was a man and she was a woman. He'd read that that sort of thing happened with identical twins, but even then he wasn't entirely sure he bought it.

"He's been tortured."

That part Murphy could believe. If the missionary hadn't been murdered outright, there was every possibility he'd been taken in for questioning. What Letty's brother could possibly have to disclose remained a mystery.

Letty felt incredibly soft and vulnerable in his arms. Almost against his will, he found himself stroking her hair away from her face.

"We've got to find him."

"We will," he said as if he believed it were possible.

Letty sighed audibly, releasing her warm breath against the skin at the hollow of his throat.

"Promise me," she insisted. "Promise me we won't leave Zarcero without finding Luke."

He couldn't do that. "Letty, be reasonable."

"Please, we've got to rescue him."

Murphy said nothing. He wasn't being cruel, just realistic. He'd like to give her all the reassurances in the world, but he couldn't, not this time.

Not that he opposed lying to a woman in bed. He'd done it plenty of times. He simply told a woman what she wanted to hear and saved himself grief.

But he couldn't make himself do it with Letty.

"Luke's going to die unless we rescue him." Her words trembled from her moist lips. Murphy felt the action of her mouth against his skin and the slick feel of her tears as they rolled down her cheeks.

"You don't understand," she said. "Luke's dying."

Murphy struggled, not knowing what to say.

"Promise me."

Instead of comforting her, his silence agitated her, and she moaned softly, her pain and grief overwhelming her.

"All right, all right," he whispered against her hair. "You have my word of honor. No matter what it takes, we'll get Luke out of here."

"Thank you. Thank you," she repeated again and again until her voice faded completely.

Murphy didn't know how long he continued to hold her. Long after she'd returned to sleep. Much longer than was necessary.

He'd find her brother for her. Dead or alive. If nothing else, Murphy was a man of his word.

11

Letty woke with her head nestled against Murphy's shoulder and his arm tucked protectively about her. She felt both cozy and shielded from harm until she remembered her dream.

A sense of urgency filled her, and she rolled away from Murphy and sat up. She tried to think, tried to remember the dream. Luke, poor Luke, had called out to her to tell her he wanted to die because the pain was too much to endure any longer.

She sensed that he was already close to death. They had to get to Managna and find him before it was too late.

Brushing the wild array of hair from her face, she recalled the way she'd clung to Murphy last night and pleaded with him to find her brother. And he'd given his word. From the hesitant reluctance in his voice, she'd known he would rather have ignored her fears, but in the end he'd vowed they wouldn't leave Zarcero without finding Luke.

The man was an enigma. In the two full days that they'd been together, he'd been impatient and sometimes cruel. Yet last night he'd taken her in his arms and agreed to rescue Luke, even if it meant putting his own life at risk. Letty simply didn't understand him, but then she suspected that no one really did.

She felt his movement at her side as he stirred. He didn't look at her, and she sure as heaven didn't glance at him. The scene from the night before mortified her now.

"We need to get out of here," he muttered, "the sooner the better."

Letty realized Murphy was concerned about putting Carlos's friend in danger, and she shared his fears.

"How far from San Paulo are we?"

"A hundred miles, maybe more. There's a village close by. I'll get us a car there."

It went without saying that he'd have to steal it. Letty never would have believed she'd condone such an action, but she did. Her heart sagged with relief. With a vehicle and a bit of luck, they could reach San Paulo and Luke before the end of the day.

Murphy left her for a short time while he scouted out the surrounding countryside. She used the minutes effectively and was packed, ready and eager to leave the protection of the barn, when he returned.

He held open the door for her. Sunlight spilled into the cool, dim interior of the outbuilding, heralding another picture-perfect day in Zarcero.

They left the farmyard and walked through a field of tall grass, avoiding the road. For the better part of two hours they traveled without communicating.

Murphy seemed aware of every sound and stopped abruptly a couple of times. He pressed his finger over his lips and waited before proceeding.

When they came to a grove of large Guanacaste trees, Murphy stopped and reached for his canteen. He drank first, then handed it to Letty. The water tasted terrible. She'd seen Murphy add a capsule to it and knew it must have been some form of purification pill. It was difficult for Letty to estimate how far they'd traveled. It felt like five miles or farther, but she couldn't really say.

Murphy wasn't any friendlier than he had been earlier, which disappointed her, following his promise from the night before.

A conversationalist Murphy wasn't.

He seemed to have reached a decision, because he sat down near a tree. Without a word he unfolded a map, pressed it down upon the ground, and studied it intently.

"How much farther is it to the village?" she asked.

He didn't look up. "Not far." He refolded the map carefully and placed it inside his knapsack. He stood, and Letty reluctantly came to her feet.

"I want you to stay here."

"Why?"

He answered by removing the pistol from his shoulder holster and handing it to her.

She stared at it, almost afraid it would explode in her palm. "What's this for?"

"I want you to keep it with you from here on out. Understand?"

"But—"

"Do you want to find your brother or not?"

"Of course, but—"

"Then do as I ask." His eyes cut her to the quick. "You probably couldn't hit the broad side of a barn, but it's the only security I have to offer you."

"What should I do while you're away?"

"Wait quietly," he suggested impatiently.

He started to walk away, but a terrifying thought came to her. "Murphy?" she called out.

He glanced over his shoulder, looking none too pleased with her.

She implored him with her eyes, nervous and more than a little afraid. "What if . . . what will happen if you don't come back?"

A slow, easy smile claimed his face as if he found her question comical. "I'll be back."

She nodded and offered him a shaky smile of her own. "Okay."

Holding on to the gun with both hands, she glanced around her suspiciously, wondering if there might be guerrillas hiding in the bush, ready to attack her the minute Murphy was out of sight.

She started to call out to him a second time, but he was gone. He'd virtually disappeared from one moment to the next. Vanished like a puff of smoke.

Truly alone, Letty walked the circumference of the grove and glanced at her wristwatch. Murphy had been away all of five minutes and already she was worried.

She shifted the pistol from one hand to the other,

wondering if she was actually capable of killing another human being. And doubted it.

As far as she was concerned, Murphy's lessons on firing the .45 had been for naught. Apparently it made him feel better leaving her with some form of self-defense, despite the fact she found it useless.

By five o'clock, nine hours after he'd left, Letty forced herself to stop looking at her watch. Murphy had been gone far longer than she'd expected.

He could have been captured. Could have been killed.

He had no means of letting her know his predicament. True, he'd given her specific instructions to remain right where she was, but just exactly how long was she supposed to wait? Nine hours seemed far too long.

As unpleasant as it was, she had to accept the possibility that he would never return. True, he was an expert at what he did, but that didn't make him invulnerable.

The chance existed that he'd met up with a group of guerrillas and been taken captive himself. Perhaps he'd been caught attempting to hot-wire a vehicle and thrown in jail by the local authorities.

Fearing the worst, Letty wondered what she should do. If anything.

The option of retracing her steps and going back to the farmhouse presented itself, but she didn't want to backtrack. Not after her nightmare. If she intended to reach Luke in time, it meant making her way into San Paulo or Managna, and she couldn't do that waiting days on end for Murphy. Especially if he was no longer able to come for her.

On the other hand, Murphy had been specific about her following orders. She'd never seen a man so hardheaded or unreasonable. Just exactly what was she supposed to do?

The decision was made for her several minutes later when gunfire sounded in the distance.

Murphy was in trouble. She could sense it. Not in the same way she knew Luke was in trouble. This time it was woman's intuition.

She had to find a way to save him.

Praying she was doing the right thing, Letty reached for her backpack and placed it on her shoulders. With the gun clenched in her hand, she headed in the same direction she'd seen Murphy go.

12

Jack Keller decided to let Marcie wait and wonder. Her cool reception had come as something of a shock. In the beginning he'd been angry, but he'd since changed his tune. Actually, he understood.

It'd been months since they'd last seen each other, and a woman had her pride. Things changed. People changed. He'd left her without a word. She had every right to be displeased with him, but he intended to make it up to her. Once he'd soothed her ruffled feathers, things could go back to the way they'd always been between them.

Marcie was a sensual woman, and it was rare to find one as uninhibited and generous in bed as she was. It was even more rare that she'd never asked or hinted for anything in return for her favors.

This time when he stopped off to see her, he brought long-stemmed roses. Floral shop ones that came in a box with a fancy silk ribbon, not a cheap bouquet comprising carnations and a few other common flowers.

He dressed up, too. Not a suit and tie, but in a shirt fresh from the cleaners and pressed slacks. If he'd been more certain of his reception, he would have phoned first.

When he arrived at her apartment he found her car parked at the curb. He smiled. One thing about Marcie, she was consistent. As he recalled, she wasn't keen on a lot of change. Keller liked that. She'd lived in the same apartment for ten years and drove the same car she'd had when they'd first met.

He rang the doorbell and waited. He half expected her to answer, wearing her robe and little else. As he remembered, when she arrived home she habitually changed out of her uniform and into something more comfortable. He definitely approved of her choice.

To his surprise, she answered wearing white shorts and a high-necked, sleeveless blouse. "Johnny." Her voice was decidedly even, and he couldn't tell if she was pleased or not to see him.

"I came to apologize for the other day," he said, looking and sounding contrite. "You must think me a Neanderthal to come on to you the way I did."

She stood on the other side of the screen door, her hand on the knob as if she weren't sure she should let him in.

Keller decided a little underhanded persuasion just might be necessary. "I would have contacted you sooner, but I was in an accident." It was necessary to stretch the truth now and again, although he didn't make a habit of it.

"An accident?" Her pretty eyes widened with concern.

"I'd really like to talk to you, Marcie. Nothing more, I promise." He raised both hands in a gesture of surrender.

She hesitated.

"Please," he added with a sincerity few could refuse.

His plan worked; she unlatched the screen door.

"It's good to see you," he said as he walked into the apartment. He made it sound as if he were damn lucky to be alive.

To Keller's surprise, he found the interior of her apartment markedly different. The furniture was the same, but everything else had changed. The drapes were bright, the windows sparkled. A knitting basket filled with yarn was next to the chair. Several magazines were fanned out across the top of the coffee table.

Without waiting for an invitation, he sat down. Again he made it look as if it were a trial for him to remain upright for any length of time, which wasn't far from true. His ribs had been killing him for weeks.

He set the box of roses on the coffee table and all but collapsed against the back of the sofa.

"What happened?" she asked.

Keller hid a smile at the gentle concern in her voice. "Car accident," he whispered. He thought to tell her there was a metal plate in his head but feared that was carrying the story a bit too far. "If you don't mind, I'd prefer not to talk about it."

"Of course." Her warm, caring voice was a balm after her earlier rebuff.

A moment of strained silence passed between them. Everything was going as planned, except that Marcie remained standing on the far side of the room almost as if she feared what would happen if she sat next to him. Keller wished she would. If he had the chance to kiss her once or twice, they might get past this awkwardness. All she really needed was a little gentle persuasion.

She seemed to be waiting for him to say something, so Keller brought up the first thing that came to mind. "The reason I stopped by, other than to apologize for the other day, was to personally thank you for bailing me out of jail."

"It's all right, Johnny."

"I'd like to show you how much I appreciate our friendship, Marcie. I don't know what I would have done without you." Several months back he'd been foolish and gotten himself arrested in a bar fight. Charges had later been dismissed, but Keller had been stuck in the clinker and would have spent the night if it hadn't been for Marcie. Normally he would have done the time, but Murphy had needed him, and he'd had a plane to catch.

"You don't owe me any money," she claimed as he withdrew his wallet. "You must have forgotten with the accident and all."

"You're sure?"

"Oh, yes. A cashier's check arrived a week later."

"Good." She'd reassured him of that earlier, but wanting to make sure she'd been reimbursed put him in a good light.

Again he confronted a short, awkward silence.

"You're looking wonderful." That was no exaggeration. Marcie did look good. Better than he remembered. "What's different?"

"A lot of things."

He leaned forward, bracing his elbows against his knees. "I don't suppose you have something to drink?" As he recalled, Marcie kept a full liquor cabinet.

"Coffee?"

At first he thought she was joking, but it was clear she wasn't. "Sure."

"Sugar and cream?"

"Just black."

She walked out of the living room, and he was left to twiddle his thumbs. Keller waited a moment and then followed her into the compact kitchen.

Marcie was busy assembling a pot and glanced over her shoulder when he entered.

"Johnny," she said, and seemed nervous as she continued in a hurried, rushed voice. "There's something you should know. I'm seeing someone else now."

So that was it. Well, it didn't come as any real surprise.

"He's real good to me."

"In other words he doesn't disappear for months at a time."

She shrugged, as if his disappearances had never really concerned her.

"I'm happy for you, sweetheart." Keller wanted to shove his fist down the other man's throat, but he didn't let Marcie know that.

"You are?" She visibly relaxed.

Keller nodded. "You deserve the best."

The coffeepot made a gurgling sound, and the dark liquid drained into the glass pot. Marcie turned and opened the cupboard doors and reached for two cups.

Keller moved behind her, pressing his body intimately against her backside. "Let me do that for you," he whispered. She was soft, warm, and womanly. Her buttocks cushioned him as if she'd been custom-made just for him. Normally he wasn't a jealous man, but Keller felt a flare of the ugly green monster just thinking about Marcie in bed with another man. The emotion came as an unwelcome surprise.

Gradually he eased himself away from her and brought down two ceramic mugs. "Tell me about your new boyfriend," he encouraged. The more he knew, the better he could undermine the other man.

He noticed that Marcie's hand shook ever so slightly as she poured the freshly brewed coffee. Keller smiled inwardly. She'd enjoyed the brief intimacy as much as he had. She didn't like it, but she couldn't deny it.

"His name is Clifford Cramden and he's a plumber."

"A plumber." Something was wrong. The Marcie he remembered would be bored to tears with a man named Clifford Cramden. It didn't add up.

"Is he the jealous type?" Keller asked, helping himself to a kitchen chair.

"Clifford?" She raised questioning eyes to his. "I don't know. I've never given him any reason to be jealous."

No reason to be jealous? Marcie?

"Do you think he'd mind if I took you to dinner to thank you for your bailing me out of jail?"

"That's not necessary."

"It's the least I can do," Keller insisted, sounding as sincere as he could. "If you think it would help, I'll contact your boyfriend myself and explain. The last thing I'd want is a misunderstanding between you two."

Marcie lowered her lashes, and it was clear she was tempted.

"The Cattleman's Place," he said, mentioning the most expensive steakhouse in town.

Her pretty eyes met his. "I've always wanted to have dinner there."

It was on the tip of his tongue to tell her that a plumber wasn't likely to be able to afford it.

"How about it, Marcie? Tomorrow night. I'll pick you up at six."

She closed her eyes, shook her head, and answered hurriedly. "I can't."

"The next night, then," he pressed, unwilling to drop it. "If that doesn't work, then you choose the day and time."

A long moment passed before she spoke. "Saturday?" The lone word was breathless, as if she weren't sure even now if she should.

"Saturday it is," he said cheerfully, feeling as if he'd won a decisive battle. "I'll be by for you at six."

"Just between friends," she said, her eyes holding his.

"Of course," he lied. But then friends made the very best lovers.

13

Night had settled over Zarcero, and Letty would have been lost completely if not for the village lights that gleamed in the distance like small beacons, guiding her. She made her way down the steep incline into the town as carefully as she could, fearing she might lose her balance with each step. Intermittent bursts of gunfire could be heard in the distance.

The moon and stars offered little in the way of illumination. As she drew closer to the town, she heard boisterous music and singing. It took a bit more time for her to make out the words of the raunchy song, and she blushed as she translated them. Apparently the civil unrest hadn't disturbed the civilians as much as she'd assumed.

Once she reached the outskirts of the town, Letty hid, to assess her options. She'd been traveling four or five hours at this point and had seen no trace of Murphy.

He'd come for a vehicle and apparently hadn't succeeded, which meant he'd probably been captured. She'd steal a car first and then find him. Although she knew next to nothing about cars and engines, she did hope that with a bit of patience and a hairpin in the ignition switch, she might coax an engine to life. She'd heard a credit card could open a locked door, and if that was true, then surely a hairpin could start a car.

A number of vehicles would surely be parked outside the cantina. But stealing one of those and driving away undetected would be next to impossible. She had no choice but to scout around.

Flattening herself against the side of an adobe building, Letty silently made her way down a deserted alley. Sweat broke out across her brow as she feared discovery. Perhaps she should wait . . . . After a moment she decided against it. She'd already wasted an entire day, fruitlessly anticipating Murphy's return. She tried not to think what had happened to him or what those gunshots had meant.

The thought he might have been killed produced a tightness in her chest, and she banished the worry from her mind. She'd go after Luke first, she decided, then return for Murphy.

Once she'd had the opportunity to scout out the town, she'd weigh her options, make her choices, and move.

The entire village appeared to be deserted except for the cantina. The music was growing louder and more boisterous.

Eventually she was able to maneuver herself between two buildings and look out onto the main road that ran in front of the local bar. From the laughter and good cheer, one would never guess the country was in chaos.

As Letty suspected, six or seven jeeps and a variety of dilapidated American cars thirty years or older were parked in front of the bar. Thus far they were the only vehicles she'd seen.

The people inside didn't seem to have a care in the world. The doors were wide open, and tables spilled into the streets. A number of women paraded around in tight-fitting skirts and low, elastic-style blouses. Some delivered drinks, others brazenly touted their wares and openly invited attention.

Out of the corner of her eye, Letty watched as a soldier grabbed a woman's waist and dragged her onto his lap. The young waitress squealed with delight before he slammed his mouth over hers. Soon the two were all over one another. The woman squirmed in the soldier's lap and straddled his hips. Panting, she threw back her head, and he buried his face in her ample bosom. His hands cupped her full breasts as he licked and sucked at her neck.

Letty was mesmerized, unable to make herself look away. The two were all but making love in full view of the entire cantina. Letty's mouth felt dry, and she couldn't understand why she found such a blatant display of sexual activity so fascinating.

All at once it came to her.

That wasn't a soldier with the waitress. It was Murphy.

The shock was enough to make Letty's knees go out on her. With her back against the building, she slid to the ground until her buttocks landed in the hard dirt.

Murphy. The dirty son of a bastard had left her to wait in the hot sun for hours on end while he was making love to a . . . a floozy.

Rarely had Letty been more furious. All this time she'd fretted and stewed, certain he'd been captured or worse. The afternoon had been hell, worrying about him.

She'd risked her life in an effort to find out what had happened to him. Anything might have befallen her as she'd made her way into the village. Not that Murphy would have cared. He'd have been grateful to have her out from under his hair.

She'd made a drastic mistake trusting Murphy. The man had no morals. No decency. She hoped he died a slow, painful death. She relished the thought of him suffering.

Her anger was enough to motivate her into action. Whereas before she'd been almost afraid to breathe for fear of discovery, now she moved freely from one building to the next, being sure to remain in the shadows. She was careful, very careful, but not stupid.

Still uncertain about the odds of successfully stealing a jeep, she made her way to the far side of town, thinking that she'd hide in the church until the wee hours of the morning. By then the soldiers would be too drunk to realize what she was doing.

As she neared the church, she heard the soft, almost soundless approach of someone behind her. Her blood ran cold. Fear was an amazing thing, she realized. Never had her thought processes been more clear.

She waited until he was almost upon her before

whirling around, thinking she would startle her stalker.

To her shock Murphy stood almost directly behind her.

"Murphy?" She nearly shouted his name in her surprise.

He clamped his hand over her mouth and shoved her against the side of the church. "Just what the bloody hell do you think you're doing?"

One aspect of soldiering Murphy had learned early in his career was that emotion was as much an enemy as a gun-toting revolutionary. Murphy went into a mission with no feelings, did what he was paid to do, and got the hell out in the most expedient manner possible. In all his years with Deliverance Company, he'd lived by those rules.

Then he'd joined forces with one Letty Madden.

Everything changed the minute he agreed to accompany the postmistress to Zarcero. She caused him to see red faster than anyone or anything he'd ever known.

This latest escapade of hers, slipping down a dark alley in enemy territory, sticking out like a sore thumb, was a prime example. It didn't matter how much the rebels had drunk, they were still soldiers. It was only a matter of time before she'd be discovered.

Murphy had carefully bided his time, waiting for nightfall to make his move. He'd sat on the fringes of the cantina, in a "borrowed" rebel uniform, gathering valuable information. By the time he'd joined the rowdy assembly, most of the soldiers were three sheets to the wind. Carlotta, the shapely woman in his arms, had provided the perfect camouflage while he'd learned what he needed.

Then out of nowhere Letty appeared, as obvious as a bull in a china shop. He'd damn near gone ballistic right then and there. She was fortunate he hadn't done more than shove her up against the side of a building.

She struggled and bit down on the fleshy part of his hand between his thumb and index finger. Hard. Murphy swallowed a yelp and pinched her jaw until she released him. Despite the pain, he continued to hold her captive.

"Just what the hell are you trying to do, get us both killed?" he demanded. "I told you to wait for me." As soon as he could reason clearly, he'd deal with the fact that she'd disobeyed a direct order.

She pressed her hand against his chest and shoved, but he didn't budge.

"You dirty son of a—" She bit off the last word and glared at him with eyes that would have quelled a lesser man.

"Me?" he muttered, not understanding her fury. "Listen, little sister, let's get something straight right here and now. When I give an order it's to be obeyed."

"You've given me your last order, buster." She squirmed against him and would have done him injury had he not escaped her knee.

Her fury caught Murphy off guard. What the hell did she have to be so mad about? It took him far longer than it should have to realize Letty had seen him with Carlotta. The waitress had been all over him, hawking her goods, looking for a few extra dollars on the side.

"Let me go," she insisted, her chest heaving. At another time, Murphy might have enjoyed having her squirm against him. But not when it put them both at risk.

"Shut up before you get us both killed," he said none too gently.

Murphy relaxed his grip on her wrists, but only slightly. They needed to clear the air. Unfortunately they couldn't do it in the alley with rebel soldiers partying across the street.

"I'll release you if you promise not to speak." He waited for her acquiescence, which she gave grudgingly with one sharp nod of her head.

Satisfied, Murphy wrapped his hand around her upper arm and half dragged her out the back side of the alley. He led the way out of the village, not stopping until he was confident they wouldn't be heard.

"I will not tolerate insubordination," he said heatedly, the haze of his own anger only now beginning to fade.

"You won't have to," she returned calmly. "You're fired."

He was confident he'd misunderstood her. "Fired?"

"I'll find Luke without you."

Murphy couldn't help it, he muffled a laugh. "Really?"

"I absolve you from your duty." She dismissed him with a dramatic wave of her hand, in an action befitting royalty.

"Just how far do you think you'll actually get before you're discovered?"

"Farther than I did today. How long did you intend to leave me baking in the sun while you and that . . . that woman were—"

"That woman kept me from being discovered." Letty seemed to conveniently forget he'd placed himself in considerable risk on her behalf.

"I know exactly what that woman did for you," Letty spat, disgust dripping from every word.

Murphy didn't need this, not after the day he'd had. If she wanted him off the mission, it was fine by him. As far as he could see, it was a waste of time anyway. "Great," he returned. "Wonderful. I couldn't be more pleased." He turned and started to walk away.

His mind buzzed with fury and outrage. After all he'd been through, this was the thanks he got. The woman was a candidate for a mental hospital. For that matter, so was he for ever having agreed to escort her to Zarcero.

Well, he was finished. He washed his hands of her and her do-good brother. He didn't need this kind of grief.

He hadn't taken two steps when she stopped him.

"Wait."

It didn't take her long to come to her senses, he noted, mildly pleased. She needed him, and rehiring him wasn't going to be as easy as she seemed to think. He'd set a number of things straight. First off, she couldn't follow the simplest instructions. One thing he wouldn't tolerate was insubordination. Not from anyone, much less a fickle-hearted woman.

He turned around to discover Letty kneeling on the ground, digging through her backpack. "I won't be needing this," she said, retrieving the .45. She held it between two fingers as if it were something dead she'd rather not touch.

His weapon. She'd flustered him to the point he'd forgotten his single most valuable survival tool, the very one he'd voluntarily left behind for her protection.

"Before you go," she said, shoulders squared, "I want you to know I think you're the most unprincipled, unscrupulous, immoral man I've ever met."

Murphy hitched his eyebrows up a notch and chuckled softly. "You mean to say it's taken you this long to discover that?"

She was seething.

Murphy loved it. He'd done his duty, gone the extra mile. Extra mile, hell, he'd gone a whole lot farther than that. Letty Madden was on her own, and he couldn't be more pleased.

He tucked the gun inside his belt. "Good luck finding your brother."

"I don't need luck," she said, righteousness echoing like thunder from her lips. "God is with me."

"If that's the case, I don't know why you ever felt you needed me," Murphy returned without malice.

"Frankly, I don't either."

With wide, determined strides, Murphy continued up the steep incline that led away from the small village. Without trouble he should be able to make his way back to the farmhouse that night. In the morning he'd talk to Juan and signal for Carlos. If everything went smoothly, he'd be in Boothill in two days' time.

14

For reasons Luke would probably never know, the beatings had stopped. The pain was manageable now, and with this unexpected reprieve came the will to continue. For the first time since his capture, he found the strength to live.

In the back of his mind, a hazy remembrance of Rosita's visit haunted him. Had it been real? He no longer knew. For whatever reason, God had allowed her to come to him, whether in body or spirit, he didn't know. Whichever form, Luke was grateful.

Try as he might, he didn't recall what she'd said, if indeed she had actually visited him.

All he remembered was that in the worst of his pain, when the agony had been more than he could bear, she'd been there, smoothing his hair from his brow, whispering reassurances. He'd felt her love and her courage as powerfully as if she'd dressed his physical injuries.

Luke's heart swelled with love for the beautiful woman and the future he'd planned with her as his wife.

When he'd been assigned Zarcero, Luke had been confident the Lord had sent him to the troubled Central American country for a specific reason. He'd been in Zarcero almost two years before he'd discovered what God had wanted to teach him.

Love.

Not for the gentle peasants who made up a large part of his ministry. His heart had been prepared to love and encourage them for years beforehand. That they had accepted and loved him in return had come as a bonus. The people of Zarcero had been both generous and gracious from the first.

No, what God had sent him to Zarcero to learn was about the love a man has for a woman. What his parents might have shared at one time but had lost.

Luke couldn't remember the first time he'd met Rosita. It wasn't her beauty that stood out in his mind, although she was more lovely than words could adequately express.

Each morning she walked her younger brother and sister to the mission school on her way to work at the market. He must have greeted her a hundred times before he truly noticed her the way a man notices a woman.

This sudden awareness had taken him by surprise. Luke had dedicated his life to God's work, and after his own parents' miserable marriage, he'd decided to remain single.

Mission work was frequently demanding, and he

didn't want to be forced to make the often difficult choice between the needs of his congregation and those of a family.

Paul Madden had never completely recovered from the loss of his wife. He'd lived with doubts and regrets the remainder of his days.

Luke's father had loved his wife heart and soul, and when she'd abandoned him with two children for another man, he'd accepted the blame as if he were the one solely at fault. If only he'd been a better husband instead of a good minister. If only he'd paid more attention to his wife and less to his congregation. He'd never forgiven himself. Never remarried. Never chanced love a second time.

Luke had vowed not to make the same mistake. Naturally he'd been tempted to fall in love. He was as human as the next man, and susceptible to the attention of attractive young women. There'd been any number who'd caught his eye.

But never anyone like Rosita. She was good and kind, gentle and caring. He noticed how the people of Managna loved her. Anyone who knew her couldn't help being affected by her goodness and delicate beauty.

It had taken months for him to pay her heed, but the same wasn't true for Rosita. She claimed her younger brother and sister were fully capable of finding their own way to school. With love shining from her eyes, she took pleasure in reminding him that he was probably the most obtuse man in the universe.

Luke didn't doubt it.

It took him months to actually get around to asking her out. The night of their dinner, he was a nervous wreck. He was twenty-seven years old and felt as though he were seventeen all over again.

When he stopped off at Rosita's house, his tongue seemed glued to the roof of his mouth. He chatted amicably with her father, patted the top of her sister's head, and joked with her brother. Then Rosita came out, wearing a lovely white dress with a flowing skirt and red belt. His heart hitchhiked straight to his knees.

Later that evening, when Luke brought her back to her family, he was convinced he was the worst dinner companion she'd ever known. Their meal had been a disaster, and he'd been the one at fault.

True, nerves had played a part in his uneasiness, but more than that Luke realized that he loved this woman. His sentiments had long since been decided. This wasn't high school or college, where he'd found himself fleetingly attracted to the opposite sex. This was love and the real world.

He hadn't come to Zarcero looking for a wife or the responsibilities of a family. He'd charted his course, confident he was doing the right thing. Then God in His almighty wisdom had hurled a wrench into his picture-perfect blueprint.

Instead of rejoicing in this wonder, instead of thanking God for this unexpected gift, Luke had decided he wanted nothing to do with love. Love would hinder his work. Loving Rosita would handicap his efforts with the people of Zarcero. Love would distract him from his purpose.

Luke decided he wanted none of it. In time, whatever physical attraction he felt for the beautiful young woman would fade.

It didn't.

Instead it grew and blossomed without so much as a touch or a kiss.

Luke wrote his sister, asked for prayers for a deep, inner struggle without telling her exactly what it was he battled. As close as he was to Letty, he feared she would never understand.

When it came to love and marriage, he and Letty appeared to be of the same mind. She'd shown no more inclination toward the married state than he did himself.

Finally, after avoiding Rosita for two months, he inadvertently ran into her while visiting an elderly widow, Mrs. Esparza.

To his shock and hers, Rosita answered the door. She'd been reading to the sickly ninety-four-year-old, and for the first time in days Mrs. Esparza was sleeping comfortably.

Luke was inclined to leave quickly, avoid temptation. A disciplined man by nature, he made his excuses, promised to return later, and headed out the front door.

For reasons he never understood, before he walked out, he turned and looked back at Rosita. He discovered her sitting by the old woman's bed, her head bowed and her eyes bright with tears.

When he questioned her about the emotion, she blushed and claimed dust had gotten in her eyes. Once more Luke turned to leave. And couldn't.

All at once he was tired of fighting what he wanted most. Tired of pretending he was strong. Tired of ignoring his heart.

That was the afternoon Luke learned the lessons God had been struggling to teach him. The lessons he had rejected. The lessons of love.

Luke was a man. But he'd been trying to live the life of a saint, with his head buried in the sand, ignoring the man God meant him to be. It had taken this slap alongside of his head to accept and appreciate the human side of his nature.

The physical part of him had been ignored and repressed for so long that when he set it free, it nearly carried him straight over a cliff.

From that day forward Luke knew it was either preach one thing and live another or marry Rosita. Two weeks before the army overtook the government, Luke had asked Rosita to be his wife and she'd agreed.

He'd known asking her to share his life and his ministry was what God intended from the minute he'd found the courage to pop the question.

He'd hungered for the day he and Rosita could be married. Silently he'd vowed to find a balance in his life, to continue his work with the mission and at the same time be a good husband and father.

Luke opened his eyes and looked around the bare jail cell, and with renewed strength he prayed for the future.

That evening, when a plate of unpalatable food was shoved into the cell, Luke forced himself to swallow a few bites. Then, because he needed to say it aloud, he sat at the end of his bunk, raised his eyes to heaven, and whispered.

"I want to live."

15

Anger was an unfamiliar and uncomfortable emotion to Letty. She sat on the dark hillside and trembled with outrage after Murphy's departure.

The sight of him with that . . . woman, burying his face in her breasts, kissing and sucking her neck, was enough to make Letty physically ill. Her stomach burned every time she thought about it.

She was well rid of him. Clearly she had misplaced her trust. It was a painful and expensive lesson, but one best learned now. Murphy had already delayed her an entire day. Who was to say how much more time he would have wasted while he entertained himself with that hussy.

Undoubtedly he considered her a fool for having dismissed him. The decision had been made in the heat of anger, but that didn't mean she was without resources.

The church steeple silhouetted the moonlit sky. Although Luke had been in Zarcero only a little over two years, he was well known and loved in the religious community. All she needed was to contact another minister or priest, and they would lead her to her brother.

Careful to avoid detection, Letty made her way toward the Catholic church. The street was dark and silent in front of the hundred-year-old structure. Tall, thick doors marked the entrance.

Letty studied the street a long time, fearing that the moment she moved into the open, she'd be caught. Her concern was unjustified. Murphy had apparently paraded around all day in that silly looking uniform and no one had noticed him.

Drawing in a deep breath, she walked out of the shadows and stepped smartly toward the church. By the time she'd made it up the few short church steps, her heart felt as if it were about to explode inside her chest

To her relief, she found that the building wasn't locked. The moment she applied pressure, the thick wooden door creaked open.

She stepped into the vestibule and heard an eerie clicking sound. Blinded by the light, she raised her hand to shade her eyes.

The first thing she noticed was that the pews were missing. Instead the church was filled with desks. And soldiers. Lots of soldiers.

The strange clicking noise she'd heard earlier was the sound of rifles.

Letty froze. The barrels of a dozen guns were pointed at her heart. This place no longer served as a house of God; it was a command center for rebel soldiers.

The farther he walked, the angrier Murphy became. Soon he found himself swearing, first under his breath and then louder, until he had to restrain himself from shouting. But even that didn't make him feel better.

And he knew why.

Despite the fact Letty had fired him. Despite the fact he cursed the day he'd ever laid eyes on her. Despite his better judgment, he was going back.

He couldn't think of a single reason why he should, except his conscience. If anything happened to her, and it would—the woman was not only stupid, she was as naive as they came—he'd never be able to live with himself.

In addition, there was the small problem of his promise. He'd assured her, again knowing he'd regret it, that he'd find her brother.

While it was true he'd have a hell of a better chance rescuing Luke Madden without Letty, in good conscience he couldn't leave her behind to an uncertain fate.

As much as he'd like to do exactly that.

The woman exasperated him. She was God's revenge against a life of not giving a damn.

As he made his way back to the village, Murphy brought his emotions under control. He was going to need his wits about him. He'd have to deal with the rebels, true, but he'd managed to stay alive in these types of situations for years. He excelled in the art of disguise, of blending into the background. The unknown element, what gave him the greatest concern, wasn't the rebels. It was Letty.

It would be just like her to give them both away the minute she laid eyes on him. The woman didn't possess a nickel's worth of common sense.

As he reentered the town, he noted that the music continued to blare from the cantina. The festivities had yet to wind down and wouldn't, he suspected, until the wee hours of the morning.

He walked down the street with purpose, as if he were under important orders. No one stopped to question him, and he doubted that they would.

He paused as he neared the far end of the main street. The last structure left on the block was an old church. He almost discounted it, almost looked past the obvious.

Lights on at this time of night? In a church?

Something was very wrong.

Letty was forced into a chair, and her arms were tied behind her. She glared up at the rebel leader, whose name was Captain Norte, and refused to allow him to see her fear.

"How did you get into Siguierres?" he demanded in broken English.

She told him the truth. "I walked." She said it without emotion, without sarcasm.

He backhanded her across the face. Blood filled her mouth, and she blinked up at him, shocked and stunned by his violence. He looked as if he'd relish hitting her again.

"Put her in jail. Let her cool her heels with the rats for the time being and see if that loosens her tongue," he instructed two guards.

Her hands were untied, and with a soldier at each side she was half lifted from the chair and escorted out the front door. The cool air felt good against her burning, stinging face. She moved her lips carefully. She'd never known a slap could be so painful.

The two men at her side spoke in whispers. At first Letty couldn't make out what they were saying, then she understood that they'd agreed not to take her directly to the jail. They intended to have a little fun with her themselves first.

"No," she said, jerking her elbows first one way and then another. She spoke rapidly in Spanish, telling them that their captain would be greatly displeased when he learned what they'd done. She reminded them that officers expected their orders to be carried out without question and that their captain had ordered them to escort her to the jail.

Desperate now, she told them that if they were to rebuild their country, they must do so with honor. Not with despicable acts of violence against innocent women.

She spoke fast, reasoned hard, and with each frantic plea she realized she might as well have saved her breath. The two weren't about to be cheated out of their pleasure.

They dragged her kicking and screaming behind a building and threw her down upon the hard ground.

She fell against her backpack, and the wind was knocked out of her.

One man held her shoulders, pinning them to the ground. It took both men to restrain her. They allowed her to kick and writhe until her energy was spent before the larger of the two men knelt and ripped open her blouse.

Letty closed her eyes, refusing to look at him. She nearly gagged at the rough feel of his hands over her smooth skin. She kicked and bucked with renewed effort, but to no avail. Soon he straddled her legs and began to unfasten the snap of her jeans.

When the man holding her shoulders urged the other to hurry, Letty started to sob, her ability to fight, to resist, nearly depleted.

The first man positioned himself atop her, his weight crushing her to the ground.

At that precise moment the night exploded around them. The ground trembled, and a blast rocked the entire town. Flames shot into the sky, followed by a low rumble that grew in intensity.

"The fuel dump!" one of the men shouted in terror. He released her and ran. The soldier atop her was only momentarily fazed. Using his forearm for leverage, he rammed his arm across her throat, cutting off her oxygen supply. Her struggles ceased as a new, immediate need took over. She needed to breathe.

Just when Letty thought she was about to pass out for lack of air, the pressure was gone. The rebel went limp. His arm fell from her throat and she gasped, drawing in a deep, fresh breath of air. He was propelled away from her, his eyes frozen open, an expression of shocked horror on his face.

Sobbing, she looked up at her savior, certain what she saw must be an apparition.

Murphy leaned forward and offered her his hand. "Come on," he shouted, "we've got to get out of here, and fast."

For the life of her, she couldn't move. Not giving her the option, he reached down and brought her to her feet. Impatiently he swept her into his arms. The next thing Letty knew, she was tossed in the front seat of a jeep with its engine running.

Within seconds they were barreling out of town, leaving a huge dust trail in their wake.

Murphy continued at a dangerous pace. It was all Letty could do to keep from being hurled onto the road.

By the time he slowed down, reaction had set in and Letty was trembling from head to foot with a chill that came from the inside out.

Murphy glanced at her. "You all right?"

She answered him by slamming her fist against his upper arm and sobbing, "You came back. . . ."

"Well, don't thank me or anything."

She wrapped her arms around herself as the cold, brutal reality of what had nearly happened refused to let go.

"Answer me," Murphy snapped. "Are you okay?"

She closed her eyes and nodded.

"You sure?"

"Yes, damn it, I'm sure."

"It's going to be all right," Murphy said with surprising tenderness.

Letty had dealt with his anger, his harshness, his unfriendliness. She didn't know how to deal with his gentleness. She brushed the tears from her face and sniffled.

"Thank you," she whispered.

16

As Marcie sat at an elegant linen-covered table next to Johnny, the irony didn't escape her. This was their first real date, yet they'd been enthusiastic lovers for almost two years. They'd shared fabulous sex, good times, and fast-food meals, but they'd never gone out. Not in the traditional sense.

Occasionally Johnny brought her gifts, inexpensive baubles and trinkets, as a means of thanking her. Of paying her, she realized sadly, reluctantly. Until recently she'd never looked upon his presents as payment, but it was long past time to be honest.

The stuffed teddy bear Clifford had brought her represented the first time a man had ever given her anything without her sleeping with him first.

Up to this point ninety-five percent of her communication with Johnny had taken place between silk sheets. She knew very little about him and his life. He was a physical man with physical needs, and those needs had dominated each brief rendezvous.

Although she'd agreed to this dinner date, she wasn't sure that she was doing the right thing. Because she felt guilty, she'd casually mentioned the outing to Clifford, making light of it. An old friend, in town for a day or two. Hoped he didn't mind.

Sometimes it was difficult to know what Clifford actually thought about things. His one failing, if she could call it that, was his interminable politeness.

While Marcie was certain he wasn't pleased, Clifford had chivalrously told her to have her dinner with Johnny and to enjoy herself. He'd be talking to her again soon. The conversation had ended with that.

"Have you decided what you'd like to order?" Johnny asked, setting aside his menu.

Marcie couldn't believe the prices. A single meal at the Cattleman's would pay for her weekly supply of groceries. "The small filet?" she said questioningly.

He grinned broadly, as if she'd made the only intelligent choice on the entire menu.

It surprised Marcie how nervous she was. Not because she was with Johnny; he was an easy person to talk to, when they took time to talk. But she wasn't accustomed to sitting in an ultrafancy restaurant where the waiters wore tuxedos. Nor had she eaten anyplace where the flatware comprised more than two spoons.

"Did you have any problems explaining our date to Clifford?" he asked as if he were sincerely concerned.

"Clifford's not the jealous type."

Johnny reached for the wine menu. "He sounds like a decent sort."

"He's very good to me." Better than anyone.

The waiter arrived, and in gentlemanly fashion, Johnny ordered for her and then requested a bottle of expensive French wine, a Bordeaux.

As the meal progressed they chatted comfortably. Generally when a man asked her out, Marcie was subjected to a long, self-serving monologue. At times she'd wonder if these men feared that she didn't have a brain, or an opinion. In the end she'd decided that they were afraid of what she'd say. They came to her, she suspected, to recover from the weenie roasting they'd suffered at the hands of the feminists.

The men in Marcie's illustrious dating career endlessly touted themselves in an attempt to impress her, to reveal how fascinating or intelligent or wonderful they were. Mostly what they really wanted was to get her into the sack as quickly as possible with the least amount of fuss and prove what a magnificent lover they were. And often weren't.

By the time she'd reached her late twenties, Marcie had learned a lot about the dating scene. She realized that single men often felt an unmarried woman her age was desperate to find a husband. While it was true Marcie wanted a husband and children, her standards were higher than just any man with a pair of sperm-producing testicles. She longed for companionship, shared goals, and the dirtiest word of all. One that caused fearless men to run screaming into the night. Commitment.

Marcie didn't need the wine to relax. By the time

the steaks arrived, she was as happy as she could ever remember. Johnny was both intelligent and generous.

In comparison, Clifford, dear, dear Clifford, seemed stodgy and a little dull. His idea of a fun evening was a night at the movies and a shared bucket of popcorn. Clifford was the salt of the earth, and Johnny was the spice of life. Unfortunately her diet had been bland for a long time, and she was ready for a taste of cayenne.

Marcie had known the minute Johnny walked into her beauty salon that she wanted him, but until their dinner date she hadn't realized how much.

Subtly he altered the course of their conversation, reminding her of how fabulous the lovemaking had always been between them. His deep blue eyes sparkled with devilment as he continued to speak of the raw excitement they'd experienced in each other.

His voice was low and seductive, coaxing. Marcie felt as if she were slowly being drawn into a vortex, trapped in the memories. Soon she was a willing, eager victim, adding her own remembrances.

His eyes bored into hers relentlessly as he regarded her with a look of wonder, as though she were the only woman alive with which he'd shared this incredible marvel.

Marcie battled the fluttery beat of her heart. Johnny slowly extended his arm to her and opened his hand. His meaning was unmistakable. He wanted her. Needed her. Was going crazy without her.

Marcie experienced a bevy of contradictory feelings. She'd come so far, learned so much; but then Johnny had always made her weak.

"Marcie . . ." Her name was a soft plea that fell from his lips. A way of saying he'd go mad without her. Marcie needed to be needed, wanted to be wanted.

Her love, her body, would ease his pain, would heal his suffering, would soothe away his troubles. He'd come to her. Only her.

In the morning, she reminded herself, she'd feel like a fool, used and abused. But the promise of pleasure outweighed any threat of remorse.

Slowly she placed her hand in his. Johnny closed his eyes and sighed, as though his relief and gratitude were great. Clasping his fingers around hers, he carried her hand under the table. With his eyes holding hers prisoner, he pressed her palm against the hard bulge in his crotch and grinned.

The oxygen fled her lungs as she flexed her long nails over the strength of his erection.

Johnny heightened the anticipation for them both by insisting upon dessert, then coffee, lingering over each. His eyes filled with promise, he paid the bill and left a generous tip.

By the time the valet had brought around the car, Marcie was breathless with anticipation. The only indication Johnny gave that he was as eager for her was the speed with which he drove back to her apartment.

Neither spoke.

Marcie didn't make the pretense of inviting him inside for coffee, and he didn't ask. He parked the car, got out, and followed her to her front door.

The minute they were inside, he turned her into his arms. Their first kisses were filled with hot urgency.

He ravaged her mouth until she had to break away in order to breathe. Soon, however, the blistering, sweet fire altered as the fierce edge of their hunger abated.

His mouth and hands were unbelievably erotic as he explored her body, familiarizing himself with her breasts, hips, buttocks. He removed her sweater and bra, then sucked greedily from each of her nipples while lowering the zipper to her skirt. He was like a boy given free rein in a candy store, unable to decide which delicacy to sample first.

It didn't take him long to decide, and soon he elicited a series of soft, impatient moans. Their bodies writhed against one another, burning with need, until they threatened to burst spontaneously into flames.

Marcie helped him discard his own clothes. Between wet, wild kisses she steered him into her bedroom. Johnny picked her up and gently laid her across the top of her mattress.

As he had over dessert and coffee, he prolonged the anticipation, using his hands and his mouth until she was sobbing with need, wanting him with a desperation that made her fear she was going out of her mind.

"In time," he promised with a husky whisper. "We have all night, dahlin', all night."

Impatient, Marcie held out her arms to him. Inadvertently her head hit something soft and fuzzy.

Johnny reached for the teddy bear and tossed it off the bed.

The teddy bear. Clifford's gift. The one he'd given to remind her how much he loved her. The only gift she'd ever received from a man who didn't expect payment in return.

Johnny might as well have poured a bucket of ice water over her head.

He went to kiss her, but she jerked her head away. "I can't do this."

Johnny went stock-still. "Can't do what?"

"Make love with you."

"Sweetheart, it's a little late for regrets. We're already making love." He laughed good-naturedly, as if this were all a bad joke, but one he was willing to overlook.

While she possessed the strength, Marcie rolled off the bed. Unsteady on her feet, she walked to her closet and hurriedly donned her robe. "You got a cigarette?" she asked shakily. She'd given up the habit, but she needed a smoke now, worse than any time since she'd quit.

"A cigarette?" Johnny sat at the end of her bed and scratched his head. "Don't we generally wait until afterward for that?"

"I don't smoke anymore," she whispered, then realized she'd been the one to make the request. "I do sometimes when I'm under a lot of stress."

Johnny plowed all ten fingers though his hair. "I'm apparently missing something here. Maybe you could clue me in? What the hell just happened?"

"It's a long story." Remembering that she might have an old pack of Salems around, Marcie walked over to her dresser and searched through the top drawer until she found a cigarette.

Her hands shook so hard, she had trouble lighting up. She inhaled deeply, blew the smoke at the ceiling, and then coughed until she thought she'd heave her guts out.

She went into the bathroom and tossed the lit cigarette into the toilet.

"Marcie, sweetheart, tell me what's wrong?"

"You have every right to be angry," she said, walking back into the room and retrieving the teddy bear. She held it against her abdomen like a shield.

"I'm not mad," he said gently, "just confused."

"It's Clifford."

"Clifford," Johnny repeated as if he weren't quite sure he remembered the name. "Your new boy-friend?"

"Right." She nodded once, profoundly. "He's never asked anything of me." Her gaze skirted back to the bed. "He's been kind and good—"

"I'll be good to you, too, sweetheart." His words were heavy with insinuation. "Give me a chance to show you exactly how good it can be."

"It's not that kind of good," she said, and realized she was doing a poor job of explaining herself. She swept the hair away from her face. "Clifford doesn't ask anything of me," she said bluntly.

Johnny's eyes rounded with offense. "Hey, I didn't buy you dinner because—"

"I know. I know," she interrupted. "I don't know how to explain it. He's kind and steady and—"

"You're still talking about Clifford, right?"

"Right. I can't hurt him like this because you turn me on." She continued to clench the stuffed animal against her middle.

Johnny didn't respond.

"You have every right to be furious. I wouldn't blame you if you walked out that door and never saw me again. It'd probably be best for both of us if you did."

Again Johnny didn't say anything. Buck naked, he stood and retrieved his clothes.

"How about putting on a pot of coffee," he suggested.

"Coffee?"

"Make it strong, all right? Real strong."

She nodded.

Then he headed for her bathroom. "You don't mind if I use your shower, do you?"

"Not at all." Johnny was closing the door when she realized she hadn't told him about the problem with the hot-water knob.

"Don't worry about it," he muttered after she explained, rubbing a hand down his face. "I won't be using the hot water."

17

Murphy parked the jeep on the side of a rut-filled dirt road and studied the map. He'd managed to stay off the main thoroughfares, but he wasn't fool enough to presume they'd made a clean escape.

Blowing up the fuel dump had created the diversion he'd needed in order to rescue Letty, but it wasn't something Captain Norte was likely to forget or forgive. Captain Norte, however, was the least of his worries.

Murphy's neck was on the chopping block, and consequently Letty's was too. But the good captain and his band of murderous cutthroats had to find him first, which was something Murphy intended to make damned difficult.

Once he'd found his bearings, he folded the map and replaced it inside his knapsack.

Letty slept fitfully at his side. It had taken several

hours for her to fall asleep. She'd curled up and rid-
den in stone silence until pure exhaustion had taken
hold.

Murphy's experience with comforting women was
limited. He didn't know what to say to ease her mind,
so he'd said next to nothing. Mainly he heaped the
blame for the near rape upon his own shoulders, and
he cursed himself for ever having left her. In his
defense, he reminded himself that Letty had been
unreasonable and stupid and he'd responded in kind.

He didn't calculate how long he'd been away. Not
long, thirty, forty minutes. In that time she'd managed
to walk waist deep into a pile full of shit.

Murphy refused to continue to beat himself up.
The ordeal was over, the soldier who'd attacked her
was dead, and he and Letty were miles away from
Siguierres.

Letty stirred, sat up, and rubbed her hand along the
back of her neck in an effort to work out the kinks.
"How long have I been asleep?"

"A couple of hours."

He felt her stare and her hesitation.

"I . . . I was wrong," she said.

Murphy shifted the gear into first. "Which time?"

"I should have waited like you instructed. It was a
mistake to go after you. It's just that ten hours can be
a terribly long time when one is waiting. I heard gunshots and I didn't know what had happened to you
and . . . It doesn't matter now. I made a mistake. It
was all my fault and . . ." She let the rest fade away.

"As I recalled, you fired me," he remarked stiffly.

"I shouldn't have done that, either."

"True." He wasn't going to argue about the obvious. She'd learned her lesson the hard way. "What are you prepared to offer me to come back?"

She closed her arms protectively around her torso.

"Don't worry, the terms will be different this time."

"What do you want?"

He noted the apprehension in her voice.

"One thing, and one thing only." He held up his index finger for emphasis. "You will do what I say, when I say, without question. If you disobey an order again, it's over. Understand?"

She nodded.

"Good. Now that that's clear, let's find your brother and get the hell out of here."

The road was filled with ruts large enough to swallow small animals. They were far enough off the beaten path that Murphy didn't worry about being detected. He slowed to a crawl in order to manipulate the vehicle around problem areas.

He worried about Letty. He didn't like a lot of chatter on a mission and up to this point had discouraged conversation. Although she'd abided by his unwritten demand, he'd felt her eagerness to ask questions. Not this day. Her silence was a good indication of how badly the attack had shaken her.

"You hungry?" he asked after a while.

"A little."

"We'll stop soon." If he was a different kind of man, he'd take her in his arms. Tenderness was as foreign to him as comforting distraught women. Besides, he was fairly certain that the last thing Letty needed or wanted was a man's touch. Murphy frowned. Much more of this and he'd turn into one of those men seeking to find their inner child.

"Would it be possible for me to have a bath?" she asked after a while.

A *bath?* Judas H. Priest, what did she expect? They weren't likely to run across a luxury spa in the jungle.

As he remembered from the map, there was a small lake close by, and he told her so.

The higher the elevation, the more lush the vegetation, and they'd been climbing steadily since leaving Hojancha. The terrain was dramatically different from the hot, dry area they'd left two days earlier.

Murphy found a decent spot to park the jeep, and while Letty nibbled at breakfast, he made a half-mile circle around the lake to be sure they hadn't plopped themselves down in the middle of a rebel-infested area.

"Go ahead and take your bath," he said when he returned. He removed his hat and wiped the sweat from his brow with the back of his arm.

Letty hesitated. "Is there a chance anyone will be watching me?"

"No one human," he answered confidently.

She thanked him with a weak smile and walked behind a low-lying bush to remove her clothes.

Murphy climbed inside the jeep, scooted the seat back as far as it would go, and tried to sleep. He'd been up the better part of thirty hours and felt it.

He heard water splash as Letty stepped into the lake. A picture of her body formed in his mind, and he struggled valiantly to banish it. To no avail.

Try as he might, he couldn't expel the mental image

of her lush breasts and her milky white skin from his mind. Sweat broke out across his brow.

"Murphy . . ."

Her cursed under his breath. "What now?" he answered gruffly.

"I'm sorry to bother you, but do you happen to have any soap?"

The next thing he knew, she'd be asking about face cream and deodorant. He bit back the sarcastic question and reached for his knapsack.

"Just a minute," he said with a decided lack of enthusiasm.

"Thank you. I really do hate to bother you."

He'd just bet she did. Murphy located the soap and walked over to the water's edge. It lapped lazily against the sandy shore, inviting. Birds chirped merrily nearby. He was pleased someone was happy.

Letty had squatted down in about three feet of crystal blue water so all that showed was her neck and creamy white shoulders. It was enough. His jaw clenched at the angry-looking bruise her blouse had covered. The acid in his stomach burned along with his hate for the men who had inflicted those bruises.

"I'll catch the soap if you throw it," she volunteered, and lifted her hands out of the water. In doing so, she inadvertently exposed the top half of her generous breasts.

Murphy heaved the small soap bar in her direction, turned abruptly, and headed back toward the jeep.

"The water's wonderful."

He grumbled some nonsensical reply under his breath. He was in no mood for her chatter.

"You should come in yourself," she offered next. "I'll be out of your way in no time."

The temptation was strong, far stronger than it should have been. Murphy knew better, but he was hot and overly tired and in need of something. Exactly what remained a mystery.

Before he could question the wisdom of his action, he sat down in the sand and removed his boots. He peeled off his clothes in record time, leaving on his briefs, and walked out to meet her.

Letty's eyes rounded with each step he advanced toward her. "I thought you'd wait until I'd finished," she mumbled.

"I decided not to." He wasn't entirely sure what she expected him to do. Once he was waist deep, Murphy dove headfirst into the cool water and swam below the surface until his lungs felt as if they would burst.

Damn, but it felt good.

He turned around and found Letty exactly where he'd left her. "Do you want the soap?" she asked timidly, her back to him.

"Yeah." He swam toward her and stopped a respectable distance away, offering her a semblance of privacy. His feet touched the bottom and he stood. The water lapped at his chest.

Letty held on to the soap bar as if it were gold. "Murphy?"

The emotion in her voice caught him off guard. "Yeah?"

Her throat worked convulsively, as if she were trying to swallow something too big to go down her esophagus. "I . . . need to say something."

"Now?"

"Yes," she cried, half laughing, half weeping, "now, while I still have the courage."

A woman's mind was a mystery to Murphy. Why she'd choose this precise moment, when they were both near nude, for this tête-à-tête made no sense to him.

"I want to thank you for saving me from those soldiers." Each word appeared to be a struggle for her to enunciate.

His inclination was to make light of his role. He'd been hired to protect her, to get her in and out of the country as quickly and as safely as he could. She seemed to conveniently forget that none of this would have happened if they'd both done as they should. It was a lesson well learned.

She swabbed at the moisture on her face. "Could you . . . would you mind very much holding me for a moment?" she asked brokenly.

Before he could react, Letty was in his embrace, clinging to him as if he were a rope dangling over the edge of a cliff. Her arms circled his neck, and she buried her face in his shoulder, sobbing softly.

"I was so frightened."

"I know, I know." Unsure what else to say or do, Murphy gently patted her slender back, doing his best not to notice how soft her skin was.

"If you hadn't come when you did—"

"It's over now."

"He meant to kill me," she said with conviction. "He was going to rape me and then strangle me. He pressed his arm against my throat and I couldn't breathe."

"It's over, honey."

She clung to him, her skin cool and slick, her body nestling against him. Murphy wasn't made of stone. He couldn't ignore the way her breasts teased his chest any more than he could ignore her legs rubbing against his.

Gritting his teeth, he wrapped his arms around Letty's waist and held her firmly, securely, in his arms. What she needed was his strength, his protection, his confidence. That was what she sought.

"Come on," he whispered, and used his jaw to caress the side of her head. "We need to get out of here."

She nodded and wiped the tears from her eyes. "Friends?" she asked.

The question was one he preferred not to answer.

Raising her head, Letty met his eyes. "Friends?" she asked a second time.

Letty Madden and him. Not likely. His friends were few. Carefully chosen. He was a hired gun, and he didn't want her painting him as her personal knight in shining armor because he'd killed the bastard about to rape her.

"No thanks, sweetheart. I got all the friends I can handle." He knew, even as he spoke, that his words would insult and offend her, but that couldn't be helped. They'd come to Zarcero to do a job. When it was finished he'd be out of her life and she'd be out of his.

Letty's head snapped back, and she glared at him. "You're a nasty son of a bitch, aren't you?"

"Yes." He wouldn't deny it. "You'd best not forget it."

He stalked toward the shore. "It's time to get back on the road," he said evenly. "We leave in five minutes."

Letty plowed out of the water, making more noise than a Sherman tank, sloshing and kicking, venting her frustration like a woman scorned.

Murphy quickly donned his clothes and had a hell of a time hiding his smile.

His amusement quickly faded when he realized they were being watched. He didn't know where or who was out there. Not yet. Over the years he'd developed a sixth sense about such matters.

"Letty . . ." He kept his voice low and calm.

She ignored him.

"Without being obvious, walk over to me."

Something in his voice must have alerted her to the danger. She picked up her clothes and walked directly to his side. "Someone's out there," she whispered.

He grinned. "Yeah, I know."

18

Jack Keller returned to his condominium around two in the morning. He let himself inside, tossed the keys on an end table, and strolled aimlessly through his living room while rubbing the back of his neck. His night certainly had taken an unexpected turn. He'd had Marcie in the palm of his hand, whimpering for what they both wanted, and then whammo, the next thing he knew she was asking for a cigarette and listing Clifford's sterling traits.

Jack should have been angry. A woman couldn't lead a man to the point of no return and then call it quits. But Marcie had done exactly that. Naturally he'd been frustrated. It'd taken ten minutes under an ice-cold shower to cool his libido. The disappointment had been as sharp as his frustration. Damn it, he wanted her. It'd taken half a pot of strong coffee to clear his head.

Even now he wasn't entirely certain he understood about Marcie and Clifford. He was fairly certain she wasn't in love with the plumber. Marcie wanted *him*, and that wasn't his ego talking, either. He loved the way her eyes lit up when she saw him. His touch flustered and fascinated her. She was both sensual and honest, a rare combination in a woman, he'd discovered. It distressed him to realize that if he didn't act soon, he was going to lose her. Not to any fast-talking shyster, either, but to a plumber.

Jack openly admitted that he'd underestimated Marcie. She deserved far more credit than he'd given her. He had assumed he'd easily be able to manipulate her into bed. Dinner, a little sweet talk. A kiss. Hell, it hadn't even taken that much. By the time their meal had arrived they could hardly stay in their chairs for want of each other. All that had changed, however, shortly after they'd arrived back at her place.

Right up to the moment Marcie had rolled away from him, Jack had thought it'd be a snap to have her. Not so, but then he always had enjoyed a challenge. It stirred his blood. Marcie was a hell of a woman, in bed and out, and it'd do him well to remember that.

His mind was filled with thoughts of Marcie and the pleasure that awaited them. Jack was determined to have her. Hell, just how difficult could it be? No woman in her right mind would choose a plumber named Clifford over him. Women needed excitement, pleasure, adventure, and he offered all three.

Okay, okay, Clifford had won round one, but the championship fight had only just begun. Jack fully expected to gain the prize, and frankly he didn't expect it to take much longer. A little subtle planning, and he'd close in for the kill.

He got excited just thinking about it.

Too keyed up to sleep, he turned on the television and plopped himself down in front of the boob tube. No sooner had he finished a complete surf of the channels than his doorbell chimed long and loud.

"What the hell?" he muttered, glancing at his watch. People generally didn't make social calls this time of the morning.

His peephole revealed two clean-cut men standing on the other side of his door. They might have been twins if one hadn't towered a good six inches over the other. The two had "the law" written all over them. Officious. Pompous. Self-important. Both looked as if they were struggling to hold in a fart.

The taller of the two impatiently pressed the buzzer a second time.

The temptation not to respond appealed to Jack. He was already short-tempered, and having to deal with a couple of tight-ass federal agents didn't rate high on his list of ways to pass the wee hours of the morning.

On second thought, he had to concede that their temperaments wouldn't improve if he left them sitting on his porch all night. Forcing himself to disguise his irritation, Jack opened the door.

"We're sorry to bother you this time of night," the shorter man said. He pulled identification from inside his suit jacket and flipped it open. Ken Kemper. CIA. The second man, Barry Moser, showed his identification as well.

Unimpressed, Jack folded his arms and leaned against the door frame. And waited. "What do you want with me?"

"We need to ask you a few questions."

"Now?" Jack asked. He pointedly looked at his watch, stating silently that he had better things to do with his time. After all, he had company. *Nick at Night* was waiting for him.

"We can do it here, or we can take you downtown," Barry suggested, his voice monotone, making it sound as if it made no difference to him. "The choice is yours."

The fact that Jack had supposedly been given a choice when he had none didn't escape him. Sighing loudly, he made a sweeping gesture toward the living room. "Make yourselves at home, *gentlemen*," he said.

The two agents walked across the room and then like robots simultaneously sat on the sofa.

Jack reluctantly reached for the controller and turned off the television.

"I understand you're a friend of a man who goes by the name of Murphy."

Jack rubbed his jaw and played dumb. "Murphy?"

"Let's skip the bullshit," Kemper said impatiently. "We know all about you and Murphy and Deliverance Company."

"We're not here about covert activities," Moser added.

Jack just bet. "Then what do you want?"

"Where's Murphy?"

"I don't know," Jack told them, which was true enough. The last time he'd heard anything at all had been that phone message, in which he'd learned that Murphy was headed toward Zarcero with the Madden woman. He hadn't seemed any too pleased about it, either.

"You don't know where Murphy is?" Ken Pompous asked a second time.

"Did you check Boothill, Texas?" Jack asked.

"He's missing," Moser, the one with the tighter of the two asses, replied. "By sheer coincidence, so is Letty Madden."

"Letty who?" Jack asked, continuing to play dumb. At this point it wasn't difficult. He was getting slow in his old age, and careless. Stupid mistakes. He'd learned the hard way that mistakes cost lives. It was apparent the two men had been sitting outside his condominium waiting for his return. And he hadn't noticed.

"Letty Madden," Barry repeated. "She's Boothill's postmistress."

"Never heard of her."

The two men exchanged knowing looks, but they didn't challenge him.

"Don't you find it the least bit curious that these two people both disappeared at the same time?"

Jack didn't respond for several tense moments. "Do you think Murphy kidnapped her? If that's the case, shouldn't the FBI be handling the case?"

Both men ignored his suggestion. "Have you ever heard of Zarcero?" Ken asked next.

Jack pretended to roll the name around in his mind. Then, like a schoolboy who'd done his homework, he replied, "It's the country in Central America that's going through all that political upheaval, isn't it?"

"Letty's brother, Luke Madden, served as a missionary in Zarcero."

Both men appeared to wait for some kind of reaction to this. Jack gave them none.

"From what we've been able to learn, Ms. Madden is determined to locate her brother. Determined enough to ignore the advice of her country and go after her brother herself."

"Is that a crime?"

"It depends on what she does about it."

Jack stifled a yawn, swallowing it loudly, and hoped the two took the hint. They weren't going to get any information from him. Even if he had some to offer, he wouldn't share confidences with the likes of them.

"What's all this got to do with Murphy?" he asked, pretending to find their conversation taxing.

Neither agent seemed particularly interested in answering him. Apparently they preferred to be the ones asking questions.

"We believe Ms. Madden may have hired your friend to help her locate her brother."

"Really?" Jack arched his eyebrows as if to suggest this was news to him. "Do you really think a postmistress could afford Deliverance Company's services?"

"Not Deliverance Company," Kemper, the shorter one, informed him primly. "We believe she hired Murphy."

"Why would she do something like that when all she need do is contact the helpful people employed by the State Department? Surely the State Department would be able to assist a worried postmistress hoping to locate her long-lost brother. All you people need do is apply a few sanctions and a little diplomatic leverage, and Luke Madden will be coming home singing the praises of a democracy. Hallelujah, brothers," he sang, raising his arms above his head and waving his hands.

Neither man appeared to find his antics amusing. "Have you ever heard of Siguierres?" Kemper asked, scooting forward on the cushion, narrowing the distance between them.

"Siguierres," Jack repeated, and shook his head in complete honesty.

"We've received word of an explosion."

"A fuel storage tank," the second agent supplied.

"The work is suspiciously like that of your friend Murphy."

"Is that right?" Jack swallowed a grin and lazily leaned against the chair's cushion. He cupped the back of his head, his elbows fanning out on each side of his face.

"We don't know if your buddy's in contact with you or not," Ken said stiffly, and stood. Barry followed. "But if you are, we have a bit of information for him."

"What makes you think Murphy would contact me?"

"Birds of a feather, perhaps," the taller agent suggested.

"For all I know, Murphy could be sport-fishing in the Gulf of Mexico." Jack shrugged as if to say his friend's whereabouts remained a mystery to him.

"If you do hear from Murphy, tell him he's in over his head this time."

"Just a minute," Jack said, and leaped out of the chair.

He rushed to a side table, where he withdrew a pad and a pen. "What was that again? I want to make sure I got it right. Far be it from me to miscommunicate this important missive. *In over his head?* Is that what you wanted me to tell him? Anything else, fellows?"

Both men glared at him and then wordlessly walked out of the apartment.

Jack followed and closed the door, struggling not to laugh outright. It certainly sounded as if his pal were up to his old tricks. Briefly Jack wondered what kind of mess Murphy had gotten himself into. From the sound of it, he was taking care of matters nicely.

19

"*Don't move,*" *Murphy instructed* Letty in an urgent whisper. He crouched behind the jeep himself. "Don't even breathe."

She nodded as her muscles tightened warily. Her heart was lodged in her throat. Even the birds in the trees seemed to have quieted. The stillness that fell over the area took on an eerie quality.

Murphy reached for his weapon and carefully took aim.

Hunkered down against the four-wheel drive, Letty tried to think clearly. Her senses fine-tuned, she heard every noise as if it were announced over a public broadcasting system. A scarlet macaw flew from one tree to the next, its brilliantly colored wings flapping against a backdrop of blue sky and lush green jungle. Birds called, their cries loud and discordant in the sudden silence. Thick green leaves wavered and weaved in the breeze, stirring the fresh morning air. The day was indescribably beautiful. And deadly. The sounds fit together like intricate puzzle pieces, creating a graphic picture in her mind. Except for one distinct sound: hushed voices.

Letty froze with fear. She didn't move, didn't breathe, didn't make a sound. Murphy was poised beside her. He'd heard the same thing she had and leveled his pistol in that direction. She studied him and knew that he was calculating their chances of escaping, weighing their alternatives. It was either flight or fight.

If they were caught, Letty was well aware of what would happen to her. She'd received a foretaste of that the night before. Although her mind was hazy with fear, she had the presence of mind to murmur a silent prayer. If she was to die, she preferred to go quickly. She wasn't afraid of death as much as the process of dying.

The flicker of hope that they might escape faded as she studied their situation. They were trapped by the lake and had nowhere to go. Each soldier, and there was no telling how many there were, would be heavily armed. Murphy would hold them off as long as he could, but there was only so much one man could do. She was useless to him and, consequently, herself.

Her throat went dry, making it impossible to swallow. She thought about Luke and her father. Grammy. Surprisingly her mind was sharp, clear, alert.

All at once a muffled sob broke the tense silence. Like that of a small child. One terrified and lost.

"Murphy," she whispered, making a clumsy effort

to dress. Somehow she managed to slip the dress over her head and insert her arms into the short sleeves. "It's a child."

"I heard." But he kept his gun poised and ready. "Come out," he shouted in Spanish.

Letty rolled her eyes. The poor thing was terrified. Murphy's gruff voice wasn't going to encourage anyone into the open.

"We mean you no harm," she added on a gentler tone, again in Spanish. "You're safe."

No sooner had she spoken than a bronze-skinned girl of about twelve appeared, a baby propped against her hip. She walked into the clearing, barefoot, her dress in rags. Her large brown eyes sought out Letty, her look empty, weary, afraid.

"Sweet Jesus," Murphy whispered when four other children, who looked to be between the ages of five and ten, stood, revealing themselves one by one.

They were terrified, Letty noted, trembling, shaking, huddling together, uncertain of what awaited them.

Murphy barked a number of questions, but they appeared to be too frightened to answer.

Letty moved from behind the jeep while Murphy slipped into his pants and followed.

"Where are your parents?" Letty gently asked the oldest girl.

The youngest boy, who was about five, started to sob, and the girl who held the baby placed a protective hand on his shoulder. "We don't know."

"What are your names?" Murphy demanded.

Letty glowered at him. The children were frightened enough without him shouting orders at them. The oldest, the girl, introduced herself as Maria and her brothers as Vincente, Esteban, Rico, Dario, and the baby, Pablo.

"The soldiers came," Vincente explained, his dark eyes bright with weary defiance. "Early in the morning, they stormed into our village. Our mother woke us and helped us escape out the window . . . . She told us to run and hide in the jungle, and we did."

"Then we heard the guns."

"After the soldiers left," Maria whispered, her eyes glazed over with the horror of what had happened, "we returned and everyone in the village was gone."

"All the houses were empty."

"Except for Carlos and Juan and Ernesto. They were dead." Vincente, who was no more than eleven, stiffened his shoulders as if to say had he been there he would have helped save the men. What struck Letty was the way in which the youth mentioned the three dead men. He made it sound as if soldiers routinely plundered the village, as if the happenings were an everyday occurrence.

"We buried them as best we could," Maria whispered, comforting her baby brother by bouncing him gently on her hip.

"Everyone was gone?" Letty repeated. "Where would the soldiers possibly take them?" She looked to Murphy for answers. He'd been through this sort of thing countless times, unlike her. He'd know what to say and do. Expectantly, the children turned to him as well.

He shrugged as if he were as much in the dark

about all this as they were. "Generally they're only interested in the men."

"For what reason?" Letty asked, before she realized he couldn't possibly answer. Whatever the answer, it was sure to distress the youngsters.

"When did this happen?" Murphy asked, ignoring her inquisitiveness.

"Three days ago."

"Three days," Letty cried. No wonder the children looked so wretched. "You must be starving." Without waiting for Murphy's approval, she took the baby from the girl's arms and cradled him against her side. "When was the last time the baby had anything to eat?"

At the mention of food the children gathered around her like small chicks fleeing a storm. Letty half expected Murphy to disapprove, but he didn't. Nor did he complain when she dug through their own meager supplies.

The children ate like animals, stuffing the food into their mouths and tucking what they couldn't manage just then inside their pockets. Letty's heart ached as she watched them. She wished she had more to give them. When they'd finished, the six thanked her with wan, pitiful smiles.

Murphy continued to ply the youngsters with questions, extracting as much information as he could. Again and again he interrogated the family, until she glared at him, silently reminding him that these poor children had suffered enough.

She took them aside and helped them wash. While she combed their hair, she mulled over what they should do. It wasn't possible to take the six with them into San Paulo; the risk would be too great. But her first priority had to be Luke. She wanted to discuss the matter with Murphy, but he was sitting apart from her and the children, studying the map.

"Vincente," Murphy called after a few moments.

The next time Letty glanced in his direction, he'd squatted down in the sand. Maria and the four boys huddled around him while Letty gave the toddler a sponge bath. She watched as the girl found a stick and drew a diagram in the sand. Now and again she nodded and answered Murphy's questions. The boys added details.

Busy as she was washing the baby, Letty couldn't make out what the exchange was about. But she did learn that the children were lost. They'd been walking for days, seeking their grandmother's village, and had somehow gone hopelessly astray.

"Our mother told us to go to our grandmother's," Maria said, fighting back tears. "*Abuela* will know what to do."

Letty rose and walked over to place an arm around the girl's thin shoulders and smooth the hair from her brow. Not even a teenager and already the girl carried the heavy burden of caring for her five younger brothers.

"Everything will be fine," Letty whispered, praying it was true.

The girl smiled weakly and nodded.

The minute Letty was able to separate herself from the children, she confronted Murphy. The baby rode her hip as if he'd spent the majority of his life there.

"What are we going to do?" she asked. "We can't take the children with us. It's much too dangerous."

His eyes held hers. "I agree."

"Nor can we leave them here." The small family was hopelessly lost, half starved, and terribly frightened.

"Luke . . . I don't think he's going to last much longer." She wanted Murphy to supply the answers, to reassure her, but he did none of that.

"This is your call," he said evenly.

"My call," she repeated, wanting to weep with the agony of it. Her brother's life hung in the balance. But she couldn't just abandon six children.

Murphy stared at her. "You ready?"

"Ready?" Letty glanced toward the children. He gave her little enough time to make the most important decision of her life.

"We can't sit around here and debate the issue all day. Decide."

She leveled her face to the sky, letting the sun warm her. Hardly aware of what she was doing, she closed her arms protectively around the toddler. All at once he felt incredibly heavy.

Murphy glared at her. "What's your call?"

"Luke's my brother," she cried. Then her gaze fell upon the five small boys, Maria's brothers. The weight of the girl's responsibility made her far older than her years. The twelve-year-old was left to see to their very survival.

"Fine, we go without them," Murphy said, and started toward the jeep.

"Wait." Letty bit into her lower lip. She couldn't do it.

Murphy paused.

"We'll take the children to their grandmother's village," she whispered.

"You're the boss." A slight movement of his mouth might have been an approving grin, but it was difficult for Letty to tell with Murphy. He was quite possibly the most complex man she'd ever known.

Murphy estimated that Questo, the village the children had been trying to find, was approximately fifteen miles from the lake. However, with the roads in the condition they were, Letty feared it would take them the better part of a day. That meant delaying their arrival into San Paulo.

"This was what Luke would want me to do," she mumbled as she climbed into the jeep. She knew this to be true, but it hadn't made the decision any easier, convinced as she was that Luke was close to death. But she couldn't leave the children to an uncertain future. Not when it was within her power to help them.

Murphy helped the two smallest boys inside the jeep. He crowded them between Letty and Maria. The older boys rode on the hood, hanging on to the windshield, and pointed the direction from which they'd traveled.

Exhausted, the baby slept in Letty's arms. She found it strangely comforting to hold the toddler. His head was nestled close to her heart, his chubby fist pressed to her breast. Although she loved children, Letty hadn't given much thought to being a mother. She suspected her hesitancy had a great deal to do with her own mother and her parents' failed marriage.

A ready excuse was that she hadn't found the right man.

There was always Slim, of course. He'd proposed to her on a semiannual basis and was profoundly patient with her. She'd always told herself that she would marry sooner or later, but she was in no rush.

Unbidden, her gaze scooted to Murphy. Letty didn't know how he was able to drive with two small boys poised on the jeep's hood, but he managed admirably. The poor little ragamuffins looked self-important to be riding in such a choice location.

Murphy must have sensed her scrutiny because he glanced in her direction. He didn't smile. She suspected he wasn't the kind of man who often did, but in his own way he told her he approved of her choice.

Without explanation, she experienced a rush of warmth. A feeling of peace and rightness. Of tenderness. She was with this man, a paid soldier, in the thick jungles of Zarcero with a baby in her arms, and she'd never felt more right. She kissed the child's chubby cheek, smiled softly at Murphy, and looked away. He'd openly disliked her, rejected her friendship, and maintained a wide emotional distance from her and just about everyone else. Yet he was an honorable man. He'd come back for her, even after she'd fired him. He'd held her, comforted her.

Murphy might not choose to have her as his friend, but she was beginning to think of him in those terms. He quite possibly was the best friend she'd ever had.

The back roads were in deplorable condition, and the jeep pitched and heaved its way along the rough-strewn path. At this rate, the thirty-mile distance would take the majority of the day and possibly part of the night.

They stopped to rest late in the afternoon, when the sun was directly overhead and the heat was at its worst. The children were exhausted and cranky. The eight of them shared a meal meant for two adults, then lay down in the shade of a sprawling tree. Letty stretched out in the cool grass with the children, who promptly fell asleep.

Murphy sat apart from her and the others, his back propped against the tree trunk. His rifle rested atop his bent knees.

Again, Letty found herself scrutinizing him, fascinated by every aspect of his personality. He was gruff and impatient and at times surprisingly caring.

She didn't view him as handsome. He was too rugged, too hard, for that. With several days' growth of beard, he resembled the roughest kind of redneck. A Texas specialty. Perhaps that was the reason he'd chosen Texas as his home.

"When was the last time you slept?" she asked, sitting up.

"I forget."

She stood and moved toward him. "If you want, I'll stand watch and you can rest."

"I appreciate the offer, but no thanks."

"How much longer do you think it'll take before we reach Questo?"

"Four, possibly five hours. It would be almost faster to walk."

She sank onto the grass across from him and crossed her ankles. "Why Texas?"

"Texas?"

"Why did you choose to live in Texas when you could live anywhere in the world?"

His gaze left hers, and when he spoke it was with reluctance. "Because it's home."

"You were born and raised in Boothill?" This surprised her. Having lived there most of her life, she thought she knew everyone.

"No."

"But you bought that piece of property."

Again it was a long time before he answered. "Those thousand acres belonged to my grandfather several years back," he murmured, almost as if he were uncertain he should tell her that much.

"Mr. Whitehead?"

He shook his head. "Long before Whitehead. My grandfather lost the farm during the Depression, sometime in the early thirties. I wanted to buy it back for him, which I imagine is fairly illogical since he's been dead now far more years than I can remember."

"It isn't unreasonable in the least. I, for one, am grateful to your grandfather, otherwise I'd never have found you. Once we get Luke safely out of Zarcero, he'll be grateful, too."

"Don't jump the gun, we haven't found him yet."

"But we will," she said with absolute confidence.

"Your top button's unfastened," Murphy said, gesturing toward her dress.

"It is?" She looked down and noted the small V created by the opening. She'd purposely left it unbuttoned, allowing the breeze to cool her.

"When I first met you, you'd have had that thing fastened all the way to your nose."

"That's ridiculous."

He didn't answer, but she knew he spoke the truth. She'd lowered her guard with him. With herself.

"It's too hot to keep it buttoned," she said, hoping the explanation would satisfy him. She should have known better.

"No hotter than Boothill in August."

She pinched her lips together, and to her surprise he laughed outright.

"What, might I ask, is so funny?"

"You. Damn it, woman, we've been lovers. Loosen up a bit, will you?"

She blinked rapidly, furious with him for announcing such a thing in front of the children, even if they were sleeping. "I'd like to remind you," she said, seething with indignation, "that our one and only night together was the fee I paid for your services and nothing more."

Murphy picked a blade of grass and chewed on it casually. She could tell that her reaction to his gibe had amused him. Frankly, she didn't take kindly to being the brunt of his jokes.

"You could be a hell of a woman if you gave yourself half a chance."

"You mean if I lifted my skirts to you or any other randy man who took a liking to me?" she tossed out angrily.

"No," he snapped back. "One man. What the hell's wrong with you, anyway? I saw you cuddling that baby. You're a natural. You should have been married long before now, raising a houseful of your own kids."

"I don't care to discuss with you the manner in which I choose to live my life."

"With anyone, I'd imagine." He spoke casually, chewing on the grass as if he hadn't a care in the world.

Murphy had ruined everything. She'd been enjoying this moment of tranquillity, this peaceful interlude, and he'd purposely set out to rattle her. And succeeded. She wanted to stand up and slap him, but that was what he expected of her. Quite possibly, it was what he wanted. Out of pure stubbornness, she stayed exactly where she was.

"How was it?" His voice dropped to a seductive level, warm and yet strangely weary. "The lovemaking between us?"

Letty could feel the heat rising up her neck, like floodwaters racing toward a levee. "Let me assure you, Mr. Murphy, what we experienced wasn't lovemaking, it was sex."

"Fine, how was the sex?"

Apparently he had no interest in arguing semantics. Hardly aware of what she was doing, Letty started uprooting the grass at her sides by the handful. Her breathing grew deep and slightly labored.

Murphy chuckled softly. "That good, was it?"

"I beg your pardon?"

"Look at you. You're getting all hot and bothered just thinking about it." He appeared to be highly entertained by her discomfort.

"Do you mind if we change the subject?" she said primly.

"Why? I'm perfectly content with the way our discussion is going. You enjoyed yourself. Hell, sweetheart, there isn't anything wrong with that. For the record, so did I."

Her eyes met his. "You did?"

"What I remember of it." He scratched the side of his head and frowned. "I usually don't have a memory problem. Either you were the finest piece of ass I've had in years or it was so incredibly bad, I've blocked it from my mind."

Letty had had all she could take. She roared to her feet and balled her hands into tight fists at her sides. "You're the most disgusting, vulgar man I've ever known. Every time I start to believe you're capable of being noble and good, you go out of your way to prove otherwise."

His smile faded. "It'd serve you well to remember that."

"Don't worry, I will."

20

Marcie, dressed in white cotton pants and a blue sailor top, watched outside her living room window for Clifford's truck. He was picking her up on his way to the baseball game that evening and was due any minute.

When he'd phoned earlier, she'd heard the hesitation in his voice, as if he expected her to tell him something he didn't want to hear. She promised to be ready on time. And she was. Physically. But mentally was an entirely different story. This was the first time since she'd started dating Clifford that she wasn't pleased to see him.

Marcie needed time to sort through what had happened with Johnny and her feelings for him. She'd expected him to be angry, cutting him off the way she had. Naturally he hadn't been overly pleased, but he hadn't yelled at her, either. Instead they'd sat at her kitchen table and talked everything out. She told him about Clifford, and he'd listened and understood.

Then, before he'd left, he'd kissed her gently. The kiss itself had been almost brotherly, but not quite. It had lasted too long to be considered a show of affection between friends. With the kiss had come the hint of a promise. That was what had kept her awake most of the night: the promise. And when Johnny made a promise, verbal or otherwise, he delivered.

Consequently her day had been one disaster after another. For some unexplainable reason, Mrs. Hampton's auburn dye had become a Lucille Ball red. Mrs. Hampton, a longtime customer, was furious. So were the three clients Marcie kept waiting while she worked frantically to tone down Mrs. Hampton's hair color.

The problem, Marcie realized, all stemmed from what was happening between her and Johnny. She'd thought she was strong enough to resist him. She wasn't. She'd assumed that a dinner date under the pretense of "for old times' sake" was innocuous enough. It wasn't.

The measure of her desire for him could be calculated in the length of time it had taken him to convince her to go to bed with him. It distressed Marcie to admit they'd barely ordered their meal when she realized exactly what was going to happen. And damn near had. She may have called an end to their lovemaking, but it was the hardest thing she'd ever done. She wanted him. Loved him. Slipping back into that old mode of pleasuring a man had come effortlessly with Johnny.

Clifford's large Ford pickup rounded the corner and pulled to a stop in front of Marcie's apartment. She reached for her purse and headed out the door.

Clifford was strolling up the pathway when he saw her. He stopped, and his eyes widened the way they always did when he saw her. Widened with warmth and appreciation.

"You look pretty," he said, and leaned forward to kiss her, his movement slightly awkward. His lips grazed the edge of her mouth and part of her cheek.

He was a big man, tall and stocky, but not fat. He wore his baseball uniform, complete with cleats. *Kansas City Plumbing* was embroidered across the back of the blue-striped jersey in bold red letters.

A crop of thick, unruly hair stuck out from beneath his cap. It was time for her to give him a trim again, she noted. That was how they'd first met. Clifford had come into her shop late one Friday afternoon, looking to make an appointment. His barber had recently retired, and he hadn't gotten around to finding another. Although it was close to quitting time, Marcie had taken the appointment.

He'd seemed uneasy sitting on a chair in a beauty salon, so she'd chatted away, hoping he'd relax. She'd been surprised when he'd asked her to dinner. In retrospect she wondered if he'd surprised himself. The invitation had come in the form of a negative, tentative question. "I don't suppose you'd consider having dinner with me, would you?" He'd seemed shocked and pleased when she'd agreed.

Soon they were seeing each other on a regular basis. Clifford wasn't like other men she'd dated. He wasn't suave or sophisticated. Her experience with a blue-collar guy was limited. Clifford was a regular Joe, a nice guy without an agenda.

"How'd your dinner go with your friend?" he asked casually, sounding almost indifferent.

Marcie wasn't fooled. Clifford was worried about her date with Johnny. "Good," she said, wanting to play it down and avoid his questions. It wasn't as if she could tell him she'd been so hot for Johnny that she'd practically torn her clothes off in a rush to make love to him.

"Where'd you go?"

Marcie had hoped he wouldn't ask and sighed inwardly. The Cattleman's was one of the most expensive restaurants in town. She toyed with the idea of lying to him or claiming she didn't remember. The temptation was strong, but she'd made a promise to herself early on in their relationship that she wouldn't lie to him, nor would she stretch the truth.

The truth had an amazing elasticity. There'd been a time when she could have stretched it to the moon and back and not batted an eyelash. No more.

"The Cattleman's Place."

Clifford let out a low whistle. "This must be a rich friend."

"I assume he must be."

"How was the food?"

Marcie had foreseen Clifford's curiosity, that would be natural, but she hadn't anticipated his prosecuting-attorney list of questions.

She must have hesitated a moment too long, because he asked again. "I asked about the food. How was it?"

The truth be known, she'd barely tasted a bite. "Wonderful."

"That's what I've heard. Someone told me you can't get a cup of coffee there for under five bucks." He opened the passenger door for her, and because it was something of a hike upward, he offered his arm.

Once she was inside the cab, Clifford jogged around the front and joined her. He started the engine, his gaze trained straight ahead. Then, out of the blue, he announced, "I'm never going to be a rich man, Marcie."

"Johnny's just a friend," she murmured, and immediately felt guilty because she'd been far more than pals with Johnny. She'd said it because she didn't want to hurt Clifford, but she knew that she already had.

"Have you known him long?" he asked at the first red light.

"A couple of years. I told Johnny I was dating you now, and he said you sounded like a good person and he was pleased for me."

Clifford didn't change his expression, but she noted the way his hands tightened around the steering wheel. "Will you be seeing him again?"

That was what it all boiled down to, she realized. Would she be seeing Johnny again? Honesty was the best policy, Marcie reminded herself. "I don't know."

Clifford glanced at her, and it seemed that his eyes bored holes straight through her. "I guess what I'm really asking is if you *want* to see him again."

If she thought the first question was difficult, the second was impossible. She glanced out the side window in an effort to be truthful not only with Clifford, but with herself.

What she realized almost made her sick. She did want to see Johnny again. He was like dessert, scintillating, enticing, but ultimately unhealthy and bad for her.

Johnny whistled in and out of her life on a lark. He was always generous with her, but he wasn't the type of man who was interested in a permanent relationship, nor had he ever expressed a desire for a family. Marcie made no apologies for wanting to be a wife and mother.

"Marcie?" Clifford pressed anxiously.

"I don't know," she admitted miserably. "I just don't know."

Clifford grew quiet after that. Marcie wanted to reassure him, wanted him to know she considered him her future. But she couldn't very well tell him that when she was half crazy for Johnny, even when she knew it was a dead-end relationship.

Clifford parked the truck at the baseball field. Several other team members had already arrived and were on the grass doing stretching exercises.

He turned off the engine and kept his hand on the key. "I can't say that I'm happy knowing you want to see this other guy."

Marcie didn't imagine he would be. She wasn't particularly pleased herself.

"Would you like for me to step out of the picture completely?" he asked.

"No," she said automatically, forcefully. She didn't want to lose Clifford. On the other hand, she wanted to be fair to him, too. Although she hadn't made any specific plans to see Johnny again, he'd be back. They both knew it.

Clifford's dark eyes held hers.

"Perhaps I should leave that up to you," Marcie offered, appalled at her own lack of grit. She couldn't promise him she wouldn't see Johnny again. How he responded to that would determine the course of their relationship.

Naturally she could lie, lead him on, tell him what he wanted to hear. She could always feed him a line, one she'd swallowed a hundred times herself. But she refused to do that to the one decent, kind-hearted man she'd ever dated.

Clifford inhaled a deep breath and held it inside his chest a long time. "I'm sure all those self-help people would advise me to make a stand," he said finally. "It's either him or me, that kind of thing. But I'm afraid if I did that, you'd choose him." He paused and released his breath forcefully. "I'm probably not going to be able to afford to take you to dinner at the Cattleman's Place for another ten years or so, if then. I've got a business I'm building, a future, and that doesn't leave a lot of money for discretionary spending."

"Clifford, it isn't the fact he's rich."

"I know," he threw out crisply, "he's probably a hell of a lot better looking than I am, too." Not waiting for her to respond, he opened the truck door and hopped out.

Even though he was hurt and angry, he came around to Marcie's side and offered her his hand.

Clifford was right. Johnny was by far the better looking of the two. But there were other ways of measuring the worth of a man than his sex appeal. Now if she could only make herself do it.

21

At dawn Letty woke and discovered Murphy
had built a small fire and was heating water for coffee.
She sat up and stretched her arms high above her
head and swallowed a yawn.

The children slept peaceably about her, innocent as
lambs, exhausted from their ordeal, clinging to each
other.

Her heart softened as she studied them.

Her gaze drifted to the beast of a jeep, which had
decided for no apparent reason to stop running.
Murphy had spent two frustrating hours attempting
to find and correct the problem and had finally given
up. At his best estimate they were five miles outside
Questo, but it might as well have been a hundred.

Delivering the children to their grandmother had
required far more time and effort than Letty had
intended. She had hoped to deliver the children and

be on their way long before now. Instead they'd been forced to spend the night in the jungle. Her heart pounded with dread, fearing what was happening to Luke while she was delayed.

She also had a strong desire to be rid of Murphy. She wanted him out of her life. Just looking at him, with that smug smile of his, disgusted her. The man was completely lacking in moral decency. Because of Luke she was willing to tolerate his presence, but she wouldn't for a moment longer than absolutely necessary.

The night before, when the decision was made to wait until morning to travel, Murphy had gruffly ordered her to set up camp. Then he'd promptly disappeared, leaving her to deal with all of the children alone.

To his credit, an hour after he'd abandoned her with the children, Murphy had returned with two dead iguana and announced this was to be their dinner. Letty had heard that iguanas were often referred to as tree chickens because of their taste, but she'd never actually sampled one.

The roasted meat was delicious, and after the evening meal she'd readily fallen asleep and slept like a dead woman until morning.

Taking her backpack with her, she walked away from the clearing into the protection of the woods in order to change clothes. It had been a mistake to wear the dress, one that she intended to correct.

Once she'd changed back into her pants and shirt, she returned.

"There's extra hot water if you want coffee," Murphy offered. He sat close to the small fire, holding a tin cup. He swirled the liquid around a couple of times and then raised it to his lips.

"Thank you, no," she said primly.

"Very well, Your Highness."

He was baiting her, and she knew it. So she did the only sensible thing: she ignored him. She did, however, need to discuss one small item with him, however embarrassing.

"I'm afraid," she said tentatively, "that I might have given you the wrong impression."

Unconcerned, he glanced up at her. "You probably have any number of times."

His attitude rankled, but she was woman enough to overlook that. "The other morning . . . when I . . . when we were in the lake, I . . . I guess you could say I cried on your shoulder."

"You could say that." He tipped back the tin cup and downed a swallowful of coffee.

"My fear is that you might have been misled into thinking that I'm attracted to you."

"Physically, you mean?"

"Yes," she said quickly, perhaps too quickly.

A smile edged up one side of his mouth. "That worries you, does it?"

"Not exactly. I just felt it would be best to clear the air, so to speak." This was far more difficult than she'd imagined. His attitude wasn't helping, but then she knew better than to expect any assistance from him.

"What are you afraid of, sweetheart?"

She resisted the urge to ask him to refrain from calling her by any terms of affection, especially since that wasn't the way he intended them.

"I'm sure there are plenty of women in this world who are . . . who would be strongly attracted to you, but I don't happen to be one of them. No offense meant."

He arched twin eyebrows as if to cast doubt on the sincerity of her words. The edges of his mouth quivered with the effort to suppress a smile. "None taken," he said. She had the impression he would have laughed outright if he had.

"The entire incident was an unfortunate one."

"I understand perfectly," he returned, "however . . ."

"What?" she pressed when he wasn't immediately forthcoming.

"How do you explain the night before we left Boothill?"

She stiffened. "Exactly what do you mean?"

"You want me to spell it out for you? You seemed hot enough for me then. Would you care for me to elaborate?"

Letty bristled. "I think not."

"That's what I assumed." He threw what remained of his coffee onto the fire. The water hissed against the burning wood. Murphy stood. "You'd better get the kids up. We've got a long walk ahead of us."

Letty turned to comply.

"By the way," he said, stopping her, "the top button of your blouse is fastened."

Her fingers reached automatically for the button before she realized what he'd said. Mortified, she whirled around, in such a hurry that she nearly stumbled.

It took the better part of an hour to get the children up, fed, and ready to travel.

To Letty's surprise, Murphy lifted the baby into his

own arms. The toddler didn't so much as protest. If anything, the little boy seemed deeply curious about Murphy, staring up at him in wide-eyed wonder.

They marched silently in no real order. By the time they arrived outside the Questo city limits they were tired, dirty, and hungry.

"Our grandmother lives next to the grocery store," Maria told Murphy when he stopped them a safe distance outside the city. The hill where they stood looked down into the town, which to Letty's surprise was a respectable size. Large enough to have a decent-size post office, she noted. From the number of businesses, she'd guess the population to be equal to that of Boothill, around five thousand.

Murphy handed the baby to Letty. "Wait here with the children," he instructed.

"Where are you going?" She could tell from the way his mouth tightened that he wasn't accustomed to having to answer for his actions. She didn't care. Since she was footing the bill for this little adventure, he could darn well tell her.

"First off I want to make sure the grandmother is still around to take the children."

Good point, and one Letty hadn't paused to consider.

"Secondly, it might behoove us both if I checked out the streets before either one of us goes parading down the center of them."

Another bull's-eye.

"We didn't exactly go out of our way in the last village to make friends," he reminded her.

That was true as well. Murphy never had told her what he'd blown up, but from the force of the explosion she knew it had to be something big. Something expensive that Captain Norte wouldn't easily dismiss.

"Anything else you care to know?" His eyes filled with impatience.

"No," she said, but as he turned and walked away, she changed her mind. "Murphy," she called, and stepped forward. "Please be careful."

He cast her a cocky smile and headed down the road at a half trot. "I'll be back before you know it," he promised.

He wasn't.

An hour passed and then two.

After the last episode in which she'd gone against Murphy's orders, Letty didn't dare investigate what had happened this time. Clearly something had.

All Murphy had planned on doing was checking out the town. For safety's sake.

"Your man is gone a long time," Maria commented as the sun rose steadily toward the middle of the sky.

Letty didn't correct the girl. Murphy was most definitely not her man. Nevertheless, she worried. What could possibly have gone wrong? The possibilities were endless. He could be dead, dying, wounded, unconscious, captured.

"I'll go," Vincente suggested.

"No," Letty objected.

"I'm just a boy. No one will ask questions. No one will know that I'm there," he explained with perfect logic. "I do it all the time."

"He does," Maria assured her.

Letty bit into her lower lip, undecided. If Murphy found out that she'd sent a child into town, searching

for him, he'd have her hide. But what else was she
to do?

All the children were looking to her for guidance.
Letty felt at a loss. She closed her eyes and prayed
sending Vincente was the right thing to do.

"All right," she whispered, "but please be careful."

Maria chuckled. "That's what you said to Mr.
Murphy."

Letty swore the next hour claimed a year of her life.
She paced and fretted and worried and stewed. The
children grew restless as well, squabbling with each
other, impatient and irritable. Letty knew she'd trans-
mitted her own fears and regretted that, but she
couldn't seem to help herself.

Just when she was about to give everything up for
lost, Vincente appeared with a short, stocky woman at
his side.

The instant the children saw her they raised their
arms, cried, *"Abuela!"* and raced toward her.

The woman was breathing heavily after climbing up
the steep hillside. She wore a white blouse and black
skirt. Her hair was pulled back into a tight bun, and
her face was red with exertion. The children's grandmother sat on a large rock to catch her breath. The
youngsters all spoke at once. Even the baby took it
upon himself to let out a piercing yell just then.

Abuela hugged and kissed each child in turn, then
took the toddler in her arms, squeezing him protectively against her. His chubby hands clung to her neck.

Letty caught Vincente by the shoulders. "Did you
find out what happened to Murphy?" she asked.

The boy's eyes went to his grandmother.

"*Abuela*," Letty said, having no other name by which to address her.

"Your man," the older woman said, struggling still to talk. She wiped the perspiration from her face with a white handkerchief. "The most unfortunate thing has happened."

Letty's heart stopped. "Unfortunate thing?"

"He came into town just as the local police received notification to be on the lookout for an American man and woman." She paused, her eyes dark and serious. "Our police chief is a conscientious man who seeks to please the new powers-that-be in our country. On receiving word that there was an American man and woman in the area, he organized a patrol." She paused to take in a deep breath. "As it happened, two officers were opposed to joining a search party without first having a cold beer. It was just bad luck that they spotted your friend in the cantina."

"Murphy went to the cantina?" Letty cried, forgetting her concern. The mercenary appeared to have a penchant for such establishments and a weakness for the women who frequented them. Just thinking about him holding and kissing another woman caused her blood to boil.

He'd done it again. He'd left her to sit and twiddle her thumbs in the hot sun with six children while he quenched his thirst and his sexual appetite.

"Where is he now?" she asked, none too gently.

"Jail."

As far as Letty was concerned, he could sit there for a good long while. She was so furious that she found it impossible to stand still.

"I've asked a friend to give me what information he could." The woman's eyes grew dark with concern. "He told me that a man by the name of Captain Norte has been notified of your man's capture."

Letty pressed her fingertips against her lips to hold back a gasp.

"The captain is said to be very pleased. He is sure to arrive before nightfall."

"Oh no," Letty whispered. She sank onto a rock and tried to think.

"There's other bad news, I fear," the older woman continued gently. "Your man put up a fight."

"How badly is he hurt?" Letty cried. She might find Murphy's behavior despicable, but she didn't want to see him suffer. Especially when he'd come to Zarcero to help her find Luke.

"This much I don't know." A soft smile touched the older woman's lips. "But from what I learned, the other two men suffered more than your friend."

"I have to break him out of jail," Letty announced, purpose making her words loud and strong, "and I have to do it before Captain Norte arrives."

The woman placed her arms around the two oldest children. "My family and I will do everything we can to help you."

Murphy spat out a mouthful of blood and worked his jaw back and forth, testing the tenderness. All in all he wasn't in bad shape. This was one exchange in which he'd given worse than he'd got. Not bad considering it was two against one, and then three. By the time he was in jail it had taken five men to hold him down.

Talk about a lack of luck. He hadn't been in town ten minutes when two local police strolled inside the cantina. He hadn't given them much concern. His fight wasn't with the local authorities, but with the rebels who'd taken control of the army. In small towns that dotted the countryside, it was difficult to detect which direction the political winds blew. It wouldn't have been unlikely to find loyalists in Questo.

With one eye on the officers, Murphy had made himself as inconspicuous as he could. Unfortunately it was too little, too late. The next thing he knew, the pair were strolling toward him. Before he knew it he was slapped around and tossed inside the city jail.

Such as it was. The building seemed to have been built by the same outfit that constructed the jail in the old television series *Mayberry RFD*. The entire adobe structure was one large room, which contained three cells divided by thick metal bars. Two desks lined one wall so that he could be kept under constant surveillance.

Murphy tried not to think about Letty, sitting in the foothills, awaiting his return. He just hoped she had the common sense not to do something stupid, like decide to come look for him herself. It would be just like her to investigate matters on her own.

The woman had no patience. That wasn't the only virtue in short supply, either. So prim and proper, she was; it had taken more restraint than he cared to admit not to kiss her senseless that very morning.

She seemed to find it important to inform him she

wasn't the least bit sexually attracted to him. And pigs
flew. She wanted him, only she was too damn proud
to admit it. Naive too, he realized. She didn't know
what was happening to her. One thing was clear: she
didn't like these feelings.

Well, she wasn't alone. Murphy wanted to make
love to her again, too. He knew better than to mix
business with pleasure, but nothing was ordinary
when it came to this mission.

Without even trying, Letty Madden was the most
alluring, enticing woman he'd ever known.

Murphy didn't like admitting that, and probably
wouldn't have, if he hadn't been sitting in a jail with
nothing but time and worry on his hands.

Desiring her brought out the worst in him. He'd
been crude with her earlier, wanting to shock her,
punish her for being so damn desirable. He didn't like
being attracted to her, didn't enjoy being turned on by
a prim sister of a missionary. But he was, more than
by any woman in a hell of a long time.

Suddenly the front door to the jail swung open and
a dumpy-looking policeman walked into the room. He
was short, with a belly that looped over his belt
buckle. Other than a cursory glance in Murphy's
direction, he ignored him.

The two guards spoke in a rushed flurry of Spanish,
most of which Murphy was able to catch. Apparently
there was something important that demanded the
other officer's attention. Moose-Gut had been assigned
to take his place guarding the prisoner until an important man arrived. Some captain, hopefully not Norte,
Murphy thought.

The first officer left, and a plan began to form in Murphy's mind. The replacement didn't look any too swift mentally, and physically a slug moved with greater speed and dexterity.

He groaned, testing the waters.

The guard ignored him.

He was about to ask for a doctor when the door opened a second time and two meal trays were delivered by a tall, thin woman. One was for the officer, and Murphy suspected the second was his.

Murphy's stomach growled. It had been a long time since he'd last eaten. To his surprise, the meal looked downright appetizing. A nice green salad with plenty of vegetables, refried beans, warm tortillas, rice, and chicken. Murphy's mouth began to water.

The guard glanced once in Murphy's direction, tucked a napkin into his shirt collar, and proceeded to eat. Murphy watched in disgust as the pig downed both dinners.

About twenty minutes passed, perhaps longer, and the outside door opened again. Lying on his back on the thin cot, Murphy stared at the ceiling with his hands tucked behind his head. More out of curiosity than any real need to know, he glanced toward the door.

His breath jammed in his lungs and he damn near fell off the cot. Poised inside the doorway was Letty. Only she wasn't dressed as when he'd left her or at any other time he'd seen her.

Letty had disguised herself as a whore.

22

Murphy didn't know what the hell kind of game Letty was playing, but whatever she was up to, he didn't like it. It required all the restraint he could muster not to stand up and demand just what the hell she was doing. As it was, he bolted upright and watched in shocked amazement as she strolled lazily inside the jailhouse.

She had on a traditional Zarcero dress, a white elastic blouse with a large ruffle. Hers, however, seemed to be a couple of sizes too big and dipped low enough to expose the top half of her magnificent breasts. The tiered skirt reached midcalf, but one side was pinned up with a red flower, revealing a healthy portion of smooth thigh. Her hair spilled down across her shoulders like a silken waterfall. Her red lips pouted perfectly as she placed her hand upon her hip and sauntered forward until she stood directly in front of the fat guard's desk.

Murphy noticed the way Letty's eyes avoided his. She wasn't looking at the guard, either; instead her gaze lingered on the two empty dinner plates. A slow, relaxed smile came over her.

"What do you want?" the officer barked.

"Everyone left you, didn't they?" she said in perfect Spanish, her tone sultry. "They always leave you with the dirty work, while the others take the credit."

"Who are you?" he asked, his voice less antagonistic.

"A friend," she said, her voice low and suggestive. "I'd like to become a very good friend."

Murphy couldn't believe she was actually naive enough to think she could walk into the jail and seduce the keys off the guard.

"I need a friend, and it seems that you've got lots of time to play." Her voice dipped seductively. "And I'm the kind of friend who'll play any game you want." She bent forward and planted her palms against the side of the desk. As she did, her breasts all but tumbled out of the blouse.

Like a lightning bolt, Murphy was off the cot. He stood with his hands biting into the steel bars. The woman was certifiable. This was a dangerous game, and he'd wager she had yet to figure out the rules.

"We could have a lot of fun," Letty continued. "Just the two of us. Just the way you like it." She straightened and planted her bare foot on the desk and slowly edged back the hem of her skirt. Her leg was long, sleek, and smooth. The guard seemed entranced by the shape and texture of her pale skin. For that matter, Murphy was equally enthralled. He'd known she was a natural beauty, but he'd forgotten just exactly how beautiful.

The guard moistened his thick lips, and Letty hastily removed her foot from the desktop.

"Later," the fat man suggested hopefully.

She whirled around so quickly she sent her hair spinning, backed her buttocks against the desk, and sighed regretfully, pouting. "I'm busy later, but I have plenty of time now."

The guard hesitated.

"Delma told me just the way you like it best."

He gave a nervous laugh and shifted uncomfortably on his chair. "You . . . you don't object."

"No," she said in a comforting sort of way, moistening her lips once more.

Murphy couldn't quite make out what she whispered next, but he understood enough. Apparently Letty claimed the guard's particular sexual deviation just happened to be her specialty. He wiped a hand down his face. He couldn't believe she was actually getting away with this.

"How much?" the guard asked suspiciously, dragging his eyes down the length of her.

Murphy's gut tightened. He didn't like that look one damn bit.

Letty named a figure. The corner of her blouse slid down her shoulder, and she nervously raised it back up. Then, as if she suddenly remembered the role she was playing, she cocked her chin and allowed the elastic to slip back down once again.

If Murphy had been watching Letty from a purely objective view, he'd have called this the worst acting job he'd ever seen. Except for one small thing. Letty had the body of a starlet—young, supple, naturally seductive. Without her inhibitions getting in the way, she was instinctively provocative. He'd noticed some of that early on when they'd first met in Boothill. Murphy had known intuitively that just beneath the surface of her self-righteous facade lay the heart of a carnal, captivating woman.

Even though it was all an act, Letty managed to have an effect on Murphy. He was as mesmerized by her sleek, enchanting body as the guard appeared to be.

Murphy's body tightened with desire as Letty maneuvered herself about the room, skillfully avoiding being fondled by the jailer. Murphy didn't know what she had in mind, and he didn't want to know, because whatever it was had to be asinine. If she thought she could overpower a man who weighed three times as much as she did, then she was about to learn a painful lesson.

Although he'd investigated every avenue of escape a thousand times, he did so again. Within minutes Letty was going to be screaming her head off, requiring help. She hadn't seemed to figure that out yet.

He glanced at the guard and saw that he'd followed her around the room a couple of times in a crazy cat-and-mouse game, then walked over to the door, where he twisted the lock.

"My oh my," Letty cooed, "you're already big and strong."

Murphy's knuckles cracked against the steel bars as his grip tightened. If the pig of a jailer so much as touched her, he swore he'd find a way to kill the man.

"Are you ready for the time of your life?" Letty whispered, leading the way into the open cell. She looked over her shoulder.

It might have been his imagination, but it seemed to him that the guard's step wavered slightly as he followed Letty into the cell.

Murphy's gaze followed them both like a hawk. He was seconds from coming unglued. The two danced around each other. Letty's skirt rustled against the guard's pants, her breasts achingly close to the fat man's chest.

The jailer lunged for her once, but she laughed and ducked. Then, by some miracle, the guard staggered, his eyes rolled back into his head, and he collapsed face first onto the cot. It seemed as if all the strength went out of him at once.

Letty closed her eyes in abject relief and clenched her hand to her breast. "Thank God," she whispered.

"What the hell happened?" Murphy demanded.

Letty pressed a finger to her lips and hurried out of the cell. Frantically she searched through the drawers until she found a set of keys. First she locked the guard inside one cell and then she unlocked Murphy's.

"We've got to get out of here," she whispered frantically. "Norte's on his way."

"Shit." Murphy grabbed her hand and half dragged her across the floor.

"Maria and Vincente are outside."

"The children?" She'd brought them into this as well. He would have thought she'd know better.

Sure enough, the two oldest children waited in the bed of a rusted-out pickup. A woman he didn't recognize sat in the driver's seat. As soon as they appeared she cast him an anxious smile and started the engine.

"Hurry," Maria urged, glancing down the street.

"The children will cover us," Letty explained, hopping onto the tailgate and slithering into the straw.

Murphy followed. As soon as they were safely concealed, he felt the additional weight of the straw, then heard the two children scramble into the front. Soon the truck took off at a leisurely pace.

"What the hell was going on back there?" Murphy demanded.

The front right tire hit a pothole and Letty was thrown against him. "I'll explain later," she promised.

"Explain now," he returned, refusing to be thwarted. They were tossed about like potatoes tumbling down a conveyer belt, but he didn't care. He wanted answers.

"We got you out, didn't we?" she reminded him.

"That had to be the craziest stunt I've ever seen. You had to dress up as a hooker. Judas Priest, you'd play the role of a nun more effectively."

"I'd think you'd be grateful instead of complaining," she muttered, sounding none to pleased with him.

Well, he wasn't exactly happy with her, either. She'd been stupid, and damn lucky she'd come out of that jail unmolested. He'd like to know what happened to the guard. As far as he could see, she hadn't slipped him anything. There were any number of ways to have broken him out of jail that didn't require her to play the role of a hussy.

The jostling continued, and Murphy inadvertently slammed against Letty once more. This time she released a yelp of pain.

Murphy cursed silently and looped his arm around her, pulling her tight against him. At least now they weren't ramming into one another. Beneath the thick load of straw the heat was stifling and the air stale; nevertheless Letty felt soft and feminine pressed up against him.

Murphy held his breath and tried not to think about the woman in his arms. Tried not to notice how soft her breasts felt against his forearm. Or how her buttocks were tucked snugly in the notch between his thighs. Complicating everything else, she smelled good. Real good. Murphy wasn't much for flowers, but the scent reminded him of lavender.

Hardly aware of what he was doing, he turned his head and nuzzled her ear with his nose. It might have been his imagination, but Letty seemed to ease her head back to him.

Imagination or not, he relaxed for the first time since he'd been arrested. He loosened his hold on her and rubbed his forearm beneath the weight of her breasts. Damn, but she felt good. Their heaviness fell against his arm, and his senses went into overdrive. It didn't do any good for him to lie to himself. He wanted her.

He pressed his lips against the back of her neck and whispered, "Thank you," close to her ear.

She sighed audibly and rolled over so that she faced him. "What did you just say?" She sounded incredulous.

"Thank you," he repeated gruffly, and because being obliged to anyone was foreign to him, he added, "You know, for breaking me out of jail." Later, when the time was right, he'd discuss her methods.

What seemed particularly right at the moment was to kiss her. Testing the waters, he lowered his mouth to hers and brushed his lips across hers. He felt her soft gasp as he stroked the width of her mouth with the tip of his tongue.

Her hand gripped hold of his shirt collar when he kissed her again, only this time he held nothing back. Groaning, he thrust his tongue deep into her mouth, probing the inside with slow, gentle forays that pitched his senses into outer space.

Letty whimpered softly and tentatively touched his tongue with her own. Murphy thought his heart was going to slam straight out of his chest at the heady excitement that filled him. He'd never been so hot for a woman. Had it been anyone else, he would have flipped them on their back and done away with any other preliminaries.

With Letty everything was different. He wanted matters to be right with her. He wanted to please her, to pleasure her. With other women he'd never felt such a keen responsibility.

Wrapping his arm securely around her, he dragged her hips against his swollen front and sighed audibly when she rotated her softness against him.

Without a lot of finesse—little was afforded him in the moving vehicle—he glided his hand up her front to her breast. Her ripe fullness overfilled his palm. It didn't surprise him that her nipple had already tightened into a bead of arousal.

"The whole time in the jail . . . ," she said between soft kisses.

"Yes?"

"I pretended . . ."

He lowered his mouth to her bared breasts, kissing, sucking, and licking her nipple. "You pretended," he prodded.

"That I was enticing you."

He chuckled softly. "Count your blessings you weren't."

"My blessings?"

"Yes." He captured her nipple between his lips and sucked greedily. She moaned and buckled beneath him. "Trust me, sweetheart, I'd have had your skirt up over your head so fast you wouldn't have had a chance to tell me about your specialty."

She stiffened. "Everytime I begin to think . . ." She hesitated, then added on a priggish note, "You're unbelievably crude, Mr. Murphy."

It seemed incredulous to him that they were practically making love and she insisted upon referring to him as "Mr. Murphy." "It's the truth, sweetheart. If you're honest with yourself, you'll admit you want me just as much."

There was no telling where their discussion or their love play would have taken them. Just then the pickup came to a rough, abrupt stop. Letty buried her face against Murphy's shoulder and exhaled sharply. They weren't given more than half a second to compose themselves, right her blouse front, and untangle their arms and legs.

"You okay?" the children's grandmother asked.

"Fine," Murphy said in a growl.

"Letty?"

"I'm . . . fine too." She sounded anything but.

"Where are we?" Murphy asked, looking around.

The old woman didn't answer. "Come. Quickly," she urged.

Murphy helped Letty down from the tailgate. He noticed that her legs weren't any too steady on the ground. His senses had taken a wallop as well, but he didn't allow it to show.

"Stay here," the woman instructed. She left them standing in the shadows and approached the house alone.

"This is the home of *Abuela*'s brother, Aldo," the youngster explained.

"He's a fisherman," Vincente added.

Several minutes later *Abuela* walked out of the house with a short, white-haired man. He looked to be well advanced in years and suffering with curvature of the spine.

"My brother, Aldo," the old woman said.

Murphy exchanged handshakes with the man.

"I understand you and your woman saved the lives of Elena's grandchildren. Our family is grateful. Now it is time to repay your kindness. Follow me."

He led them down a narrow, winding path. The only light came from the moon and stars. The dirt pathway curved a meandering trail through the dense vegetation toward the river.

"We're looking for my brother, Luke Madden," Letty said, not losing sight of the reason for this mission. "Do you know him?"

The old man paused and rubbed his chin, his look thoughtful. "What city?"

"Managna, near San Paulo."

Aldo scratched his chin a second time. "San Paulo is a large city, and I don't know any Luke from Managna."

"He's a missionary. He has a church and a school there. He's been missing ever since the coup."

"I wish you well in finding him," the old man said

when they reached the water's edge. The water slapped against the shore like a woman washing clothes by beating them against a rock.

They were going to need a lot more than luck to find Luke, Murphy mused, but he didn't want to think about the difficulties that faced them in the future when there were enough problems to deal with in the present.

"The soldiers won't think to look for you on the water," Aldo said. As he spoke he walked over to the small vessel, powered by a tiny engine. "Take my boat."

Although the offer had been made casually, Murphy was aware that in accepting the watercraft, they would be floating away with the family's source of income.

"We can't do that," Murphy protested.

"We can't?" Letty looked at him with round, pleading eyes.

"Please," Aldo insisted, directing his comments to Murphy alone. "The boat is our gift to you in appreciation for finding Elena's grandchildren. I have many friends in San Paulo who can return it to me."

Murphy didn't budge. It didn't matter how many times Aldo insisted he and Letty take the boat, it didn't change the facts. The old man was giving them his only means of livelihood. Murphy would find another way of getting Letty to San Paulo.

"You must," Elena insisted. "The roads are blocked, and the jungle is full of dangers. How far do you expect to get on foot?"

"Norte has the entire countryside searching for us," Letty added.

Murphy sighed. If he was alone, he would have handled matters differently; but he had Letty's safety to consider. "Thank you," he said, disliking indebtedness, especially where there was every likelihood that he would never be able to repay the kindness.

Letty hugged Elena and the two children.

"You forgot your pack," Vincente cried, and raced back to the pickup. He returned a moment later with her backpack and handed it to her.

"Thank you, Vincente."

"The potion worked?" Maria asked.

Immediately they were hustled inside the boat and Murphy had the motor going. Aldo and Elena insisted upon loading them down with food and other supplies. While Letty and others dealt with that, Aldo drew Murphy a detailed map of the river. With luck they could be in the capital city within a day's time.

Murphy was already several days longer than what he'd hoped to be. This was supposed to be an in-and-out mission. But he'd learned early on that missions rarely, if ever, went exactly as planned.

Not until they were making their way down the dark, silent river did Murphy have the opportunity to address his questions to Letty.

"What did Maria mean when she asked you about the potion?"

"It was nothing," she said dismissively, but she looked away—a sure sign she was uncomfortable with the inquiry.

Murphy wasn't fooled. He heard the apprehension in her voice. She sat as far away from him as she could, which seemed a bit silly after the heated kisses they'd shared earlier.

"What'd you slip that guard?" he demanded.

Her head came up, and even in the dim light he read her anxiety. "I gave him something that would make him fall into a deep sleep."

"When?"

"Ah . . . earlier."

Murphy frowned. The only thing the guard had eaten or drunk had been at dinner. "How?"

"That isn't important. It worked, didn't it?"

He wasn't going to drop this. "Tell me, Letty."

"Well . . ." She leaned forward and cradled her middle with both arms. Watching her was like watching a butterfly folding its wings, closing itself off from the world. "You might think that getting you out of that jail was just me, but there were several people involved. It wasn't easy, Murphy, and you don't seem to appreciate everything we went through for this."

"You're not answering the question." He didn't like the scenario his suspicious mind had formed. The guard had keeled over like a felled statue and was out like a dead man. When he woke, Murphy pondered, would the guard be left to wonder exactly what had transpired between him and the hooker? The way Murphy had been left to wonder about his night with Letty?

"You have to understand," she said, speaking fast and rushing her words together. "We had to get that particular guard into the jail first."

"Why?"

"Because he's stupid and weak. Delma said he'd be our best chance."

That piqued his curiosity. Delma? . . . Ah, that was the name Letty had mentioned to the guard. "How'd you get him there?"

"I left that part to Elena and her relatives. I didn't fully understand what they were doing, but apparently they feigned some kind of emergency that involved the bank. That sent the first guard out. . . ."

"Go on." He started to clench and unclench his left fist, something he did only rarely in an effort to ward off anger.

"Then Mrs. Alamos cooked up her special dinner, only you didn't eat yours the way you were supposed to."

"I didn't get a chance. Mr. Wonderful decided he deserved both dinners."

"That explains it."

"Explains what?" he demanded gruffly.

"Why . . . Never mind."

"I do mind," he snapped. "Exactly what did you put in the dinner?"

"Herbs." Her voice was so small he had to strain to hear it above the noise of the boat's engine.

"Herbs?" he shouted.

She nodded.

It didn't take him long to make the connection. "The same herbs you placed in the dinner you cooked for me the night before we left for Zarcero?"

Nibbling on her lower lip, she nodded a second time.

Murphy's fist tightened around the helm. "We never made love, did we?"

She didn't answer him.

"Did we?" he shouted.

She jumped an inch off the rough wooden seat.

"You cheated me."

"Not exactly."

"What the hell do you mean, 'not exactly'?"

"We spent the night together," she reminded him timidly. "That was what you requested, remember?"

Impotent rage filled Murphy. When he thought about the grief she'd given him over the last few days, he saw red. He should have known better than to trust a woman. Despite the fact she was the sister of a missionary, the daughter of a preacher, and holier than thou, she'd lied and cheated him.

She looked small and scared.

He didn't trust himself to say a word. Rarely had he been this close to exploding with outrage. It would serve her right if he left her right then and there— docked the boat, climbed onto the shore, and walked away from the cluster fuck she'd created. He would too, if he could figure a way to live with himself afterward.

"You owe me." He spat out the words, which sounded like sawed-off bits of steel even to his own ears.

Letty said nothing.

"I intend to collect, Letty. Don't think you're going to come out of this a virgin. You sold that right a long time ago. I fully intend to collect my due."

She raised her head, and her large, round eyes revealed her fear.

"Just remember, you owe me."

23

Luke gained strength each day. He hadn't seen Rosita since his capture. At least he didn't think he had. There'd been that one night early on when the torture had been at its worst and his mind had been fogged with pain and grief. But he couldn't trust the memory.

Nevertheless, Rosita's love was with him. He felt it as keenly as he did God's. It was his strength. What got him through each day. What gave him the courage to face the unknown.

His cell was dank and dark. Solitary confinement in hell. One thin ribbon of sunlight was all that was allowed him. He waited each day for the sun to move that precious strip of golden light to his bed, then he lay there as it washed over him, cleansing his heart, giving his soul hope. He'd come to feel that those few glorious moments in the sun was God's hand stroking him.

The days merged one into another. Luke had lost track of time, and because his memory was unreliable, he'd invented his own calendar. Today was Saturday, according to his week.

He missed his books dreadfully. His Bible most of all. He missed his life, his friends, his church. He filled his waking hours with prayer.

The sound of footsteps slapping against the concrete walkway brought him upright on the bed. He hadn't been tortured in several days and had thought the worst of it had passed.

His stomach knotted, and he tried to remind himself that God wouldn't ask him to endure anything beyond what he was able. The fear of another beating all but squeezed the oxygen from his lungs.

He couldn't bear the pain. Not again.

He slammed his eyes closed and prayed the men weren't coming for him. Immediately he felt guilty. If they didn't torture him, it would be another man. He'd heard the screams. He knew what was happening because he'd been subjected to those very atrocities himself.

The lock on the thick cell door clicked open.

Luke thought he would vomit until he saw the man who filled his doorway. It wasn't a soldier. He introduced himself as Luke's attorney.

An hour later Luke stood before a kangaroo court. His leg ached terribly, but he had no choice. The judge was the officer who'd killed his friend Ramón. A kind, elderly man who'd never hurt anyone. A saint. Luke's only comfort was knowing that Ramón had left the cruelty of this world for the glory of the next.

The room was crammed full of locals. People Luke knew from Managna and San Paulo, people he'd worked with and helped over the last two years. His gaze skimmed the crowd and he prayed for a glimpse of Rosita, his love, his heart. His disappointment was keen when he didn't see her.

"How do you plead?" asked the soldier who mocked the role of judge.

"What are the charges?" Luke asked.

The list that was read off by the prosecuting attorney was so ludicrous that Luke almost laughed aloud. He'd been charged with everything from arson to rape.

"Do you understand these charges read against you?"

The formality of the question produced a smile. "Yes." He almost added, "Your Honor," but it would have been a travesty of justice to call the man presiding over the court honorable.

"How do you plead?"

"Not guilty," Luke said without emotion.

A murmur rose from the crowd.

"Bring in the others."

Others? Luke twisted around as the door in the back of the room opened. Four boys were led into the room single file. Their faces were swollen and bloodied. It took Luke several moments to recognize them as teenagers who lived close to the mission.

"Hector." He breathed the young man's name. Emilio, Juan, and Roberto all stared with blank eyes into the distance.

Luke felt as if his heart would break. The room

started to spin as the charges against his friends were read. Their crimes, from what he could make of this mockery of a trial, stemmed from an effort they'd made to break Luke out of the jail.

"Please," Luke pleaded. "I'll tell you anything you want to know."

A sick, almost eerie smile lit up the prosecutor's face. "It is too late for confessions."

"I have nothing for which to confess," Luke cried.

"Your crimes are numerous."

"Fine. Charge me with what you wish, but let these innocents go. They're boys."

"No longer, señor."

Luke slammed his eyes closed. The weight of the world felt as if it rested solidly on his shoulders. It was real, he decided. It had actually happened. Rosita had come to him. He remembered how she told him that Hector had a plan to free him. She hadn't listened when he'd pleaded with her to let him die. As a result, these four young lives would be forever marked. The reason: their love for Luke, their desire to rescue him from this hell.

Hatred filled him, so dark and so black that it consumed him. This was what evil did. This was what greed reaped.

The prosecutor stood, his smile glib as he elaborated on the crimes Luke and the youths were said to have committed. The defense attorney sat at the table beside him and made a number of notations.

By his own estimate, Luke counted seventeen contradictions in the short testimony. Not that it would matter. This wasn't a trial. It was an excuse.

He didn't bother to listen as the defense presented its case, weak as it was.

When the time came for him to testify, Luke looked around the courtroom and viewed a sea of anger. One with a tide that swung with popular opinion. One that followed the fickle winds of who was in power and the hope of personal gain.

Disgusted as he was, discouraged and battling bitterness, Luke looked into that sorry crowd and tried to find it in his heart to forgive them.

Forgiveness and love were what he'd been preaching for the last two years. He didn't know that God would be giving him such a vivid lesson in the virtues.

"Stand."

The attorney at his side helped Luke to his feet. He wavered slightly, braced his feet apart in order to maintain his balance, and looked the judge square in the eye.

"After weighing the evidence before me, I find you guilty."

The same verdict was repeated for Hector, Emilio, Juan, and Roberto.

It came as no surprise.

"I hereby sentence you to stand before a firing squad at dawn."

Luke's eyes drifted shut as the words fell upon him like stones.

The gavel slammed against the desk, and the room erupted into applause.

24

Letty could feel the anger coming off Murphy in waves as they continued down the river. They were guided by the moon and stars and the single light of a flashlight. The heat radiated off him until the tense silence was almost more than she could bear.

She shifted painfully on the hard, wooden seat on the boat, but it wasn't the lack of comfort that caused her distress. Guilt ate at her like caterpillars chewing away on new plant growth. She had duped Murphy. Cheated him. These weren't crimes he was likely to forgive.

His accusing eyes ate holes straight through her, his look unwavering. Letty thought to speak, but she could think of nothing to say. Her excuses, which had seemed reasonable and sound back in Boothill, rang false now.

Without him saying a word, Letty knew what

Murphy was thinking. He viewed her as a hypocrite, one who spouted off her beliefs and then fell short of her own ideals when it suited her purposes. She swallowed at the tightness in her throat when she realized that was exactly what she'd done. She'd used him.

Explaining matters would be impossible, but she forced such a list in her own mind. She hadn't misled him for selfish reasons. Luke's life was at stake. Her brother was in trouble, and she couldn't sit idle and not help. Even if that meant cheating Murphy. Until he'd discovered what she'd done, he'd been content. He hadn't known the difference.

Besides, Letty felt he deserved what he got. That Murphy would demand such an outrageous payment in return for his assistance was nothing short of despicable. The only reason he'd made such an offer was because he'd assumed she'd refuse. He'd been looking for a means of salving his conscience and was furious when she'd thwarted him.

To her credit, she had followed through with the letter of the agreement and spent the night with him. She was willing to agree that she'd broken the spirit of their contract. Nevertheless, their lovemaking had progressed much farther than she'd planned.

Looking out over the dark waters, Letty vented a deep sigh, her thoughts filled with regret and doubt. It would have been better if she'd followed through with their bargain and given herself to Murphy. But she'd barely known him then, and he'd frightened her. The same way he did now. In their time together she'd come to trust him. Now and again, to her amazement, she found herself actually liking him.

After the tender kisses they'd shared earlier, she could only wonder what it would have been like if she'd followed through with their arrangement. Certainly it would have been pleasurable. If for nothing else, Letty would be grateful to Murphy for the surprising gentleness she'd found in him.

Or should she be? Murphy had proven her worst fears that she was like her mother, a slave to her own passions. A wanton. A woman with an inclination to promiscuity.

Letty's fears multiplied a hundredfold. Once she'd given herself to a man outside of marriage, she feared it would be like opening Pandora's box. There was no telling where such behavior would lead. If she married, if she gave her body to another, it would be a man she respected and admired. A man who stirred her mind. A man like Slim. The rancher wouldn't be a demanding lover. For years now he'd been satisfied with the crumbs of her affection. Murphy was dangerous, the least safe man she'd ever met.

It wasn't his soldiering ways that distressed her, but her ready and often heated response to his touch. The tender exchange of kisses was evidence of his skill to arouse her to a fever pitch. The danger seemed to heighten her desire, and that frightened her all the more.

All at once Letty couldn't bear this terrible tension any longer. "It's because of my mother," she whispered, knowing that probably confused more than helped the situation. She swallowed hard and held her chin at a proud, lofty angle, hoping he'd appreciate what it had cost her to share this.

Murphy ignored her.

"She abandoned Luke and me when we were five. My father was devastated. . . . He never remarried."

His eyes flickered once.

"She ran off with another man. Apparently this wasn't the first time she'd become involved. My father confessed that over the years there'd been several other men."

She lowered her head, afraid to look at Murphy, afraid of what he'd say if she did make eye contact with him. "My grandmother told me that my mother had a weakness for men. That she was to be pitied." Her voice trembled slightly, and she paused long enough to regain control.

"I don't think you have anything to worry about," Murphy responded gruffly.

"I don't?"

"Trust me, sweetheart, you're nothing like your mother."

In essence he was telling her what a cold fish she was, which was as great an insult as the other. Letty bristled but refused to argue with him. She couldn't very well confess how weak he made her feel. To do so would be handing him a weapon he was sure to use against her. So she held her head high, battled down the emotion, and said nothing.

"So that was what worried you?" He didn't seem to require a response. His eyes glowed in the dark night, his anger replaced with silent amusement.

"I regret having tricked you." She felt she owed him that much. "Telling you about my mother doesn't condone what I did, but I hope it explains why."

"Does it?"

"I . . . we have a long way to travel together, and I think it's important to air this once and for all. You're right, I lied and I cheated you. You have every reason for being angry. If it's any consolation, I deeply regret it. You've been more than fair with me. I can only imagine what would have happened to me alone. I am sorry, Murphy."

"Enough to give yourself to me the way we agreed?"

She glared at him. "Does everything boil down to sex with you?"

"Pretty much."

"Don't you think you're being just a little ridiculous about all this?"

"Hardly. I named my price, you agreed. What else is there to discuss?"

The man was unreasonable. "It was a contemptible thing to ask of me. You're little more than a stranger."

"You were willing to trust me with your life."

"I needed your help. I still do. How was I to know what kind of person you are?"

"Rationalize it all you want, sweetheart, but the bottom line is that you cheated me. You sold yourself to me for a price. The terms were set, and you agreed. All I'm asking is for what's due me." His anger was woven into each syllable.

"I agreed in order to save my brother's life."

"Sugarcoat this any way you want, but that doesn't change the facts."

"But I didn't cheat you, not entirely—"

"True," he interrupted, "you defrauded your way out of it. Tell me, does that make everything better?"

Letty bristled at the harshness in his voice. "All right, so you want your pound of flesh, and you'll have it." It did no good to reason this out. Not with Murphy and his one-track mind. She'd hoped that explaining her past, laying the pain of her fears at his feet, would dent his hard-ass attitude. She should have known better, should have left matters well enough alone.

"You're going to agree?"

"Yes," she all but shouted.

"When?"

"Right now." She stood, and the boat wobbled precariously from side to side. Ignoring the danger she'd be putting them in if she capsized the small vessel, she jerked the elastic-necked blouse over her head and tossed it aside.

"Letty, sit down." He hissed the words between clenched teeth.

"Not until the agreement is met. You've been terribly wronged. If you want me so damn much, take me." She started to remove the skirt, lifting it over her head the way she had the blouse. Somehow, when the material covered her face, she lost her footing. Her arms shot out in a desperate effort to maintain her balance, waving madly about. She could feel the boat rocking dangerously from side to side.

Murphy swore loudly and shouted, "Damn it, sit down!"

Before she had time to think, before she could save herself, Letty tumbled backward into the dark, cold water. As she hit the surface, the loose skirt fell over her face.

The last thing she heard before she went under was Murphy's fury.

Immediately her mouth filled with water and she started choking. Fear paralyzed her, and the current carried her, somersaulting her one way and then another, twisting the material of her skirt around her face.

When she surfaced, she screamed, terrified she would drown. Terrified she'd be lost before she saved Luke. She'd read that a drowning person's life flashed before his eyes. She felt nothing, only a crippling, horrible fear. Not even this last final rundown of her life was to be granted her. The pain in her lungs from lack of oxygen burned like nothing she'd ever known.

Seemingly out of nowhere, she felt herself being lifted out of the water. One moment she was convinced she would die, and in the next her head was above the water and she was breathing again.

She coughed and spat, then choked some more. Murphy's hand manacled her wrist. Somehow he managed to control the boat and at the same time hold on to her.

"Give me your other arm!" he shouted.

It demanded every ounce of strength she possessed to comply. His grip on the second wrist was as tight and firm as on the first.

"Come on, sweetheart," he challenged, "you've got to help me."

She heard the extreme effort it cost him to hang on to her.

The river swirled around her as if to say it had been cheated and wanted her back. The waters pulled at her from one end and Murphy from the other. She felt as if she were on a rack, being stretched apart by two opposing forces.

Once he was able to lift her shoulders above the waterline, Murphy worked on getting her back inside the motorboat. The task was incredibly difficult. The boat was in danger of flipping a number of times. Letty was able to prop one foot onto the side, but when she attempted to lift her full weight inside the vessel, she discovered she was too weak. Finally Murphy was able to fit his arms beneath hers, and with the two of them working together, he hauled her out of the murky water and back into the boat.

She fell like a dead fish into the middle of the craft, which continued to teeter precariously.

Exhausted, Murphy fell back against the helm, his breathing ragged and deep. His chest heaved with exertion.

It didn't take long for reaction to set in and for Letty to start weeping. She hated tears and the weakness she experienced when she succumbed to the emotion, but she couldn't help herself. It wasn't the first time she'd broken into sobs in front of Murphy, and each time it was more embarrassing, more difficult.

She expected him to rant and rave at her for being so incredibly stupid. She'd risked both their lives because she was hurt and angry and outraged.

She'd stripped her soul bare for him and been subjected to his sarcasm. For all the good telling him about her mother had done, she might as well not have spoken. Sitting, she draped her arms around her bent legs and hid her face in her knees. Silent sobs shook her shoulders.

The last thing Letty expected was for Murphy to take her in his arms. He sat in the bottom of the boat next to her and wrapped his arms around her nakedness.

Sobbing, she clung to him, accepting his warmth, his solace, his nearness. He repeatedly ran his hand over her wet head, saying nothing. The thunderous sound of his heart pounded into her ear. He'd been as frightened as she, perhaps more so.

She felt him press his cheek against the top of her head and then forcefully release his breath.

"Go ahead," she whispered when she was able to control her emotions.

"Go ahead and what?"

"Yell at me. I deserve it."

"I think the river said it far more eloquently than I could." Somehow in the craziness that followed her near drowning, Murphy had managed to cut the engine and steer them to the bank.

Wordlessly they clung to each other. After a long time, Murphy spoke. "You don't need to worry that you're like your mother," he said. "Any man would treasure a woman as loyal and faithful as you. It's not every sister who would risk what you have to find her brother."

She lifted her face to look up at him. He swept a wet strand of hair away from her brow. "My own mother wasn't any paragon of virtue," he admitted hoarsely. "She made her mistakes and paid dearly for them. I imagine your mother did as well. We're each our own person, we live our own lives, make our own mistakes, learn from them, and move forward."

"Does this mean you're absolving me from our agreement?" she asked hopefully.

His laugh was filled with wry amusement. "Hardly. I look forward to collecting what's due me, but all in good time. All in good time."

25

Jack had decided to ride it out a while, let
Marcie cool her heels waiting to hear from him. His
patience lasted all of one day. To his surprise he found
himself wasting a good deal of time thinking about the
beauty shop owner.

Although he wasn't thrilled with the way she'd broken off their lovemaking, he realized it had cost her
plenty. When he was able to overlook his own disappointment, he felt a certain admiration for her.

Jack had experienced his share of women over the
years. He loved them, was generous with them
because he could afford to be, and then he left them.
Not without certain regrets. Generally, when he went
off on a mission, he did so on good terms with the
woman of the moment. That way when the time came
for his return, the lady friends in his life would welcome him back with open arms. Marcie had done
exactly that a number of times.

He'd been attracted to her for the simple reason that her sexual appetite was as vigorous as his own. She was one of the few women he could spend two or three days at a time in bed with.

This was the way he'd played the game for a good many years. Women floated in and out of his life, often two or three at a time. He loved them all.

Lately, however, Jack had been giving serious consideration to a monogamous relationship.

It wasn't anything he'd voiced aloud. Certainly not to Murphy, who would have laughed himself silly. He appeared to have reached this decision in the last couple of weeks. It might be that Cain and Mallory had influenced him. When the two former mercenaries had married, it'd shocked the hell out of everyone at Deliverance Company.

This was slightly different. Jack wasn't considering marriage. No need to go overboard on this one-man, one-woman idea. It was important for him to keep his options open. But that didn't mean he'd be cheap about the arrangement. He planned to lavishly set up the woman of his choice and gift her with an abundance of his attention.

In return he'd ask for certain considerations. First and foremost was complete and absolute faithfulness. Until Marcie had broken off their lovemaking, he wasn't sure a woman was capable of such steadfast devotion. Marcie had proved otherwise. By her own words, she'd admitted that she wasn't head over heels in love with her plumber friend, yet she'd refused to betray his trust.

Jack was impressed.

He wasn't sure what had changed Marcie, but

whatever it was, he found himself liking the woman she'd become. True, he wanted her in his bed and had almost from the first moment he'd laid eyes on her. But now he wanted her in his life.

He waited until he knew she'd be home from work and then reached for the phone and dialed her number. She answered on the second ring, almost as if she'd been waiting for his call.

"It's Johnny." Sooner or later he was going to have to tell her his name, but for now he'd let that slide.

"Johnny." Her voice had that breathless, excited quality about it. She made it sound as if the highlight of her day had been hearing from him. As if he were the most special, the most wonderful thing that had ever happened to her. A man could grow accustomed to this kind of welcoming.

"I felt we needed to talk," he said.

He sensed her hesitation. "Talk? About what?"

"Anything. Everything. I don't want to lose you, Marcie."

"Johnny, don't, please."

He could see her clenching the phone, her eyes closed, her conscience fighting him as she battled down her desire for him.

"Did you tell Clifford about our date?" he asked.

"Yes."

"Did you promise him you wouldn't see me again?"

She paused, as if she didn't really want to answer him. "No. I should have, but I didn't."

Jack smiled knowingly. She hadn't promised Clifford something she wasn't sure she could deliver. Another admirable trait. Honesty. "I need to see you."

He dipped his voice to a throaty, seductive level and emphasized the word "need." It wasn't any stretch of the truth. Just hearing her voice had made him hard. He hadn't been this randy in months, and he wasn't willing to settle for second best. He wanted Marcie. The burning inside him grew hotter until it became an exotic torture to merely talk to her.

"All right," she whispered after he remained silent, "but someplace public."

"Fine. You name where." The restaurant hadn't hampered him any. Their naked hunger wasn't going to cool simply because they happened to be around other people. If anything, that could well enhance it.

"When?" She asked this with the same breathless quality as before.

"Now."

She hesitated.

"I need you, baby," he whispered into the receiver.

"Oh, Johnny, I don't think this is such a good idea."

"I do. Nothing's going to happen, I promise. Just let me see you."

Again she paused, then sighed and said, "Have you ever played putt-putt golf?"

Now he was the one who hesitated. He frowned and scratched the side of his head. "You want to play miniature golf?"

"Yes."

He heard the hint of defiance in her voice and grinned. He knew a challenge when he heard one. She seemed to think if they were involved in something silly, they'd be able to keep their minds off what they both wanted most: each other.

"Sure. Name the time and place and I'll be there."

He was waiting for her when she arrived in that rattletrap of a car she drove. Replacing her vehicle would be one of the first things he'd do for her. She'd look good in something deep blue, he decided. Ah, what the hell, he'd buy her a little red sports car.

Marcie's gaze nervously skirted his as she approached him.

"Thank you for coming," he said, and leaned forward to brush his lips across her cheek. She was wearing a sleeveless, full-length summer dress with a scooped neckline, and she smelled of roses and sunshine. It was all he could do to keep from closing his eyes and inhaling the warm, fresh scent of her.

"I should warn you, I'm good at this," she announced while he paid for their tickets.

"Do you want to place a small wager on the outcome of the match?" he suggested.

She eyed him speculatively, as though she weren't sure she'd like his terms. "Like what?"

"An ice-cream cone."

A smile lit up her face. "You're on."

What Jack didn't tell her was that he hoped she'd allow him to lick the ice cream, and when his tongue was good and cold he'd suck her breasts. It was a game they'd played in the past, one she'd apparently forgotten.

The first hole was a windmill contraption. The object was to putt in time so that the golf ball would miss the windmill blade as it circled past the hole.

Marcie went first and bent forward, holding the golf club. It may have been his imagination, but it seemed that she purposely projected her derriere toward him. Then she wiggled it in such a manner to entice him beyond endurance.

"Marcie . . ." He squeezed his eyes closed and groaned aloud.

"What?" she asked, twisting around to confront him.

"Do you have to hold the golf club like that?"

"Like what?" She batted her eyes at him in a gesture of innocence.

"Never mind," he returned brusquely. "It doesn't matter."

It didn't take Jack long to realize she'd been telling the truth. She beat him handily and enjoyed every minute of it. The surprising thing was, so did Jack.

"I suppose you're going to make me buy you that ice-cream cone?" He made it sound as though this were insult on top of injury.

"You're darn tootin' I am."

They walked next door to the small parlor, where he ordered triple-decker cones for them both. They sat across from each other at a picnic table in the shade. Jack reached for her hand, turned it upward, and drew lazy circles in her palm with his index finger.

"You said you wanted to talk," Marcie reminded him, tugging her hand free.

"Yeah." Now that the time had come, he wasn't sure where to start. "We've been good friends the last couple of years."

"Have we?" she challenged softly.

Her question caught him by surprise.

"We've been lovers and little else, Johnny. There's

more to a relationship than a two- or three-day love fest every few months."

"Okay, okay, you've got a point. But I want all that to change."

She stopped licking her cone and regarded him with large, round eyes. "How do you mean?"

His gaze held hers. "I like you, Marcie. A lot. You're one hell of a woman. I'm ashamed to admit that I took you for granted until recently."

"You mean until Clifford entered the picture."

He didn't have much ground to stand on with that argument. "You've got a point, but this time is different."

"You're right it's different. I'm not falling into bed with you the minute you snap your fingers. I'm crazy about you, Johnny, I have been for a long time, but it hasn't gotten me anywhere."

"Jack Keller," he said softly. The time had come to lay his cards on the table, expose his hand, and deal honestly and fairly with her.

"Jack Keller?" she repeated.

"My name isn't Johnny, it's Jack. I felt it was time you knew that."

She didn't say anything for the longest moment, and then, to his shock, he noted that her eyes brimmed with tears. "Marcie?" He reached into his hip pocket and produced a clean handkerchief. "What's wrong?"

She stood, walked over to the trash receptacle, and tossed her ice-cream cone inside, then folded her arms around her middle.

He'd expected a number of reactions to the truth, but tears wasn't one of them. He followed her, threw away his own cone, and then gently placed his hands against the curve of her shoulders. "You can still call me Johnny if you like," he suggested softly.

"You didn't even tell me your name."

"I did," he rushed to tell her. "But we were in a bar, remember? The music was loud, and you must have misunderstood me. I meant to tell you later."

"But you couldn't very well announce that I'd gotten your name wrong when you'd just finished screwing my brains out."

"Wrong. I didn't care what you called me as long as you let me stay with you," he whispered. He pressed his lips to her neck. "I want us to start over, Marcie. This time let's do it right."

"Why should we?" she whispered. "We both know that there's only one thing we have in common, and that's a healthy physical appetite."

"Agreed, but if we get along so famously in bed, can you imagine how well we could get along outside of it?"

Her shoulders lifted in a half laugh. She smeared the moisture across her face with the back of her hand. "Okay, let's say I agree to getting to know you better outside of bed. In other words, you want us to become friends, right?"

Jack bit his tongue. This wasn't exactly what he was suggesting, but close. He wanted her to move in with him, but he didn't intend for her to take up residence in his guest bedroom. The impatience he felt to have her back in his bed was keen, but he realized if he moved too quickly, he might lose her.

"That is what you want, isn't it?" she asked, twisting around and confronting him.

"Yes," he agreed emphatically. "Friends."

"Then what?" she pressed.

He hesitated, not sure what she wanted him to say. "Whatever you want, baby. We'll let this relationship go however you say. You're the one at the helm."

This appeared to shock her. Her eyes were wide and expectant, as if she weren't sure she should believe him. Then, as if she wanted to test the waters, she said, "Let's start with a little honesty, then. If I had your name wrong, there might well be a few other matters we should set straight."

"I agree." He raised both hands, indicating that she should ask away.

They started to walk with no real destination in mind. Because the temptation to touch her was strong and he was fairly certain she didn't want him to, Jack clenched his hands behind his back.

"Are you married?"

"No," he returned adamantly.

"Have you ever been?"

"No."

She studied him as if to gauge the truth of his response. He met her gaze boldly. "It's the truth, I swear it."

"You're away so much of the time."

"True." He didn't elaborate until he read the skeptical look in her eye and realized she was testing him and if he failed now, he could lose her. "But I'm not a salesman the way I've led you to believe."

"You're not?"

He dragged deep breaths through his lungs. The truth might be too much for her to accept. This was a gamble he had no choice but to take. "You probably won't like this. There's a danger in that, but if the truth is what you want, then I'll give it to you."

"You're an IRS agent, aren't you?"

He laughed, and because she was so damned cute, he leaned over and gently kissed her lips. "No. I work for Deliverance Company. We're a group of highly trained professional soldiers who specialize in rescue operations."

"You're a mercenary?" She sounded incredulous.

"Yes."

"Oh, God."

"Sweetheart, listen, I've been doing this for a lot of years. I'm damn good at what I do. I'm alive, aren't I?"

She nodded, but he noted that some of the shine went out of her eyes. She found a park bench and sat down.

"Say something," he said, sitting beside her.

She studied him for a long moment, then flattened her hand against the side of his face. "If I asked you to change jobs for me, would you?"

The woman went straight for the kill, he noted, and at the same time he respected her for it. No need beating around the bush if they deadlocked over an important issue.

It took him a couple of moments to compose his reply. "I don't know."

"That doesn't tell me anything."

"Let me put it like this. I'd be willing to give it a try, if you felt you couldn't live with my profession. Two men in the company were married a few years back. They both left Deliverance Company, and appear to

be content. If Mallory and Cain can make the adjustment back into civilian life, then I imagine I could as
well."

"They both married?"

"Yes. Happily, it seems." This didn't seem the time
to announce he wasn't considering such a drastic step
himself. He wanted Marcie in his life, but the legal
ramifications of marriage were more than he wanted
to ponder at this point.

Marcie's shoulders drooped, as if the weight of her
thoughts had burdened her.

"I need to think about all this, Johnny. Jack," she
said, quickly correcting herself.

"Do that, baby."

"There's Clifford to consider." She sounded worried.

"I know."

"He's been so good to me."

"I'll be good to you, too," Jack promised.

"You don't understand about Clifford."

"I'm sure I don't." Belittling the other man wouldn't
be smart at this point.

"I'll need time to think this over."

"Of course you will." It would behoove Jack to be
patient. He wanted Marcie. Without too much trouble he could see himself falling in love with her.

26

Luke heard the sound of the guards' footsteps outside his cell at dawn. He was ready to die. He'd had weeks to mentally prepare himself for death. That the day would come on the feast day of St. Paul, the patron saint of Zarcero's capital, was an irony of its own.

After he'd first been arrested, when the torture had been at its worst, when the unrelenting pain had kept him awake day and night, Luke had prayed for death. Later, when the agony became tolerable, he realized how very much he wanted to live. Thoughts of Rosita and their future together had lent him the strength to continue. To hope. To believe. To trust.

Now his life was about to be snatched away from him, along with the lives of four loyal youths. Innocents, whose only crime was their desire to save him from the hands of these butchers. There would be no last-minute reprieves. No dramatic rescues. This was the end.

The cell door opened, and despite the pain in his leg, Luke stood proud and tall. Soon he would be robbed of his life, but he refused to go kicking and screaming before his executioners. With his head held high and with as much dignity as he could muster, he placed two letters on top of the cot and boldly met his escorts. With one last glimpse of his cell, he prayed silently that his letters reached Rosita and Letty.

The smaller of the two guards roughly bound his hands behind his back and then shoved him forward with the butt of his rifle. Luke walked through the dark stone passageway into the light. Perhaps he was becoming fanciful in his final moments, but he felt that within minutes he would leave the ugliness of hate and vengeance and walk into the light of God's love and forgiveness.

The sun blinded him as he was led out of doors. He squinted until he saw that Hector, Emilio, Juan, and Roberto were already in place. They stood against the wall, their hands tied behind their backs. Apparently they weren't to be afforded the luxury of a blindfold.

Despite his determination to be strong, Luke experienced a painful tightening in his chest. He didn't want to die. He didn't want to leave all the things life might have held for him. He thought about Rosita and the love he felt for her and their unborn children. For the mission work he'd hoped to complete in Zarcero. For Letty, who would be completely alone now. He hoped that his death would be the catalyst that would convince her to marry Slim. The rancher had been more than patient with her.

Shoved forcefully by his captors toward the others,

Luke stumbled and his head bounced against the concrete wall. Pain shot through him, and for a moment he saw double.

When his vision cleared he noted that Juan and Roberto were both sobbing with fear. They were little more than boys. Neither one was yet sixteen. Hector looked as if he were in a state of shock and stared blindly into the distance. Sixteen-year-old Emilio had slumped to the ground, his legs no longer able to support him.

Background noise filtered toward Luke. The sound of women sobbing and pleading for mercy rose from outside the compound. The boys' families, he guessed sadly. Luke knew that Rosita would be there, and his last thought before the firing squad raised their rifles was of her. He closed his eyes and prayed that God would take the love he felt for Rosita and place it in the heart of another man. One who would cherish her the way Luke would have had he been allowed to live.

He closed his eyes, prepared to meet the God he served.

"Wait."

Luke's eyes flew open as an officer marched across the compound with wide, purpose-filled steps. His gaze centered on Luke as he spoke to the soldier in charge of the execution. Luke didn't know what was happening, but he noticed the way hope lit up his friends' eyes. They stopped and looked to Luke as if he might be able to explain these strange happenings.

"Faith, my friends," he whispered, wanting to encourage them.

During his captivity, Luke had met many of the army's leaders, but he didn't recognize this latest addition.

The two officers held a short conference. Soon a soldier marched forward and grabbed Luke by the upper arm and dragged him away from the others.

"Proceed." The order was issued by the officer in charge of the firing squad.

"No," Luke shouted, struggling. "No!"

His scream was obliterated by the sound of firing rifles. The shots echoed into the early morning, mingling with screams of terror. Luke twisted around to see the bloody, lifeless bodies of the four youths slumped against the wall. The scent of sulfur and death hung in the air.

His grief and horror, his sense of loss, were so keen that his knees gave out on him and he fell to the dirt. His stomach rioted and the contents surged up his throat. He gagged and vomited. He was no longer in Zarcero, he was in hell, in the very hands of Satan himself.

When he'd finished heaving, Luke was lugged into the commander's headquarters and slammed onto a chair. He looked at the faces of the two men and felt nothing. No fear. No pain. Nothing.

The compound commander and the second man spoke quietly, but Luke paid them no mind. He felt as if his mind had isolated itself from the inhumanity of what he'd just witnessed, from the travesty committed against his friends. He dared not think about the lives of these innocents or he would go mad, so he sat completely numb.

"I've come to ask you about your family," announced the officer who'd stopped the execution.

Luke glanced briefly in the rebel's direction.

"Answer Captain Norte," Captain Faqueza, the camp commander, shouted when Luke wasn't immediately forthcoming.

"My family," Luke repeated, still numb, still dazed.

"Tell me about your family," the captain pressed.

"I belong to the family of God."

His response warranted him a slap across the face.

"You have a wife?"

"No," he whispered.

"A sister, then?"

Luke said nothing.

"These were found on his cot," Commander Faqueza said, and placed the two letters Luke had left inside his cell on top of the desk. The other man reached for the first note.

"Letty."

Luke's head snapped up and he narrowed his gaze. "What's my sister got to do with this?"

"Letty Madden," Captain Norte repeated, having trouble pronouncing the English name. "I believe that was what the woman said her name was."

"Letty's here?" Adrenaline shot through Luke's bloodstream, and he bolted upright and out of the chair.

He was forcefully shoved back down as Captain Norte paced in front of him. "I've met your sister and her friend."

Her friend? Luke hadn't a clue who that would be. Not Slim. Luke couldn't imagine the rancher in Zarcero. Not now. Letty's man friend would be completely out of his element in Central America at the best of times.

"What have you done with her?" Luke demanded.

"Nothing," Norte said, and then added with a soft, demented laugh, "Yet, that is. Your sister has proven to be something of a nuisance. With the help of her troublesome friend, she's managed to destroy a fuel dump, kill two of my men, and steal a jeep."

"Letty?" Luke was incredulous. "You must be mistaken. My sister works for the United States Postal Service."

Norte snickered.

"It's true."

"We had word of her friend's capture recently, but unfortunately before we were able to question the man, he escaped. We believe your sister was behind that as well."

"Letty?"

"Apparently she managed to drug the guard."

"You have the wrong woman," Luke said without emotion. He didn't know what Letty was doing in Zarcero, but he prayed she'd leave while she could.

"I have a score to settle with your sister."

Luke said nothing.

"And it seems to me that the way to get to her is through you."

"He was sentenced to death," Commander Faqueza complained, apparently upset that Luke hadn't been shot with the others.

"He will die," Norte replied confidently, "you have my word on that. But first I will use him as bait to trap two enemies of our people."

27

Letty *woke with a start* and bolted upright. She exhaled slowly and glanced around, finding her bearings. Yellow-cheeked parrots, egrets, and frigate-birds chirped a cheery greeting. She saw the boat and realized they were still on the river, but Murphy had secured it so they could both catch a few hours of badly needed sleep.

She wasn't entirely sure what had woken her. For several moments her groggy mind refused to function. Then all at once a terrible sadness, a deep, soul-wrenching grief, pressed heavily against her chest. Alarmed, she flattened her hand over her heart, wondering at the strong, powerful sensation. It was Luke, she realized with a start. He was feeling this pain, and it was almost more than he could take.

"What's wrong?" Apparently she'd inadvertently woken Murphy. He propped himself up on one elbow and studied her.

"I don't know," she whispered, battling back the waves of mind-bending sorrow. "All I know is that it has something to do with Luke. Something's happened, something terrible. I feel his agony, his grief." She didn't look at Murphy, knowing he was skeptical of the emotional link she shared with her twin brother. "Murphy, we have to find him soon. Something really awful has happened. . . . Whatever it is has broken his heart."

"We'll be in San Paulo by afternoon," Murphy said.

"We have to hurry," she whispered, and buried her face in her hands until the sensation dwindled and faded.

"Take it easy, sweetheart, we'll get there all in good time."

"I'm worried." She straightened and looked down the river, eager to be on the way.

He sat upright, yawned, and rubbed a hand over the side of his jaw. He hadn't shaved in a couple of days, she noted, resisting the temptation to reach out and stroke his face. The desire surprised her. They'd shared a number of small intimacies since beginning this trip. Letty felt comfortable with him in ways she hadn't with any other man, save her father and brother. Even Slim, the man she'd once felt she would marry.

"You've got that look," Murphy muttered, and frowned at her as if he weren't sure what to expect next.

"What look?" she asked, reaching for her backpack and running a brush through her tangled hair.

"I don't know, but I don't like it."

Letty pinched her lips together. "You don't need to worry. We'll find Luke and be out of here soon enough, so you say. Then I won't harass you with unpleasant looks."

"I didn't say it was unpleasant," he snapped, reaching for his weapon. He leaped from the bow of the boat to the shoreline. "All I said was that I didn't like it." With that he disappeared into the bush.

Letty continued brushing her hair, convinced Murphy was by far the most disagreeable human being she'd ever had the misfortune of meeting.

She didn't understand him. One minute he was snapping at her like a cantankerous turtle and another time he was holding her, comforting her, reassuring her that she wasn't responsible for the sins of her mother.

At one point she'd offered him her friendship, which he'd soundly rejected, yet he was quite possibly the best friend she'd ever had. In the past week Letty had shared more confidences with this soldier of fortune than she had with her closest, dearest childhood friends.

Letty realized Murphy wasn't interested in listening to her worries. He probably would rather she'd left them unspoken. Her concerns must have embarrassed him. She knew they did her and vowed that whatever was to follow, she would no longer burden him with her past.

Within half an hour they were chugging down the river once again. Letty sat at the far end of the boat, her back straight, fervently avoiding him. If Murphy had any complaints about her attitude, he left them unsaid.

They must have traveled two hours or more without speaking. Letty swore she'd swallow her tongue before she'd be the first one to speak. This too appeared to suit Murphy's purposes. He had never seemed more content. He leaned back and whistled merrily, as if they were on a Caribbean cruise rather than a rescue mission to save her brother's life.

"That's the look I detest the most," he said, stretching his long legs out in front of him. He leaned against the side of the craft with one hand on the engine.

"What look?" she flared, immediately angry with herself for reacting.

"That uptight prude look of yours."

"I'm not a prude!"

Murphy laughed.

Letty folded her arms and glared at him. "Isn't there anything you like about me?"

"Sure," he returned lazily. "You've got one of the finest pairs of tits I've ever seen."

Letty closed her eyes. "You are by far the most vulgar, crude man I've ever known."

"Sweetheart, that's a compliment."

"Then kindly keep your *compliments* to yourself. You disgust me."

Murphy grinned broadly, apparently well pleased with himself. "Yup," he announced, "this is the way I like it best. You madder than a firecracker and me enjoying it. It doesn't get any better than this."

"Well, far be it from me to raise your level of consciousness out of the gutter. Not when you seem to enjoy it there so much."

Murphy chuckled. "Don't be so quick to dismiss the gutter, sweetheart. You meet lots of interesting people."

"I can just imagine."

"You know, it's downright pleasurable baiting you." He chuckled softly. "I don't know what I'm going to do for fun once we're finished with this mission."

"I imagine you'll find some other form of sordid entertainment."

"I'm sure I will," he said, continuing to be amused with himself, "but I have the feeling it won't be nearly as enjoyable as my time with you."

The long stretch of silence between them had seemed intolerable, but this conversation was worse. "How long before we reach San Paulo?" she asked, more as an effort to funnel the topic away from herself and to the matters at hand.

"An hour, possibly two."

She sighed expressively. "Are you going to abandon me again?"

"Abandon you?"

"Yes," she said sternly. "Twice now you've insisted that I stay outside the city while you go on alone to investigate. I'd like to remind you that both times have turned into unmitigated disasters."

"Is that a fact?"

"Yes," she returned emphatically. "You left me for ten hours outside of Siguierres. When I felt I had no choice but to check up on you, I discovered you making love with a whore in some sleazy cantina."

"Just to set the record straight, I was gathering information."

Letty rolled her eyes. "I can only wonder what you learned. When I found you, it was more than apparent that you were talking to her bosom."

Murphy snickered loudly. "Don't worry, your breasts win hands down over hers. She didn't have near enough to satisfy me."

"Would you kindly shut up?" He chuckled, and she knew he was baiting her, but she couldn't help herself. "You know what your problem is?" she flared, unable to keep silent.

"No, but I bet you're about to tell me."

"First off, you don't know how to talk to a woman—"

"I beg to differ. I can sweet-talk the best of them."

"Hookers, you mean. But when it comes to dealing with a real woman, a lady of refinement and culture, you're at a complete loss."

He didn't disagree with her, she noted.

"And so you do what you've always done," she continued, "what has become, I would say, your expertise. You insult and berate what you don't understand."

He arched his eyebrows as if impressed with her insight. "From listening to you," Letty went on primly, "I strongly suspect that you don't have a clue of what it really means to make love."

"Now just a minute—"

"You think of sex as a bodily function, sort of like shaving or brushing your teeth. Something mildly enjoyable when the mood strikes you. I sincerely doubt that you've ever really been in love. You're absolutely ignorant of what it means to make love to a woman on an emotional level. The only plane that exists for you is the physical. You might well be the greatest lover in the world, or assume you are, but in reality, I pity you."

The amusement faded from his eyes and he

clamped his mouth closed. Letty had said far more than she'd intended. Well, it would do him good to sample his own brand of medicine.

The rest of the morning they traveled the river, communicating only when it was necessary.

When they passed a fishing boat, Letty knew they must be nearing San Paulo. Her heart slammed against her chest with excitement. Soon they'd find Luke. And once Luke was safe, she'd be rid of this obnoxious, ill-tempered, unreasonable mercenary.

Unless, of course, he insisted on claiming his fee.

Murphy's mood had turned foul after his discussion with Letty. She'd proved to be an easy mark. He enjoyed provoking her, indulging himself. This time, however, she gave as good as she got. What surprised him was how accurate she'd been.

What she'd said hit home. He didn't know how to talk to a woman. His dealings with the opposite sex were generally linked to women of the night. He'd avoided relationships. The most meaningful time he'd spent with the opposite sex generally didn't last longer than a pleasure-filled hour or two.

As for what she'd said about making love . . . there, too, he suspected she was right on. He'd been having sex for years, but he'd never really made love. Not that it plagued him, but he was left to wonder at the difference.

It was just past noon when Murphy found a safe spot to dock the boat. He considered leaving Letty while he ventured into the city, but he dared not. The woman had a penchant for finding trouble, and the city would be a prime spot. He wanted her near so he could protect her if necessary.

They carried everything with them. Murphy found an honest-looking laborer who, for a fee, promised to return the boat to Aldo. The man agreed, claiming he had relatives in Questo, and personally guaranteed its safe return.

Following that, Murphy led the way into the city, taking the back streets, keeping Letty close to his side. It wasn't long before he realized they'd walked into some sort of religious holiday. The streets were decorated, and an air of festivity floated about them. The natives were dressed in their best attire. Musicians played their instruments on every major street corner.

"What's going on?" Letty asked.

"Hell if I know. It looks like a celebration." All the better, Murphy felt. This was the first piece of good luck they'd had.

"We're going to buy ourselves some clothes and join in," he said, steering her toward an open-air shop.

The entire inventory hung from the shop's ceiling. Blouses, shirts, dresses in a variety of sizes and colors, swayed in the gentle breeze.

Murphy wandered around, checking out the merchandise, hoping he'd find something to fit his bulky build. If he didn't change out of the fatigues, he'd stand out like a pumpkin in a rice field.

No need announcing to the rebel troops that he'd arrived. With a fresh set of clothes, he'd be able to manipulate his way around town and blend in with the crowds.

He left Letty while he tried on a shirt and a pair of pants. There wasn't a mirror inside the dressing room, but the transformation must have impressed her because she took one look at him and burst into giggles.

When Murphy saw his reflection, he understood why. The white cotton pants and shirt with multicolored embroidery on the wide pockets made him look something like a karate expert. The shop owner added a colorful cloth belt, insisting it was a necessary addition because of the feast day. The wide sombrero completed the transformation.

Luckily Letty already wore the traditional Zarcero dress. On impulse, Murphy bought her a lace shawl and a new pair of shoes. He paid for their purchases with cash.

"Where to now?" she asked once they were back on the street.

He grinned. "To the celebration, where else?"

"But—"

"Trust me, I know what I'm doing."

The center of town was a madhouse. The city square was jammed with citizens who were badly in need of an excuse to celebrate.

Soon after they'd made their way into the town square, a religious procession moved past. An altar boy carrying a large gold cross led the way, followed by the priest, dressed in full orthodox regalia. Behind him was another boy carting a three-foot statue of the Blessed Virgin. Following up the rear, in perfectly matched rows, were twenty other young altar boys.

As the priest walked past, those gathered in the city square blessed themselves. The priest waved a pot of incense. Behind the religious procession came a platoon of marching soldiers. The gaiety fizzled, and a somber mood took root as the uniformed men filed past.

Letty edged closer to Murphy, and he could feel her fear. He placed his arm around her shoulder. "Don't worry," he whispered for her ears alone. "They don't see us."

As soon as the small parade continued down the street and out of sight, the music started up once again. Men played guitars and sang, children raced across the lawn, and women congregated.

"Let's get something to eat," Murphy suggested. He was famished and knew Letty must be, too.

She nodded.

Taking her hand in his, Murphy led the way. If they were to get separated in this crowd, it would be close to impossible to find each other again.

He found a vendor and purchased a meal that consisted of a mixture of rice and meat, tasty and filling.

"Don't talk," he instructed as they sat on the grass.

"My accent is perfect," she insisted, sounding downright insulted that he should suggest otherwise.

"I want to listen."

"Listen?"

He nodded.

"Just what are we supposed to be doing?"

This woman was driving him nuts. "Pretend we're lovers."

Predictably, Letty blushed.

"We only have eyes for each other, understand?"

She nodded.

It wasn't difficult to feign an infatuation for Letty, Murphy discovered somewhat to his chagrin. In fact, the role came far more naturally than he would have liked.

Every now and again he'd lean forward, brush the hair from her shoulder, and kiss her neck. Soon his head was nestled in her lap as he lay in the cool grass and stared up at the bright blue sky as though he hadn't a care in the world.

Within an hour he'd learned the whereabouts of the military compound and the commander's name. News of the execution of four teenage boys was rampant. A day meant for joy had been tainted with grief.

As the two women who strolled past talked about the execution, Letty's eyes met his. "They executed children?"

"So it seems." Murphy stood and helped Letty to her feet. "Let's mingle."

As he edged the way outside of the town square, he found two well-armed soldiers advancing in his direction.

"Let's dance," he said, taking Letty's hand firmly in his.

"Dance?"

It was close to evening, cooler. A row of Japanese lanterns was strung between trees, defining the area meant for dancing. Murphy turned Letty into his arms. He wasn't exactly light on his feet, but he did a fair job of faking waltzlike steps.

It had been one thing to sit with Letty, but it was another to hold her in his arms. She moved against him as naturally as if they were long-standing partners.

Her warm breath tickled the base of his neck. The need to close his eyes and soak in her gentle softness was strong, but he resisted. Lordy, she tempted him.

He found her staring up at him, and her eyes smiled into his. They continued to sway to the music. What information they might have learned in those moments was lost on him. Murphy all but drowned in the depths of her eyes.

Unable to resist, he lowered his head and his mouth touched hers, tasting the softness of her lips, outlining their shape with the tip of his tongue. Letty moaned softly, and her arms crept about his neck.

"We have to find Luke," she whispered huskily, and hid her face in his throat.

"We will," he promised. He closed his eyes momentarily and breathed in the fresh, womanly scent of her. An educated guess told him the army held Luke Madden at the military compound with the other political prisoners. If the executions had already begun, there was no time to lose. He sincerely hoped, for Letty's sake, that it wasn't already too late.

Murphy wished he could protect her from what they might discover, but he could see no way. Her brother was all the family she had.

When the music ended, he led her off the dance floor. What they needed now was a vehicle. However, because of the festivities, the streets were barred from traffic. There didn't appear to be a single car in sight.

His idea about blending in became increasingly difficult as the soldiers filtered into the crowd. They appeared to be on a quest, searching for someone.

"We have to get out of here," Murphy whispered. "Come on."

They hadn't gone far before he instructed her to cover her head with the shawl. She readily complied.

Pretending an absorption with her, he managed to hide his face. Another pair of soldiers advanced toward them, and Murphy turned Letty into an alley.

"Kiss me," he instructed.

"I beg your pardon?"

"Just do it, and pretend you've wanted nothing more for hours on end. Understand?"

She nodded. He had his back to the wall, and Letty slanted her mouth over his. She didn't possess a lot of finesse, but to her credit, she gave it all she had.

With one eye open, Murphy watched as the soldiers walked past. He closed his eyes and took control of the kiss, deftly switching positions so that she was the one with her back against the wall.

His mouth was hard on hers. She whimpered softly and then parted her lips to admit his tongue. Her arms slid around his neck, and she was fully involved in the exchange.

Both were breathing hard and heavy before he ended the kiss.

"Are they gone?" she asked.

"They were gone a long time ago," he whispered.

Letty muttered disparagingly under her breath, then asked, "Is everything a game to you?"

"No. I just wanted to see how much you wanted me. Now I know. You're crazy for me."

"Don't be ridiculous. All I want is to find my brother and get the hell out of here." She wrapped the shawl around her shoulders as if it were a plate of armor, her dignity sagging and badly ruffled.

"Don't worry, we'll get Luke out," Murphy said with a confidence he wasn't feeling. He slipped her hand around his arm. Night was just beginning to settle in. The real celebrating would begin soon, and passage through the streets of San Paulo would become impossible. They'd best make their escape now while they could.

They'd gone a short ways when Letty stopped, staring. "Look," she whispered, awed.

Murphy caught a glimpse of two men on stilts, dressed in outlandishly colorful outfits. Each carried a flaming baton, and at intervals they would stick the batons down their throats and then blow flames into the sky.

"I've never seen anything like that."

"I did once in Rio during Mardi Gras."

Suddenly her arm slipped from his. "What is it?" he asked.

"I think I see someone I know."

Before he could stop her, she slipped into the crowd. Murphy attempted to follow her, but it was impossible.

"Letty," he shouted, uncaring who heard him. "Stop."

He skirted his way between, around, in and out, but it was useless. Within seconds he had lost her completely.

28

Marcie picked up her polished pink bowling ball and enthusiastically approached the pins. She studied the shiny hardwood alley and stepped forward, swinging her arm back and then releasing the ball.

It rolled off her fingertips and coursed down the middle of the lane, zeroing in on the head pin. Then, at the last possible moment, just before the ball slammed into the pins, it veered sharply to the left, knocking down three out of the ten pins.

Her shoulders sagged with disappointment. She'd done everything exactly the way she should. The ball had zeroed in on the head pin, then had chosen a path of its own. All she'd managed to knock down were three lousy pins.

"It's all right, honey," Clifford called from behind her.

Marcie pushed down the sleeves of her thin knit sweater. The air-conditioning in the bowling alley had always been too cold for her.

"I was cheated," she cried.

"You can get a spare."

Clifford spoke with the utmost confidence. His smiling eyes reached out to her, and Marcie did her best to smile back, but it was difficult.

If her bowling was off, then she blamed Johnny . . . Jack Keller for that. Their meeting the night before had stunned her. He'd been so open, so sincere, so forthright. When she'd discovered that all this time she hadn't even known his name, she'd been hurt and angry. Only later did she appreciate the risk he'd taken to set the record straight.

"You can do it," Clifford called when the ball return spat out her pink ball. "Here."

He joined her and, gripping her by the shoulders, gently eased her two shorts steps to the right. "You should be fine now."

Marcie poised the ball in front of her and stared at the remaining pins, determined to pick them up. She wasn't going to let a little thing like Jack's proposition unsettle her from the really important matters in life, like bowling.

Smiling to herself, she started down the alley, putting some energy into her swing and delivery. This time when the ball left her fingertips it headed straight as a bullet down the right-hand side of the alley. The way it looked, she would leave the six middle pins standing.

Disappointed she turned around, not wanting to watch.

"That's it, that's it!" Clifford shouted. He waved his hand to the right as if that would influence the direction of the bowling ball.

Marcie turned around, and to her surprise she noticed that just as it'd happened before, the ball took another dramatic sweep to the left. Only this time it solidly hit the head pin. The remaining pins exploded as if they'd been hit by a blast of dynamite.

"I did it, I did it," Marcie cried, jumping up and down as if she were on a pogo stick.

Clifford joined her, wrapped his burly arms around her waist, and lifted her over his head. "That's my girl," he said, grinning up at her, his face filled with pride and happiness.

Marcie returned to the bench as proud of this one small accomplishment as she was of anything she'd ever done. It was as simple as mind over matter.

Clifford walked up to the ball return and reached for his own bowling ball. The smile on Marcie's face faded as she studied him. The plumber would never be poster boy-toy material, but he was gentle and charming.

Marcie knew how difficult it must be for him not to question her about what was happening between her and Jack. He'd asked about Jack only once, and then just to inquire if she'd be seeing him again. When Marcie had admitted that she didn't know what she'd be doing, he'd praised her honesty and hadn't pressed the issue again.

If the situation had been reversed, not knowing would have eaten Marcie alive.

Clifford threw the bowling ball and scored a strike.

She applauded wildly, reached for her beer, and saluted him. He bowed eloquently and marked the score sheet.

Marcie couldn't imagine what it would be like to bowl with Jack. They'd never so much as attended a movie or a football game together. She didn't even know if he liked sports or cheered for the Kansas City Chiefs.

Other than their lone dinner date, their entire relationship had revolved around their time in bed. Not that she hadn't enjoyed herself. The sex had been incredible, but there was more to everyday life than a quick tumble in the sack.

Now Jack claimed he wanted her on a permanent basis. Marcie noted that the word "marriage" had never come up. At least not in regard to their relationship.

True, Jack had said something about two of his friends having recently married, but she'd noticed how he had carefully avoided the topic when it came to the two of them.

Men generally avoided the M word when it came to her, Marcie realized. A small pain stabbed her heart, and she shoved thoughts of Jack from her mind. It wasn't fair to Clifford to spend time with him and stew about another man.

"How about catching something to eat?" Clifford asked when they'd finished with the game.

"That sounds great." She feigned enthusiasm, although she wasn't hungry.

Clifford carried both their bowling balls out to the car. He seemed a bit edgy, Marcie noticed, but she suspected his uneasiness had to do with the uncertainty of what was happening with them.

They pulled into an all-night diner, one of his favorite spots. The waitress motioned them to the booth in the corner, and Marcie slid across the red vinyl seat.

Clifford reached for the menus tucked behind the sugar canister and handed her one. "I'm in the mood for a cheeseburger," he announced. "How about you?"

Marcie shook her head. "I'm not that hungry," she murmured absently. "I think I'll just have a piece of lemon meringue pie."

The gum-chewing waitress stopped for their order a couple of minutes later.

"So," Clifford said, holding on to his water glass with both hands, "how's life treating you this week?"

"Good," she said.

He cleared his throat and briefly met her eyes before lowering them once more to his water glass. "I got to thinking this afternoon about you and this other friend of yours."

"You want to know if I've seen him again, is that what this is all about?" .

Clifford shook his head. "No," he said with emphasis. "It's probably better if you don't tell me, and not because I'm burying my head in the sand, either. If you are seeing him, which you certainly have every right to do, I'd dwell on it more than I should and risk screwing up Mr. Wallace's remodeling project." He smiled tightly and focused his concentration on the tabletop once more.

"Clifford, maybe—"

"I don't mean to interrupt you, but if you'd let me finish what I have to say, it would be easier. Okay?"

"Sure." He was so adorable that Marcie had to work not to slip out of her seat and join him on the other side of the table. Instead she reached across the table and squeezed his hand.

"When I left it up to you to date this old friend of yours, I got to thinking that maybe you assumed I didn't really care if you did date this other guy."

"Oh, Clifford, I know better."

"I'm not much to look at, I realize that. There's grease under my fingernails, and I could stand to lose a few pounds."

Marcie had never seen anything but a gentle, kind man who was good for her and to her. Clifford would never pretend to be something he wasn't. He'd never lied to her. He was thoughtful, sweet, and generous.

"You're my teddy bear."

A smile quirked one edge of his mouth upward. "No one's called me a pet name before. At least none that they were willing to say to my face." He sat up straight and rubbed his hand along the backside of his neck.

"When I met you I'd given up the hope that I'd meet someone special," he continued. "Hell, I'm close to thirty-five now. My younger brother's got four kids. His oldest is going into junior high in September."

"Bobby?"

Clifford nodded. "I've never been good with women, talking with 'em and stuff like that. It seemed every time I was around an attractive woman my tongue would get all tied up and I'd say something stupid that would sound like an insult. Then I met you." He chanced a look at her.

"You came into my life at just the right moment as well," Marcie said. She'd never mentioned her past. Never told him about the mistakes she'd made. The time, energy, and esteem she'd squandered on users and losers. For all Clifford knew, she was as white and pure as lambs' wool.

"I did?"

"I'd given up on finding a decent man."

"You?" He seemed incredulous. "But, Marcie, you're beautiful. There must have been a hundred men who wanted to make you their wife."

She hadn't the heart to tell him the truth. Men didn't marry a good-time girl. They'd had their fun and their kinky sex with her and then gone home to their wives and girlfriends.

Clifford lowered his head once again, then arched his back and stuck his hand inside his pants' pocket. He brought out a diamond ring, which he held between his thumb and index finger. The stone was small and glittered in the light.

He cleared his throat and looked skeptically at her. "I've been trying for the better part of a month to find the nerve to ask you to marry me, Marcie. This here diamond's been in my pocket all this time."

"A month?"

"Everytime I'd try to come up with the words, my tongue would stick to the roof of my mouth. I must have rehearsed what I wanted to say a thousand times. Then your rich friend came in the picture and, well . . . I decided I'd wait to see what happened with him."

"But—"

"I know, I know. This guy's still in town, and I figure you're probably seeing him. I called you last night and there wasn't any answer."

"You didn't leave a message on the answering machine?"

"No," he admitted reluctantly, "I figured I was going to lose you to this fancy guy even before I had a chance to propose."

"Clifford, please." Her throat was closing up on her at the unexpectedness of the proposal. She didn't know what to say.

"I know this is probably the worst thing I could possibly do to you now. The truth is, Marcie, I was afraid this diamond would be burning a hole in my pocket when you told me you were going back to your old boyfriend."

"Oh, Clifford."

"I love you, Marcie. I have from the day I first walked into your shop and you gave me a haircut. It was the first time a woman had ever cut my hair. You were so friendly and nice and chatted away like I was someone special. Women generally treat me like a husky Forrest Gump. I suppose that's because sometimes I don't make a whole lot of sense."

"Clifford, you're smart and kind. . . ."

"Yeah, but I don't fit the image of the tall, dark, handsome hero, and so . . . Never mind, none of that is important. What is important is that I love you. I want to marry you, and if you agree, I promise I'll do everything within my power to make you happy."

Marcie covered her mouth with both hands as tears blinded her eyes. "There's so much you don't know about me."

"I know everything that's important."

Marcie wiped the moisture from her face as she saw the waitress arrive with their order. She sniffled and smiled at Clifford.

"Would you mind very much if I took a day or two to think it over?"

He grinned and nodded. "I thought that was what you'd say. Take as long as you need. I'm not going anywhere."

Then, with barely a pause, he reached for his cheeseburger and ate it like a man on the brink of starvation.

29

Hopelessly lost, Letty wandered aimlessly through the streets of San Paulo. She'd gotten separated from Murphy when she'd thought she'd recognized a young woman from Luke's mission. Letty couldn't remember her name. Rosa. No, Rosita. Something along those lines.

Letty had met Rosita the previous summer. She remembered her specifically because the lovely young woman was so clearly infatuated with Luke. Her twin, being obtuse and completely blind to matters of the heart, seemed blithely unaware of this woman's devotion.

Letty had caught a fleeting glimpse of her. There was every likelihood Rosita could tell Letty what had happened to Luke. In her excitement Letty had broken away from Murphy, then twisted and curled her way though the throng, calling to Rosita.

There'd been so many people. Soon Letty had become caught up in the crowd, trapped in a sea of moving humanity. The last look she'd had of Rosita, Letty had found herself steered in the opposite direction.

In that brief glance, Rosita had looked pale and drawn. The deep shadows beneath her eyes spoke of pain and fear. It looked as though the beautiful young woman hadn't slept in a week.

Once Letty realized she'd lost sight of Luke's friend, she'd wanted to weep with frustration. Then she'd remembered Murphy.

"Oh, shit." She'd actually said the words aloud.

By this time he was nowhere in sight. The very least he could have done was keep up with her, she thought, exhausted and alone. She wrapped the shawl he'd purchased for her more tightly around her shoulders. Not because she was chilled, but for the security it afforded her. Which was pitifully little, she realized.

Again and again, as the evening progressed to night and the night to morning, Letty had tried to think of where he would be. Where he would think to look for her or meet her.

Every logical place had turned up empty. She'd gone back to the apparel store and waited outside the locked doors, certain Murphy would think to check for her there.

She'd even traipsed all the way back to the river where they'd docked the boat. That had been a big mistake. Not only was there no sign of Murphy or the fishing vessel Aldo had lent them, but she'd run headlong into a group of drunken soldiers.

Luckily she'd escaped their interest and slipped away. Even more fortunate was that not one of them was in any condition to chase after her.

The city square had also turned into a dead end. She'd lingered around there for hours, hoping she was inconspicuous, knowing she wasn't.

As the sun crept over the horizon, Letty realized she had nowhere else to go. Nowhere else to look. They'd lost one another irrevocably, and it was her fault. The only thing for her to do now was look for someone else to help her locate Luke.

That little shit, Murphy mused as he stalked through the dark alleyways. One minute Letty had been within his grasp and the next thing he knew she was gone.

The frustration was worse than heartburn. He'd been up and down the streets of San Paulo without so much as a trace of her.

Of all the stupid, idiotic things for her to do, this topped everything. As best he could figure, she'd chased after someone she'd *thought* she recognized. Someone she recognized from where?

He should have known better than to get involved in this fiasco. Women like Letty Madden lay awake nights thinking up ways to ruin men's lives.

When Letty had first approached him, he'd recently returned from a mission and was in no mood to take on another. In the few days he'd been home, he'd actually started to enjoy the role of the gentleman rancher. Not that he was tempted to make anything permanent of it.

The sedate life wasn't for him. Then again, he'd thought the same of Cain and Mallory when they'd retired from soldiering. His two friends were as high on adventure as he was himself, and he'd been sure they wouldn't last long in civilian life. But he'd been wrong.

Mallory perhaps he could understand. The hulk of a man had stepped on a land mine and nearly lost his leg and his life. When he'd returned to Deliverance Company, whatever element had made him a good soldier was gone. Sometime between the accident and his recovery he'd lost his thrill for adventure. Murphy suspected the injury coupled with meeting Francine were what had led to Mallory's retirement.

Cain was an entirely different story. Cain had been their leader, the most fearless, intrepid man Murphy had ever met. It was difficult to believe that a woman was solely responsible for Cain's unexpected retirement, but it was the truth.

A lovely San Francisco widow had turned his friend's life upside down. Before Murphy could account for what happened, Cain had set up house in Montana and was raising cattle with the best of them. More shocking to Murphy was the fact that Cain was happy.

Unlike Mallory, who'd taken to raising llamas and children on a Washington State island, and Cain the rancher, Murphy didn't know anything but soldiering.

Why such thoughts would come to him while he traipsed through the rebel-controlled streets of San Paulo on a wild-goose chase seeking Letty, Murphy didn't know. Frankly, he didn't want to know.

At this point, he promised himself, if he ever found the pest, she'd be fortunate to escape with just a good tongue-lashing.

He'd looked everywhere. The streets. The city square. The river. He'd even walked into a women's rest room, thinking she might be there.

His patience, limited in the best of times, was gone. It'd evaporated in the time he'd spent searching for her. The only thing left now was to locate Luke Madden. Her brother was the best chance Murphy had of finding Letty.

If the little shit was still alive.

Letty surrendered all hope of ever finding Murphy. She simply couldn't waste any more time looking. In her search, she'd kept an eye out for Rosita or anyone else she might recognize from the mission in Managna.

At nine the evening of the second day, she found herself standing in front of a Catholic church. Earlier, in Siguierres, she'd walked willy-nilly into just such a church, thinking she'd be safe. Instead she'd stumbled into a rebel command post. To say she'd learned her lesson was an understatement.

The large wooden door creaked as she gently pushed it open to peek inside. Her relief was palatable when she realized this was no military headquarters.

She stepped inside quietly. The church's interior was lit with several candles. Rows of thin pews with bare wood kneelers formed uneven lines down both sides of the sanctuary.

The altar was an ornate wooden structure, painted

white and trimmed in gold, that stretched two floors to brush against the ceiling. As she stared at the front, at the floor level, she realized that a body lay adorned in a white robe.

Letty remembered Luke telling her that many people believed that the cathedral in San Paulo possessed the actual remains of St. Paul. Not the original St. Paul, the one popularly known as the thirteenth apostle, but another one who had followed several centuries later. The practice of displaying the decayed bodies of dearly beloved saints was common in Central America.

Holding her breath, Letty carefully moved forward and slipped into the last pew. Seeing that the kneeler was down, she knelt and bowed her head for prayer.

If ever she needed divine intervention, it was now. Everything was a mess. Even if Murphy did happen to find her, he'd be so furious that he'd never feel he could trust her again. Then there was Luke and the time she'd wasted looking for Murphy.

Letty didn't know how long she prayed. She was exhausted, hungry, afraid. And that was only the tip of the iceberg.

She heard a movement, a creak of a shoe, a *whoosh* of air, a fragmented sigh. Even if it had been a soldier, she wouldn't have cared. Emotionally she was ready to collapse. Physically she'd gone past the point of no return.

Letty opened her eyes and raised her head. Her dark eyes met those of a white-haired priest she guessed to be about sixty. He blinked. So did she.

"My dear," he whispered in stilted English, "these are dangerous times for a woman alone."

"Yes, I know," she whispered in Spanish, knowing the language was safer for them both.

"I'm Father Alfaro. Is there anything I can do to help you?"

Letty hesitated. "I don't think so." She stood, certain he would ask her to leave, but her legs were shaky and she fell back into the pew.

"You're ill?"

"No, I'm fine," she said, dismissing his concern. "Really."

"Where are you staying?" He entered the pew and sat next to her, took hold of her fingers, and gently patted the back of her hand.

Her hesitation was answer enough, she suspected. Squaring her shoulders, she looked him directly in the eye. She had to trust him; there was no one else. "Have you heard of the mission in Managna?"

"Yes, of course."

Hope sent a shot of adrenaline into Letty's bloodstream. "Then you must know my brother, Luke Madden. He's the missionary in charge of the Managna mission." She leaned forward and gripped the priest's frail arm. "Do you know what happened to him? Have you heard anything about him? I feel certain he must have been arrested, but—"

"My dear, you mean to say that you've come all this way hoping to find your brother?"

She nodded. "Can you tell me anything about what's happened in Managna?"

The priest's eyes saddened. "Unfortunately, no. I've heard of your brother, yes, and the work he's done among the people. He's spoken of with great love."

"He's been arrested?"

The priest studied her for a long moment before answering. "Yes, I believe so."

"Then he's alive." Her spirits soared. Luke was alive. Alive. The music of relief made for a lovely song.

"My dear, I'm sorry, I can't say. I simply don't know."

Her shoulders slouched with the weight of her dashed hopes.

"It was for your brother that you were praying just now?" he asked gently.

Luke, yes, but her heart had been filled with Murphy as well. He'd come to Zarcero because she'd needed him. Despite knowing she'd tricked him, he'd continued with the mission. She wouldn't have blamed him had he dumped her then and there. Although he struggled to depict himself as a scoundrel, Murphy was an honorable man. In this instance he'd behaved more ethically than she. She'd tricked him. Duped him. All for her own purposes.

"My dear," Father Alfaro whispered, "are you alone?"

"Alone?" She glanced over her shoulder, uncertain what he was asking. That no one else was with her was obvious.

"Is there another traveling with you, perhaps a man?" he continued, his voice barely above a whisper.

"We were separated," she answered, making sure her own voice contained only a hint of sound. "How did you know?"

The faintest hint of a smile touched the corners of the elderly priest's eyes. "It is better that I don't answer."

"A friend helped me cross from Hojancha into Zarcero."

"And your friend? You say you were separated? How long ago?"

"Two days. I thought I saw someone who knew Luke, and when I turned around . . . my friend wasn't there. I've spent every minute since searching for him."

The priest frowned.

"Have you heard anything about . . . my friend?" Letty felt as though a vital part of herself were missing. Without Murphy she was lost and confused. Uncertain where to go or what to do next. All the while, Luke's life hung in the balance.

"No, nothing," Father Alfaro whispered.

"And nothing about Luke?"

"I cannot help you with your brother."

"Please," Letty pleaded, squeezing his hand. "I must find my brother."

"I'm sorry, my child."

"But surely there's someone who can help me." She had nowhere else to turn. Nowhere else to go. If Father Alfaro refused her, she might as well surrender herself to the authorities. If ever she'd been aware of her own powerlessness, it had been in the last two days without Murphy. He'd become more than her guide and protector. Much more. He'd lent her the confidence she'd needed. The courage to face the future.

Father Alfaro stared at her with unflinching regard, as if seeing her for the first time. It was the look of a man who was being asked to risk his life for a stranger on the strength of his intuition. The strength of his ability to gauge her character.

"I know a man who can get us information about your brother." Again the words were whispered so low that there was almost no sound. His breath brushed past her ear.

"Please, oh, please," she said eagerly, doing her best to constrain herself. "I'll do anything. Pay anything. Can you take me to meet him? But we must hurry. I fear Luke's in grave danger."

"No. You must not see this man, or talk to him."

"But—"

"You heard of the four boys who were executed?"

She nodded. The streets had been filled with news of the horror.

"They were all from Managna."

"No," Letty gasped.

Father Alfaro nodded sadly. "So it is said."

"Could it be that my brother was shot with them?" Letty asked, barely able to think past the anxiety she felt for her twin.

"I can't answer your questions," the priest answered gently. "But I will do what I can to help you find the information you need. In my heart, I feel God will answer your prayers and you'll find both these men you love so much."

Letty sucked in her breath. Both men she loved so much. . . .

The old priest was right, she realized with a shock. She had fallen in love with Murphy. It wasn't anything she'd expected to happen. Certainly nothing she'd planned. She wasn't even sure she was pleased about it. In the two days they'd been apart, she'd felt as if a giant hole had opened up in the area of her heart.

"Oh no," she said aloud.

"No?" The priest regarded her quizzically.

"Not Murphy," she whined, barely realizing what she was saying. Life would be so much more predictable with Slim. Safe, kind-hearted Slim. Even if she did love Murphy, that didn't mean he wanted anything to do with her.

The door behind them creaked. Letty tensed, as did Father Alfaro.

"You must go," he whispered, "and quickly. Return to the church tomorrow morning. I will find out what I can about your brother."

"Thank you," she whispered. She turned to retreat from the pew at the far end.

"Judas H. Priest. Letty."

A harsh male voice echoed like a pistol shot through the church.

"Murphy." She scrambled onto the polished wooden pew, leaped over the back, and raced toward him. He looked like hell warmed over. As bad as she felt.

He held his arms open, and laughing and crying, she flew into his embrace.

His arms closed over her and held her with such strength that she couldn't breathe. Letty didn't care. Her lungs might not be able to function, but her heart was in fine shape.

"Where the bloody hell have you been for the last two days?"

"Me?" she gasped. "Where were you?"

He didn't answer. "You try this kind of stupid stunt again and I'll—"

"Yes. Yes."

Slanting his mouth over hers, he kissed her with an urgency and hunger that robbed her of what little breath remained in her.

"I should kill you after what I've been through the last two days."

"This hasn't exactly been a picnic for me."

He didn't stop kissing her. Again and again his mouth roughly claimed hers. His teeth ground against hers, and when she sighed, his tongue swept the moist interior until they were both panting and breathless.

She twined her arms around his neck and stepped onto her tiptoes. "I didn't know what to do."

"I couldn't make myself stop looking for you," he murmured between kisses.

"I was so afraid."

Murphy chuckled. "You? I don't believe it for a moment."

Father Alfaro cleared his throat pointedly. "Perhaps you should introduce me to your friend, my dear."

30

Keeping his arm around Letty, Murphy turned to face the man of the cloth. He wasn't going to let Letty out of his sight unless he could be certain exactly where he could find her again. In the last two days he'd turned San Paulo upside down looking for her, worrying about her damn fool neck and risking his own in the process.

"Murphy, this is Father Alfaro." Letty gestured toward the priest.

"Pleased to meet you, Father," Murphy muttered, leaned forward, and offered the older man his hand.

"Father has a friend, someone who might be able to find out what's happened to Luke."

Murphy studied the priest, wondering exactly how much they should trust this man. His instincts were generally good, and it seemed to him the priest could be counted as an ally.

While Murphy had roamed the city, he'd made a few subtle inquiries of his own and learned that Commander Faqueza, the man in charge of the military complex, was a real bad-ass. Faqueza had a reputation for torturing his prisoners and enjoying the process of crippling them mentally. If by some miracle Letty's brother was alive, Faqueza might well have broken him. Letty could be risking her life for a brother gone mad with pain.

"I'll learn what I can," Father Alfaro assured Luke, "but I can't make any promises."

The priest's gaze held his a second or two longer than necessary, as if to say he didn't personally hold out much hope Luke was alive.

"I can't tell you how much we appreciate this," Letty responded for them both.

Murphy's hand tightened around her shoulder. The relief he'd experienced when he'd walked into the church and found her was beyond description. He'd given up, convinced himself the only way he'd connect with her again was through Luke.

For two solid days the uneasy restless sensation in the pit of his stomach had persisted. Try as he might, he couldn't shake the feeling he should be able to find Letty.

Not until the sun had set and night had blanketed the capital city had Murphy recalled that when they'd separated briefly in Siguierres, the first place Letty had gone to had been the local church. As soon as he'd remembered that, he'd quickly stalked from one house of worship to another, looking for any trace of her.

"We've got another problem," Murphy told her

grimly. Now that he knew Norte was in town, the sooner they found Luke the better. Murphy was smart enough to recognize that Norte's presence was no coincidence.

"What?" Her anxious eyes met his.

"Norte's in town."

"You know Captain Norte?" Father Alfaro's voice dipped with tension as he mentioned the other man's name.

Murphy nodded.

"I don't think you'd say we were two of his favorite people," Letty said, and Murphy felt the tension tighten her shoulders.

The priest shook his head sadly. "Captain Norte does not make a good enemy."

Murphy had already determined as much.

"You must not be seen together." Father Alfaro rubbed his hands together nervously. He shot them a look and seemed to come to some sort of decision. "Come," he ordered. "You'll be safe with me. Hopefully by morning I'll have some news of your brother."

Murphy knew the priest was taking a substantial risk on their behalf and hesitated to place the other man in danger. If not for Letty, he would have refused.

Father Alfaro seemed aware of Murphy's concern. "You needn't worry. I've placed my life in God's hands many times." Expecting them to follow obediently, the priest led the way out of the sanctuary.

Once outside, Father Alfaro walked in the shadows around the side of the church to the two-story structure next door. They entered the back of the building and made their way through the kitchen and down a long hallway.

Murphy noticed that Father Alfaro moved as silently as possible and didn't turn on any lights. He paused at the bottom of the stairs and glanced upward, waited a moment, then escorted them into what looked to be a library. Once inside, he closed the door softly. The moonlight that filtered in from the windows was minimal.

Murphy smelled lemon oil and old books, not an unpleasant combination. The priest flattened his hand against the fireplace mantel and appeared to be searching for something. After a moment Murphy heard a soft clicking sound and then watched in amazement as a bookcase swung open like a door inviting them into a magical, fictional world. Only all that was inside the compact space was a cot and nightstand.

"You'll be safe here for the time being," the old priest told them. "I'll come for you in the morning as soon as I can. Until then I must ask you to be as silent as possible."

Murphy nodded, and with Letty at his side the two entered the secret room. Letty sat on the side of the bed, and from the way her shoulders slumped forward, Murphy could see that she was exhausted. He wasn't in much better physical shape himself. The emotional and physical demands of the last two days had taken their toll on him as well.

"Rest well, my friends," Father Alfaro whispered before the bookshelf silently slid back into place.

The space was instantly dark and smelled of old

books, dust, and mildew. The little light afforded them came through narrow cracks in the bookcase.

Murphy stood for a moment and found his bearings. Locked inside a secret room in a priest's home wasn't something handled in any military handbook. It sure as hell wasn't anything he'd run into in all his years of soldiering. But his main concern was Letty's safety, and he figured they'd be secure enough.

He heard her stretch out on the narrow cot and half expected her to insist that since there was only one bed, he should take the floor. Unwilling to argue with her, he was about to do exactly that when she whispered, "There's room enough for you, too." Her voice was reed thin and inviting.

Something was definitely wrong. Murphy resisted the urge to slam his palm against his ear and clear his head. He actually hesitated, unsure if it was a good idea for them to be that close. Tired as he was, it would be damn difficult to resist making love to Letty. This, he decided, was a symptom of utter exhaustion.

This woman owed him. She'd promised him. He wanted to make love to her more than he'd ever desired any woman. And yet . . .

"Murphy?"

Silently he moved toward the cot. She'd scooted as far as possible to one side and still remained on the bed. Murphy removed his gun and set it on the nightstand within easy reach.

"How is it," he couldn't resist asking, "that of all the churches in San Paulo you stumble upon the one priest involved in covert activities?" He wasn't accustomed to dealing with this kind of incredible luck. Talk about a needle in a haystack.

Letty took an elongated moment to answer him. "I believe God sent me to Father Alfaro."

Had there been more light, Letty would have seen him scowl. Murphy wasn't comfortable with her response. If God was willing to allot favors, there were a number of more important ones he wanted. Then again, it would be just like this God of Letty's to see fit to place them both in the path of temptation. If having them sleep together was God's idea of a joke, Murphy wasn't laughing.

He reluctantly eased himself down on the cot. Although she'd insisted there was plenty of room for them both, there wasn't. He twisted, rolled from one side to the other. Together they discovered the most comfortable position was for him to lie on his back and for her to sleep on her side with her head tucked against his chest.

Murphy's eyes drifted closed as he hugged Letty to him. Her arm came around his waist and she released a soft, feminine sigh of contentment. This was about as close to heaven that Murphy intended to get. This woman felt incredibly good in his arms. The kind of good that had as much to do with the emotional as it did the physical. The kind of good a man like Murphy feared most, because it meant he cared.

Caring was an expensive emotion for a mercenary. It had cost the life of more than one good man. He'd seen Cain take a bullet because his thinking was muddled with thoughts of Linette. He was determined not to let the same thing happen to him.

"Father Alfaro knew about you," Letty said, cutting into his thoughts.

"What do you mean?"

"He asked if I was traveling with a man."

"When?"

"Early on, when we first started talking."

Murphy had to give the matter some thought. He suspected the priest had connections with the CIA, which was good news as far as Murphy was concerned. He might well be in need of those alliances.

"I'm so tired," Letty whispered, and nestled deeper into his embrace.

"I know, sweetheart."

"I'm not sure what I would have done if I hadn't found you." She yawned a second time.

"Me either," he admitted. He could feel himself giving in to the demands of his body. Before he fell completely asleep, he cupped her shoulder and lowered his chin just enough to touch the top of her head. Dropping his guard completely, he wallowed in the rightness of having her in his arms. He might as well own up to the truth. He cared deeply for Letty.

31

"*Luke.*"

His name came to him on the faintest breath of sound. He rolled his head to one side and opened his eyes. Rosita's face was framed in the small square box of his metal cell door.

"Rosita?" Was it possible that she could be real? His heart slammed against his ribs as he carefully eased himself off the cot, trying to ignore the pain. He moaned with the effort it cost him to move. The agony went deep, but he would have suffered far worse for the chance to see Rosita.

"I'm here."

Little more than her beautiful dark eyes showed through the box. But it was enough to send joy crashing through him. This gift, this wonder of seeing the woman he loved, brought him incredible happiness.

"How is it you're here when—"

"Don't ask. They won't let me inside your cell. Not again."

"Then you *were* here before?"

"Yes." She blinked back tears. "Please, let me touch you." The only part of her hand that she could get past the steel bars were two fingers. Luke pressed his lips against the pad of one and nearly wept. Her fingers worked against his face, caressing his unshaven cheek. He closed his eyes, savoring the simple pleasure of her touch.

"I'll always love you," he told her, choking on emotion. He paused, fearing if he spoke again, he wouldn't be able to keep from sobbing.

"And I'll always love you."

For the longest moment they did nothing but cherish this unguarded gift of being together. The thick metal door couldn't bar the love he felt for Rosita or hold hers back from him.

"Are they beating you?" Rosita asked in a voice that said she feared the truth.

He couldn't lie to her. "Some. Not as bad as in the beginning."

He watched as the tears crowded her eyes, making them bright and clear; then the moisture spilled down the side of her face.

"Hector and the others?" he asked.

"They were given a decent burial." Her voice cracked slightly.

He was almost afraid to mention his sister's name. "Have you heard from Letty?"

"Letty, no. Is she here? In Zarcero? How is that possible?"

"I don't know, but I'm afraid she must be. It was the reason I wasn't killed with the others."

"That explains why—" Rosita stopped abruptly, as if she'd already said more than she intended.

"Tell me," he ordered.

"My uncle . . . the reason he let me in to see you was to tell you good-bye. Commander Faqueza has ordered a public execution in two days' time."

"It's a trap. You have to find my sister and tell her."

"But how? Where?"

Luke pressed his forehead against the door. It felt cool against his skin. Cool and hard. He needed to think and couldn't. His mind clouded with concerns and worries. Anyone he knew who might have helped Letty into the country was either dead or already in prison.

"I'll try to find her, Luke," Rosita promised, "I just don't know where to start looking."

"Do what you can." He couldn't worry about Letty now. Later, when he was alone, he'd dwell on his twin sister and pray God would keep her safe. These moments with Rosita, quite possibly his last, were too precious to waste.

He kissed her fingertips once more. "After I'm dead, Rosita, you must—"

"No," she cried. "It was a miracle you were saved. You aren't going to die, my love."

"We don't have time for denials. We have to face the truth now, while we can." If he wasn't gunned down by a firing squad or hanged, as some of the other political prisoners had been, there was every likelihood that the beatings would kill him.

"How can a God let this happen to us?" She wept openly. Her voice trembled with the force of her sobs.

"How could He allow Hector and the others to die such a horrible death?"

Luke had repeatedly asked these same questions himself. "God isn't the one responsible for the hate in this world," he assured her, wanting more than anything to hold Rosita one last time. He would die a happy man if he could feel her softness against him. If he were allowed one last opportunity to touch her sweet face and feel her heartbeat against his own.

She glanced over her shoulder, and he saw a flicker of fear. "I must go." Wiping the moisture from her face, she offered him a brave smile, turned abruptly, and was gone.

Luke heard the gentle fall of her footsteps as she sped away. The physical effort it cost him to stand caused him to tremble violently. He barely made it back to the bed before he collapsed.

He was suffocating with the weight of his worries. Norte was going to use him to trap Letty.

Luke knew his sister well. She'd do anything to rescue him, including placing herself at incredible risk. He couldn't allow that to happen, but he didn't know any way to prevent it.

Letty would come racing in on a white charger, believing she could save him, and in the process sacrifice her own life. His sister hadn't a clue what these men were like. She'd never seen evil on this level. Neither had Luke until he'd been taken captive.

The only way he could thwart Captain Norte was to die before the public execution could take place. With his eyes open and raised to the heavens, Luke looked to God.

"Let me die," he pleaded, "before it's too late."

32

"*As of two days ago your* brother was alive."

Her heart in her throat, Letty whirled around to face Father Alfaro. "He's alive?" The priest had come for them bright and early that morning and led them to the home of a friend, someone he trusted. Murphy had disappeared with Father Alfaro shortly after their arrival. She wasn't keen on their being separated so soon after finding each other, but she wasn't given any choice.

Murphy looked to Father Alfaro and then to Letty.

"What is it?" she asked. She was beginning to know Murphy, and there was something he wasn't telling her.

Neither one seemed eager to elaborate. "Luke's hurt," she cried, certain the news was bad. "How seriously? Can we move him? Does he need a physician?"

"Letty," Murphy said, and gently wrapped his hand around her forearm. "It isn't that."

"My source wasn't able to learn of your brother's physical condition," Father Alfaro continued. "All he could tell me was that your brother is alive."

"There's more," she insisted, unwilling to be protected from the truth. Murphy should know her well enough by now to recognize that. "Tell me," she insisted. "I need to know."

Once again the two men exchanged looks.

Murphy was the one who spoke next. His eyes held hers and his words were low and even, without emotion. "Luke's been sentenced to death."

Letty closed her eyes and held her breath until her chest tightened and her lungs ached.

"His execution is to be held publicly at noon in two days' time."

"Two days," she repeated. The blood seemed to rush from her head, and the world started to spin. For an instant she feared she was about to faint. The need to sit down became urgent; she reached out blindly and lowered herself onto a rough wooden chair.

"Letty?"

"I'm okay." But she wasn't. She hadn't felt right all morning. Although she'd slept better in Murphy's arms than she had in weeks, she'd awakened exhausted, weary to the bone.

The ill feeling had intensified as the morning had progressed. She probably should have said something, but she'd been fairly certain the feeling would pass. It hadn't.

"We've got to save him," she said, looking to Murphy. She'd found herself doing that more and more often. Along with her heart, she'd given him her trust. In her eyes, he was capable of the impossible. As obstacles in saving Luke became more and more insurmountable, she relied heavily on Murphy's talents.

"I gave you my word I'd find your brother, Letty, and I will." His jaw was clenched with grim determination.

The need to touch him was strong. To flatten her palm against his cheek and thank him. Those two days wandering about the city without him had taught her valuable lessons. As much as she wanted to find and free Luke, she could do nothing without Murphy.

The priest cast the mercenary a worried glance. The atmosphere in the small adobe house reeked of tension. Not understanding, Letty looked to Father Alfaro.

"We fear the execution might be a trap," the priest explained.

Murphy chuckled. "Norte wants us. And really, can you blame him? We made him look like the fool he is. What he doesn't realize is that he hasn't got a prayer. Not only are we going to escape his clutches, but we're going to steal Luke right from under his nose."

"The word on the street is that Commander Norte will richly reward the person who captures either of you."

"I see." And Letty did. As Father Alfaro had told them the night before, Captain Norte didn't make for a good enemy.

"You should be prepared for the worst," the priest told her gently. "We'll do everything within our power, but it's possible we won't be able to save your brother."

"You must," she cried. Her heart desperately wanted to believe it was possible to rescue Luke. Her brother deserved so much better than this. He'd given his heart to the people of Zarcero, dedicated his life. Without Luke, she'd be completely alone and lost. Without him, her anchor would be missing.

"You have my word that I'll do everything I can to free Luke," Murphy said, the intent look back in his eyes.

"I can't ask for anything more than that," she returned.

The rest of the morning was spent with Murphy and Father Alfaro talking and making plans. The two appeared to come to some form of agreement, and soon afterward Murphy left. He didn't tell her where he was going or how long he'd be away.

Letty sat in the shade of a tree, trying to analyze what was wrong with her. The achy, restless sensation persisted into the afternoon. She attempted to put some name to what she felt. The physical symptoms resembled a low-grade case of the flu, but she knew it was more than that. In some ways it seemed as if this queasiness were connected with her twin.

Letty waited impatiently for Murphy's return. Several matters needed to be discussed and decided. Her mind was so occupied with that, she wasn't aware of the subtle changes going on about her.

At first.

It came to her all at once that she was being watched. She wasn't sure how she knew, but she trusted this sixth sense. For a long time she remained motionless, afraid to move, fearful of attracting attention to herself. The same sixth sense that told her she and Father Alfaro were no longer alone warned her that if she did move, she'd be a dead woman.

As soon as the thought went through her mind, fear drifted in like a thick fog, the haze of it making it difficult to reason out exactly what was happening.

With her breath held tight within her chest, she glanced across the yard. Father Alfaro sat inside the house at a table. He appeared to be reading.

A vision flashed into her mind of a jail cell, of torture and death. For one single instant she could smell the filth, taste the horror, and feel the pain. Then it was gone.

The next moment, a picture of Murphy hell-bent for leather surged like gangbusters into her mind. She seized the image and held on to it, needing him just then. If he were here, he'd know what to do. She had the pistol with her—he'd insisted she carry it at all times—but reaching for it now would be useless. She'd be dead before she could even point it. And even if she could get her weapon without drawing attention, she wasn't sure about firing it. She'd done so the one time, and only because Murphy had insisted. She wished she'd paid more attention now.

Maybe it was because she was thinking of Murphy and the gun that she was prepared for what happened next. His voice, soft and urgent, drifted from behind her.

"Letty, when I shout I want you to drop to the ground and cover your head. Have you got that?"

She gave a small, imperceptible nod. Every muscle in her body went tense.

Soon after Murphy whispered, Letty saw three soldiers hiding in the vegetation close to the house. Two of them had pointed their rifles directly at her. The other man had his trained on Father Alfaro, through a window.

Dressed in camouflage, they blended in perfectly with the scenery. It was a wonder she'd been able to pick them out at all.

The taste of fear filled her mouth, attacked her senses. A humming sound roared in her ear, and the scent of anticipation, the choking swell of the afternoon heat, settled over her like concrete blocks. Her throat felt as dry as a crusted, empty lake bed.

"Do it!" Murphy's cry cut through the hot, still afternoon air like a razor-sharp scissors through paper. Swallowing a scream, Letty fell face first into the dirt. Remembering what he'd said about covering her head, she brought her arms up to protect herself.

The quick, staccato bursts of Murphy's weapon roared over her. Letty froze with fear, unable to scramble to safety even if he asked it of her.

Three soldiers lay dead outside the adobe structure. Three good men, downed by their own sloppy work, Murphy mused. Letty and the priest had been sitting ducks. The guerrillas could have had them any time, but Norte's men had been overly confident and forgotten one small thing. Him.

When Murphy had arrived on the scene, he'd recognized instantly that Letty had sensed the soldiers' presence. Their interest had seemed to be focused on the priest. Not until later had they realized Father Alfaro wasn't alone.

Murphy thanked the powers above that Letty had had the presence of mind to remain silent and still. He was convinced it had saved her life.

When he'd happened upon the scene, he'd been scared spitless. Letty in grave danger. He'd strongly suspected his feelings for her had changed. Little by little she'd chipped away at the wall of his defenses until he'd fallen hopelessly in love with her. The moment he'd recognized he could lose her to a guerrilla's bullet had removed all doubt of the sentiment he felt for her.

Murphy wasn't being immodest by claiming he was a good soldier. Furthermore, he understood the reasons that made him good. Death had never been any big threat to him. It held no terror. His world consisted of a few carefully chosen friends and Deliverance Company. And that was it. The full extent of his existence. He was a man with little to lose.

His life to this point had been devoid of contentment, of joy, and, most profoundly of all, of love.

He wasn't particularly happy to own up to the fact he loved Letty. It wasn't an emotion he was comfortable with. He feared loving her might mean he'd need to surrender a part of himself, and frankly that worried him. He'd die for her in a heartbeat. Stop a bullet in order to save her life. But he wasn't sure he should let her know how much he cared.

The silence that followed the blast of gunfire was louder than a cannon burst. He stepped out from behind Letty and walked over to where the guerrillas lay. With the boot of one foot, he turned them over and checked to be sure each one was dead. They were.

He experienced no emotion, no sense of regret, no sense of loss. This was what he did. He found no pleasure in killing, no thrill.

"Murphy . . ." His name was a weak cry from Letty's lips as she raced toward him and into his arms. He scooped her up and held her against him. She trembled violently, her arms holding his neck so tightly that it was close to becoming a stranglehold.

"It's all right, sweetheart."

He derived such a simple enjoyment from holding her that he momentarily forgot about the priest.

Father Alfaro looked pale and drawn as he walked outside the adobe house. Murphy noted that the other man's steps weren't any too steady. The priest removed a white kerchief from his pocket and mopped his brow.

"Mother of Jesus," he whispered, staring at the dead men.

"You all right, Father?" Murphy asked, releasing Letty.

"Fine. Fine." He glanced over at the dead soldiers again. "They're Norte's men."

"Then he knows where we are."

The priest closed his eyes. "Alphonse," he said as though in deep pain. "He would never have betrayed me without first being tortured."

"We've got to get out of here," Murphy said, in a hurry to get Letty to a safe place. Only he wasn't sure where.

"Letty," he called. Only seconds earlier she'd been

in his arms. Now he caught a glimpse of her inside the house, sitting with her face in her hands as if the scene outside the door were more than she could bear to view.

He wanted to comfort her, explain that he would have spared her this if it had been within his power.

"Letty, we've got to get out of here," he called again. He knew he sounded gruff and impatient, but it couldn't be helped. She was in danger, and he'd die before he'd let anything more happen to her.

Suddenly he caught a movement out of the corner of his eye. He threw the priest to the ground and fell for cover himself, but he couldn't reach Letty.

Rolling in the dirt, firing as he went, Murphy counted two other guerrillas. He heard one muffled shout of pain, then silence. The eerie, unnatural silence that often followed gunfire and death.

"Let's get the hell out of here!" he shouted, eager to get Letty and the priest to safety. His steady gaze scanned the jungle, his senses on full alert.

Letty's scream caught him off guard. The sound of a single gunshot filled him with a crippling terror. Dear God in heaven, not Letty. *Please, don't let them have Letty.* He bargained with everything he had. His life. His heart. His soul.

He roared to his feet with a cry of outrage and raced into the house. He was ready to kill or die, whatever the situation demanded. He discovered Letty standing with a .45, the one he'd given her at the start of the mission. The pistol dangled from her hand.

A soldier lay dead no more than five feet from her.

She looked to be in a state of shock. Deathly pale, she stared sightlessly at the dead man on the floor. He lay in a pool of blood, his eyes open. The rebel was dead, but even then Murphy could feel his hate.

He walked over to where she stood and gently pried the pistol free from her fingers.

"You all right?" he asked gently.

She shook her head, walked outside, and promptly vomited.

33

Rosita walked into the dimly lit room and looked at the body of the man stretched out on the table. A piercing pain cut through her heart as she realized what her uncle had told her was true.

Luke was dead.

A sob wrenched itself from her throat, and she covered her mouth in an effort to hold back a cry of bitter anguish. It wasn't supposed to have happened like this. They should have been married, she should have borne his children, and they should have spent many long, happy years together. He'd loved her, and she'd loved him more than any man she'd ever known. More than she would ever allow herself to love again.

"Quiet," came the husky voice of her uncle. "If anyone finds you here, I'll be in trouble."

She answered him with a strangled sob of grief. "What happened?" she asked, needing to know.

"The guard told me he died in his sleep."

"His sleep?" Rosita didn't believe him, although he was her uncle and the one who'd helped her see Luke two other times before.

"No one knows the exact cause of his death. He was alive when the lights went out, and then in the morning he was dead. Commander Faqueza questioned the guards, and no one went into your friend's cell all night."

Gently, in a gesture of farewell, Rosita touched Luke's face. He looked serene, at peace. Beautiful in a way that words could never describe.

"Captain Norte is said to be very angry," her uncle informed her. "He'd planned to use your friend to trap the others."

Rosita studied Luke and realized this was what he'd prayed would happen. It was the only way he could save his sister and spare them both the terror of witnessing a public execution. He'd always put the concerns of others first.

Luke Madden had stolen her heart the first year he'd arrived in Zarcero. For months Rosita had kept her feelings to herself, afraid to let him know how much she cared.

Later, when Luke came to love her, her heart sang with joy. As deliriously happy as she'd been then, she suffered now. The pendulum of love swung in both directions, she realized. The depth of her love was equal to the deep, emotional agony she suffered at his death.

"We must go," her uncle warned.

"A minute more," she pleaded. She wanted to look

at him a bit longer, memorize the peaceful look on his face, sear it into her heart for the long, lonely years she would have without him.

"Are you ready?"

She nodded, and the hot tears continued to stream down her face.

"I could do nothing more to save him," her uncle said sadly. "I tried."

"I know you did." She pressed a gentle hand to his arm. "Thank you for the risk you took to bring me here."

"Your friend was a good man."

Rosita wiped the tears from her face. "I wish you could have known him."

"I did in some small ways. He did not curse when they tortured him. He had only love. If any man is with God, it is your friend."

34

Letty knew that Murphy was worried about her. She'd killed a man. She hadn't wanted to do it, and she would live with the agony of regret the rest of her life.

The guerrilla had given her no choice. It had come down to a simple equation: him or her. The shock came for Letty when she realized how desperately she wanted to live.

She hadn't so much as hesitated, and it was that quick thinking, that pure instinctual desire to live, that had saved her.

Father Alfaro had hurriedly ushered them to another house of a friend he could trust. This night they were in a space under the floor of a barn. The room was only slightly larger than the space afforded them in the priest's secret room in the rectory library.

Murphy sat across from her, eating the dinner that

had been provided them. He used the tortilla to scrape up the beans, downing the food hungrily. He'd almost completely finished before he noticed she hadn't touched her meal.

"Letty, eat."

She shook her head. "I can't. I'm not hungry."

He set aside the tin plate and moved so that he was sitting next to her on the mattress. "Honey, listen, it was self-defense."

She closed her eyes, willing him to stop talking. The strange sick sensation that had been with her since morning returned.

" . . . probably saved my sorry ass as well," Murphy continued. "He wouldn't have stopped after killing you."

"Murphy." Blindly she reached out and gripped his arm.

"Are you going to be sick again?"

"No. Oh, Murphy . . . no, please, no."

"Honey, what is it? Don't go soft on me now, kid."

"He's dead."

"Sweetheart, you didn't have any choice."

"Not that soldier," she said sobbing. "Luke." She bent forward and pressed her forehead to her knee. That was what was wrong. All day she'd felt it. All day she'd struggled with this horrible sick feeling in the pit of her stomach.

"But Father Alfaro assured us that as of two days ago he was alive."

The grief she felt overwhelmed her. It felt as if she'd been weighed down with bricks and then thrown over the side of a boat. She was going down, deeper and deeper and powerless to stop, powerless to help herself.

Not until Murphy wrapped his arms around her did Letty realize that she was clinging to him. The sobs went so deep they produced a physical pain. She rocked back and forth, sobbing, gasping for breath, mourning for the twin brother she'd lost.

"Letty, honey, don't cry like this. We don't know what's happened to Luke."

"I know. My heart knows."

"But Father Alfaro said—"

"He's dead. My brother is dead. We're too late. We can't save him."

Murphy held her until she had no more tears to shed. She clung to him, her fingers pinching his flesh in her grief, in her desperation. Still he held her, still he comforted her.

When Letty's tears were spent, he gently laid her down on the mattress and sat with her. He whispered reassurances, but Letty couldn't hear them. Couldn't. Her heart felt as if it would melt inside her chest with the overwhelming weight of her sorrow.

At some point she must have fallen asleep because the next thing she knew it was dark. The room hidden below the barn was pitch black.

She knew Murphy was beside her because she heard the even rhythm of his breathing. Then she remembered her brother, and the anguish and pain returned.

"Letty . . ."

She rolled over and buried her face in his neck. "Make love to me," she whispered. "I feel so alone, so empty. I need you. Please, Murphy, please, make love to me."

Murphy closed his eyes and prayed for strength. Letty in his arms was temptation enough, but for her to plead with him to make love to her was more than any man should have to refuse.

"Honey," he whispered gently, brushing back the hair from her face, "you don't know what you're asking."

"I want you. I need you, Murphy, please." She moved against him, rubbing the tips of her nipples against his chest, their hot tips searing him until he felt as though he'd been branded. He gritted his teeth and willed her to be still.

He needed her, too. His body had been telling him so in punishing ways for weeks. But not now. Not like this, with her heart heavy and out of her mind with grief, certain she'd lost her brother.

Murphy didn't know what to make of this mental link she shared with her twin. He was far more comfortable dealing with hard, cold facts. The two-day-old information given them that morning claimed Luke Madden was alive. He preferred to put stock in that and not some intuitive notion Letty had come up with that her brother was dead.

Earlier, Murphy had promised her he'd find Luke, and he wasn't giving up until he had the evidence he required. Dead or alive, he was determined to locate Letty's brother.

She continued kissing his neck, her moist lips sliding across his skin in instinctively sensual ways. Murphy closed his eyes and battled down the desire that had begun to throb through his body.

"Letty, please . . . "

"I feel so alone."

"You aren't alone. We don't know Luke's fate. Not yet."

"I know what's happened," she whispered, and sobbed softly. "He's dead. I feel it in my head and in my heart." Her hands roamed his chest, spreading moist kisses down his abdomen. He gripped hold of the blanket, clenching it with both hands as he struggled to resist her.

"You don't know what you're asking." His voice rumbled with the effort it took to reject her. If there was a God in heaven, Murphy sincerely hoped his sacrifice would be richly rewarded. This was far and above the most noble deed he'd ever done.

Only Letty was capable of raising him to this level of do-goodness. He'd known she was trouble the minute he'd met her, but he didn't know she would affect his heart.

Unable to restrain from touching her any longer, he rubbed his hand down the length of her spine, stopping short of her buttocks, savoring the warm, smooth feel of her.

He needed her. His mind and his body had been telling him the same thing from the beginning. But the strength of his desire was more profound than the evidence straining against his fatigues. She was like sunshine in a closed-up room, revealing the dust and neglect. Without warning she'd stormed into his life and with her prim and proper ways exposed him to what he really was. Exposing his heart to what he'd become.

Her gentleness was an absolution to the cruel, often severe world of soldiering. He hadn't understood why Cain wanted Linette in his life. Why he'd given up so much of himself for the chance to marry the widow. It all made an ironic kind of sense now.

Cain needed Linette for the same reasons Murphy needed Letty.

Letty's love helped cancel out the things he'd done, the horrors he'd seen. The cruel hate of man's inhumanity to man. It helped absolve the things he'd been forced to do. What he would do again come morning if necessary.

"Don't you want me?" Letty asked.

"Want you? Honey, you have no idea."

"Then why won't you make love to me?" She snuggled closer to his side, torturing him more than if he were trapped in the hands of a sadist. She was so damned sexy and was too naive to know it. So damned innocent she took his breath away.

"Don't make me say it," she whispered, burying her face in his shoulder.

"Say what?" He was completely perplexed.

"Damn you, Murphy." She slammed her fist against his chest.

"What is it you don't want to tell me?" He flipped her onto her backside and gazed down at her, not understanding. Her eyes, bright with tears, stared up at him with more than a hint of defiance. Her rebellion was short-lived, and she looped her arms around his neck and raised herself enough to kiss him.

He'd taught her well, he realized as her mouth settled over his. Her tongue stroked his, renewing the battle of wills in which he was willingly conquered.

"Letty, say it," he breathed, forcefully breaking off the kiss.

"I love you," she whispered.

His heart went berserk. "Oh, honey." He rolled away from her and onto his back.

"That's exactly why I didn't want to tell you. You don't want my love, don't need it. Having me say it only embarrasses you. I didn't want you to know, didn't want to tell you."

He swore once and hauled her back into his arms, hugging her tight against him. But when they kissed this time, he was the one in control, he was the one directing her mouth to his.

"Oh, Letty," he muttered against her lips. "Don't you know how much I love you?" His tongue met hers, and he pressed her body intimately to his, flattening her breasts against the hard wall of his chest. She felt so damn good. Too good. What strength he possessed to resist her was fast dwindling.

With a reluctance that drained him, he pushed himself away from her. He threaded his fingers through her hair. Just looking into her beautiful eyes made him realize how much he cared. Enough to hold off making love to her because the time wasn't right.

Hers were filled with surprise, with question. "You love me?"

"More than my own life."

"When did you know?"

Leave it to a woman to ask a question like that. "This afternoon."

"With the guerrillas?" she asked.

"Yeah. Probably sooner, but I didn't want to own up to it."

He kissed her then for the sheer pleasure of it. Because denying himself what he wanted most was the purest form of hell he'd ever known.

"You love me." She repeated it with an incredulousness that he found amusing.

"Is that so difficult to believe?"

"Yes. . . . I thought, I assumed you saw me as a damned nuisance."

"I do. But I love you more. When this is over, I want us to marry." He couldn't believe he'd suggested marriage, hadn't known it was coming until the proposal slipped out.

"You want to marry me?" This too came in a manner that suggested she wasn't sure she should believe him.

"I love you so damn much." He kissed her again, greedy for her mouth, showing her in the physical what he felt in his heart. "So much that I'm going to wait until we're married to make love."

"You want to wait?"

"All right, all right, that was a rash statement. We'll wait until we get back to Boothill." He sat up and removed the silver chain from around his neck. "Here, this is your engagement ring." The tiny gold angel made a clanking sound against his dog tags as he slipped it over her head.

Letty fingered it.

"The angel belonged to my grandmother. It's the only thing of hers I own. I've thought of it as my good-luck charm—now it's yours."

"You're giving me your good-luck charm?"

"I'm giving you my heart. You're going to be my wife, Letty."

"What about Deliverance Company?"

"I don't know," he answered. "We'll figure all that out later." He hadn't stopped to consider that she might not want him. When it came to husband material he wasn't much, but he loved her.

"Good idea."

"Can you go to sleep now?" he asked brusquely.

She didn't say anything for a long moment, then nodded. "Can I call you Shaun after we're married?"

He grinned. "I suppose you'll have to. It wouldn't be seemly for a wife to call her husband by his surname."

She nestled into his arms as if they'd spent half a lifetime sleeping together. He'd just started to drift off to sleep, happier than he could remember being at any other point in his life, when Letty spoke again.

"I want children."

"Children," he repeated. That was another aspect of this marriage business that he hadn't stopped to consider. "Can we discuss that later?"

"No. I won't sleep unless I know you want the same things as me."

"Children," he repeated, thinking of his married friends. Both had become fathers and revealed no regrets. "Why not? Before I know it you're going to have me completely domesticated."

"I hope so." He heard the smile in her voice.

Murphy closed his eyes and drifted off to sleep. He kept Letty close to his side all night. She woke him once and whispered something about being thirsty. He found her some water, which she drank greedily, and then they both returned to sleep.

In the morning Murphy knew something was terribly wrong with Letty. Her eyelids fluttered open and she stared up at him sightlessly.

"Letty?" He pressed the back of his hand against her forehead. She was burning up with fever.

He roused Father Alfaro, who contacted a doctor friend of his he could trust. By the time the physician arrived, Letty was delirious. She recognized Murphy but no one else, and she clung to him.

"What's wrong with her?" he demanded when the doctor had completed his examination.

"I don't know, but it doesn't look good. Her fever is very high. I have seen such a fever and rash one time."

"Yes?"

He didn't respond right away. "We must get her to a hospital."

A hospital. The man was asking for the moon.

The doctor's eyes were grave. "Otherwise she will not live more than two days."

35

"*Marcie, did you order* the Apple-Smith perm?"

Marcie stopped counting the money in the till to think. The beauty supplier had stopped in earlier that afternoon, and she'd ordered an extensive list of items. "I can't remember."

"I specifically asked for the Apple-Smith perm, don't you remember? You know Gladys Williams insists on it, with her thin hair." Samantha sounded justifiably upset.

Marcie vented a deep sigh. "I'm sorry, I can't recall what I asked Vickie to send us. I'll give her a jingle in the morning and check to be sure I ordered the perm."

"I've got to take care of my LOLs."

"I know." Samantha was a whiz with the little old ladies, and a large section of her clientele consisted of the over seventy crowd.

Her friend hesitated. "You sure you're all right, Marcie? You've been in never-never land all day. What's bugging you?"

"I'm fine." She managed to scrounge up a smile.

"It isn't just today, either. You've been preoccupied for days now."

Marcie set aside the stack of one-dollar bills. She'd tried counting them three times and each time had come up with a different number. "I have, haven't I?"

"Are you sure this isn't something you want to talk about?" Samantha set aside her purse and leaned against the glass counter, crossing her arms. "I got the time. It used to be that we'd talk for hours on end, remember?"

That was true enough, but those had been during Marcie's bar-hopping days. The two had often gone out together after work and then traded war stories in the morning. But times had changed. Marcie had abandoned that lifestyle, and Samantha was a single mother with a kid to support.

"Clifford proposed," Marcie confessed.

"Clifford! All I can say is that it's about time. I was ready to hog-tie that man and ask him when he was going to pop the question."

Marcie laughed, but it was forced.

"Gee, honey, aren't you happy?"

"Sure," Marcie said, and meant it. She was ecstatic. She'd waited the better part of her life for a man to ask her to be his wife. This was a dream come true.

"Oh." The happiness drained from Samantha's face. "You're in love with Johnny, though, aren't you?"

"Yes . . . no. Oh, Sam, I don't know anymore."

"Have the two of you been . . . you know?" Her voice lifted slightly with insinuation.

"You want to know if I'm sleeping with him, right?"

"Listen, honey, if you don't want to say, that's fine, because it isn't any of my business."

Marcie stuck the money back inside the till and slammed the drawer shut. "No, not that I haven't been tempted. Johnny always did have a way about him that made my knees go weak."

"You mean to say you *haven't* slept with him lately?" Samantha sounded incredulous.

"How could I, and look Clifford in the eye?"

"I suppose you're right." Samantha plunked herself down on one of the padded chairs by the washbowl and crossed her long, slender legs. "Johnny's the one you're crazy about, but it's Clifford who proposed."

"Actually, Johnny mentioned something about the two of us setting up housekeeping."

Samantha's head snapped up, her eyes wide. "He did?"

Marcie was sorry she'd told her friend this part because she knew exactly what Samantha would say, and she was right.

"Then what's the problem? There's no contest, is there? I mean, Clifford's sweet and everything, but, honey, Johnny's the kind of man who'll make your blood run hot just looking at him."

"I know, but . . ." Marcie let the rest fade. Clifford was the Rock of Gibraltar, while Jack Keller was like shifting sands. Intellectually she knew this, but emotionally she struggled. She panted after Jack, but she cared about Clifford.

"Uh-oh," Samantha whispered. "Speaking of the devil. Look who just pulled up."

Marcie didn't want to look. It could only be Jack, and she didn't want to see him. When she was with him she couldn't think clearly, couldn't trust herself to do what she knew was right. He knew that too and used it against her. Little by little, bit by bit, he was chipping away at her defenses.

She'd told him she needed to think about moving in with him, the same way she'd told Clifford she needed time to consider his marriage proposal. It'd been several days now, and Jack had obviously grown impatient.

"I'm out of here," Samantha whispered, winked at Marcie, grabbed her purse, and was out the door.

"Howdy, Sam," Marcie heard Jack greet her friend, his voice husky and deep.

Marcie didn't turn around. She closed her eyes and summoned her defenses.

Jack stood behind her. She could feel his presence as keenly as if he were touching her.

"Marcie."

"Hello, Jack." Her fingers dug into the glass counter.

"How's my girl?" he asked next, and cupped her shoulders. His hot breath warmed her as he bent forward and kissed the side of her neck. He sucked gently and ran his tongue brazenly over her smooth skin.

Marcie curled her toes at the fiery sensation that shot through her.

"I've been thinking about you day and night," Jack confessed, "wondering if I was going to ever hear from you again."

"I . . . I said I'd call."

His lips continued to nibble away at her. "I couldn't wait any longer. I had to know."

Marcie's eyes drifted shut, and she drooped her head to one side, exposing her neck to him. The desire to turn around and bury herself in his arms made her weak when she desperately needed to be strong.

"I haven't come to a decision yet," she told him, struggling to keep her voice even. "I have to think of every aspect. This is important, very important."

"It's what I told you, isn't it?"

"No," she denied, and the breathless quality was back in her voice. "It's everything."

"Let me help you make up your mind," he whispered.

"That's not a good idea." Although her lips said one thing, her body said another. Her head was lolling back, and she rocked it gently from side to side to give him greater access to her skin.

"Baby, I'm going crazy wanting you." He slipped his arm around her waist and fitted her backside to his hard, masculine front.

"Jack—"

"I know I shouldn't be here." His hands were busy with the front of her uniform. Before she could find the strength to stop him, he'd unfastened her blouse and eased his hand inside, cupping her breast. Her nipples turned traitor and beaded instantly. She couldn't keep herself from trembling and rotating her buttocks against his throbbing erection.

"Easy now, baby, easy." A wealth of satisfaction

echoed in his dark whisper. His free hand cupped her crotch, rubbing the junction between her legs.

Marcie couldn't believe she had allowed him to do this to her. She'd lowered the venetian blinds at closing time, but the slats remained open. Anyone passing on the sidewalk could look in and see what they were doing.

It was hard to believe that any man was capable of reducing her to this level, and she sobbed softly, willing herself to find the strength to resist him.

Jack misunderstood her cry of distress as one of need. "The couch is still in the back room?" he asked urgently. His hot breath branded her ear.

"Yes, but I don't think—"

"That's been our problem," he countered huskily, "we both been thinking too damn much. It's time to recapture the fire we once shared."

"Oh God."

Marcie never intended for them to end up on the couch in her back room. She wasn't entirely sure how he got her there. One moment she was in front of her shop, battling back her own treacherous body. The next thing she knew, she was in her back room, lying across the sofa. Within seconds Jack had her blouse peeled open and her breasts exposed. He knelt on the floor and buried his face in her bounty, cupping her fullness in his palms. His mouth locked on to a nipple and he sucked greedily.

The instant his mouth closed over her nipple, the pulse throbbing between her legs intensified and she lifted her hips from the sofa.

"That's good, baby, real good. Let me see how ready you are." His voice was hoarse with need.

No sooner had the words parted his lips than he stuck his hand up her skirt and swept aside the crotch of her panties.

Marcie stiffened in his arms. It'd been so long since she'd made love, so long since a man had touched her this intimately. Her body reacted and she gave a strained cry at the unexpected burst of pleasure. She was stunned, dizzy, almost delirious as he began to work his fingers inside her, stretching her, readying her for him.

"No—"

He cut off her cry of protest by kissing her. His tongue echoed the stroking movements of his fingers, the rhythm fast and hard.

The sensation he created was like fire, spiraling into a tighter and tighter coil. It threatened to break through and take control any moment.

Marcie knew what he was doing, what he'd intended from the first. He was using her body against her, bringing her to climax, pleasuring her first. She also knew that afterward he would expect the same relief. This was more than heavy petting, it was an unspoken agreement to have sex with him.

"Jack, no." Her voice was a weak wail of anguish as she broke off the kiss and struggled to a semisitting position. Breathing heavily, she leaned on one elbow.

Jack's breathing was equally ragged. His head drooped forward as if her words hadn't fully broken through the fog of his desire.

"You don't mean it. Tell me you don't mean it?" he pleaded.

It took her several moments to compose herself to where she could look him in the eye again, let alone speak. "I'm sorry, truly I am. I never intended for matters to progress to that point."

Jack leveled himself off the floor and sat at the end of the couch, his elbows on his knees. He glanced at her and exhaled sharply. "I'm the one who needs a cigarette this time. You got one?"

She shook her head. "Not with me."

He rubbed his face.

"How about a shower?"

She wasn't much help with that, either. "I could stick your head in the washbasin."

He chuckled. "I'll pass."

She sat up and took a couple of minutes to catch her breath. Her fingers refused to cooperate as she fastened the small white buttons in the front of her blouse. "I can't think straight when you touch me."

Jack laughed. "I disagree. You seem to find a means to thwart me without much of a problem. Don't misunderstand me, I'm frustrated as hell, but at the same time I'm a little in awe of this newfound control of yours. You've changed, Marcie."

He couldn't have paid her a better compliment. "I'm not the same Marcie anymore. I haven't been in quite some time."

"Live with me, Marcie," he said, reaching for her hands. "Baby, we're good together."

"In bed, you mean."

"Within six months we'll know each other like only married people do," he countered.

"But we might not even like each other."

He captured her face between his hands. "I've always liked you. You're sweet and gentle and good."

Marcie bit into her lower lip.

"What is it?" he asked gently. "Tell me and I'll do anything within my power to fix it."

"I want children, a home, a family." Her eyes held his. "I want a husband."

"You're looking for me to marry you, aren't you?"

"Yes," she whispered, unwilling to take second best. She didn't tell him Clifford had proposed. This was not a contest to see which one could buy her the biggest diamond.

"Marriage," he repeated as if it were a dirty word.

The bell above the door chimed, and Jack looked to her. The CLOSED sign was in the window, but she hadn't locked the door.

"Marcie?"

Clifford. She bolted off the couch so fast, she nearly tripped over her own two feet.

"Clifford, hello." Her cheerful greeting sounded false even to her own ears. She was sure her cheeks were flame red and that he must know she had another man in her back room.

"I hope you don't mind my stopping in unexpectedly like this." He removed his baseball cap and held it in both hands. His gaze drifted toward the back room.

"No, of course not." She leaned against the glass counter and avoided looking him in the eye.

"I realize I haven't given you much time . . . "

"You want to know if I've reached a decision yet?"

"Yeah." Again he looked past her toward the back of the shop and the drapes that separated the two main parts of the business. "I don't mean to pressure you," he added.

"I know that."

His gaze focused on the front of her uniform, and he edged his way backward toward the front door. "I can see that I've come at a bad time. . . ."

"I'll call you," she promised, "okay?"

"Sure." His eyes filled with an incredible sadness. "Sure," he repeated. "Whatever you say." Having said that, he turned hurriedly and walked out the door.

Marcie had the incredible urge to cry. She'd seen the look in Clifford's eyes and recognized it all too well. It was the same look of disappointment and hurt she'd felt a number of times in her dating career. It generally came when she learned the man she'd been seeing for three months was married. Or how she felt when a guy asked her for a small loan for his ailing mother and she knew damn well it was for booze.

She returned to the back room and slumped onto the couch.

Jack stood above her. "All right," he said impatiently. "Let's get married."

36

Letty was only vaguely aware of what was happening to her. She felt herself walking down a long narrow corridor. Doors opened from each side of the hallway, and each one seemed to beckon to her.

She stopped and read the nameplate and was tempted at each door to enter, would have if not for Murphy, who stood at the end of the hallway, calling to her. He sounded angry and desperate. When she hesitated, he commanded her attention. He refused to allow her to rest or to stop. His demands on her became relentless.

Once she reached him, he didn't seem satisfied. He wanted something from her, but she couldn't figure out what it was. Because she loved him, she tried to give him whatever he asked, but he made no sense to her befuddled mind. He seemed to think it was terribly important for her to drink something bitter tasting.

Later his voice became gentle as he spoke to her. His hands cooled her face and washed her face and neck. She couldn't remember being so dirty. With everyone else he sounded urgent and impatient, but with her he was uncharacteristically tender.

She slept and had trouble waking. A discordant noise interrupted her rest. It sounded like the roar of an engine. Like that of an aircraft. She felt the sun on her face and the force of the wind. It felt cool when she was so terribly, uncomfortably hot.

Then he held her against him and told her again how much he loved her. He promised to find Luke for her.

Luke. A sob obstructed her throat at the mention of her brother. He was forever gone to her. Forever lost. She'd found him too late. The intense grief was mingled with the memory of an unexpected gift. Murphy's love. Her hand closed over the tiny gold angel.

"Remember, I love you," Murphy whispered.

Letty wouldn't soon forget.

She was wrenched out of his arms and set inside a seat. But this wasn't like any car she'd ever known. She realized as she gazed at a row of panels that she was inside a plane and Father Alfaro was with her.

The sound of guns and angry shouts interrupted their farewells. Murphy reacted immediately, leaped back, and slammed the door closed.

"Go, go, go!" he cried, but he wasn't speaking to her. "Get the hell out of here!"

Letty's head lolled to one side, and she saw Murphy racing across a grass field. She gasped with alarm when she saw a band of guerrillas surround him. Her gasp became a cry of frustration and anguish as red tips of fire exploded from the end of a machine gun and she watched, helpless, as Murphy fell.

"No . . . no, not Murphy . . . must go back."

"We can't," Father Alfaro said, his words marked with sadness.

"He didn't have a chance," the pilot said in a strong American accent. Letty tried to focus, tried to think clearly, but everything was cloudy, obscured from her as if she were trapped inside a deep fog.

"Why didn't he come with us?" So little of this made sense to her.

"He made himself the target instead. He saved our lives," Father Alfaro told her, gripping her hand. "No greater love has a man than he who lays down his life for his friends."

Soft sounds drifted toward Letty. The distinct click of a clock, counting off the seconds. The padded footsteps against a tile floor, the scrape of metal rings against a rail. The scent was that of disinfectant and something else she couldn't name.

It cost her a surprising amount of energy to lift her eyelids and look around. The first thing she saw was a round clock on the wall, then a television mounted in the corner. A railing, like that for a shower, looped around her bed.

If she didn't know better, she would think she was in a hospital. The view outside her window looked decidedly like that of Texas. But that didn't seem possible.

The last thing she remembered was being in

Zarcero and of Murphy holding her. She remembered something else. A small, worrisome fear niggled at her conscious. A plane and gunshots and Murphy putting his own life on the line for her.

Murphy. She smiled, closed her eyes, and reached for the chain around her neck.

It was missing.

Frantic now, she forced herself to sit up. Stretching awkwardly, she reached for the button that rang for the nurse. A disembodied voice responded.

"Miss Madden, you're awake. That's wonderful. I'll be right in. You've got an anxious gentleman here, waiting to see you."

Murphy. It had all been so confusing. Murphy wouldn't abandon her. Not after giving her an engagement necklace. The whole episode with the airplane had been part of some terrible nightmare. She closed her eyes and whispered a prayer of thanksgiving.

The nurse arrived moments later. Her wide, friendly smile put Letty at ease. Then, when she least expected it, she thrust a thermometer in Letty's mouth and took her blood pressure.

"You said my friend . . . ," she asked the minute the temperature gauge was out of her mouth.

"In a minute, dear." The nurse smiled graciously and reached for Letty's wrist to check her pulse. It was all Letty could do not to mention that her heart was in fine working order. She wanted her necklace and to see Murphy, in that order.

The friendly nurse retrieved the dog tags and seemed surprised when Letty kissed the angel and placed the set over her head. It wasn't much of an engagement ring to anyone else, but it was worth more than any diamond to her because it had come from his heart.

"Would you like me to send in your friend now?"

She nodded enthusiastically, then changed her mind. "No, wait. I must look a sight."

"You look a thousand times better than when they brought you in, dear. For two days we didn't know if you were going to live or die. You've been very ill."

The kindly nurse ran a brush through Letty's hair. "Are you ready for your friend now?"

"Please." Letty was so eager to talk to Murphy. So eager to learn what he'd discovered about Luke in Zarcero. Eager to show him how much she loved him.

She heard the heavy footsteps before he entered her room and closed her eyes briefly in anticipation of seeing him again.

But it wasn't Murphy who entered her hospital room, grinning from ear to ear. It was Slim.

"Welcome home, Letty," he greeted her, his ever-present Stetson in his hand. "My, but you're a sight for sore eyes. I can't tell you how glad I am to see you."

"Slim," she murmured, unable to disguise her disappointment.

"From what I understand, we're lucky to have you."

"Hello." Hiding the devastating disappointment was more than she could manage. "Do you know anything about Murphy?"

"He didn't come back with you?"

"No. I don't know." She lay back against the pillow, overwhelmingly tired and broken and alone. Slim was her friend, but Murphy was her heart. Her very reason for being alive.

Jack loved her. He hadn't realized his feelings for Marcie until after he'd proposed. Then he wondered why it had taken him so long to recognize the truth. Contacting her after a nine-month silence had been a fluke. But once he saw her again, he'd been completely taken by the changes he'd seen in her. Their intermittent love fests were based on something more than sexual satisfaction. True, it had taken her refusal to bed him again for him to see the light. In the weeks since, he'd enjoyed spending time with her. He found Marcie to be intelligent, well read, and well versed in political affairs. Not only did she have a decent head on her shoulders, but she was warm, witty, and fun.

What Marcie did for him sexually was something else. If ever there was a woman who equaled him sexually, it was Marcie Alexander. Now she was about to become his wife.

He resisted the urge to phone Cain and let his friend know he would soon join the ranks of the married himself. He might even ask for a little maritial advice from his former boss—although the way he felt right then, he didn't need anyone or anything but Marcie.

She'd let it be known she wanted kids. He hadn't actually given any thought to the matter of a family. There was no reason he should. But now that the subject had been introduced, he was excited at the prospect of becoming a daddy.

Jack had visited Cain not long ago and been amazed at how well his friend had adjusted to fatherhood. Fact was, Jack had never seen more startling changes in anyone.

Cain fussing with dirty diapers was as much of a shock as Cain herding cattle. Now *that* was a sight to behold.

Apparently Mallory was into this baby thing in a big way. The last Jack heard, Mallory and his wife, Francine, were already planning a second addition to their family.

Now he was next. Damn, but it felt right. In retrospect he didn't know why he'd taken so long to take the plunge. He guessed he'd been waiting for the right woman. Well, he'd found her in Marcie.

He walked into the kitchen, opened the refrigerator, and popped a green olive in his mouth. She was due to stop off at the apartment at any time.

Earlier that afternoon he'd picked out a diamond that had set him back ten thousand. Jack never thought he'd spend that much money on a wedding band, but he wanted Marcie to know he loved her. He was proud of her, of the person she'd become in the last several months. Proud that she hadn't fallen into bed with him the minute he'd showed up at her beauty shop.

If she insisted, he'd wait until after the wedding ceremony, he was that crazy about her. He sincerely hoped she wasn't going to put him off again, but he'd cross that bridge when the time came.

The doorbell chimed, and he did a quick visual on the apartment. Marcie was early, but that was a good sign. Very good. She was eager to see him, too.

To his surprise, it wasn't Marcie standing on the other side of the door, but another woman. She wasn't bad looking, either. A little on the thin side and pale, as if she'd recently recovered from a bad case of the flu.

"Are you Jack Keller?"

He leaned against the doorjamb. "Depends on who's asking."

"Letty Madden."

Madden. Madden. The name rang a bell, only he couldn't remember from where.

"Do you have a minute to talk?" she asked. From the look in her eyes she wasn't going to be easily turned away.

He hesitated. It wouldn't do well to have Marcie arrive and find him with another woman. Well, she needn't worry; she was the only woman for him, and he'd take a great deal of pleasure in proving that to her.

"I've come a very long way to find you, Mr. Keller," Letty Madden announced primly. "It has to do with Murphy."

That was where he'd heard the name. Letty Madden was the name of the irritating postmistress who'd hired Murphy to find her brother in some hell-hole Central American country.

"Come on in," he said, gesturing toward the living room.

She hadn't gone more than a couple of steps when she faltered. Jack feared she would have collapsed right then and there if he hadn't caught her. He gripped hold of her elbow and then slipped an arm around her waist.

"Easy now," he said gently, and guided her to a chair.

"Sorry. I was released from the hospital yesterday. They didn't advise me to travel, but I had to talk to you."

"You know about me?"

"Murphy mentioned you frequently."

This was interesting, since he'd always known his friend to be closemouthed.

"Have you heard from him lately?" she asked eagerly.

"Not in some time."

It was pathetic to see the light fade from her eyes. "I thought, I'd hoped he'd be in contact with you."

"He mentioned you as well," Jack announced. "You're the one who wanted to hire him to take you to Zarcero. Right?"

She nodded, and a hint of a smile touched her mouth. "I don't suspect he mentioned me with any real affection."

Jack didn't answer right away. Murphy had considered the woman to be a thorn in his side. "Did you find your brother?"

She swallowed tightly and looked away. "We were too late, he'd been killed."

"I'm sorry."

"So am I. Luke was a decent, God fearing man." Her hand went to her neck and she fingered what looked to be dogtags and a small gold angel. Jack had seen only one such angel in his life. It had belonged to Murphy. His friend had called it his good-luck charm.

"Where'd you get that?" he demanded.

Her eyes widened, as though she weren't sure what he meant. It seemed to take her a moment to realize he was referring to the necklace.

"Murphy gave it to me." Her eyes held his. "I haven't heard from him. Not a word. Nor will anyone tell me what's happened to him. I've lost my brother, I can't bear to lose Murphy, too."

Jack frowned. These were the words of a woman in love. Her hand closed around the dogtags as though she were clutching a lifeline, the only thing that kept her from losing control of her emotions.

"I'm afraid he's dead," she whispered, and her voice cracked.

"Murphy dead?"

"I didn't know where else to turn."

"Tell me what happened." He sat across from her and listened as she related the details of their adventure in Zarcero, pausing only when he asked questions. She stopped at an incredible point, explaining that she'd been half crazed with fever and Murphy had gotten her and a priest friend to an airstrip, then held off rebel troops himself while they'd escaped to safety.

"The priest?"

"I never saw him again," she murmured sadly.

"He was in the plane with you?"

"Yes, I think so. I don't remember anything after that. The next thing I knew, I woke up in a Texas hospital. A family friend had been notified and was waiting to speak to me. As soon as I was released from the hospital, I came to find you."

"You haven't a clue where the plane landed?"

"None. I'm sorry. I was too sick. Apparently I'd been bitten by a particularly dangerous spider, but I'm fine now." She brushed the hair away from her face, a gesture of nervous anticipation. "Will you locate Murphy for me?"

Jack didn't need to weigh the decision. There'd been a time a couple of years back when he'd been captured and tortured. It'd been Murphy who'd led the team of men who broke him out of prison. He wouldn't hesitate to repay the favor now.

"I'll be on a plane as soon as it can be arranged." He'd need to talk to Marcie first, explain everything. But she was sure to understand.

Letty's eyes drifted closed with supreme gratitude. "Thank you," she whispered.

"Hey, I owe Murphy big time."

"So do I." But she didn't elaborate.

Jack couldn't help wondering exactly what had happened between those two in that jungle.

Letty left, and not five minutes passed before Marcie arrived.

"Hello, Jack," she said softly.

He looped his arms about her waist and dragged her inside the apartment, ready to kiss her good and proper, show her how crazy he was about her. He would have, too, if she hadn't turned her head aside at the last minute.

"Baby?"

Not until then did he notice that her eyes were bright with tears. "Marcie, what is it?"

"I'm so sorry," she whispered.

"Sorry?"

She clenched her hands together and lowered her head. "I can't marry you, Jack."

He almost laughed. The woman had to be joking. Marriage was what she'd said she'd wanted. He'd gone out and purchased a diamond. Something was very wrong with this picture, and he had yet to figure out what it was.

"Not going to marry me?"

"I decided," she said, her voice low and breathy, "to accept Clifford's proposal, if he'll have me."

37

Marcie closed her eyes briefly in an effort to calm herself before she rang Clifford's doorbell. She'd been to his house only one other time, and that had been for a short visit.

He lived in a two-story house close to Olathe, a suburb of Kansas City, in a house that had once belonged to his parents. He'd moved in after he'd been forced to put his father into a nursing home. It was a solid old house with flower beds out front and space for a small garden in the back.

No one answered, and Marcie had begun to fear she'd made the trip for nothing when the door abruptly opened.

To say that Clifford was surprised to see her would be an understatement. He stared at her as if seeing a ghost.

"Marcie, what are you doing here?"

Good question. "I thought we should talk."

He held open the screen door for her. "Sure."

The house was dark and cool on the inside. The furniture was large and bulky, sturdy, like the man himself. An old upright piano that probably hadn't been played in years stood against one wall. Framed photographs were arranged across the top.

It caught Marcie's attention because she'd always wanted to learn how to play the piano as a girl. There'd never been money for that sort of thing. Her father tended to drink up more than he contributed to the family's income. By the time she was thirteen her parents had divorced and she'd seen her father only intermittently since.

"You want something to drink? I got a pot of coffee on, if you're interested."

She was nervous enough as it was without having to hold on to a coffee cup. "No thanks."

Clifford gestured toward the overstuffed sofa. He was still in his work clothes but had removed his boots. His white socks were a stark contrast with his black short-sleeved shirt and jeans.

Marcie figured he must have come home, started reading the newspaper, and fallen asleep on his chair. That was what probably had taken him so long to answer the door.

"I figure I know why you're here," he said, sitting across from her. He sat close to the edge of the chair and leaned forward. Something on his hands demanded his attention because he couldn't seem to make himself look at her.

Clifford knew? Marcie sincerely doubted that.

"I apologize about the other day. I should never have dropped by the shop, but I was anxious for your answer," he murmured sadly.

Marcie almost smiled. "Is it the ring that's bothering you or the marriage proposal?"

"Both, I suspect. In retrospect, I imagine that little diamond isn't much of an incentive for you to marry a guy like me. Forgive me, Marcie, I gave it to you for all the wrong reasons."

"I hope that's not true. I came here to tell you something," she said, hurrying her words in an effort to say what she must.

"I know you were with that other guy, if that's what's worrying you."

Marcie shifted uncomfortably. "You're right, I was." She couldn't lie. Not to Clifford, who'd only been kind and honest with her.

"I could see when I came that I'd arrived at an inconvenient moment." His voice was heavy with sarcasm.

Marcie inhaled deeply, regret tightening her voice. She clenched her hands nervously. Having him find her with Jack made everything she had to say so much more difficult. "We didn't make love. I swear to you, Clifford, we didn't."

"But you were tempted."

"Yes." Her voice was small and wobbly.

Clifford leaped off the sofa with a dexterity that surprised her. He walked over to the window and rammed five fingers through his hair. "That seems to be answer enough for me. You can keep the diamond, Marcie. I bought it for you. I don't know how this other guy will feel about you keeping it, but I hope you will."

"He won't like it."

Clifford's shoulders tensed. "No, I don't suspect he will. I sure as hell wouldn't want my wife wearing a ring another man gave her."

"Don't misunderstand me, I fully intend to wear that diamond ring."

One shoulder lifted in a jerky laugh. "You always were a stubborn woman." He turned to face her, and his eyes held hers for a long moment, as though he intended to memorize her features. "I love you, Marcie. I knew from the first that I was probably going to lose you. You're too good for me. You loving this other guy doesn't come as any shock."

"It doesn't come as any great shock?" she repeated softly. Marcie hadn't expected to cry. When the tears clustered in her eyes and dribbled onto her cheeks, she was taken by complete surprise.

"Marcie?"

"You're an idiot, Clifford Cramden," she shouted, "an idiot. Don't you know the kind of woman I am? Men don't give women like me diamond rings."

He looked like a man in shock.

She was on her feet and not sure why. She didn't want to leave, so she started pacing in front of the old upright piano. "Don't you dare tell me you're not good enough for me. It's the other way around." Her arms cradled her middle. "There've been more men in my life than I can count. I made love with so many men that eventually I stopped loving myself."

Wordlessly, Clifford continued to stare at her.

"For years I was convinced that all men really

needed to change was the love of a good woman. Only I wasn't smart enough to realize that when I dove into the ocean to save a drowning man, I risked going down with him." She sniffled and angled her head toward the ceiling. She rubbed the moisture from her cheeks and sat on the piano bench, curving her hands over the smooth polished-wood edge.

"It took me a long time to realize that when a man slapped me around, then claimed he didn't know why I put up with him, that he knew what he was talking about."

"A man beat you?"

"Men, sweetie, more than one. I'm a slow learner."

"This guy you were with tonight? Has he ever laid a hand on you?" he demanded, his fists clenched.

"Jack? No, never."

Clifford relaxed. "Good."

"Don't you see, Clifford?" she cried, having trouble keeping her emotions in check.

"See what? What type of person you are? I saw that right off, Marcie."

She stared at him, uncertain she understood what he was saying.

"You're a warm, generous, loving woman."

She sniffled. "Didn't you hear a word I said? I have a history with men, Clifford. An endless, boring history with a number of users."

"Yeah, well, we all have a history, don't we? I knew about yours a long time ago."

"You did?"

He glanced away from her and lifted his shoulders in a half shrug. "There were any number of so-called friends who felt it was their duty to let me know you had something of a reputation."

Marcie closed her eyes at the sick feeling that attacked the pit of her stomach. "Other than that one time, you never once tried to get me to bed."

"Do you know why, Marcie? Because with me you were always a lady. You never gave me reason to suspect anything else. I was proud to be with you. You're warm and funny, and you made me laugh. Some of the best times of my life are the ones I've shared with you."

"You're an idiot."

"For loving you? Hardly. It means a great deal that you'd come here to personally tell me you were going with this other guy. I don't blame you. He can give you a hell of a lot more than I ever could."

She couldn't believe what he was saying.

"You see, loving you means that I want whatever you do."

"Clifford Cramden, I love you. It's you I want to marry, not Jack Keller. You."

"Me?" He narrowed his gaze, as if he weren't sure he should believe her. "You came here because you want to tell me you're marrying me?"

She walked over and stood directly in front of him and leveled a threatening look directly at him. "Don't even think about changing your mind."

"Changing my mind. I . . . you're sure?"

"I'm more positive about this than I've been about anything else in my life."

"But—"

"Don't be making up excuses to talk yourself out of it, either. Understand?"

"Yes, but—" His eyes lit up like lampposts.

"I've been waiting all my life for a man as good as you."

With an infectious grin on his lips, he pulled her down and into his lap. "I'm crazy about you, Marcie. You don't have a clue how damned difficult it's been not to make love to you."

"We've got plenty of time for that," she said, slipping her arms around his neck.

"A lifetime," he said, kissing her with a hunger that left her breathless and clinging.

She smiled up at him and knew they were both going to be very, very happy.

38

The week that passed was the longest one of Letty's life. She sat by the phone, leaped on it the minute it rang, waited breathless for word about Murphy. She didn't care who delivered it. Jack Keller. Father Alfaro. Even Captain Norte himself.

Not knowing was driving her mad. She didn't sleep, and she had absolutely no appetite. No news wasn't good news; it was no news—and she was desperate to learn Murphy's fate.

When she couldn't bear the silence any longer, she took matters into her own hands. This time she went directly to where she was sure to get information: the Central Intelligence Agency in Washington, D.C.

It took her the better part of two days to work her way through the bureaucracy. She had to shout before anyone heard her; now she suspected they would tell her everything just to get her off their backs. On the third morning she was ushered into the office of Agent Ken Kemper.

"Ms. Madden." He escorted her into his office, moved behind his desk, and gestured for her to take a seat.

Sitting down himself, he reached for a file. "You're inquiring about Reverend Luke Madden and a mercenary by the name of Shaun Murphy."

"That's correct." She clasped her hands together and waited. Early on, she'd learned that the less information she volunteered, the better.

"Reverend Madden is your brother?"

"Yes."

"A missionary in Zarcero?"

"That's correct."

"What is the basis of your interest in Mr. Murphy?"

"He's the man I hired to find my brother," she stated matter-of-factly.

"I see."

His mouth thinned with evident disapproval. Letty said nothing. She made no excuses for hiring Murphy. The federal government had given her no choice. She'd done everything within her power to get some kind of government intervention. Her pleas had been ignored, so she'd had to take matters into her own hands.

"Was hiring Mr. Murphy wise?"

"What else was I to do?" she cried, losing her patience. "I begged and screamed for our government to help me find Luke."

"Surely you understand that would have been impossible."

"So I was repeatedly told. That's the reason I hired Mr. Murphy." She angled her chin proudly, refusing to give one inch.

"Then you located your brother?"

Letty's throat was in danger of closing up on her. "I'm fairly confident he was killed." Just saying the words was difficult. "I don't have any solid proof of that, but nevertheless I'm afraid there's no hope for Luke."

The agent lowered his gaze. "It's our understanding as well that your brother was murdered."

She didn't speak until the emotion dissolved in her throat. "Since you have information regarding my brother's fate, then you must also know what's happened to Mr. Murphy. You people have ways of learning the truth, of finding out what you want to know." She tightened her jaw. "You have my word that if you don't tell me, I'll make the biggest pest of myself you've ever seen."

"Bigger than you have already this week?"

"Yes," she returned furiously. "I don't know if you're aware that I'm a federal postal employee."

"I believe that was in the letter you wrote."

Letty, who rarely raised her voice, did so now in frustration and anger. "Don't you know it's a dangerous thing to irritate a disgruntled postal employee?"

"Ah . . ."

"Tell me what you know about Murphy!" she shouted.

A stark silence fell between them. "If you'll excuse me a moment . . ."

"No. Tell me."

He hesitated, then pushed a button on his inter-
com. "Send in Agent Moser."

Within five minutes a second agent arrived. He
walked into the room, shook hands with Letty, and sat
on the chair next to hers.

"What we're about to tell you can never leave this
room," Agent Kemper said in warning.

"It would put innocent people's lives in danger,"
Agent Moser added. "Is that understood?"

Letty nodded.

The two men exchanged looks, as if they were
deciding which one would deliver the information.

"We had word about your mercenary friend."

"Yes," she whispered. Her throat went dry with
anticipation.

"I'm afraid it isn't good." The second man pushed
up the glasses that had scooted down the bridge of his
nose.

She hadn't expected it would be. She would have
heard from him otherwise. "Is he dead?" she asked
starkly. "That's all I want to know."

"I'm afraid so."

Letty closed her eyes, and it felt as though her
heart had stopped completely.

"We're very sorry, Ms. Madden," Kemper said gently.

"Apparently he was captured on an airfield?" Agent
Moser made the statement a question.

She nodded. So that part had been real and not
some fever-induced dream.

"He was taken prisoner and executed the following
day. I believe he was hanged."

39

Letty sat in the cool evening shade on her porch and shelled peas, watching thick clouds drift effortlessly across the deep blue Texas sky. It had been a month since she'd returned from Washington, D.C. Longer since she'd contacted Jack Keller. She hadn't heard from him, but she had the answer now. There was no reason to hope. Her brother was gone. And she'd lost Murphy as well.

In time she'd be able to look at a sunset and not feel crippling emotional pain. In time she'd rebound. Time was the great healer, the great comforter.

Because he was worried about her, and because in his own way he loved her, Slim had stopped off to visit every night for two weeks. Although she appreciated his concern and friendship, she'd finally, gently, asked him to stay away.

She hadn't returned to the post office yet. Hadn't

decided if she'd ever go back. She'd found a certain solace puttering around her garden, living from one day to the next without demands, without a schedule. This leave of absence from responsibility would aid the healing process, Letty decided. She needed it.

Evenings were her favorite time, when she sat here and soaked in the beauty of the sunset and relived memories of the days spent with Murphy, traipsing through a Central American jungle. In years to come she fully expected to experience the joy of having loved him instead of the maiming sorrow of his death.

A fragile peace had come regarding the loss of her brother. The pain cut deep, deeper than any grief she had yet to experience. She'd lost so many loved ones. For all intents and purposes, her mother had been out of her life when she was five; her grandmother had died when Letty was eleven; and her father's death had come when she was a young adult. But her brother, her twin . . . that was by far the greatest loss.

She accepted Luke's passing. She'd done everything humanly possible to help him, to reach him in time. Even before she'd gone in search of Luke, she'd been warned to prepare herself for the worst. But she'd refused to give up hope.

What others didn't seem to realize was that no amount of mental preparedness would have equipped her to deal with the death of her twin.

She believed Luke had asked God to take him for some greater purpose. His death, like so much of his life, had been a direct answer to prayer. Try as she might, she couldn't begrudge her brother that.

It was for Murphy she grieved. Murphy she would

miss. Loving him had brought her such unexpected joy. It had been the surprise of her life.

Falling in love had caught them both unaware. At first she'd found him vulgar and offensive. He'd gone out of his way to shock and incense her, but it had all been an act. Inside he was one of the most compassionate and thoughtful men she was ever likely to meet.

She treasured the memories of him playing with the children in Questo. Her only regret was that he'd never have the opportunity to tease and laugh with their children.

His gentle side had revealed itself when he'd held and comforted her after her near rape in Siguierres. Those moments in his arms were ones she'd hold in her heart through the years. She'd been so foolish and idiotic to have fired him after seeing him with the woman in the cantina. She recognized now that the real reason was that she'd been jealous. Her heart must have known even then.

A smile played over her lips. Murphy had taught her so much about herself, lessons she wouldn't soon forget.

In the distance she saw an approaching plume of dust, and she sighed. Slim again, she suspected. Keeping a vigil over her wouldn't help the way she felt about him, but the rancher hadn't seemed to realize that.

But it wasn't Slim's pickup that made its way down the long dirt driveway that stretched between her house and the road.

Setting the bowl of peas aside, Letty stood and looped her arm around the porch column. She blinked, and her heart quickened as the silhouette of a man became visible. Soon the man, one lovingly familiar, became recognizable. A man she loved more than her own life.

Murphy.

Her heart refused to stop banging against her ribs, like sticks against a tin drum. He remained in her thoughts so much of the time, it was understandable for her mind to conjure him up. Perhaps she was hallucinating.

The pickup pulled to a stop, and the dream continued. The driver's door opened, and he climbed out of the cab.

Letty's arm around the post served as a desperately needed anchor.

She didn't know if she dared believe what her eyes were telling her. Greedy for the sight of him, her gaze roved from his dark, thick, military-style cut hair to his cowboy-booted feet.

He stood at the bottom of the steps, and a slow, lazy smile eased up the edges of his mouth. His gaze slid longingly to hers, and the love she read there convinced her this was no dream, no aberration. This was Murphy, and he was real and alive.

A strangled cry escaped her throat, and she literally sailed from the top porch step and into his arms.

He caught her and threw back his head and released a deep-throated laugh. "For a minute there I was wondering if you remembered who I was."

"Murphy . . . oh, Murphy." She directed her mouth to his, not giving him time to explain or respond while she roughly planted wet kisses over his face, not caring where her lips landed. All that mattered in those moments was holding him, kissing him, and glorying in the truth that he lived.

"Letty, sweet Letty." He growled her name and wrapped his arms about her waist, then lifted her several inches off the ground. He buried his head in the delicate curve of her neck and exhaled sharply.

"I love you so much, so much, so much," she chanted again and again, unable to say it enough times.

"I love you," he insisted. Cupping her face with his hands, he made love to her with his mouth and tongue until they both trembled and clung to each other.

Letty felt the reluctance with which he ended the kiss, inching his lips from hers. He smiled down on her and brushed his thumbs across her cheeks, moist with tears she hadn't realized she'd shed.

"I was told you were dead," she said when she could.

Still clinging to each other, they sat on the top step. Tucked in his arms, Letty pressed her head against his shoulder.

"Who told you that?" he demanded.

"The CIA."

His soft laughter stirred the hair close to her temple. "One thing you need to learn, sweetheart, is never to believe the government."

"But I saw you shot down . . . at least I think I did."

"You were in no shape to remember much of anything."

"Were you . . . shot, that is?"

He hesitated. "Yeah, a couple of times."

She gasped and would have anxiously investigated his injuries, but he stopped her.

"I'm fine."

"I know, but—"

"Hey, I'm here, aren't I? Thanks to Jack and a few other of my closest friends."

"Jack Keller did find you?" She would be forever grateful to Murphy's friend. Somehow, all in good time, she'd come up with a way of repaying him personally for bringing Murphy home to her. "Tell me everything. I need to know it all. What did you learn about Luke? Don't hide anything from me."

He kissed her, his mouth lingering over hers as if he needed to feel and taste her once more before he continued.

"After you were shot they took you to Norte, didn't they?"

He tensed, then nodded. "Yeah."

"Did they . . . torture you?"

"Let's just say Norte was very pleased to see me, but furious that I'd been shot. You see, he'd been so eager to do the deed himself. Now it seemed I was to die and deny him the sadistic pleasure. He didn't want to simply finish me off, he wanted me to suffer for the error of my ways first."

Letty tensed, knowing he must have been in terrible pain.

"The two shoulder wounds quite possibly saved my life."

"How?"

"I was thrown in prison."

"Without medical attention?" That was criminal, inhumane . . . but exactly what she would have expected from Norte.

"A woman by the name of Rosita saved my life."

Luke's friend, the woman she'd thought she'd seen in San Paulo.

"Apparently she had someone on the inside willing to assist her on a limited basis. She came to me seeking information about you." He hesitated and planted his hands on either side of her face as his gaze delved into hers. "You were right. Luke is dead. I'm sorry, honey, I would have done anything to spare you that."

"How?" The word had a difficult time making its way out of her throat.

"She believed he went peaceably in his sleep, but she doesn't know for sure."

Murphy's arms tightened about her. "Apparently, before he died, he'd learned that the two of us were in Zarcero, and he asked her to do whatever she could to locate you and get you out of the country."

Tears welled in her eyes. Even with his own life about to end, Luke's thoughts had been for her.

"She loved your brother."

"I know." Her voice came out frail and trembling. Although Luke had never mentioned his feelings for Rosita, Letty knew in her heart that he'd come to love her as well.

Murphy gathered her close.

"I probably would have died if Jack and company hadn't arrived when they did. I don't suppose you'll feel any sadness when I tell you Norte's dead. I would have taken a great deal of pleasure in doing him in myself, but Jack beat me to it. As it happened, I wasn't in any condition to manage it."

Murphy was right, she didn't feel the least bit of

regret. The world was a better place without his hate.

All these long, lonely weeks she'd been left in the dark, believing the worst, suffering. "Why did you wait so long to come to me?"

"I couldn't, love. I was in pretty bad shape by the time Deliverance Company got me out of San Paulo." He brushed the hair aside from her neck and kissed her there. Raising his eyes to meet hers, he encountered the chain. "You're still wearing the necklace."

"It's my engagement ring, remember?"

"Engagement? We're engaged?"

"You proposed," she reminded him, not taking kindly to the fact that he'd apparently forgotten.

"I proposed marriage? Me? You've got to be joking." His look was skeptical. "I sincerely hope you didn't take me seriously."

"I most certainly did. Listen here, Shaun Murphy, you may think you suffered in Zarcero, but that's nothing compared to what I'll do to you if you've changed your mind about us."

Laughing, he wove his fingers into her hair, his eyes smiling into hers. "Unlike certain people I know, I keep my word."

"Are you suggesting I don't?" she grumbled, infuriated that he'd imply such a thing. She stopped abruptly. "Are . . . you're talking about our agreement."

"I fully intend to collect my due."

She wrapped her arms around his neck, sighed deeply, and pressed her head to his chest. "And I intend to deliver."

Epilogue

Letty stood on the porch with her hands braced against the wood railing. Her gaze traveled to the night sky, ablaze with a million blinking stars. A full moon stood guard over the earth.

Letty would have liked to believe Luke was looking down on her and smiling from one of those stars. She hadn't been able to sleep for thoughts of her brother.

Out of the blue, Luke's letter had arrived a month earlier. It had come as a shock to receive something penned almost a year ago. Rosita had enclosed it with a note to explain that the envelope had been found in Commander Faqueza's office shortly after the legal government of Zarcero had been restored.

Letty had read it countless times, so often she'd committed it to memory.

My dearest Letty,

It grieves me to write and tell you that by the time you read this letter, I'll be dead. A few days ago I stood trial and was condemned for crimes committed against the people of Zarcero. The trial and all that has befallen this country deeply distress me, but I can do nothing.

Don't weep for me, Letty. I leave this world confident that I've completed the work God set out for me, but I don't go without regrets. There's such irony in all this. You see, for the first time in my life I'm truly, deeply in love. My hopes for the future are but ashes now, for God has called me for a greater purpose.

I know you, Letty, almost as well as I do myself. Please, don't be bitter. Forgive my killers. I am leaving, but I promise that you will never be alone. My love will always be with you. In your darkest hours, and in your greatest joys, I'll be there. The military can take my life and all that I have, but nothing could destroy the closeness we have always shared.

Do you remember when we were kids and you sometimes claimed you could feel if something was wrong with me? I was never sure what to make of that "feeling" of yours. I'm ashamed to tell you I didn't believe you. Now I understand, because I've felt it too. For you. God has such wonderful plans for you, Letty. Such grand adventures. I can leave you now, because in my heart I know that you'll find happiness. I'm no prophet, but it wouldn't surprise me if you mar-

ried within the next few months. How I wish I could see you as a wife and mother.

You were always smarter than me. At least you liked to think so! For the first time I'll know something before you do. Heaven. The next time you look up in a night sky, look for me, Letty. I'll be up there smiling down on you.

I remain . . .
Your brother

The child moved within her womb, and Letty pressed her hand against her abdomen and smiled softly to herself. She'd learned so much about herself this last year without Luke. She missed him dreadfully, but it was as he'd always said. God closed one door and quickly opened another. She was a wife now and soon to be a mother. The fears that had crippled her about her own mother had long been laid to rest. It was as Murphy had assured her in the jungle. She was nothing like her parent, but it had taken his love to prove what she should have recognized long before.

The screen door opened. "Letty?"

"I'm here." She glanced over her shoulder at her husband.

Murphy joined her. "You couldn't sleep?"

"I was just thinking about Luke."

He stood behind her, slipped his arms about her waist, and flattened his palm against her rounded tummy. "Although we never met, I would have been proud to call him friend."

"Luke would have shook his head in wonder over

the two of us." And marveled at the changes love had wrought in them both.

"Hey, from what I read, your brother seemed to know about me."

Letty sighed softly. "I think he did." Luke had been right, too. She was truly happy. Despite her concern, Murphy seemed to find contentment outside of Deliverance Company. The security company he'd formed had more business than he could handle.

"What about Jack?" she asked, thinking of the company and Murphy's proposal. "Will he come to work for you?"

Murphy kissed the side of her neck. "It doesn't look that way." He levied a deep sigh that rumbled inside his chest. "If I didn't know better, I'd say Jack fell in love."

"What's so odd about that? You did too."

"Yes, but I have a wife and Jack doesn't. He's been in a foul mood for months. From my experience, when a man goes around self-destructing there's generally a woman at the heart of the problem."

Letty didn't disagree with her husband's assessment of Jack's troubles because she suspected he was right. "Jack's going to be fine."

"Oh?" Murphy chuckled. "And how would you know that?"

"I don't, for certain, but I wish him well." She owed Murphy's friend a great deal and wanted him to be happy.

"You ready to come back to bed?" Her husband yawned loudly.

"Yeah." She turned, and together, arm in arm, they walked back inside the house.

As they turned away, a shooting star blazed a fiery trail across the black satin night.

With more than 70 million copies of her books in print, **DEBBIE MACOMBER** is a favorite author of romance and women fiction readers around the world. Officing in a Victorian-style building that also houses an ice cream parlor and a bookstore, Debbie writes heartwarming stories about small-town life, home and family, women who knit, enduring friendship and humorous angels named Shirley, Goodness, and Mercy, who tackle their  earthly missions with zeal. The Washington author demonstrates an almost uncanny ability to see into the souls of women and to express their emotions, values, and concerns.

Debbie's writer's journey began in 1973, when she journaled these prophetic words, "Since the greatest desire of my life is to somehow, some way, be a writer, I'll start with this journal." Today, the *New York Times* bestselling author, who overcame dyslexia to achieve her success, says, "No one should underestimate the power of a dream."

Debbie's devotion to her craft and her readers has brought her many awards. Her more recent honors include a RITA®, romance publishing's prestigious "Oscar," from the 9,500-member Romance Writers of America for *The Christmas Basket*. In 2005, Debbie's *44 Cranberry Point* was named the winner of The Quill Award for romance in the first year of this nationwide "readers' choice" competition.

Debbie and her husband, Wayne, live on Washington's Kitsap Peninsula and winter in Florida. They have kayaked in Puget Sound, river rafted with their four children, and crewed an Americas ship. With her passion for adventure, it is no wonder that Debbie penned her Deliverance Company romantic suspense series that includes *Someday Soon* and *Sooner Or Later*.